MYTHS & REVENANTS

WARHAMMER
AGE OF SIGMAR

MYTHS & REVENANTS

DAVID GUYMER • ANDY CLARK • EVAN DICKEN
DAVID ANNANDALE • NICK KYME • GUY HALEY
C L WERNER • JOSH REYNOLDS • GAV THORPE

A BLACK LIBRARY PUBLICATION

First published in 2019.
This edition published in Great Britain in 2019 by
Black Library,
Games Workshop Ltd.,
Willow Road,
Nottingham,
NG7 2WS, UK.

10 9 8 7 6 5 4 3 2 1

Produced by Games Workshop in Nottingham.
Cover illustration by Lewis Jones.

A CIP record for this book is available from the British Library.

ISBN 13: 978 1 78193 949 9

See Black Library on the internet at

blacklibrary.com

Find out more about Games Workshop
and the worlds of Warhammer at

games-workshop.com

Printed and bound by CPI Group (UK) Ltd, Croydon, CR0 4YY

From the maelstrom of a sundered world, the
Eight Realms were born. The formless and the divine
exploded into life.

Strange, new worlds appeared in the firmament, each one
gilded with spirits, gods and men. Noblest of the gods was
Sigmar. For years beyond reckoning he illuminated the realms,
wreathed in light and majesty as he carved out his reign. His
strength was the power of thunder. His wisdom was infinite.
Mortal and immortal alike kneeled before his lofty throne.
Great empires rose and, for a while, treachery was banished.
Sigmar claimed the land and sky as his own and ruled over a
glorious age of myth.

But cruelty is tenacious. As had been foreseen, the great
alliance of gods and men tore itself apart. Myth and legend
crumbled into Chaos. Darkness flooded the realms. Torture,
slavery and fear replaced the glory that came before. Sigmar
turned his back on the mortal kingdoms, disgusted by their
fate. He fixed his gaze instead on the remains of the world he
had lost long ago, brooding over its charred core, searching
endlessly for a sign of hope. And then, in the dark heat of
his rage, he caught a glimpse of something magnificent. He
pictured a weapon born of the heavens. A beacon powerful
enough to pierce the endless night. An army hewn from
everything he had lost.

Sigmar set his artisans to work and for long ages they toiled,
striving to harness the power of the stars. As Sigmar's great
work neared completion, he turned back to the realms and saw
that the dominion of Chaos was almost complete. The hour
for vengeance had come. Finally, with lightning blazing across
his brow, he stepped forth to unleash his creations.

The Age of Sigmar had begun.

CONTENTS

THE SEA TAKETH

David Guymer

> '*Oh, ware the day the fishing folk come,*
> *To no barrier will they concede,*
> *Their lures will entice both the strong and the frail,*
> *And lo will the good fishes bleed...*'

'What is that ditty she sings?'

Ingdrin Jonsson had no idea at what age humans considered their offspring to be competent adults, as per Artycle Nine of the Kharadron Code, but the girl was as winsome and waifish a thing as he could imagine, and so addressed his question to the father.

'Tis an old song, Master Jonsson,' Tharril bellowed, his words timed to the rhythm of his oars and the crash of spray across his back. 'Her ma sang it to her, as my ma sang it to me.'

'It gives me the creeps.'

'Any honest song should.'

Jonsson clung grimly to the port gunwale as freezing saltwater sprayed his face. It was not like plying skyborne currents. His dusky beard stuck to his skin and to his light sky-captain's leathers. He could taste the ocean on his breath. Holding fiercely to the slimy wood, he peered back into their star-speckled wake. The surface of the ocean bulged and receded, as though something vast and primordial breathed. Where waves crested, they caught starlight. Where waves sank, they folded under, taking that captive light back with them to the depths. The oceans were realms within the realms, forgotten by time, history and gods. Ancient magic dwelled there, unformed, untouched by hands mortal or divine since the formation of the aetheric cloud itself. With every precipitating crash against the hull, he was reminded of its elementalism. With every tug of current on the keel, Jonsson conceded a little more that he had placed his fate in the hands of a dark and unruly god.

> *'They crave what's within,*
> *'neath flesh and 'neath bone,*
> *Sparing only the young...'*

Tharril was effectively enthroned in the wooden prow of the boat, an oar in each hand, controlling the boom of the lateen sail with a pedal-like noose of rope about his left foot. Beneath the bench there was a massive warhammer, and in his lap, a spear. Tharril and his folk were fishermen, but there were plenty of fish around Blackfire Bight that would consider a single-sail like this one small prey. Jonsson too was armed, a skyhook on a strap across his shoulder and a privateer pistol loaded in his holster.

Thalia, the girl (Jonsson had also heard her father call her 'spratling' or oft times just 'sprat'), sat against the starboard gunwale, across the centreline from Jonsson. A plaid net lay in sodden folds over her knees as she sang her ballad, extricating wriggling fish as long as her arm or longer. Silver, nightshade-blue and bone-white shimmered under starlight as they flapped and squirmed, only to disappear into buckets of cold brine. Jonsson watched as she pulled another fighter from the net. Smaller, this one, its tail barely reaching her elbow with her hand clamped expertly about its gills. She tossed it over the side.

The ocean accepted its return with a faint splash.

'And when they grow old and grandchildren forget,
That will be the day when the fishing folk come.'

Jonsson wondered if he was paying Tharril and his girl too much to sail him out there, if they were just going to pursue a normal day's take along the way.

'Why do you throw back the small ones?'

'They are young,' she replied.

'But why?'

She shrugged. 'You just do.'

With a grunt, as disturbed as much by the company of the odd girl as by her brute of a father, Jonsson pried his fingers from the gunwale and leant forwards. His chest of equipment had been stowed inboard.

With exaggerated care because his hands were numbed with cold and shrivelled by salt spray, he worked the combination lock and lifted the lid. Unrolling the now-wet fleece packing, he assembled his zephyrscope and arktant.

Bringing the rubber eyepiece to his eye, he trained it on the twinkling dot of Sigendil. The night sky might vary from realm to realm, and even within a realm, and with the movements of Ulgu-Hysh within the aetheric cloud, but the beacon star of Azyr was a fixed point in every sky. With one eye on the High Star, he manipulated the sliders on his arktant to account for the position of the local constellations.

'Can you hold this thing steady?'

'Ha!' Tharril barked, rowing.

'*Bokak*,' Jonsson swore, as a sideswipe wave spoiled his measurements.

'What are you doing?' Thalia asked.

'Taking a position, girl.'

'Why?'

'Because!'

'I thought Kharadron lived in the sky.'

Jonsson sighed. 'Aye, girl, we do, seeking our fortunes on the aether winds.' He leant across the open chest and winked. 'But every now and again, some careless soul drops something.'

'You are looking for treasure?'

'It won't look for itself.'

The girl sniffed, with the iron rectitude of the very small. 'No one takes from the sea.'

'Good. It'll still be there then.'

'No one takes from the sea.'

'What about these?' Jonsson nodded towards the nets and buckets full of splashing fish.

'That's what the sea gives.'

Her deathly earnestness brought a snippet of a smile to Jonsson's face. 'A sour face like that aboard an aether-ship is almost always a sign of something trapped in the ear. Very serious if left untended.' He reached out as though to tug on her ear, but then pulled his hand back with a flourish at the last moment, presenting her with a copper comet and a toothy grin.

She frowned.

'Hah!' said Jonsson, slapping his thigh. 'Would you see that? Somebody raised this girl right.' He passed one hand over the other, the copper coin disappearing. Then he unfurled the palm of the crossed hand to reveal a larger, golden coin. The girl's eyes lit up, as if in reflection. 'A quarter-share, from the aether mints of Barak-Thryng, girl. Legal tender under any of the six great admiralties.'

'Take the coin, spratling,' grunted Tharril. 'Afore he makes it disappear again.'

Jonsson winked as the girl scraped it off his palm.

'What's that?' she said.

Jonsson followed her gaze down.

'Now *that*,' he said, patting the hard object that lay safe beneath the second layer of fleecing, 'is something that will really amaze you.'

Jonsson's heavy boots thudded to the ocean floor. His legs bowed, his shoulders bunching, the monstrous pressure of the sea bottom crushing down on the weak points of his armour. The rigid plates of the deep-sea-adapted arkanaut suit creaked like a metal pipe being squeezed by a gargant.

'*Oh, ware the day the fishing folk come.*'

He turned on the spot, ponderous as an armoured beetle. His headlamp sent a speckled beam into the pulverising blackness. Bubbles issuing from the seams in his armour and the rings of his air hose – a mile of collapsible metal flexing from the back of his helmet towards the surface – cut up his light. Every one was a tiny mirror held up in the completeness of the dark.

'Ingdrin Jonsson isn't afraid of the deep!'

He lowered his skyhook warily.

Almost nothing lived at these depths.

He knew of the merwynn and the kelpdarr, fiercely isola-tionist and protective of their territories, but even they rarely plumbed beyond the sunlit layer. The great beasts that preyed on such folk, lurkinarth and kalypsar and the like, prowled the richer waters of the coastal regions and shipping lanes accordingly. The ocean floor was a desert.

Spiny encrustations of rose-coloured coral glittered everywhere his lamps passed.

There was nothing here.

Bracing himself against the awesome weight of water on his shoulders, he thumped down to one knee. Bubbles and silt puffed up around the armoured joint, but the cloud stayed compact and low. With his beams angled tight to the opalescent reef around him, he ran his gauntlet over its surface. He had never seen a mineral like it. His light seemed to be trapped by the structure of it, spreading outwards through veins of denser crystal. Piece by piece, the reef lit up, and street by colonnaded street, the turrets and spires of a drowned city was lifted out of darkness.

'Tromm...' he breathed, bubbles squirming through the gaps in his mask.

The structures were of coral and lime, as if grown out of the reef itself, the lustre of nacre gleaming from monuments and domes. There were high towers. Great bridges. Palaces. Walls. Statues of what looked like aelves stood sentry over squares and gardens, armoured in opulence in pearl and shells and mounted upon monstrous piscine steeds. For all its obvious former glory, however, the place was a ruin. Pallid, light-shy vegetation strangled the life from the great works, the camouflaged wings of bottom-feeding rays rifling through the debris that littered the grand avenues.

'Aighmar.' Jonsson stared over the coral-lit city with something like reverence. 'Lost city of the Deepkin aelves. I found it.'

'Their lures will entice both the strong and the frail.'

Jonsson gripped his skyhook and looked back. His helmet could not freely rotate about his shoulders. It took a moment.

'And lo will the good fishes bleed.'

Behind him again.

'Who's there?'

He plodded around another half-circle, bubbles exploding from his helmet's seals as he cried out in alarm. While his attention had been fixed on the lambent city of the aelves, the blunt nose of something gigantic had emerged from one of the larger hollows in the reef. Jonsson did not see much. A dull flash of cartilaginous teeth. A silvery ripple of gills. Then there was an explosion in the water, spined fins seething, monstrous grey muscle writhing, and the beast was surging from its lair towards him.

He reacted on a hair-trigger. It saved his life.

In a storm of bubbles, the heavily adapted aether-endrin bolted onto his shoulders pushed him up and back. Shudders ran through the water as the beast's jaws crashed shut on the effervescence where he had just been.

Jonsson got a horribly good look.

The beast was as long as a short-range gunhauler, grey as battle-damaged iron. Its eyes were glassy yellow knotholes of alien hunger.

With a powerful stroke of the tail, it twisted into Jonsson's bubble trail, dorsal blade-fin carving the water as it closed the distance, fast. Jonsson swung his skyhook between them and fired. The harpoon launched in silence, a red cloud billowing from the side of the monster's snout.

The beast thrashed in pain and fury, almost ripping the skyhook, still tethered to the harpoon by a taut length of steel chain. Jonsson pulled the release bolt before the gun was ripped out of his hands and the chain twanged off towards the wounded creature. Jonsson drew his pistol from its thigh holster. He had no expectation that it would fire under water, but it was all he had left.

The monster jerked about the middle, gnashing at the chain that its own movements flicked tauntingly over its head, missed, and drove its head through a coral wall. The reef crumbled around it, blood fountaining as the coral worked the harpoon embedded in the beast's snout like a well pump, and something in its animal mind said 'enough'.

It swam away, churning a thin river of red with its tail.

Jonsson let out a relieved breath.

That had been an allopex.

'You have the best bad luck of any duardin born, Ingdrin Jonsson,' he told himself.

He had never heard of an allopex hunting alone, and a school of them could bring down a krakigon.

'They crave what's within, 'neath flesh and 'neath bone.'

With a snarl, he swung his pistol towards the source of the voice, twisting his head prematurely so that he was looking into the back of his helmet. He almost laughed when he realised. It was the air hose. That girl, Thalia, must have been sat near the inlet, singing. He gave the base of the hose a rap as his boots sank inexorably back towards the ocean floor. 'Nothing to fret over,' he said loudly, hoping that his voice would carry back up. 'Just like I promised.'

But when he started towards the ruins of Aighmar, he did so quickly.

There was blood in the water.

One night and another day later, Thalia had a knife in her hand, blood as far up as the elbow.

She sighed, opening the ghoulish bream from mouth to tail

and emptying its guts into a pail. She enjoyed filleting. Normally. She liked the sliminess of the fish in her hands. She liked the smell, the sound of the brothing pot bubbling inside, waiting for the tailfins and the heads, listening to the hens in the back patch clucking their goodnights.

She squinted across the shingle to where the sunset was slowly turning the ocean an amethyst-tinged red. The water was placid, as still as the brass mirror that da had never removed from ma's dresser. It looked bigger to her somehow, swollen. Waves lapped at the pebbly promontory, like the village cat at the fish juices on her fingers.

She blinked herself awake, realising that she had been about to nod off. Right there on the porch step, her chores unfinished. She shook her head. The air was thick. Her eyelids felt like honey.

Stifling a yawn, she found herself facing in a direction that she had scarcely given a moment's consideration to before today. The inland road. It was the way to Toba Lorchai, the greatest city in all the realms next to fabled Azyrheim itself, or so her da had told it. Da had never been there though. Neither had she.

Jonsson had gone there.

Thalia had slept all night and most of the morning, but the Kharadron had been packing his chest into his strange metal caravan, pushing a clinking pouch into da's hand and disappearing up the inland road almost as soon as they had drawn the boat up onto the beach.

'A black wind in his sails,' da had said that night.

A sudden shriek from the direction of the water snapped her head up.

The sound lingered on the air for a moment before being abruptly silenced. She strained her ears, but could hear nothing but the crash and tumble of waves on the shingle. The tide was in too high, washing about the boat sheds and net stores. The sea was too red. Brown-and-white kelp bobbed with the action of the waves like bodies.

'Da?'

She bent down to deposit the un-gutted fish back into its bucket as an arrow thudded into the porch post in line with where her eyes had just been. She looked back at it, quivering in the split wood, and gasped, too shocked to scream.

A woman with a dripping shortbow stood waist-deep in the shallows, buffeted from behind by pliant waves. At first glance she might have passed as human, but she was not human. Wet robes the colour of an ocean under moonless skies clung to a slender physique, fish-scale armour cladding her forearms and torso. Her face, shoulders and midriff remained bare, her skin as pale as a dead fish's eyes. Thalia thought her beautiful, but it was a haunting, pitiless kind of beauty, the sort that would drive mere mortals to distraction and despair.

The woman nocked another arrow to her bowstring. She raised her bow to draw, sighting down the shaft. Thalia noticed with horror that she had no eyes. Just smoothed, perfect skin over shallow sockets.

From the first shot to now it had probably been about a second.

Thalia did scream then. She screamed and she ran.

Da would have wanted her to go inside and bar the door. That was what he had always told her to do when the dead and the drowned came. But that was not what she did.

The second arrow whipped past her face, splitting the wood nearer the bottom of the porch post, as Thalia leapt onto the loose stones and tore towards the pier.

Set at the lip of the promontory at the outskirts of the village, the pier served both as a wave breaker and as a mooring for a dozen one- and two-berth boats on its leeward side. It was also where da and the others would sit out and drink beer when the nights were warm.

She started to hear noises as she got closer.

Shouts. Metal.

Fighting.

'Da!'

She sped around the last cabin, a third arrow thudding into the corner boards at her heels, and saw it.

The jetty speared outwards into the still, swollen water, a zigzagging half-bridge of wood, forested with masts and lines. Eight women and three men – most of the adults in the village – were there on the boardwalk, hemmed in by an ever-circling tide of lissom warriors wielding two-handed swords. Like the bow-woman they were sightless. Like the bow-woman it did not seem to matter. The village had always prided itself on being well armed, and had been taught by harsh necessity how to use its weapons well. But they were accustomed to fighting off the seasonal deadwalker floods, enemies that could not flow around a cudgel or a spear-thrust like seaweed in the currents of a passing fish. These warriors seemed almost to be dancing rather than fighting, the huge blades in their hands willing partners instead of tools to be directed.

Old legends, myths and songs skipped through her mind. Frightful tales of the dark ocean and hungering aelves.

'Deepkin…'

Thalia picked her da out from the fighting.

Her heart almost stopped beating in relief.

Her da was as broad across the chest as the keel of a boat, browned by sun and sea, and caulked with scars. He could lift Thalia in one hand and cousin Rollin in the other, and throw

them both, squealing, off the end of the pier. He was a champion, the God-King of her world.

With a roar, he smashed his warhammer into an aelf's chest.
The blow shattered the swordsman's armour. The aelf crashed
to the decking a dozen feet back and did not rise.

'Da!' Thalia screamed in exultation, but he did not hear her.
His full attention was on his enemy.

Seawater was seething up through the planking of the jetty,
causing the downed aelf's arms and head to lift up. Thalia
gasped, for she was well used to the horrors of necromancy,
but this was different. Wasn't it? Something compelled her to
keep watching as a ghostly light shrouded the body. It seeped
into the aelf's skin through the half-heart brand on his forehead, and mere seconds after hitting the deck a ruin, the aelf
was vaulting athletically back to his feet. Armour hung off him,
but the bruises over his ribs were already fading. He butter-
flied his moonlit blade.

Her da scowled and hefted his hammer.

Thalia's mind was racing, faster even than she was as she
tore onto the boardwalk.

A very different-looking aelf warrior emerged from the sea
on the crest of a solitary wave to be deposited onto the boardwalk beside her da. His armour was scalloped and studded
with jewels, heavier and finer than that worn by his warriors.
His helmet was tall and fluted, inhumanly ornate, and entirely
without any openings for eyes or ears. Only the mouth was
visible and it was thin-lipped and cruel. In his hands, he bore
a long-handled weapon with a serrated edge that fell somewhere between scythe and spear. A small lantern globe hung
from its head. There was something about its light that pulled
on Thalia, behind her eyes, inside her chest, that was desperate to take leave of her and be one with the source of that light.

The newcomer turned his spear, his *light* towards her da.

His eyes softened as the light bathed his face. He lowered his hammer as though his arms could no longer lift it. He stared into the light. Something horrible and golden seemed to lift from his shoulders, streaming towards the aelf's lantern.

Then her da collapsed to the deck.

'Da!'

Small and desperately quick, Thalia darted through the melee, avoiding friends and hard-faced aelves both as she splashed onto the flooding jetty and threw her arms over her da. She shook him, crying, 'Da. Da! *Da.*' His eyelids quivered as if he were asleep and dreaming. His chest rose and fell beneath her body. Relief choked off her sobs. He was not dead. He was not dead. She wiped the tears from her eyes, feeling the sting of seawater. 'Wake up, da.' Taking a shoulder in each of her hands, she shook him. 'Wake up!'

'I think that I am... feeling,' said the aelf with the light, looking down on Thalia and her da through the faceless metal of his helm. His lips remained straight lines, but he steepled a hand over the ridged plate of his breast and turned his blade aside. 'Pity. Sorrow.'

'It is understandable, soulrender.'

Another magnificently lithe aelven warrior strode down the boardwalk. She was perfect, a queen of austerity, dark-haired and pale-skinned, armoured in black, as cruel as the ocean waves.

'Away from the crush of blackness and cold, what can we do but feel as we were made to? Trust instead that soon it will be done, and that oblivion awaits us all beneath the waves.'

The one she had named *soulrender* lowered his head. 'It is rare to find such wisdom in the souls of the *akhelian*. The martial council chose well in electing you our queen.'

Thalia's lip was trembling, but she knelt defiantly upright between the aelf queen and her da, brandishing the inch-long filleting knife that was still in her hand.

'I like you, child,' the woman said, though neither her voice nor her face expressed any emotion. 'I would see my *namarti* children take souls like yours.' With a scimitar that glowed the colour of rose coral, she tilted Thalia's jaw so that their eyes met. 'My name is Pétra. Queen of the Mor'phann, protector of Aighmar and reaver of souls.'

Thalia was suddenly painfully aware that the sounds of fighting had stopped while the aelf queen had been speaking. A tear glistened in her eye, in defiance of her pride.

She wanted her da.

'Speak to me of the one that took from my ocean.'

Jonsson woke to the crash of waves.

He started, huge fists clamping around the leather steering grips of his endrin-cart and squeezing until both knuckles and leather were whitening. He breathed, letting the tension go slowly. Just a dream. Clearing the misted glass with a sleeve, he peered out at the bleakly forested hillside. The trees were stick-thin, sparse black leaves rustling with a sound like that of the distant sea amplified through a conch shell. It was dawn. He had allowed himself to sleep for too long. The expedition to Aighmar had wearied him more than he had admitted to the girl. But he had not been prepared to linger in that village a moment longer than he had to.

Cursing under his breath, he wiped the nightmare sweat from his palms on his trouser leg, and pulled open the door.

A rush of chill morning air displaced the stale, fish-breath odour that had been allowed to stew in the cabin overnight.

Too long.

Too, *too* long.

He clambered out, stretched his back, stretched his legs, then hurried around to the front of the cart to crank the endrin. Once the vehicle was awake and purring he hauled himself back inside and pulled the brake lever.

He made it another six hours before the endrin packed in with a wheezing sputter. He got out again, tense and muttering, to crank it one more time.

One last time. Another six hours ought to do it.

He stopped for nothing. Not for food. Not for drink. *Definitely* not for sleep. When the sun again began to sink below the barrow hills, he got out to light the lamps and climbed right back in.

Blackfire Bight was a vast and lawless expanse of grim hills, moribund coastline and bone-coloured sands, but it was neither banditry nor undeath that worried him.

He had already slept too long.

Jonsson did not know much about the sea-aelves. No one did. They were a myth, and in some cases even less than that, and from every scrap of information he had been able to uncover, they were quite brutal about ensuring that remained the case. *Deepkin*, some called them. *Idoneth*, those scant records suggested they called themselves. Some fragments of text claimed them to be descendants of the *cythai*, the first, mythical race of aelves to have been drawn into the realms by their creator, the god of learning and light, Teclis. Legends. If there was even a nut of truth to them, then the cythai had fallen a long way indeed. Such stories as existed in the inherited consciousness of coastal communities across the Bight were of settlements scoured overnight, ships vanishing, armies disappearing without a trace of an enemy, wars of migration as entire nations were driven inland by a sudden, inexplicable terror of the sea.

Jonsson did not know much.

He knew enough to move inland, fast.

He tried to avoid thinking of Tharril and the girl.

If Jonsson's mind was a keenly running endrin, then his conscience was that oil-stained bit of machinery that presumably
did something of tremendous import, and which Jonsson had
managed very well by never interfering with. He patted idly at
his jacket pocket, cursing himself for giving the girl a whole
quarter-share. What had he been thinking? What was she going
to spend it on? He scowled. This was exactly what his old
endrinmasters had always tried to teach him. Know every bit
of your endrin. If you did not, then it was liable to hiccup at
the most inconvenient of times.

The endrin-cart grumbled as it continued to climb.

Walls. That was what he needed. High ones. And guns. And
an airship. Grungni, did he want his feet back on his airship.
The Deepkin were coming for him, he could feel it in his water,
and the one place nearby that was as far beyond the reach of an
angry sea as it was possible to get was Toba Lorchai.

Skyport of the Kharadron.

Toba Lorchai was a thriving free port, a small city or a large
town, depending on how one interpreted the finer Points and
Artycles of the Code, and the stubbornly still-beating heart
of Barak-Thryng's various interests in Blackfire Bight. While
trade was administered (and, more importantly, taxed) by the
admiralty, it was a stridently independent frontier port in most
respects. The bulk of its labour force were human, which was
true of many such ports across the realms, with a sizeable
contingent of duardin craftsmen, traders and oath-soldiers, as
well as a peripatetic community of orruks of a more mercan-
tile bent. They traded in meat and in bone, and in the spoils

of their constant warring on the restless lands of Skulldrake and Wither and Deathrattle Point. Most Kharadron authorities would have run the greenskins off long ago, but as long as there were other foes to fight – and Toba Lorchai had plenty – then their belligerence was an even greater boon to the town than their trade goods.

Its streets were gutters for the filth of the realm, its timber buildings climbing roughshod over the black rock of the hills and each other, as inconsiderate as the people that lived within them. Factionalism was rife. Kharadron and Dispossessed. Dispossessed and human. Orruk and absolutely everyone else. The detritus of brawls and base trades littered every doorway and corner. Draft animals that had to be blinkered and distracted with belled harnesses lest they go mad, lowed their distress in alleys. Giant vermin and hillfowl, war-bred beasts and skeleton birds, shrieked in cages. Smoke stuffed the winding lanes like a gag in the mouth.

It stank of cheap spices, night soil and endrin greases. It stank of ten thousand living, stubbornly still-breathing souls.

Jonsson thought that Toba Lorchai was probably the basest and worst den of iniquity in the eight Mortal Realms. If a fellow traveller or sage had told him authoritatively that it was, in all truth, the basest in all of creation then he would have been amused, but unsurprised.

But right then, that unpleasantly acidic burn in the back of his mouth was the taste of sanctuary. The timber stockade might have been ugly, but it was thick and it was high, and the populace, by virtue of being crooks and felons to a man, duardin or grot, were satisfyingly well armed. Better even than that, however, was the sheer freneticism of the markets, of the bawdy houses, of the excise forts and the smithies. It killed the sound of the sea that had been rasping in Jonsson's ears right up to the point that he guided his dying endrin-cart through the town gates.

Brushing off the yellow tobacco-stained fingers of an ancient and drunk-looking duardin offering to trade a tale for a coin, Jonsson pushed into the bustle.

Every grain of good sense was telling him to get back to his airship, but there was one duty he couldn't leave without observing.

The building that he was looking for was on the corner of a three-storey tenement in one of the most lightless and lawless wards of the lower city called the Greys. The skyports and grand houses of the Kharadron admiralties projected over the township beneath, like a gargantuan two-pronged fork suspended over their heads by the hand of Grungni himself. It cast large shadows and, situated right at the base of the old port's supporting columns, there were few places where they fell deeper than in the Greys. The building seemed to sag. Its roof drooped, its walls bulging imperceptibly. As if it were a plant withering for want of a ray of light. Its gritted windows displayed a piecemeal collection of faux-Nulahmian crockery and antique tableware. A spiderghast grot stood on the porch step. His body had been painted entirely in lime-white, except where carapace and mandibles had been scraped from the underlying green. He slapped a cudgel in his small palm, glaring menacingly at the handful of passers-by.

Most of the Greys' residents knew Murrag's place well enough to avoid it, but there was always the possibility that a stranger important enough to be missed might come innocently browsing for faux-Nulahmian crockery or antique tableware. The grot made sure that never happened.

Jonsson had known Murrag for decades.

When he had first deserted the venerable ironclad *Angrin-Ha!*

(an incident involving a looted Nagashi idol and a few misplaced coins that the admiral had entirely overblown), it had
been Murrag who had seen a place for him in her enter-
prise. Over the following decades, he had proven his eye
for antiquities and his knack for acquiring them, generally
from the cold hands of their former owners. The coin that
had purchased him a small dirigible, the *Fiskur*, and a crew
of his own, had been hers. Whenever he unearthed a treasure that he felt was too well protected for him to handle, he
made sure that word was passed along, and she would find
someone with more guns or fewer scruples. Any acquisitions
that he did make went first through her. Always. It was an
agreement he knew better than to renege on, even had he
not been Kharadron with contractual obligation writ into his
blood.

Aye, he knew Murrag well.

The miniscule enforcer glared at Jonsson as he approached.
The insanely potent blend of narcotics that was currently hol-
lowing out the grot's nervous system caused his eyes to cross
and his head to jerk violently on his neck.

'It's me. Jonsson.'

'S-s-s-s.'

Jonsson was unsure what the grot was trying to say, but he
shuffled aside obligingly. Jonsson pushed in the door.

To one who had never ventured inside (and most would
have considered themselves lucky to be amongst that group),
the shop would have seemed surprisingly spacious. The interior walls had been knocked down to leave just one large
front-of-house area and a small living area at the back. The
ceiling had been elevated, abolishing the second floor entirely.
Jonsson was not sure what had become of the third floor. He
had never been up there, nor seen any sign of stairs.

A handful of heavily intoxicated grots lounged about on chitin-stilt chairs that were small even to Jonsson, but in the context of this space seemed positively minute. It was as though they, the grots and Jonsson had all been shrunk and had ventured into a normal-sized room.

The effect was as disconcerting today as it had been the first time he had been admitted.

The grots largely ignored him, gazing in wonderment at the ceiling or eyeballing each other, a competitive spiderghast custom that Jonsson knew from experience could go on for days. One of them, however, was sufficiently lucid to lurch upright and stagger towards the knuckle-bead curtain that partitioned off the back of the shop.

Jonsson waited, fiddling nervously with his pistol grip. He did his best to ignore the ingrained fungal aroma. A muffled squawk and a *crunch* sounded from the other side of the curtain. He did his best to ignore that too.

'*Ingdrin Jonsson.*'

Murrag swept aside the curtain and, leading with the vastness of her belly, stomped into the shop.

The gaggle of opiated grots sprang suddenly to attention.

They saluted.

Murrag was the undisputed sovereign of all semi-legitimate and downright illegitimate business in antiques, artefacts and relics in Blackfire Bight. Her word was law, her utterances waited upon with bated breath, her needs, wants and every interest catered to any man who cared for the distinction between life and death, rich or poor.

She was also an ogor. And huge.

Each of her arms was thicker than Jonsson's waist. Her hands were like shovels, studded with bracelets and torqs that she wore as rings. He had once seen her rip a man in half.

Literally. *In half.* And then eat him. Her gut was gargantuan. It was almost a second entity, as if she had smuggled a hand-cart full of ripening produce under the mountain of her skirts. Her eyes were jet-black spigots, furrowed down into a slab of brow. Her hair was coarser than goat's wool, braided and decorated in the Kharadron style. Her appearance was brutal, but she was clever, very clever. When first they had met, Jonsson had thought he would be clear of her debt and free with her dirigible in a month. He had underestimated her, as almost everyone did. Her insatiable greed was just another manifestation of her ungodly hunger.

She was chewing as she entered.

Amongst unlicensed traders and petty crooks in every port of the realms, an ogor bodyguard was the ultimate symbol of status. The grots, then, had always been Murrag's idea of a poke in the eye to convention.

'*Gnollengrom*, Lady Murrag,' said Jonsson, unclasping his hands to give a respectful tug on his beard. He bowed.

'I always liked you duardin,' Murrag rumbled. 'So respectful.'

Jonsson bowed so low that his beard swept the floorboards.

'You are back so soon, Ingdrin. You found it then.'

Jonsson nibbled on his lip, trying to ignore the grumbling noises coming from Murrag's belly, so powerful they were shaking her skirts. 'Aye, lady, I did. Aighmar. Home of the Deepkin aelves in Blackfire.'

She gestured Jonsson towards a side table. 'Show me.'

The table was scaled for the anatomy of an ogor, and Jonsson was forced to stand on a chair in order to tip the contents of his satchel over its top. Rings and chalices and blades and glittering chunks of coral spilled over the polished wood. Murrag picked through it.

'Aelves under the sea,' she mused. 'I had tasted the rumours.

The Undying King hunts for them, you know? And the one with Three Eyes. Stealers of souls to one. Exiles of the Dark Prince to the other. They hide from them, but not from Murrag. She crunches the bone and gristle of legend and myth, devours through to truth inside.'

Jonsson bowed again.

'How did you find them?' she asked.

'We waylaid a sky-cutter flying the colours of Barak-Zon. Its own fault for straying so far from the patrolled lanes. Anyway, they had recently boarded and scuttled a Skyre clan ruinship that had been running repairs after a battle of its own. They didn't know what they had taken from its holds – not everyone reads Queekish – but it was a written record of a skaven invasion of Aighmar.'

'Records?' Murrag's brutalist features slipped into a broad grin. 'Not very... skaven.'

'Very detailed records too. The site was easy to find once I'd translated the skins. My guess is that they meant to pass them on to someone.'

'So, Nagash?' She licked her lips. 'Or Archaon?'

'I'd prefer not to think about it.'

The ogor picked up a blade from the loose pile of treasures to examine it more closely. It was a shortsword, its nacreous blade and cross-hilt plain, but fabulously ornate around the grip – as if it were intended to impress by touch rather than sight. In Murrag's grip it looked like a supper knife.

'Pretty.' She looked up, hungrily. 'Is there more?'

'Aye, plenty more. There's a whole city down there. The skaven have picked it over, but for a race of scavengers, they're careless. You can send another crew though. I'm moving on.'

'Moving where?'

'Anywhere. Away. That was always our arrangement, lady. If

ever I feel there's a prize I can't handle then I pass it on. No fee. No trouble. That's what I signed, and that's what I'll stick to.'

Murrag frowned down at him, the enormous muscles of her face shifting. 'The Deepkin scare you. Enough for *you* to tell *me* what our deal is.'

'They're coming for me. I can feel that they are. You as well now, I'm guessing.'

The ogor delivered a booming, stinking gale of laughter and gestured to her guards. They stiffened furiously.

'I feel very safe here.'

'I'm not joking.'

'Nor am I.'

Jonsson straightened. 'Well, then. I'll take my due, then I'll take my leave.'

Rubbing her belly with one hand, Murrag carefully separated out the trinkets from the coral shards and drew the former towards her side of the table, using the blade of the Idoneth shortsword like an admiral moving ship tokens around a campaign map. Jonsson's heart sank to see the coral being pushed back towards him. The mineral was clearly a repository for some kind of aelf magic and must have been worth a fortune to someone from the Collegiate Arcane, or even an arcanite cabal for all he cared. He wanted rid of the stuff.

'Old things,' Murrag growled, stirring through the pile of jewelled conches and ornate weaponry with the pommel of her sword. 'That's what I buy. That's what I sell.' She grumbled something in a hissing greenskin language to summon one of her attendants. 'Cradz. Fetch the ledger. Five shares, made out for Jonsson.'

Jonsson gawped at her.

He could not sell his dirigible for five shares, even if Vorgaard, his pirate of a bosun, could have been persuaded to scrape off the rust.

'Get the rest of it where I can't see it,' said Murrag. 'I don't like the way it smells.'

There was something magical about gold. It was a long-standing physical principle amongst the aether-khemists and chirurgeons of the Kharadron that the placement of a sufficiently high denomination coin could cause a suppurating wound to close or a malignant growth to shrink. Meditating upon its glow could cure ills both physical and mental. Even just the weight of a coin in a duardin's pocket could make his cares evaporate, making his soul feel lighter by a ratio corresponding unerringly to the value of said coin. Jonsson might have expected the miraculous effect to become even more pronounced once he had passed through the various stairgates and customs forts into the skydock proper and could safely remove his hand from his pistol holster.

He felt no easing of his spirit.

And did not move his hand.

Something he could not tally, nor weigh out on a set of calibrated scales, had put his teeth on edge. The endrin of every patrolling gunhauler and monitor, of every skywarden and rigger, sounded to him like the roar of the ocean. From every street vendor and high-end duardin restaurant, the smell of decaying seaweed and saltwater made him want to gag.

The skyport was not the Toba Lorchai that most of its inhabitants knew, but it was the face that the admiralty lords would recognise. Here were the stone-built docks erected by the first pioneers of Barak-Thryng, long before the locals had come to build a settlement at its base. Here, shipping magnates and lords of industry of all races comported themselves in gowns, flocked by equerries and viziers, while ship captains strode about the port's wholesalers in armour.

After removing himself from Murrag's company – for the last time, with any luck – Jonsson had been of half a mind to pay a visit to a jeweller of his acquaintance in a last attempt at unloading the Idoneth coral before taking his final leave of Toba Lorchai itself. A master gemsmith of the Dispossessed, his acquaintance was as famed for his honourable approach to the business as he was for his eye for a gem.

Something persuaded him to err towards the direct route.

The thought of just dumping the coral on a bench or in a doorway somewhere and foregoing his profit never occurred – to do so would have been a flagrant violation of the Code, and Vorgaard, his bosun, would have stripped him of his captaincy had he even suspected.

Exchanging curt nods with familiar faces amongst the harbour watch, Jonsson hurried towards the docks.

The sooner he was a thousand feet above sea level with his gold and the Idoneth coral securely stowed away in the captain's cabin, the happier he would feel. He could sell it in another city. Preferably in another realm.

Then, maybe, he would feel ready to move his hand from his pistol's grip.

Across from the imposing granite portico of the endrinmaster's guildhall and bank, a fountain prattled. A scale replica of the Barak-Thryng ironclad *Thallazorn* spouted water from her gun turrets into a pool. The sound grated on Jonsson's nerves. A ring of metal benches surrounded the fountain. They were popular with lunching endrinmasters, but it was barely an hour after dawn, and there was only a handful of bleary-eyed longbeards nibbling on a belated breakfast.

Jonsson sat down.

It was only four thousand and nine steps from the Grundstok Gate to the docking tines, and he was practically a beardless scamp at a mere fifty-seven years old, but he was finding it increasingly hard going catching a breath. He exhaled slowly, looking up in astonishment at the stream of transparent bubbles that issued from between his lips and floated up towards the sky. Schools of skeletal fish shoaled about the equally astonished skywardens.

Trailing bubbles from his open mouth, he brought his gaze back down to port level, to where an allopex swam between the granite colonnades of the guildhall. The huge, grey-skinned sea monster was collared and bridled, barded in a rigid plate of darkly tinted shells. An aelf in elegantly streamlined armour and wielding some kind of net launcher rode in a standing saddle on the monster's back.

Jonsson's first thought was that he had gone mad.

The anxiety of his flight was bleeding into the reality of his five senses, his fear that the denizens of the deep ocean would come for him, and now he saw the ocean in all its horror right where it simply could not be. He would have laughed at his own broken mind had the beer-soaked endrinmaster on the bench beside him not muttered a drawled curse, tugged a volley pistol from the expanse of grey beard bundled up in his lap, and opened fire.

The hammer burst of shots snapped Jonsson out of his shock.

He jumped up smartly, drawing his own single-shot firearm.

The endrinmaster's salvo tore into the allopex's head. It crashed into the ground like a side of meat dumped from the back of a waggon, and crushed its rider's leg to the ground beneath its mass. The aelf screamed, seemingly more in anguish from being wounded, than from the pain itself. The endrinmaster casually walked over to the downed beast and shot the rider in the head, then belched an enormous bubble.

Throughout the great concourses and plazas of the skyport,

the impossible was spreading. Everywhere Jonsson turned he saw his nightmare writ in powder smoke and charging bodies. Aelven warriors flowed down the main thoroughfare as though borne along on a flood tide, sweeping aside all before them, while in the air allopex knights and grim-faced warriors mounted on fangmora, eel-like horrors that coursed with sparking energies, converged on the endrinriggers working in their high nests.

The Kharadron of Barak-Thryng, however, were far from defenceless in their home port, even when assaulted unawares. Shots rang out. The leaden booms of skycannons. The rattling chatter of aethermatic weapons. Every food hall and warehouse in view that had been host to a captain and his entourage had become a casemate from which decksweeper volleys and fumigator fire raked the aelves and their bonded nightmares. In the sky, amidst the endrin rigs and aethermatic hoists, the Kharadron spat back at the aelven cavalry with drill cannon and rivet-fire. Shields of crackling elemental power surrounded the fangmora knights, deflecting most of the incoming projectiles. A second contingent armed with energised spears swept past the first before the lightning shields had fully dissipated, rushing towards the endrinriggers' impromptu redoubts with the fury of a wave.

Jonsson did not stop to watch.

'Grungni the Maker,' he breathed.

The old master belched another large bubble, which Jonsson took for typical longbeard disdain before noticing the arrow embedded in his chest. He pitched backwards and into the fountain with a splash.

Jonsson brought his pistol up as he quickly backed away, circling around the marble bulk of the fountain's scale model ironclad.

The aelves were advancing through the columns of the guild-hall. They came with an eerie, floating gait, bounding rather than walking. It was as if they moved through water even as Jonsson, a hundred feet away from them, did not.

With a snarl, Jonsson aimed and fired.

The pistol kicked hard, annihilating an archer's shoulder and spinning him hard into the face of a column. The rest kept coming, loosing as they ran. Another old endrinmaster caught an arrow in the chin and in the eye and dropped with a gurgle, his weapon unfired.

Jonsson did not even waste time reloading his pistol.

Toba Lorchai had been good to him. He would miss the place, it was true, but for him home had always been just a port of call. And the Code was very specific on the subject of lost causes.

Artycle Four, Point Five.

He turned and sprinted for the aether-docks.

The docks were Toba Lorchai's beating heart, its higher purpose and its soul. Three great prongs of granite, like a colossal fork, protruded from the crown of the hill, busy with aethermatic winches and cranes, sky-ships docking or embarking, loading or unloading. They were a hive at any time. If not for the incessant drum of gunfire and the eerie wailing of the aelves, then Jonsson might have been able to force his way into the cussing mob of grundstok crew and longshoremen without noticing anything amiss.

A very large (and very well paid) garrison of Grundstok thunderers had responsibility for the docking tines, with a contingent of orruk mercenaries that fluctuated in strength depending on the perceived threats of the times. Fire-duels crackled into life as the aelves advanced on the docks. Howling mobs of green-skinned and war-painted orruk berserkers surged from the grundstok stockades to engage the aelves hand-to-hand. The melees that broke out were ferocious. Seven-foot-tall orruks with bulging muscles hacked at the delicate aelven warriors in a frenzy. Scores of them fell in the first seconds of the charge, but the survivors neither cried out nor broke. They sang a flat, empty lament as they whirled into the attack with graceful, perfectly controlled strokes of their hefty blades.

The anarchy consuming the tines themselves was, if it were possible, of a different order.

Stevedores and endrinriggers fought one another for right of way. Harbourmasters bellowed red-faced at unyielding captains. Arkanaut companies beat terrified humans and duardin from their vessels' boarding planks with the butts of their pistols. Frigates and gunhaulers launched with their moorings still attached, ripping giant hooks out of the granite, crashing into the back of other vessels that had not yet cleared the dock, all of it conducted under the gale-roar of cold aether-endrins being pushed hard to full power.

Jonsson's own dirigible, the *Fiskur*, was smaller than most, a humble three-gunner with an aethershot carbine mounted in the prow, port and starboard, and a bow-chaser in the aftcastle. The collection of armour-plated spheres suspended over the deck within a girder of metal housed an old but well-proven aether-endrin. The winged blades of its propellers were already humming. A crew of seven were busy releasing the mooring lines and riveting the endrin-rigging for departure.

'Don't tell me you were about to cast off without me,' Jonsson shouted over the rising howl of the endrin, striding over the boarding plank mere seconds before an arkanaut companion with a torn ear and an eyepatch dragged it in from under him.

'As per Artycle Seven, Point Three,' said Vorgaard Hangarik cheerfully. The leathery-skinned bosun wore a crown that he had lifted from a dashian tomb in Lyrhia at an angle he considered dashing, and which, on a duardin half his two hundred years, might well have been. He observed the frantic activity of his company with an unhurried ease, thumbs wedged under the belt that was buckled around his armour, sucking on the dry stem of an unlit pipe.

'Point Three pertains to the incapacity, insanity or death of the existing captain,' Jonsson panted.

'Well.' Vorgaard withdrew the pipe from his mouth and used it to gesture towards the violence that was slowly breaking through the Kharadron defences and spilling into the docks. 'What was any right-minded duardin to think?'

'I...'

Jonsson put his hands on his knees and coughed.

'You need a moment to catch a breath, cap'n?' said Vorgaard. 'I've got time.'

'Do we have clearance from the harbourmaster?'

'I wouldn't say *clearance* exactly.'

'Good enough.'

Blowing quickly and hard, Jonsson wove through the arkanauts and hurried up the sheet metal steps to the aftcastle. He nodded to the turret gunner, and took the wheel.

Vorgaard followed him.

'Get my ship out of here,' Jonsson bellowed into the pole-mounted speaker-horn that was welded to the deck plating beside the wheel. 'Full power to the endrin. I want a thousand feet between us and the Deepkin before I can count down from the five aether-gold shares in my pocket.'

A raucous chorus of 'ayes' rang out at the promise of gold as the *Fiskur* lurched into a sudden climb. Jonsson gripped tight to the wheel, pulling the dirigible's course inland and upwards. The hull plating squealed and shuddered. The endrin-rigging emitted a long, tortured whine punctuated by bangs of stressed metal as the propellers dragged the ship away from the ground. The vast bow of an ironclad hove into their course. Grumbling under his breath, Jonsson hauled on the wheel, shaking his fist at his counterpart as the *Fiskur* sailed under the ironclad's keel and continued to climb.

Throughout it all, Vorgaard remained in a solid, wide-legged posture that he could hold unflustered through aether-storm or sky-battle. He cast Jonsson a sideways look.

'Deepkin, you say?'

Jonsson set his jaw. 'Aye.'

'The old legend?'

'*Aye.*'

'*Skat,*' Vorgaard swore.

'Aye.'

'I think we're out of it,' said Vorgaard, after a moment's silence.

Jonsson nodded and loosened his hold on the tiller, reducing the buoyancy in the aether-bags and levelling the pitch of the propellers. The dirigible eased off with her complaints as she levelled out of her climb, bar the occasional cough from the endrin that the endrinmaster quickly moved to tend.

He looked back.

The monolithic tines of Toba Lorchai were shrinking behind him. Even the gunhaulers and monitors that had been patrolling the sky lanes before the attack had been sprung looked small, coming about to add aerial support to the port's defenders as the *Fiskur* pulled ever further away. Just in time, Jonsson thought. He was not so high yet that he could no longer distinguish the dark, graceful tide of aelves from the splintering battle lines of the Kharadron and their allies. From up high it looked like a black sea coming in, sweeping away the sand fortresses and metallic pebbles that had been set up around the beach in its absence. They had already swept as far in as the tines. The fighting was even spilling over onto those ships still in dock, deck watches defending their gun ridges like the ramparts of a floating castle. Those that were not already fending off boarders redoubled their efforts to be aweigh, adding to the carnage in the slipways.

'Good thing somebody had the endrin running,' Vorgaard murmured.

'It looks as though they're sparing the township,' said Jonsson. 'Trust Murrag to get out of this in one piece.'

He looked away, sick, and stared at the matt gunmetal of the ship's wheel in his hands. He could not shake the dread that this was somehow not over, that the sack of Toba Lorchai was simply incidental. It was him the Deepkin wanted, he was sure of it. He did not know how they were following him, but he did not think they were going to stop here.

Perhaps he could return to the skyhold of Barak-Thryng itself. Or Azyrheim. Gods, yes. Let the Deepkin pursue him all the way there.

'New heading, bosun,' he yelled, spinning the wheel, the prow following it slowly to starboard. 'We're heading for the Azyr Gate at Glymmsforge.'

'Good idea,' said Vorgaard.

One hand on the wheel, Jonsson shrugged off his satchel, the coral a lumpen weight in the bottom, as if he had a spiked mace against his back, and tossed it to Vorgaard.

'Throw it overboard.'

The bosun tested its weight in his hand. 'Is it valuable?'

'Cite me later. Throw it overboard!'

'Aye, cap'n.'

Vorgaard walked towards the aftcastle battlements, the satchel drawn back for an overarm hurl into the wide, blue aether, but then just stopped mid-stride. His arm dropped to his side and he just stared. Jonsson glanced over and swore.

'As aether is bloody light.'

In the sky dead ahead of their new course, in defiance of every scientific law that Jonsson cared for, there swam a gigantic armour-plated turtle. The behemoth was easily the mass of a fully gunned ironclad, but the throbbing waves of distortion rippling from the howdah mounted on its back made it difficult to make out in detail, or to accurately count the swarm of allopex and fangmora knights that ran abeam of it like gunhaulers escorting a dreadnought.

'A leviadon,' Jonsson breathed.

'Turn! Turn!' Vorgaard grabbed the wheel from him and bellowed into the speaker-horn. 'Port broadside. Aethershot carbine, fire. Skilli, why am I not currently deafened by drill cannon-fire?'

The dirigible shook to a pair of tremendous booms, falling close enough together to be heard as one. The aethershot sailed into the diffraction cloud and to all obvious purposes disappeared. The detonation drill from the bow-chaser was not so easily waylaid. It burst in the vicinity, faceted loops of explosion rippling around the leviadon as if seen from the other side of an armoured window. A couple of fangmora knights dropped out of the sky – or sank, Jonsson was not sure – becoming increasingly visible as they fell away from the leviadon's protective field.

'Brace!' Jonsson yelled as something twinkled back in return.

A razorshell harpoon as long as Jonsson was tall crunched into the rigging, perilously close to the endrin housing. The impact lurched the dirigible to starboard, smashed Jonsson's face into the wheel, and sent him sprawling back to the aftcastle deck. He groaned. Voices fought for attention in his skull.

'Endrinmaster. *Wakaz!* To your post.'

'Fire! Fire!'

'Boarders aft.'

'Stand and repel.'

'All hands to the hold.'

The clash and clamour of steel brought him back around, the scuff of armoured boots on metal planking. He jerked upright, reaching for his pistol. The repellent stench of something dank and rancid hit him halfway.

He blinked, looking up into the flat, noseless features of a nightmare with no right to exist beyond the blackest deep-sea trench. Its skin was rubbery and white, bristling with spined frills and venomous-looking barbs. It floated sinuously up and down, as if riding ocean currents that Jonsson, in his land-locked insensibility, was numb to. Its clawed fins raked Jonsson's beard with every down-movement, its triplet of tails coiling and unbunching on the deck.

An aelf woman sat bestride its back. Every part of her body, apart from her head, was encapsulated like a pearl within a shell of perfectly shaped black metal. Her skin was so gaunt and so pale that Jonsson could see the veins that webbed her face, and even make out the dark green of her eyes when she blinked. Her skin, her armour and her weapons all glistened with wetness, her voluminous dark hair billowing with unnat-ural buoyancy around the clamshell plates of her shoulders.

He could hear his crew fighting. Vorgaard, probably. Skilli in the turret. He grabbed up his pistol and swung it around. The aelf cut the barrel in half with a curt downstroke of her sword. It clicked as he pulled on the trigger.

'Boka–'

The aelf impaled him through the shoulder with the lance in her left hand, driving it through hard enough to pierce the metal of the deck, skewering him in place. The deepmare she rode opened its hideously alien mouth, but made no sound.

'Who… are you?' he said.

'Pétra. Queen of those from whom you stole.'

Jonsson shook his head vigorously, wincing as he pulled against the lance in his shoulder. 'I stole nothing. I found it. The city was abandoned. I claimed *galkhron* in accordance with Artycle Two, Point One of the– *Aaaarrgh!*'

Pétra released the butt of the lance and let it stand slack again.

'A thief's notion. To assert that a thing is unclaimed simply because it is untended.'

'My queen, here.'

Jonsson turned his head to look sideways along the deck. Vorgaard was sat up against the aftcastle wall, eyes closed, breathing shallowly as though asleep. His armour was unscratched. A tall aelf with a shining coat of armour scales and a helm that enclosed his entire face but for an expressionless mouth stood over him. He was the one who had spoken. He shook out the contents of Jonsson's satchel and held up the coral to his blank, eyeless mask. He appeared to sigh, a strange gesture when unaccompanied by any obvious outward sign of emotion.

'What have you done to my bosun?' Jonsson gasped.

The aelf ignored him.

'The lost shards of the chorrileum of Aighmar. I can feel the souls bound within.' His lips stiffened. 'I hear them wail.'

Pétra nodded, as though satisfied.

'The rest is in the township,' said Jonsson, pain making him gabble. 'I can show you who has them and where, in exchange for my life and my ship.'

The aelf queen regarded him with inexpressive eyes, a picture of untouchable beauty painted on a rock.

'I care not for the trinkets. Things can be replaced. Souls devoured by the Thirsting Prince are forever lost.'

Jonsson did not know what to say. How did you treat with creatures so alien in their values as the Deepkin aelves?

'Then... what do you want?'

'How did you learn about Aighmar?' she said.

'The city?' Quickly, Jonsson explained everything that he had previously related to Murrag, about the Barak-Zon sky-cutter, the skaven ruinship, everything.

'Then it is done,' said the helmeted aelf. 'We can return to the sweet annihilation of the senses and feel no more.' He lowered his scythe-like weapon, the light-globe swinging from its head emitting a curious pull on Jonsson's attention.

'No,' said Jonsson, trying to pull away, but for reasons other than the obvious one sticking through his shoulder, he could not. 'No.'

'You duardin are long-lived,' said Pétra coldly, hidden within the totality of the lure-light. 'Your soul will be highly prized. It will bring joy, of a kind, to the parent of a namarti who will otherwise wither in childhood and perish.'

'There's a whole city down there,' he protested. 'Thousands. You can't take them all. There will be those that remember you.'

Jonsson closed his eyes, but somehow he could see the scythe-wielding aelf's blank expression through the light. Pity. Sorrow.

And then there was nothing but the light.

Thalia hugged her knees to her chin and watched the waves break against the rocks. They were bodies, woollen and black, tumbling, ripping open, spilling their frothing white guts over the beach. She shivered, cold. She did not know what she was doing here, could not remember, only that she was alone. Her da had been taken by the sea, as her ma had been, long ago.

The memory of the more recent event slurped and gurgled from her grasp, like wet sand from between her toes as the waves dragged it away to where her recollections of the older had long been submerged.

'And when they grow old and grandchildren forget, That will be the day when the fishing folk come.'

She looked back, along the deserted shoreline. To the inland road.

Because they were not the fishing folk.

They were the fish.

BLACKTALON: WHEN CORNERED

Andy Clark

A column of armoured waggons rumbled through dusty Chamonite wastes. Stocky duardin marched beside them, their shoulders broad, their eyes hard. They wore runic chainmail and were festooned with weapons. They watched the horizon with belligerent intensity. Squat dobkine plodded along in traces near the column's rear, the chitin-armoured bovines hauling field artillery and waggons.

A doughty duardin lord led the march. He was suited in magnificently crafted armour and wore a look of ferocious determination beneath his beetling black brows. He was carried atop a broad shield, its considerable weight borne without obvious discomfort by a quartet of grey-bearded champions.

Beside him stalked Neave Blacktalon. The Knight-Zephyros was tall, even for a Stormcast Eternal, and in her sleek sigmarite armour and sculpted helm her eyes were at the same level as the duardin lord's.

'The sorcerer has been caught, and he will pay for his crimes,' said the duardin. His voice was a gravelly rumble so deep that Neave felt it in her chest.

'For that, I am sure that Sigmar thanks you, Thane Halgrimmsson,' she replied. Her tone was sharp steel to his grinding stone, tinged with the ghost of a tribal lilt.

'*You* don't, though, do you, Stormcast?' asked the duardin.

Neave didn't immediately reply. She swept her eyes across the desolate lands around them. Her supernaturally keen senses drank in every detail, their acuity only slightly dulled by an omnipresent stench. The acrid stink wafted from some distance back down the line, from the caged waggon that contained the throng's captive.

More distantly, Neave could feel the thumping footfalls of some huge beast. Predatory, she thought, from its loping gait, but not foolish enough to assail a marching column of warriors, no matter how scarce prey might be. Where would it go after dark? How did anything survive here when the ashen people came? She heard the grumbling conversations of the duardin, her quick mind easily able to sift out any given conversation from amongst the hubbub of voices, marching feet and clanking wargear.

Closer, she heard the steady thud of the duardin lord's heart, read every nuance of his posture, smelled the sharp bite of his sweat. He was eager to provoke a row, she thought, all too ready to lead her into some sleight or act of disrespect that he could then pounce on as justification to deny her claim upon his captive.

You don't so easily snare a huntress, no matter how many times you try this, thought Neave.

'Xelkyn Xerkanos has left a trail of horror and infamy behind him that stretches for thousands of miles and taints three of the Mortal Realms with its touch,' she said, finally answering the thane's barb. 'He triggered uprisings in Hammerhal Ghyra and Anvilheim. He stole the secrets of the Vault of Echoes and reduced their guardians to fleshspawn. He has insulted the dignity and authority of the God-King Sigmar time and again. I am glad that he has been run to ground at last.'

'Aye, but only because he took his blade to King Halgrimm, and I made him pay for it,' said the duardin, returning his eyes to the road ahead.

Neave heard the unspoken accusation. She had been on Xerkanos' trail for more than half a year by Azyrite reckoning, had fought him and his minions several times and come so close to slaying him that she could almost smell his foul blood upon her blades. She had been closing upon the sorcerer, sure this time of striking the killing blow, when the duardin had taken her quarry instead. That another had been responsible for claiming her mark rankled with Neave, but what troubled her more was that the mark still lived.

'Your warriors fought hard and well,' she said, keeping her tone neutral.

'They also got there before you,' said Halgrimmsson bluntly. 'Neave Blacktalon. The most famed of Sigmar's Knights-Zephyros, his arch-hunters. A warrior of the Hammers of Sigmar no less, and yet we got to your quarry before you could. I know if it were me, Stormcast, I'd feel the dishonour keen as a wound.'

With pride like yours, I don't doubt it, Neave almost said. Instead, she pressed her lips into a thin line behind her helm's faceplate. She shot a glance back along the line of march to where the sorcerer's cage-waggon rumbled along. She should have been back there guarding it, and would have been but for the necessity to once again appeal to Halgrimmsson's better sense.

'Xerkanos is caught,' she began after a moment's thought.

'His cult lies slain. It will be *my* blades that strike the fatal blow once your courts have accounted the sorcerer's guilt. I see no dishonour in such a victory, thane, only the rightful cooperation of those who have allied themselves to oppose the Dark Gods.'

Halgrimmsson gave a noncommittal grunt.

Neave had come to the battlefield in Irongrief Vale too late to swing her blades in anger, but in time to witness the duardin binding Xerkanos in runic chains and loading him into a cage-waggon for transport. The carnage of that charnel field had been hideous. The duardin had bled for their victory. Still, Neave had only had eyes for the sorcerer.

She had explained her hunt to Halgrimmsson and claimed Xerkanos as her rightful mark by the God-King's authority. The duardin had scoffed, telling her that his clan's blood debt outweighed all other considerations. He had implied that, allies or not, he would not hesitate to have his surviving warriors send her back to the heavens if she meant to stand in his way.

Rather than tell the thane just how many of his warriors would perish if he gave that order, Neave had begun what turned out to be a wrangling and hard-fought negotiation. There, amongst the dead, the Knight-Zephyros and the duardin, the thane had agreed that Xerkanos would be dragged in chains before the ancient Grudgekeepers of Clan Halgrimm, and there be tried and sentenced for the murder of Halgrimmsson's father, the king. However, it would be Neave who would act as Xerkanos' appointed executioner. Thus, she would conclude her hunt successfully and Halgrimmsson would have his justice. Just as important, particularly from the perspective of the hidebound duardin, was that no bad blood would be borne between Neave's Stormhost, the Hammers of Sigmar, and Clan Halgrimm.

It was not an arrangement that either party had delighted in. Neave was conscious that, had he not been forced to obey certain codes of honour in front of his clansmen, Halgrimmsson would most likely have refused it point-blank.

Neave knew that Halgrimmsson was young by duardin standards. He had just lost his father in terrible circumstances and it could not have escaped him that, had Neave brought her mark down sooner, that death would have been avoided. She knew she couldn't blame him for his resentfulness, his stubbornness. Neave glanced back down the lines again. I can't be blamed either, she thought, for finding his stance so damned frustrating.

And so, they had found themselves in this situation: Neave accompanying what remained of the Clan Halgrimm forces across these nameless wastes towards where the Shuddering Mountains lined the southern horizon. There lay the karak the duardin called home, a mighty fortress delved deep into the mountainside. There, Xerkanos could be put to death in a manner that would satisfy the honour of all concerned, and the matter put to rest.

Yet Halgrimmsson kept pushing, trying to edge Neave into undermining her claim.

'It *will* be my blades that separate the sorcerer's filthy head from his neck, thane,' she repeated, taking care to inject the right blend of deference and authority into her tone.

'Aye,' replied Halgrimmsson after a pause. 'Such was our bargain. But not until time.'

Neave was careful not to let her frustration show. When Sigmar gave her a mark, the sense of that quarry was imprinted upon her psyche. She felt her prey like a tingle or itch that grew more pronounced the closer she came to them, like a murmur that swelled to a ringing note. Having Xerkanos so close, just a hundred yards or so to her rear, and being unable to take her axes to his neck was almost physically painful for Neave.

She had endured worse, of course – she had been slain and reforged eight times already in Sigmar's service. Her impatience with the arrangement stemmed not from discomfort, but bitter experience.

'Thane, I ask again, can a tribunal not be convened here, now?' she asked. 'You have the authority and the good cause to try and then sentence this monster right here by the roadside. You have witnesses in plentiful supply and of unimpeachable character. You would incur no dishonour from the deed.'

Thane Halgrimmsson heard her out stolidly, as he had each time she had made this same entreaty. Then shook his head just as he had each time before.

'No dishonour, Stormcast, but the whispers would start all the same,' he said. '"Halgrimmsson allowed his anger to spur him into actions over-hasty", "Halgrimmsson had his judgement clouded by the words of some Azyrite outsider", "Halgrimmsson failed to uphold the proper traditions of his people", "Halgrimmsson's oath is unfulfilled, and he is not fit to be king like his father before him."'

After this last, he favoured her with a fierce glare, as though challenging Neave to agree with his imagined detractors.

But Neave did not. Instead, she replied, 'You know that every minute Xelkyn Xerkanos still lives, it is another minute that he is dangerous.'

Halgrimmsson snorted.

'He's bound in runic chains fashioned by Borrikh Gnarlhelm himself, and being transported under armed guard by the best part of a hundred stout duardin warriors. He's in a damned cage, Stormcast, unarmed and with his followers dead in his wake. He is no danger to us. What *would* prove dangerous is delaying our march long enough for night to come upon us and the ashen people to crawl from under the dunes. We don't halt until we reach sanctuary.'

Neave shook her head, breathed out slowly through her nostrils. If Halgrimmsson only understood what it meant to evade the pursuit of a Knight-Zephyros for so long, she thought, how diabolically devious and dangerously skilled Xerkanos had to be to achieve that feat, then perhaps the duardin would listen. She shrugged off the bleak notion that there was slim chance of that, at least until it was too late.

'I understand the dangers of these lands,' said Neave, trying again. 'But I ask you to hear me, for our alliance's sake. Xerkanos doesn't need followers, or weapons. He needs only his mind and the time to plot. The longer we allow him those things, the greater the danger that he escapes.'

'Just because he slipped your grasp, don't think that means he'll slip ours,' said Halgrimmsson. 'We ran him to ground first try.'

'I still do not believe that was coincidence,' said Neave. 'He knew I was close, that I had the measure of him this time–'

'So he let us catch him by staging the bloodiest battle I've witnessed in a century?' interrupted Halgrimmsson. 'He murdered my father just to draw my ire and then used me to keep him from your blades? He just happened to know precisely how matters would play out, and is even this moment manipulating all of us into effecting his escape yet again?'

Neave remained silent. Halgrimmsson had just voiced her every concern, barring perhaps that Xerkanos had read the son's insecurity and stubbornness in his prognostications and factored those into his scheme as well.

'*Hrukhni*,' swore Halgrimmsson. 'Why would your sorcerer be so worried about one Stormcast when he was leading an army?'

'He's led armies before, thane,' said Neave. 'They've never stopped me.' Halgrimmsson spat by way of reply.

'Xerkanos perpetrated one act of malfeasance too many when he slew King Halgrimm,' he said, his voice dangerously low. 'He'll pay for it by our laws and at the time of our choosing. You get to strike the killing blow that should, by rights, be mine. Be satisfied with that, Stormcast.'

Recognising a lost cause when she saw one, Neave inclined her head slightly and slackened her pace. She allowed the king's bearers to march on ahead as she dropped back through the column of march. Duardin flowed past in ordered blocks, clan banners flying proudly at the head of each regiment, drummers battering out a steady tattoo that kept their comrades in lockstep.

Neave drifted to the roadside and let the duardin pass her by. She stared out to the horizon and its curling dust devils. This was a truly desolate land, one of the bleakest she could recall.

Had it always been thus, she wondered, or had the Age of Chaos reduced some fertile paradise to this? Neave suspected the latter was true. If so, it was a stark reminder of why she fought, and what she battled to prevent.

Her keen eyes caught the dull edges of wind-eroded ruins in the distance, and her cloak stirred in the cold breeze as she eyed them where they lurked, half buried in dunes of dust.

'It is a sorrowful land,' she murmured. 'Good only for sorrowful things.'

Still, the spark of civilisation had been relit here, Neave knew, and they were making straight for it. There was a walled town about an hour's march ahead. Labouring under the overly optimistic title of Lightsdawn, the place had been raised by Azyrite settlers several years earlier and now acted as an outpost in this dead land. Neave had passed through Lightsdawn on her way to Irongrief Vale, had seen the underground springs and carefully husbanded crop-caverns that kept the place alive, the high walls and vast braziers that kept this land's mysterious bogeymen at bay. She had seen its hard-eyed citizens and the copious soldiers who watched over them. Neave had seen precious little evidence of the resurgence of life in the wilds that the Sigmarite priests claimed was coming, however.

She reflected that but for the alliance with the duardin, this town might well have choked on the dust and desolation that surrounded it or been overrun by the terrors that came at night. It was duardin fuel and ironwork that kept Lightsdawn together. That was part of the reason that Halgrimmsson had taken this road towards his distant karak; the column would stay overnight in the capacious cavern-barracks that his folk had dug out beneath Lightsdawn for just such a purpose, and would push on towards the Shuddering Mountains in the morning.

Before then, Neave meant to have a conversation with their captive.

Presently, Neave heard the armoured waggons rumbling up behind her. Several contained weapons and ammunition, she knew, another a complement of healers. Another was a heavy affair of iron spars and reinforced wheels with a blackened chimney protruding from its roof. That waggon housed a mobile forge presided over by Runesmith Gnarlhelm.

Amidst them all, rattling along with a knot of heavily armoured Ironbreakers marching beside it, came the cage-waggon that held Xelkyn Xerkanos.

Neave had been able to smell his acrid stench ever since Irongrief Vale. Now, as then, it swelled in her nostrils and coated the back of her throat until it made her want to gag. It was the reek of unfettered sorcery, of mutated flesh, squirming insects and caustic ashes.

It was the scent of her mark.

Neave matched pace with the cage-waggon, moving up behind it and pointedly ignoring the clanking Ironbreakers just as they ignored her. She stared in through the stout iron bars of the cage at the figure hunched within. Neave felt a violent surge of hatred swell in her breast at the sight of him. She pushed it down with an effort. This pathetic-looking pile of blue-and-yellow rags had cost her good comrades and caused grief and pain to both her and many that she cared about.

'Xerkanos,' she said, her voice cold as drawn steel. 'I see you, sorcerer. I see you clearly.'

Xelkyn Xerkanos unfolded from his crouch like a mutant spider emerging from its burrow. Insectile limbs scraped together, rune-wrought fetters clanking as he moved. The sorcerer's face was a ghastly mixture of human and dragonfly, gross mouthparts squirming in a fleshy jaw, iridescent chitin bursting in ridges through tattooed flesh. Neave saw herself reflected in the lenses of his bulbous compound eyes, each mirror image subtly different and filled with a promise of violence and horror to come.

'Do you, Blacktalon?' he asked, his warped mouth mangling his words. 'I wonder...'

'You're going to your death, you realise?' she asked. 'Whatever machinations you intended, they have landed you in chains and on the road to your doom.'

It was a crude stab, and Neave knew it, but sparring with Halgrimmsson had worn down her patience. She wanted to jog a reaction from Xerkanos. Neave's gifts allowed her to read the slightest nuance of posture, expression and response, even in a being as cunning and unnatural as Xerkanos. If he had anything to give away, she would see it, and in her experience his greatest flaw was his sense of smug superiority.

Sure enough, there it was, a very slight twitch of knowing amusement in the stretched muscles of his cheeks, a minute trip of his ninefold heartbeat.

'If you say so, Blacktalon, then it must be so,' he said, and his voice was like knucklebones clicking and insect wings rasping together. 'What is the might of Tzeentch when set against the pre-eminent majesty of your God-King, after all? How might a humble servant of the Changer of the Ways contend with so formidable a gathering of my master's foes? Surely, this time, I am doomed.'

He sounded defeated, she thought. Miserable, even. Neave knew better.

'After all the times you scried the weave of the future to evade me,' she said. 'After the armies of cultists you raised and the powerful secrets you stole, you were cornered and defeated by a host of duardin.'

'Prognostication is imprecise,' said Xerkanos. 'Fate is a scattered reflection on broken waters, not an image in a mirror, clear to see.' There was nothing false about the bitterness she heard in his voice this time.

'What were you trying to do?' she asked. 'What possible benefit could you derive from killing the duardin king?'

No response. Xerkanos' mouthparts worked, rasping one over the other in a cleaning motion. He twitched slightly beneath his ragged robes.

'I don't believe it, Xerkanos,' said Neave, her words barbed with scorn. 'I am not fooled.'

'You have never been able to see the full extent of my schemes, Blacktalon,' he said. 'Just as your idiot god cannot perceive the true breadth of my master's plan. But you tried. You tried to predict me, to pre-empt me. It is your instinct as a huntress. This was what made you easy to evade and to manipulate.'

'Not so easy to evade that I didn't slaughter your followers and foil your schemes at every turn,' she said, and was rewarded by a spasm that raced, there and gone, across his features. Neave had learned early on that Xerkanos liked his plans to run smoothly, his enemies to flounder bewildered, and to know the full extent of their defeat before he crushed them. With Neave at his heels, he had been forced to rush, to improvise frantically. It had cost him, both in terms of followers and ruined plans.

'Still you goad and second-guess,' he said, his buzzing voice sounding part mocking, part sorrowful. 'You believe that I am, what, conning my captors in some way? That I have some plan of escape that they are stupid enough to be an unwitting part of?'

At the sorcerer's words, Neave felt a couple of glares from the Ironbreakers. Just because they were ignoring her and the sorcerer didn't mean the duardin were deaf to their conversation. She suspected Xerkanos was attempting to rile them.

'I believe that you are a supremely dangerous being and that the Mortal Realms will not be safe from your taint until your head lies separate from your neck,' she said in a low growl. 'And even then, Xerkanos, you can be sure that I will see the body burned and the ashes salted and buried.'

Xerkanos hissed for a moment with what Neave realised was laughter, but then he seemed to deflate. The sorcerer rested his gnarled hands upon the wooden boards of the waggon's floor. His torn robes pooled around him.

'You give me more credit than I deserve,' he said bitterly. 'I will not give you the satisfaction of knowing how, or why, but these duardin failed to dance upon their puppet-strings as they should have. This is no ruse, Blacktalon.'

She stared levelly at him for long seconds, then Xerkanos hurled himself into sudden motion. He lunged towards the bars of his cage with an insectile hiss, blue sparks dancing to life at the ends of his taloned fingers. Chains rattled as they raced through the iron ring set into the waggon's floor, then clanged taut. The runes inscribed along their length glowed with a baleful light and Xerkanos screamed in pain. His sorcerous energies died as suddenly as they had flared, and he slumped against the wooden boards beneath him.

'*X'thazk z'threkkis aeshlech g'zarr*,' he spat, a foul curse in a daemonic tongue. The beasts pulling the waggon snorted and reared at the unholy words, and even the Ironbreakers recoiled as if struck. Only Neave remained impassive, her eyes locked unflinchingly upon the Tzeentchian sorcerer. She caught the sound of scratching talons that all others surely missed in that moment.

'Lady Stormcast, you are bothering the captive and that bothers us,' grumbled one of the Ironbreakers, a champion or leader by his helmet plume.

'My apologies,' said Neave.

'Save them and take them elsewhere, eh?' said the duardin sourly. 'We'll be in Lightsdawn within the hour. Interrogate him then if you must.' He glanced away towards where the light of Hysh was lowering towards the mountain peaks and the shadows were stretching long. It would not do to delay, that look said, for darkness brought death in this place.

Neave inclined her head and picked up her pace, sweeping past the cage-waggon and leaving its mutant occupant in her wake. She had no desire to antagonise the duardin further.

Besides, she had got what she wanted, heard the sound that indicated the sorcerer's true intentions. In the instant that Xerkanos had cursed and the waggon had jolted, Neave had caught the imperceptible motion of one of his talons dragging a long scratch through the wood of the waggon's floorboards. She had seen him nimbly lever loose a splinter of ironwood and flick it back into the ragged material of his sleeve for later retrieval. A lock pick, she thought.

Neave asked herself if she should warn the duardin, but she already knew the answer. Even if they would listen to her, even if they would halt their march long enough to search Xerkanos and remove the wooden jag from his person, she still didn't believe that they would fully appreciate the threat he represented.

She would let this play out. The moment that Xerkanos revealed himself and became a danger to them all, that was the moment in which her slaying him would be unavoidable and entirely justified. Even Halgrimmsson would struggle to gainsay a battlefield execution, though his pride and anger might push him to try.

Neave wouldn't make the mistake that the duardin had. She wouldn't underestimate her mark.

With that thought foremost in her mind, Neave settled in to match the marching pace of the duardin, holding position fifty yards ahead of the cage-waggon. She would know the moment when it came.

Lightsdawn hove into view half an hour later. Despite her position far back down the line, Neave suspected from their lack of reaction that she saw the town before any of the duardin advance guard. It was built upon a natural outcropping of night-black rock that, Neave knew from her first visit, was so hard that the settlers had never been able to carve or break it, only build atop it. An artificial road of long wooden planks and sturdy girders had been raised around the massive bedrock. It wound up in a circle from the dusty plain to the town's single gate a hundred and fifteen feet above.

A high wall of wood and iron ringed the settlement. Azyrite banners had been unfurled down its flanks, and they stirred listlessly in the cold breeze.

Neave could see the helms and spear points of town militiamen jutting above the rampart. Instinctively, she checked that they were moving, indicating soldiers on patrol instead of bodies propped upon a fire step as part of some ambush. She had been there before, she thought ruefully, remembering another battlefield, another Reforging. Only the lack of heartbeats had warned her, that time. She thought of Xerkanos, languishing in his cage at her back, a splinter of wood hidden deep in the sleeve of his robes.

She wouldn't be caught unawares.

The cry went up from the duardin shortly after as they, in their turn, sighted the town. The march picked up pace as the soldiery made for the safe haven ahead. Neave moved up the column as they went so that she was once again close to Thane Halgrimmsson by the time his bearers began to ascend the road-ramp.

'How long do you intend to stay here, thane?' she asked. Halgrimmsson spared her a glance from under his heavy brows.

'No longer than we must, Stormcast. Overnight, and leave with dawn's first light. My lads would march on through if they could. They'd do it in a heartbeat if I gave the word.'

Neave caught the defensive note in Halgrimmsson's voice. The duardin resented this halt. For all that he feigned indifference towards her, he didn't want one of Sigmar's Stormcast Eternals to perceive some lack of fortitude in his clansmen.

'I don't doubt it, thane,' she said carefully. 'It is well known that one does not chance these wastes after darkness falls. The ashen people would leave naught but bones by the dawn, no matter how stout your warriors. My own Stormhost would fare no better.'

Halgrimmsson made a rumbling sound in his chest that might have been agreement. Neave didn't know the precise nature of the terrors that haunted the plains after dark, but the arrays of huge mechanical braziers that lined the town's walls spoke to the very real threat they represented. Whatever the ashen people were, it was common knowledge in Lights-dawn that you did not chance their wrath after dark, and that equally they would not step into the light. This, also, she had learned during her first, brief visit to the town.

'So, we press on for the karak at dawn,' prompted Neave.

'Aye, and none of mine will wake you,' said Halgrimmsson sourly. 'If you miss our departure you're on your own.'

'You assume that I sleep,' said Neave, then fell quiet, leaving the thane to digest that somewhat unsettling thought.

The army's massed footfalls rang upon the wood and iron of the roadway. It flexed and shuddered under their combined weight, but Neave felt its solidity beneath her feet. As the head of the column rounded the last turn that led up towards the town gates, she spared another glance out across the plains.

Darkness was falling as the light of Hysh slid behind the distant mountains. A dark pall spread across the wastes like spilled ink. She glanced up again at the men on the walls, saw their hard-eyed gazes beneath their helms. They stared not at the darkness, but at the column of duardin approaching their walls. The garrison would be used to threats beyond the walls, she thought, far more so than those who brought them within. Still, the intensity of the soldiers' stares struck her as strange. They looked almost eager.

Neave smelled a chemical stink, sharp and acrid. She heard a rush and gurgle of fluids through hidden pipes, and a moment later the braziers along the walls roared to life. In that moment she caught another scent, strange and cloying beneath the smell of the pyre-oil. It was faint enough that, without her superhuman senses, Neave would never have smelled it at all.

Perfume, she thought, or some kind of scented oil. She tried to place the scent's origins. It was nothing of duardin make, that was for sure. Rather, she thought the smell had wafted over the walls, from within the settlement. She doubted the townsfolk would trouble themselves to scent the oils that fed the braziers.

'Thane, there is something amiss,' she said, pitching her voice just loud enough for Halgrimmsson to hear.

'Amiss?' he asked. Ahead, the town gates began to rumble open as hidden gears worked in the walls. A blocky guardhouse was revealed beyond, rising to one side of a wide, slab-floored square. Solid-looking buildings of stone, wood and metal lined the twilit street that stretched away from the square into the heart of Lightsdawn. Oil-fuelled lamps burned to saturate the streets with light.

'I smell a perfumed scent that hides a hint of corruption, and the behaviour of the wall guards seems wrong,' she said. 'They watch us like scavengers watch a sickening beast.' And there, what's that? she thought as they marched towards the gate. Was that blood she smelled? Faint, as though scrubbed or hidden? 'And I smell blood,' she added.

Halgrimmsson bristled. 'You'd have me shy at the gates with the dark at our heels because you can smell perfume?' he asked.

'I would,' said Neave, unabashed. 'I long ago learned to trust my senses implicitly.'

'They weren't much use for my father though, were they?' asked Halgrimmsson. 'You've done naught but spout words of humanish caution about our captive since we set out. Now you spook at the sight of the town that will offer us sanctuary from the night. The danger is real, but it is at our backs, not to the fore. Either your Sigmar-given gifts are overcaution and cowardice, or else you imply a lack of competence on the part of my clansmen. Which is it, Stormcast?'

They approached the gates, and Neave saw two rows of guards lining the approach into the town. Their cloaks were swept back to keep their limbs free, and their spears were held out before them, butts to the ground. More guards clustered on the walls above the gate, and yet more could be seen on the roof of the guardhouse. Those had strung bows held ready.

An army marches though their gates and they gather their guards as a precaution, thought Neave, but she was not convinced.

'Thane, I–'

'I'll hear no more, and I'll not have you offend our allies by spouting accusations about them as we cross their damned threshold,' growled Halgrimmsson. 'Leave my side or forfeit your claim on the captive. I shan't say it again.'

Neave supposed she was not the first to feel frustration at the legendary stubbornness of the duardin. Her instincts were howling of danger ahead, yet as she glanced back at the darkness now swallowing the roadway behind them, she knew that to remain outside the walls was to die.

There were too many guards, she thought. Moreover, she could see no townsfolk. Surely a few, at least, would have come out to watch their allies march through the gates, and to spit upon a captive Chaos sorcerer trussed in chains?

But Halgrimmsson wasn't going to budge. Abandoning her entreaties, Neave halted and let him march over the threshold, his clansmen stomping resolutely along at his back. Neave folded herself into the shadow of the gates and let the duardin flow past. Dust-stained warriors thumped by without a glance in her direction, the welcome light of the town's braziers playing across their leathery skin and reflecting in their hard eyes. Neave wanted to yell at them to draw their blades, to banish the looks of relief and satisfaction from their faces. She wanted to warn them that something was terribly wrong, but she knew they would ignore her.

This was a trap, and Neave knew its architect. She had tried to sway Halgrimmsson, but he was too emotionally invested in his course, and his warriors would follow him no matter what urgings she offered. In that moment, Neave discounted the duardin as lost. *The only thing that matters is to slay Xerkanos before he can escape,* she thought.

She lurked in the shadows, sliding her axes from their sheaths on her back and lowering herself into a huntress' crouch. She was ready. The moment the cage-waggon drew level, Neave would spring her own ambush. And if the Ironbreakers sent her soul back to Azyr, so long as they cut her down after Xerkanos was slain, then so be it.

Then came the scream.

The sound exploded over the marching column like the sudden impact of an avalanche. To call it deafening would be to call an inferno hot. The scream stabbed into Neave's mind like silvered blades. It seemed to reach into her body and wind coils of bladed wire around her very bones. Her phenomenal senses were overloaded by the sawing shriek that seemed to come from everywhere at once. Neave gave a scream of her own, axes clattering to the ground as she clamped her hands to the side of her skull in an effort to shut out the agonising howl.

Neave's sheer mental discipline ensured she remained aware of what was happening around her even as she dropped to her knees, her vision swimming. The duardin were reeling, stumbling into one another, dropping weapons and tearing off helms as they slapped their hands to their ears. She saw the worst affected vomit blood or give silent cries of agony as gore wept from their nostrils, ears and eyes.

The dobkine went mad. The chitinous beasts reared in their traces, antennae waving and forelegs kicking. Neave saw the team pulling the forge-waggon run mad with pain and drag the rolling workshop straight over the edge of the roadway. She could only imagine the terror and agony of the Rune-smith and his apprentices as their forge spewed hot coals across them and their workshop plunged to smash apart on the ashen plains below.

The rest of the dobkine surged and pulled, trying to flee the agony. Neave saw Xerkanos' cage-waggon rattle past her, one trace broken, a wheel cracked and spewing wooden shrapnel as it disintegrated further with every revolution. She dimly perceived Xerkanos' hunched form in the back of the waggon, sailing past her and into the town.

Neave felt rather than heard the gate's huge mechanisms engage. Gritting her teeth, she forced her hands away from her ears, enduring the redoubled agony of the sonic barrage long enough to snatch up her axes and throw herself into a dive. The huge gates swung inwards, cog-teeth meshing where she had crouched moments before.

Neave caught a last sight of duardin and dobkine still outside on the roadway. Her eyes locked with those of a clansman just yards from the gate, scrambling forward on his hands and knees in the instant before the gates slammed shut. She would remember his look of shock and desperation for years to come.

The gates closed and as they did, the scream cut off as suddenly as it had begun. Neave rolled into a crouch and surveyed the scene, the ringing in her ears swiftly subsiding. That was her Stormcast physiology at work, she knew. Others would not be so lucky.

Not that any of the duardin could be considered lucky at this moment. Around Neave, carnage and mayhem reigned. Somehow, the guards had either endured the scream or else been entirely unaffected by it; while the duardin were thrown into utter disarray, they had struck. Arrows whipped down from the blockhouse roof to punch through mail and flesh. Duardin, already driven to their knees by the sonic assault, were spitted on spear points as the guards set upon them from all sides. Here and there the clansmen tried to mount a defence, drawing together in shield walls just a handful of dazed warriors strong. Arrows fell amongst them, feathering shield bosses and flesh alike. As soon as gaps were opened the human spearmen lunged in, whip-swift, to stab at faces and guts.

Cultists, Neave thought. Xerkanos' cultists, Tzeentch-worshipping filth who had murdered the townsfolk and the guards, had stolen their uniforms and taken their place. They must surely overwhelm the duardin, and if they did, Neave would stand alone.

She allowed herself the merest moment of fury at Halgrimmsson for blundering into so obvious a trap when he should have marched his soldiers in with guns blazing and axes bared. Yet would it have helped? she thought. The duardin couldn't have stayed outside the walls lest they be claimed by the ashen people. They couldn't have predicted nor countered the scream that had shattered their resistance before it even had a chance to form.

A scream that might return at any moment, she realised grimly. Before that, she had a mark to slay.

Xerkanos' waggon had ploughed through the duardin that blocked its path and had crashed into the corner of the blockhouse. It listed at a crazed angle, its dobkine full of arrows and dead in their traces. Neave read the flow of the slaughter and realised that three bands of armed guards were closing on the cage-waggon from different directions.

When Sigmar had raised Neave up and reforged her as the first of the Knights-Zephyros, he had given his huntress many talents. Speed was perhaps the foremost. Neave rocked back slightly, tensing muscles and tendons as sparks of stormlight danced along her limbs. Then she launched herself forward with enough force to crack the stone slabs on which she had crouched.

She sped through the slaughter as a barely perceptible blur. Arrows fell around her, but she wove through them as easily as if they hung still in mid-air. A band of cultists began to turn as they sensed her approach, but they might as well have been trying to move underwater. Neave feinted right as she neared them and swept an axe in a beheading stroke before pivoting on her heel and pirouetting through their midst like a dancer. Her whirlwind axes lashed out again and again. In the space of no more than a second, she lopped the heads from two more foes, disembowelled a third and sent another sailing backwards with a thunderous kick to the chest.

Blood and tumbling bodies rained down in Neave's wake. She barely even slowed, arcing around a hard-pressed circle of duardin fighting back to back and hacking down several of their assailants as she passed.

Xerkanos' waggon was straight ahead and Neave slowed her pace. She would not simply charge in headlong, for the sorcerer was too dangerous a foe. Instead, she slid into the cover of another waggon, this one overturned within the blockhouse's dancing shadow. Firelight, blood, screams, oaths and the clash of weapons blew around her in a sensory hurricane. Neave filtered it all instinctively, registered without conscious thought the dangers nearby and their relevance to her mission.

Snipers armed with bows crowded the blockhouse roof, raining arrows down upon anything that moved. They were shooting indiscriminately, Neave thought with surprise as she saw several shafts pierce a spear-wielding guardsman even as others slew the duardin he had been duelling. Hardly the discipline and discernment she expected from the worshippers of Tzeentch.

A band of faux guardsmen were pressing in from her rear, but still a good thirty yards behind and mired in battle with a band of recovering duardin. Not so much of a threat, she thought, even as another part of her mind noted the jagged tattoos and elaborate piercings that festooned the guardsmen's exposed flesh. A number had thrown off segments of armour, she saw, had cast aside their cloaks and even flung away weapons in order to claw and strangle with bare hands. The perfumed reek was back, stronger, wafting from the attackers' bodies.

Two more bands of guards were pincering in from either side, and these truly were a risk to her mission, for they were closing upon Xerkanos' waggon. Only their drive to stop and murder each defenceless duardin they encountered had prevented them from reaching the sorcerer already.

Neave gathered herself to spring, but in that moment she felt a surge of sorcerous energies from ahead. The bars on one side of the cage-waggon glowed bright as the light of noontide. Then they simply shattered into glowing dust that skirled away on the breeze.

Xerkanos appeared in the gap, his chains discarded. He looked strong, alert, his movements sharp as a blade and his compound gaze drinking in the scene. Neave cursed herself for not factoring external attackers into her plan; slaying the sorcerer while he lay trussed in chains would have been far easier.

Still, she had to admit that the primal huntress in her nature relished a fair fight over butchering her quarry while he lay helpless. It had to be quick, though, before he linked up with the cultists who had come to–

That thought was cut off mid-flow as the lead guardsmen spied Xerkanos. They howled with murderous glee and raised their spears before breaking into a charge.

Xelkyn Xerkanos gave a buzzing snarl and raised gnarled talons. Streamers of magic gathered around his fingertips and stabbed out at the charging guards. One by one the warriors were flash-transmuted into shimmering crystal statues that tumbled to the stone floor to shatter under their own momentum.

Blood gushed from the shattered bodies, forming a slick around their glinting remains.

Arrows rained down on Xerkanos and he gave another gesture, his anger clear to Neave in the jerky impatience of his movements. The shafts transformed into flights of stinging daggerflies in mid-air, before turning back and swarming up towards those who had loosed them.

Clearly, these were not Xerkanos' followers, thought Neave. But if so, who were they and why did they want him dead? 'Blacktalon!' It took Neave a second to realise that Xerkanos was calling for her by name. 'Blacktalon, I know you're there, probably poised to take my head from my shoulders. I swear by almighty Tzeentch and upon the true name I shall never speak, that would be a mistake.'

Another rain of arrows fell, and Xerkanos ducked back into his prison-turned-shelter. Several shafts thunked into the wood of the waggon Neave crouched behind.

'Blacktalon, I know the extent of your perceptive powers,' called Xerkanos. 'You will know if I am lying, won't you? You

can tell in that infuriating way of yours. Well hear me true. If
these imposters acquire my blood, you'll be dealing with a far
greater horror than anything I can wreak.'

Blades rang behind Neave. She shot a glance back and saw
Halgrimmsson, flanked by two of his shield-bearers. The duardin fought furiously against a mass of stabbing, shrieking
cultists. For an instant, her eyes locked with the thane's, and
in that moment his expression was as unreadable as carved
granite.

More guardsmen were closing in from around the square,
dodging around the dug-in bands of duardin in their haste
to reach Xerkanos' cage. And to her great frustration, Neave
heard no lie in the sorcerer's voice.

'Slay me now, huntress, and you'll give them precisely what
they want,' he shouted, and this time Neave heard real alarm
in Xerkanos' tone. Arrows stuck, quivering, in the roof of his
cage, and fresh waves of guardsmen pressed in from both sides.

'Sigmar guide me in this,' murmured Neave. 'And if I'm
wrong, strike me down for my foolishness.'

Neave vaulted the toppled waggon and launched herself
into a sprint. She ploughed into the nearest mass of guardsmen, spinning, whirling and hacking with lightning speed. It
was as she lopped off one cultist's arm that she saw the tattoo
upon the flesh of his shoulder, exposed as her axe-blade tore
through his tunic.

It was an orb wrought in lurid purple inks and sprouting a
shaft topped with opposed sickle-moon curves. The mark of
Slaanesh.

Suddenly the perfumed stink, the deafening scream and the
wild abandon with which the guardsmen attacked all made
sense. But what did the worshippers of Slaanesh want with
Xelkyn Xerkanos?

Neave despatched the last of her attackers, then dived aside as arrows whistled down upon her. She slid under the wreck of another waggon from whose rent flanks duardin provisions spilled. Ale from broken casks dripped amidst the juices of freshly butchered meat, giving the unpleasant impression that the waggon had been disembowelled.

'Sigmar's mighty throne, Xerkanos, does *everyone* in the realms want you dead?' shouted Neave. She was rewarded by a harsh buzz that might have been a laugh.

'None so much as you, Blacktalon, and you'll all be disappointed.'

'Oh, I'll hack you to bloody flinders, sorcerer,' she shouted back. 'Only tell me why I shouldn't take your life right now.'

From across the square there rose a crescendo of baying howls. Neave shot a glance that way and saw a tide of deformed beings converging from streets that led deeper into the town. They were mutant horrors whose bulging flesh and deformed limbs were bound into hooked black leather that tore at their skin as they moved. Oversized eyes like black pearls, sucking sensory pits that took up entire faces, lamprey mouths and curled talons showed Neave at a glance why these foul abominations had not been part of the initial ambush. They could hardly have concealed such deformities.

Now, though, someone had unleashed the mutants to finish off their wounded prey, and as she watched the gibbering tide of twisted flesh hurtle towards her, she had little doubt they were up to the task.

'Whatever you have to say, Xerkanos, say it swiftly,' she shouted.

'I had a cult cell in this town,' he replied, his buzzing voice carrying over the maelstrom of shrieks and howls. 'The idiot stuntlings would give me passage across the plains safe from your blades, then my cult would spirit me away once we got here.'

'You said had, not have,' said Neave.

'Quite, I–' Xerkanos broke off as a trio of spearmen charged the hole in his waggon's bars. He spat twisted syllables and the three guardsmen's screams turned to wet gurgles as their bodies burst open like flower petals. 'I think it is safe to say my operatives are slain,' he continued. 'If I am not mistaken, these are Slaaneshi cultists of the Sixth Torment.'

'None of this answers my questions,' shouted Neave.

'They want my blood,' spat Xerkanos. '*All* my blood.'

'And I shouldn't let them have what they want?' asked Neave.

'Not unless you want them to work a ritual of surpassing power with it,' replied Xerkanos. 'A ritual of supreme divination that will light their path to their lost god. They've bled eight of my brothers already, and I am the last and greatest Tzeentchian sorcerer they need.'

'Slaanesh is dead, the aelven gods slew him,' said Neave. 'His followers are deluded, his daemons by-products of their madness.'

'Oh, Blacktalon, how *little* you know,' spat Xerkanos, and again Neave experienced the grim sensation that the sorcerer spoke the truth. Her mind whirled. She could hear the tide of mutants getting closer, the desperate curses and the clashing of blades that marked the islands of duardin resistance being overrun one by one. Closer, the guardsmen were winding themselves up for another push towards Xerkanos' waggon while arrows still rained sporadically down from on high.

And beyond the walls, nothing but darkness and certain death.

She would fight them off, she thought. Hit them as hard as she could, try to rally the duardin long enough to push the cultists back. If she could get the gates open, then she could drag Xerkanos screaming into the dark and as far from the town as possible before the ashen people came. With luck, there wouldn't be enough left of the sorcerer for the Slaanesh worshippers to work their ritual on once those ghoulish creatures had had their way.

Even as she thought this, Neave felt another surge of sorcerous power.

'Xerkanos, what in Sigmar's name are you–'

Xerkanos' cage-waggon exploded in a ferocious ball of green-and-yellow flame. Bits of wreckage cartwheeled in all directions and Neave ducked instinctively as a blazing axel ricocheted off her cover. The approaching guardsmen took the full brunt of the blast. Those not reduced to blazing cinders fell back screaming as the fires of change sent their bodies into uncontrolled spasms of mutation.

Neave felt her mark moving amidst the coiling smoke. She was out from under the waggon and running before Xerkanos could take ten paces, yet as she accelerated towards him, she saw he was running straight at a group of approaching guards. Neave cursed as she realised what Xerkanos was doing; she couldn't risk the cultists bringing him down. She would have to slay them before they did.

She hurled one of her axes and it whipped end over end past Xerkanos' shoulder to thud into the chest of the lead guardsman. The Tzeentchian sorcerer gave a buzzing cackle and dodged left, away from a wild spear thrust. That was the only blow the Slaanesh worshippers tried before Neave hit them like a thunderbolt.

'Dark Prince guide us!' shrieked one cultist just before she tore his throat out with an axe swing. He crumpled with a gasp that might have been agony or bliss. Another opened his jaws wide and spat out a coiling length of black, prehensile tongue that whipped around Neave's throat. He tried to drag her in with it, towards his mantrap maw of fangs. Contemptuous, Neave grabbed a fistful of tongue and yanked. The cultist's face smashed into her helm with a bony crunch and he fell back in a spray of blood.

The distraction had cost Neave precious seconds. She saw Xerkanos dashing into an alleyway between two high stone buildings, his ragged robes flying behind him like the multi-coloured wings of some weird insect. Neave tore her axe free from the guardsman's chest and broke into a run, crossing the gap in moments. She rounded the corner in time to see the trailing ends of Xerkanos' robes vanishing around another bend. The alleys had no lamps to light them, but Neave's eyesight was so keen that she could see perfectly well. She didn't even slow as she dashed down the rubbish-strewn alley, allowing herself to rebound hard from the wall with a clang of armour on stone so as to round the next corner all the quicker. Ahead, the alley emptied back out onto a lamplit street that swarmed with Slaaneshi mutants. Xerkanos ploughed straight into their midst, blasting assailants aside with tongues of kaleidoscopic fire.

'Sigmar's bloody *throne*,' spat Neave as she saw that the sorcerer would be overrun in moments. She ran hard, spinning her axes in her fists before launching herself into a leap. She came down amidst the mutants like the God-King's own fury, and lightning exploded outwards from her point of impact. Revolting beings were hurled through the air, their bodies convulsing and burning as her heavenly energies tore through them. Neave's axes lashed out in swift arcs, hacking through deformed flesh and sending horned heads tumbling from lumpen shoulders. A crablike claw snapped closed on her arm, hard enough to dent the sigmarite. In return, she punched its owner in the neck, caving its throat in and sending it to the floor as it choked its last.

Neave cleared a circle around herself in time to see Xerkanos vanishing down another alleyway, his buzzing laughter floating back over his shoulder.

'What are you doing, Xerkanos?' she yelled, slamming her shoulder into a rearing mutant and driving it aside. 'Where in the realms do you think you're running to?'

Xerkanos had said that his cult would spirit him away, thought Neave. What trickery did he have in mind?

She spun in a circle, beheading a goat-man hybrid and driving a rib-shattering kick into the chest of a flabby thing with too many eyes. She leapt over the toppling beastman and broke into a flat-out sprint. Neave hurtled down this new alleyway fast enough to raise a wake of swirling dust and litter, executed a one-footed spring off the wall at the far end and burst into a square flanked with glowing lanterns and dominated by a dried-out fountain.

A Sigmarite temple took up one entire edge of the square. She saw Xerkanos dashing up its steps. He glanced back, and she saw firelight reflected in his glittering eyes. She could have hurled her axes right then, hit him in the face and the chest, struck him dead in an instant. She saw the knowledge of it on his face and, infuriatingly, the smug assurance that she would not risk it. Neave could hear the howls of cultists and mutants close behind and knew that, if it was Xerkanos' blood they wanted, she could not stop them from overrunning her and taking it if he died here.

'I'm going to drag you out of this town by the throat and feed you to the ashen people,' she snarled.

'There are more futures in which you don't than in which you do,' he shouted back, before smashing the ornate temple doors from their hinges with a blast of balefire.

Neave raced up the steps and lunged, grabbing at Xerkanos

as he vanished into the cool dark of the temple's interior. She felt her hands close around one of his chitinous limbs, sensed his alarm and pain as her grip closed like a vice.

Then came the mind-shredding scream again, more ferocious and intense even than before. Neave snarled in pain, losing her grip on Xerkanos as she was bludgeoned to the floor by the sonic sledgehammer.

Xerkanos, too, gave a buzzing shriek that was all but lost in the onslaught. Neave staggered, thumping against a column as her head threatened to blow apart under the appalling pressure of the sound. She looked deeper into the temple and saw its source, squatting atop a mound of carrion.

The bodies were piled in an untidy heap, ten feet high. The few that were still clothed wore multicoloured robes that marked them out as acolytes of Xelkyn Xerkanos. All showed appalling degrees of mutilation, as though they had suffered long before they died. Their corpses dripped foul fluids.

Crouched on top of the mound of dead was a mutant several times larger than the rest. Its gender was impossible to determine, its body a rippling mass of over-muscled limbs and rolls of tattooed flab. It had six arms and two legs, and it leant forward on its many knuckles like some strange simian as it screamed. Its jaws stretched impossibly wide, permanently distorted out of shape by finely worked golden separators whose many filigreed tubes were acting as sonic amplifiers. Bulging flesh-sacs in the thing's throat puffed in and out like bellows, sucking and pumping in sequence to maintain its endless scream, and an array of disturbingly normal human eyes clustered in the veined flesh of its forehead beneath its lank golden hair.

The scream stopped. Neave let out an involuntary gasp of relief. Then the thing spoke, and she almost wished she was deafened again. Its voice was horribly human, albeit distorted. It was also horribly sane, androgynous and musical.

'The sorcerer's blood is ours, huntress,' said the mutant. 'I am Achylla of the Sixth Torment, and I claim him in the name of the Dark Prince.'

Neave pushed herself upright and firmed her grip on her axes. Her blood surged hot and angry at the sight of yet another vile champion of the Dark Gods.

'Xelkyn Xerkanos has been condemned to death by the God-King Sigmar and I am his appointed executioner,' she said. 'He is not yours to claim.'

In her peripheral vision, Neave noted that Xerkanos was edging closer to the corpse pile upon which Achylla squatted. He was half crawling, half crouching, muttering some kind of obfuscatory charm. Achylla swung its head towards him and gave a vicious screech. Xerkanos wailed in pain and collapsed, limbs shaking uncontrollably.

'This place has been consecrated with fluids unnameable on behalf of Slaanesh,' spat Achylla. 'Your warp magics will not work here, sorcerer. But...' Its laugh was a tinkling cascade of sound tainted with lascivious glee, like a beautiful brook fouled by a brothel's sewage. 'Do you seek this?'

Achylla smiled a hideous smile and held up a blue crystal talisman on a heavy gold chain.

'You will not leave here, sorcerer,' said the mutant, its leer widening until Neave thought its head must surely split in two. 'Now, my beautiful brood, come and claim him. Keep the huntress alive. Her stormflesh will make for an amusing diversion before the ritual.'

Neave's eyes narrowed at the mutant's casual tone.

'Try to take me, you lumpen freak,' she snarled. 'It will be your last and greatest mistake.' Behind her, Neave heard the scrabbling claws, the panting breath and pounding feet of Achylla's mutants surging in through the temple's broken doors. To her left, Xerkanos slumped as though stunned by the mutant's sonic assault. Directly ahead, Achylla's throat sacs puffed and bulged as they sucked in vast quantities of air. Achylla reared back, spreading its arms wide with a look of glee in its eyes as it prepared to unleash another crippling scream.

If that happened, Neave knew she would be helpless to stop the cultists from overrunning her.

Lightning fast, she spun in a circle and hurled her axes. Even as they left her hands, she was accelerating, following her whirlwind blades as they sailed across the temple in a lethal trajectory. At the last instant, Achylla managed to turn partly aside, the mutant's reactions unnaturally swift. Still Neave's axes hit Achylla's throat sacs and burst them with awful splatting sounds. Neave surged through the atomised spray of flesh and gore to drive a thunderous uppercut into the mutant's distended jaw. Bone cracked, and blood sprayed as Achylla's jaw separators tore through suddenly displaced flesh. A mouth that had spent years wired open crunched shut with a wet snap.

The mutant lost its balance and toppled backwards off the corpse mound, limbs flailing. Gold flashed in the air as it fell. Neave followed, riding the huge body down the carrion slope and driving her armoured heels into its bulging torso even as she ripped her axes free.

Achylla whipped and lashed like an injured serpent, the mutant's movements fast and violent. It let out an awful keening squeal and bucked again, throwing Neave aside to land and roll in a clatter of armour.

The mutant was up in an instant, hate and wounded pride burning in its gaze as it scuttled at Neave on all eight limbs.

With a crunch of gristle, it forced its jaws open, foot-long fangs pushing through the pink flesh of its gums. Neave hurled herself aside and Achylla's jaws snapped shut where she had stood. Before Neave could swing a blow, one of the mutant's muscled arms lashed out and a fist the size of her head hit her breastplate with a sound like a tolling bell.

Neave was flung backwards into the corpse mound. She rolled back to her feet as Achylla came at her again, useless throat sacs flapping like burst balloons. The mutant tried to grab Neave with two huge hands, but she weaved inside its reach and scissored her blades to lop off one of the grasping limbs at the elbow. Another blow opened the mutant's chest in a long gash that bled ropes of clotted gore.

Achylla fell back with a screech.

'Slay her,' it managed to croak, scrambling away as blood spewed from its wounds. A mass of mutants surged over the corpse mound and Neave spun to face them. Her axes lashed out again and again, adding more dead bodies to the heap with every passing second.

Suddenly, she felt her mark moving.

'Sigmar's throne,' she cursed as she realised that, beset by Achylla and its brood, she had taken her eye from her quarry for vital moments.

Neave took three steps and launched herself into a mighty leap, sailing over the heads of the thronging mutants and landing on the other side of the corpse mound.

She was in time to see Xerkanos snatching up the amulet where it had slithered from Achylla's grip. His mouthparts moved as he muttered a spell of awakening and the amulet glowed fiercely. This time there was no hesitation; Neave drew back her arm and hurled an axe. It flew end over end towards Xerkanos, only to sail through his shimmering outline as sorcerous energies flared. Xerkanos' mocking laughter echoed through the temple for a moment, then was gone.

It was no illusion, Neave knew. Her sense of her mark became suddenly diffuse, vanishingly distant. She would be surprised if Xelkyn Xerkanos was even in the same Mortal Realm any more.

Her flying axe hit a mutant and bisected its face. The creature thumped to the floor in a bloody mess, the haft of the whirlwind axe jutting up from its mangled skull.

Neave took a slow, deep breath and looked around at the massed Slaanesh worshippers closing in on all sides. Something large moved atop the corpse mound, Achylla dragging its mangled body over the heaped dead to stare at Neave with murderous hatred.

'Hundreds of you left,' said Neave, her tone almost conversational as she stalked across the temple floor and wrenched her axe from the dead mutant's face. Its legs kicked as she dragged the blade free with a sucking squelch. 'Only the one of me, and I'd bet Ghal-Maraz its own self that the duardin are dead to the last by now. Poor, stubborn fools.'

'You are doomed,' rasped Achylla. 'You have affronted the Dark Prince this day. How we will make you beg for death before the end.'

'You murdered a stout band of duardin loyal to the cause of the God-King,' said Neave, her voice dangerously low. She stretched out her limbs, working out the kinks and aches of battle one at a time. Warily, the mutant throng watched her, nerving themselves to attack.

'Worse, you made me lose my damned mark,' said Neave. 'Again.' Her heart thumped heavily in her chest, fury and frustration causing her head to pound in time with it. It was all she could do to prevent herself from shaking with rage. 'For that, it is you that will meet your end, Achylla. And before your hordes drag me down and send me to my Reforging, I will slaughter so many of them that your cult will be destroyed, never to rise again. This I swear upon my oath to Sigmar himself.'

With that, Neave launched herself into a blistering charge up the flank of the corpse mound. Achylla barely had time to blink in horror before Neave's axes bit deep into the mutant's throat, yet even as the foul creature's head parted company from its shoulders, it was Xerkanos that Neave was thinking of.

The hunt wasn't over, she thought as Achylla's corpse toppled sideways and a howling tide of mutants closed in from all directions. In fact, it had only now truly begun...

ACTS OF SACRIFICE

Evan Dicken

Sir Anaea knelt alone in the shadowed recesses of the chapel vault, hands clenched at her sides, head bowed in silent prayer. A muffled boom from outside caused the chapel to tremble, dust trickling from between the heavy stones overhead. Anaea opened her eyes at the sound of distant shouts, the clash of arms, but ignored the desire to leap up and join the rest of her Order as they tried to hold at bay the shrieking, gore-spattered mob that beat at the fortress walls like waves against a stony shore.

With a deep breath, she steadied herself. The Order of the Ardent Star was more than Anaea's desire for vengeance, more than the creeping loss that seemed to shadow her every thought. Master Vaskar had taught her that. But Master Vaskar was dead, cut down by the Khornate champion Sulkotha Godspite, not two hundred paces from where Anaea knelt, his body lost to the numberless horde outside. That had been three days ago, when the Chaos army was not so large, when there had been enough Order knights to sally forth in hopes that the ravagers could be driven off. The images were scarred into Anaea's memory – her comrades pulled down one by one, Vaskar falling to Godspite's vile blade as he fought to buy the other knights time to withdraw. It had been all Anaea could do to retrieve her master's sword, and the failure ached like an old battle wound.

Anaea exhaled and focused upon the statue of Myrmidia that presided over the chapel. The warrior-goddess seemed a being of deadly grace, standing triumphant although her armour was scarred by blade and arrow. The burnished gold of her shield was bright even in the fading torchlight, and her spear seemed to glitter with the blood of defeated foes.

'*Stella Invicti*.' Anaea whispered the Order's motto as her gaze fell to Vaskar's sword upon the altar. As if to echo her darkening thoughts, there came another deep rumble from outside, followed by the roar of inhuman voices and the harsh crackle of balefire.

'Blessed Lady Myrmidia, grant your loyal servant peace.' Anaea reached for the blade, its well-worn hilt fitting comfortably in her hand. She set it before her, point resting on the chapel tiles. The metal of the pommel was cool against her forehead as she bowed once more. 'Let his shining example light the way along the dark paths we must tread.'

It was a quick eulogy, far less than Master Vaskar deserved, but already more than Anaea could afford. She bowed, then turned away from the statue. Although Myrmidia cared little for genuflection and prayers, Anaea could not let her master go in silence. Moreover, she had needed time to focus, to prepare herself for what must be done. All that mattered to the Goddess of War was triumph. This time, however, there would be no glorious victory, no salvation.

All that remained was survival.

Anaea stepped from the chapel, striding across the courtyard with new purpose, but by the time she had crested the wall the ravagers had been driven off. So it had been since the siege started – Godspite raking the walls with hellcannon fire before sending her shrieking horde charging towards the fortress.

'We beat them back.' Master Karon stepped to Anaea's side, removing his helm to scrub a hand through his thinning white hair. '*Stella Invicti*.'

Anaea echoed the old master's words, but her stomach clenched as she surveyed the wreckage. Corpses sprawled across the battlement, the unholy sigils cut into their flesh marking them as followers of the God of Slaughter. Most of the newly slain wore beaten, blood-red armour, but here and there her eye caught the glimmer of knightly plate, as though a handful of golden coins had been scattered amidst the carnage.

'How many of our brothers and sisters were lost in doing so?' she asked.

'Too many,' the old master conceded with a sour frown. 'But they met a noble end.'

'And how many remain?'

'Less than one hundred.' Karon shook his head. 'Not enough to defend the eastern rampart, let alone the curtain wall. We shall have to pull back to the chapel.'

Anaea surveyed the horde, one of the seemingly numberless warbands of Chaos ravagers that had swamped the Flamescar Plateau like a bloody tide. 'Have we received any word from Sir Leta?'

Karon's silence was answer enough. They had dispatched Leta to the Burning Cliffs many days ago on a mission to seek aid from the Hermdar Lodge. The fyreslayers had never been friends to the Order, but the looming threat of annihilation made for strange alliances.

And yet, no one had come.

The Hermdar must have refused, if Sir Leta had reached them at all.

'Duardin wretches,' Karon said, echoing Anaea's thoughts. 'Hiding in their holds as if gates and stone could shield them from the end of the world.'

Anaea glanced at the old knight, but Karon's attention was fixed on the horde outside. He stood like a man steeling himself to charge into cannon fire.

Below, the ravagers had drawn up just outside of bow range. They laughed and jeered, the clash of their weapons causing Anaea's jaw to tighten. Smoke obscured the smouldering sun of Aqshy, the field of cracked basalt painted in crimson tones, red as the blood of the fallen.

As if summoned from some abyssal pit, Sulkotha Godspite stepped from the horde of muddied bronze. She was a head taller than even the largest of her mad followers, her armour set with spikes and cruel, barbed hooks, fire gleaming in the eyes of the daemonic faces etched into her breastplate. In one gauntleted fist, she carried a broken greatsword, its blade notched and pitted from hard use, foul sigils scored into its jagged length. Her other hand dragged a long, spiked chain. The barbed links writhed like a beheaded snake, lashing out at any of Godspite's followers too slow to retreat.

'Myrmidia has abandoned you!' Godspite roared, as she had every day since her horde first besieged the chapel fortress. 'Show more courage than your pitiful god. Die like warriors, not like rats cowering behind pathetic walls.'

As the champion stalked forward, Anaea could see the end of Godspite's chain was wrapped around a body in battered armour. The corpse left a smear of old blood as the champion dragged it across the stony ground.

'Come, brave knights. Join your leader.' With a heave of her massive shoulders, Godspite hauled the chain so that the corpse flopped forward.

Anaea felt a shout building in her throat, hot and furious. The corpse's armour was cracked and broken, its face a mask of dried blood, but even through the gore Anaea recognised her former master.

'*Abomination*,' Karon hissed at Anaea's side, drawing his sword. 'This cannot be allowed.'

Anaea grabbed his wrist and forced him to halt. 'You would give her what she wants,' she growled, quashing her own rage.

'And why not?' He jerked from her grip. Vaskar had been Anaea's master, but he had been like a son to the old knight. Karon shook with barely restrained fury, his scowl equal parts pain and rage. 'Cut the head from the serpent and her horde will scatter.'

'You know as well as I that killing Godspite would solve nothing,' Anaea said.

Karon gave a low, angry grunt, but slammed his sword back into its sheath. 'What do you propose?'

Anaea's gaze fell upon the battlements and towers, a long expanse of wall scattered with those few knights who survived. 'This fortress cannot be held with what forces remain to us. We must seek a more defensible position.'

'The hordes are everywhere,' Karon said. 'Where can we ride?'

Shielding her eyes from the burnished sun, Anaea scanned the horizon. Godspite's warband ranged across the cracked plain surrounding the chapel fortress, seeming to stretch almost to the Desert of Glass in the east. Although Anaea could not see them, she knew somewhere in the distance lay the Burning Cliffs. There, the Hermdar fyreslayers hunkered behind their great walls, safe in the knowledge they could weather any siege.

The Order needed to do the same, to preserve what remained of its forces, to focus on survival.

'The Redoubt,' Anaea said, at last.

Karon frowned. 'Drakemount is three day's ride across the desert, even with no enemies barring our path.'

'The Redoubt is defensible, difficult to assault, well supplied and located near the centre of the Flamescar Plateau,' Anaea replied. 'It is the logical choice, for there we will find those chapters of our Order that still survive.'

'*If* any survive.' Karon sighed, considering.

'How many more of Godspite's assaults will *we* survive?' Anaea tightened her grip on Vaskar's blade. 'This is not a war we can win, master.'

Karon winced as if Anaea's words were a knife drawn across his flesh. He regarded her for a long moment, then gave a quick nod, turning to the group of knights who had drifted over to watch the exchange. 'Gather the others and harness the demidroths. We ride for Drakemount.'

As the others hurried off to spread the word, Karon turned back to Anaea, his voice tired. 'And if you are wrong? If the Redoubt has fallen? If we cannot win through Godspite's horde?'

Anaea took a long, slow breath. 'Then you shall have your noble death, master.'

The knights waited, still as statues in the fading afternoon light. Once the Order's warriors would have filled the courtyard to bursting, bright and golden like stars fallen to earth. Now they seemed dwarfed by the high walls, diminished in number if not spirit.

'We have but one chance.' Anaea turned her mount, a reptilian demidroth, to face the assembled knights. 'The time for grand strategy has long passed. We must simply draw the savages out and create a gap. If we are lucky enough to hack our way through, we ride for the Redoubt.'

Master Karon urged his mount next to Anaea's. 'And if we are not lucky, we shall die gloriously, our blades singing Myrmidia's praises.'

Anaea looked to Karon, frowning, but the old master held her gaze.

At Karon's nod, the knights dragged open the fortress' gate. The great iron-bound doors slammed against the walls with a resounding boom.

With a grim smile, Karon turned from Anaea, raising his blade even as he spurred his demidroth forward. '*Stella Invicti!*'

The others echoed his call. Although few in number, the Knights of the Ardent Star charged as if there were an army behind them. Arranged in a serried wedge, lances lowered, they streaked west across the broken field mounted on their large, lizard-like steeds. Far smaller than their draconic cousins, demidroths lacked both fiery breath and molten blood, but were no less fierce. Anaea could feel the vital pulse of her demidroth's muscles as it bounded across the rough stone, the powerful expansion of its lungs as it drew in a great breath.

Her mount roared, and Anaea roared with it.

The Order's banner snapped in the wind as its bearer led the charge. Even now the sight of the banner filled Anaea with determination. A golden star blazing on a field of purest black, it was inscribed with the Order's war cry. Said to have been a gift from Myrmidia herself during the ancient days, the banner had been borne by the Knights of the Ardent Star in a thousand battles.

Up ahead, Godspite's ravagers laughed and brandished their cruel weapons, seemingly undaunted as they were ridden down by the wave of steel-plated doom.

The knights cut into the horde like a lava flow. Ravagers fell away, impaled by broken lances or gutted by demidroth talons. Anaea brought Vaskar's sword down again and again as if hacking through stubborn rope.

A man leapt at her from the press, axe in hand, his eyes mad with bloodlust. Anaea ducked the wild swing and drove her blade between his ribs. He fell back with a look that seemed almost disappointed, there to be torn apart by the claws of her steed.

For a moment, the combat eddied around Anaea. She sat back in her saddle to quickly scan the lines of battle. The knights' charge had cut deep into the howling mob, although not deep enough for the reavers to fully envelop them.

She waited, her throat tight. At last, the moment came, thin as a knife's edge. Frantic to spill blood, the horde had shifted to the west, following the knights' charge. Anaea caught Karon's eye and nodded.

'Withdraw!' The old knight's word rose above the clamour of battle.

With the precision of a lifetime of careful drill, the knights wheeled their mounts to charge through the closing gap at their rear. Roaring, the demidroths pelted across the pitted field, racing parallel to the ravagers' lines. The frenzied horde turned in on itself as reavers fought their own comrades, frantic to reach the knights.

For the first time in what seemed like an eternity, Anaea felt the weight lift from her shoulders. Godspite's horde was fierce, unshakeable and driven by mad bloodlust. The knights could not hope to face them in the field, but the Order could use their strength against them.

Anaea held her sword high, a wild shout building in her throat. The bulk of the horde was behind them, a few scattered bands of ravagers all that remained between the knights and the Desert of Glass.

The cry died on Anaea's lips as Sulkotha Godspite stepped from the milling crowd before them.

The Khornate champion spread her arms wide in welcome, her great blade sheathed across her back, the spiked chain writhing about her feet. Laughing, she raised Vaskar's severed head, his blood staining her armour. 'Blood for the Blood God.'

'Veer around her!' Anaea gestured with her blade, teeth gritted against the upswell of fury that screamed at her to cut the champion down. She could feel the hesitation in her comrades, her desire for vengeance echoed by every lowered lance and raised sword.

With a contemptuous shrug of her shoulders, Godspite tossed Vaskar's head to the ground, grinding it to pulp beneath one bronze-shod boot.

'*Defiler!*' Master Karon wheeled his mount to confront the Chaos champion.

'Keep formation! We cannot afford to be bogged down!' Anaea called after him, but the moment was lost as the knights followed their master. With a curse, she turned her demidroth towards the waiting ravagers.

Godspite watched them come, seemingly unconcerned. A moment before the charge connected the Chaos champion pivoted away, her spiked chain lashing up to tangle the legs of Karon's mount. The demidroth pitched forward and the old knight was tossed from the saddle. He stumbled to his feet just in time to duck a heavy slash from Godspite's blade.

The combatants were lost from sight as the knights hammered into the Chaos ranks. A pair of ravagers rushed at Anaea. The blades of their huge axes gleamed crimson in the dull red light of Aqshy's sun. Using her legs, Anaea steered her mount towards the attackers. The great demidroth lunged forward, covering the distance with a speed that set the reavers back on their heels. It pounced on the first man while Anaea shifted in her saddle as a blow cut the air where her arm had been a moment before.

Anaea's return cut took the reaver's arm off just below the elbow, flesh and bone parting like clouds before the tempered edge of Vaskar's blade. One-handed, the ravager tried to raise his axe to parry her next blow, but the weapon was too unwieldy and her stab slid easily into the hollow of the man's throat.

Drawing in a great whooping breath, Anaea glanced back. The bulk of Godspite's horde was closing in; if the knights didn't win through soon they would be surrounded and cut off.

Anaea cast about the battle, spying Master Karon.

The knight's demidroth was down, surrounded by a knot of ravagers who hacked at the dying beast with wild abandon, leaving Karon to face Godspite on foot.

Undaunted, the master launched a flurry of slashes and stabs, his blade seeking the joints of the Chaos champion's armour. With a scream that seemed equal parts joy and rage, Godspite brought her greatsword arcing around, forcing Karon to drop to one knee to avoid the slash. He responded with a cut to Godspite's knee that set her back a step. The two champions exchanged rapid blows, Karon moving like a man half his age.

Around Anaea, the charge's momentum had stalled. To her left, the Order's banner bearer was dragged from her demidroth, still slashing even as she disappeared amidst a knot of bloodspattered reavers. Anaea kicked her mount forward, and the demidroth tore into the foe just as the banner slipped from the bearer's hand.

With a cry, Anaea leaned in her saddle to catch the falling

banner, her blade arcing out to split the skull of a marauder who sought to wrench it from her grip.

'To me!' Vaskar's blade cut a bloody path through the snarling horde as Anaea urged her mount towards Karon, banner held high.

The old master pivoted to avoid Godspite's sweeping blade. Like a gargant beset by a gryphon, the Chaos champion roared and swatted at the old knight, but Karon was far too quick.

As she burst from the press, Anaea spied Godspite's chain slithering towards Karon, but her shout came too late.

The daemonic chain wrapped around the master's leg, its spikes punching bloody holes in his armour even as it pinned him in place. Unable to dodge, Karon barely parried a vicious chop from the champion's greatsword.

Anaea put her heels to her mount's flanks and it bulled into the Chaos champion, knocking Godspite from her feet. Rather than press the attack, Anaea hacked down at the chain binding Master Karon's leg. The first strike drew a spray of angry sparks and the chain writhed like a wounded snake. Godspite roared as if Anaea's blade had struck her rather than her weapon. The chain tried to unwind, but Karon drove his sword through its links to hold it in place. Anaea hewed at the chain, her nose thick with the smell of scorched metal. At last, the foul thing gave way before the blessed steel. Bleeding black ichor from its severed links, it writhed away, leaving only the portion wrapped around Karon's leg.

Godspite's howl of pain brought a grim smile to Anaea's face.

Fortunately, whatever foul sorcery had animated the chain had fled the severed length, and Master Karon was able to tear his limb free.

Suddenly, the air was full of steel-armoured forms. As if summoned by the banner, knights descended upon the struggle, sword and talon driving back the shrieking ravagers. The breaking of her chain had apparently sent Godspite into a frenzy. She hacked at those around her, seeming not to care if they were friend or foe. Other fights broke out amidst the horde as the ravagers turned on each other, the warband like a snake devouring its own tail. Sprays of blood rose like flies from an old corpse, the air thick with the stench of gore.

'We must move!' Anaea shouted at Karon, bringing her demidroth down so he could swing up behind her. The old knight sagged against her, his breath quick and ragged. Whatever holy vigor had possessed him seemed spent.

Anaea thrust the banner forward, and the surviving knights advanced, cutting through the scattered reavers to break free just ahead of the charging horde.

Anaea glanced back as they hurtled across the wide expanse of basalt. Even driven mad by bloodlust, Godspite's warband seemed a huge and terrifying thing, Anaea's surviving companions little more than a candle set against a bloody storm of destruction. The Desert of Glass would be difficult to traverse, but Anaea had no doubt Godspite would follow. There would be no rest until they reached the Redoubt.

She only hoped she was not leading her comrades to their deaths.

'Leave me here,' Master Karon said through clenched teeth. 'I can buy you time.'

'You will slay many ravagers, master, but not this night.' Anaea glanced across at the old knight's injured leg, the black-and-gold armour glistening with dried blood. Although in obvious pain, the knight had refused assistance, stubbornly riding the demidroth of one of their fallen comrades. There had been no time to treat his wound. Godspite's warband had found its feet more quickly than expected, following the warriors of the Order like gryph-hounds scenting prey.

The ragged column of knights had spent the better part of a week crossing the brutal expanse of the Desert of Glass, a vast field of volcanic obsidian left by an ancient lava flow. Although the demidroths seemed untroubled by the heat and razored spines of broken glass, their human riders were less well adapted. To wear armour was to slowly bake in the punishing sun, but to remove it was to risk being flensed by flecks of windswept obsidian.

It seemed impossible that anything could survive such cruel conditions, but the forces of Chaos were everywhere. No matter how far or fast the knights rode, they seemed unable to escape the flash of bronze on the horizon, or the distant roars carried to their ears by the furnace-hot winds. Worse, the desert had claimed a bloody toll. Knights slipped from their demidroths, overcome by wounds, their hearts stilled by the punishing heat of the sun. Those who still breathed were lashed to their saddles, while the dead were left for Godspite's monstrous hounds, which loped through the black sands, snarling and snapping at any who fell behind. Twice, Anaea had led charges to drive them off, but the beasts always returned, like flies to a corpse.

But the Order of the Ardent Star was not dead yet.

Survive.

It had become a mantra, a prayer, whispered through cracked lips as Anaea approached the smoke-shrouded peak of Drakemount.

They would be safe there. The Order would live. They would regroup, combine their numbers and defeat the foe.

'We should turn now and fight,' Master Karon said, as if reading her mind.

Anaea was about to admonish him once again when the Redoubt finally came into view.

The ancient citadel stood like a breaker against the clouds of red-tinged smoke that gave Drakemount its name.

With a hoarse shout Anaea raised the banner once more, her shoulder numb from the strain of holding it aloft for so long. She gritted her teeth at the pain – a penance of sorts – as the surviving knights urged their mounts into a shambling trot.

Anaea squinted at the flames lining the edges of the narrow path up to the Redoubt. The blaze was surely unnatural, for the rock did not melt or run like lava, nor did the fire consume it. Whatever the cause, the ancient builders of the Redoubt had placed their fortress well, the unquenchable flames making the approach treacherous.

'Our brothers and sisters await us within,' she called back to her tired companions. Unspoken was Karon's dire caveat: *if any survive.*

They came to the gates, and Anaea felt the spark of hope in her chest flutter and go dark. The great steel doors stood broken and ajar, a knight slumped in the opening, the gold of his armour almost invisible beneath scorches and burnt blood.

Smoke from the fires pricked Anaea's eyes as she dismounted to approach the knight. She didn't need to open his helm to know he was dead – the man's arm was missing, what flesh Anaea could see pocked and bloodless as old leather.

'Search the Redoubt.' Master Karon gestured at the gates, the grim lines of his face sharpened by the flickering firelight.

The courtyard was a scene of slaughter, knights and ravagers sprawled in a deathly, violent tableau. Anaea could almost picture the scene – a thin line of black and gold arrayed against a sea of hungry, blood-flecked bronze – she had lived it often enough. Heat had dried out the bodies, reducing the corpses to little more than mummified skeletons. It was a small blessing, for Anaea had fought many times alongside these chapters. She didn't think she could bear to recognise any of the dead.

Her comrades picked their way through the carnage, climbing winding stairs and forcing doors blocked by piled corpses. The Redoubt was large, but wholly dead, and in less than an hour the knights had their answer. They gathered in the shadow of one of the Redoubt's high walls, one of the few places not choked with bodies.

'The stores have been raided, the armoury emptied,' Anaea reported, conscious of the gazes of her fellow knights – the men and women she had led to their doom. 'But the treasury is untouched.'

'What use have madmen for gold and silver?' Master Karon shook his head, his scowl sharp as an axe blade. With a wince, he straightened, limping over to address the group of solemn knights. 'There is much work to do and little enough time. Repairing the gate should be our first priority.'

'This place is a grave.' Anaea met the old knight's pained gaze. 'I thought there would be other survivors, that we could hold the walls, but too many have fallen. We cannot remain here.'

'Your plan was a good one, Sir Anaea. Vaskar would be proud.' Karon's tone was firm, buttressed by a sense of solemn resignation. He took a slow step over to lay a hand on her shoulder. 'But some wars simply cannot be won.'

Anaea pulled away. Turning to the others, she shook the banner so that the star glittered in the crimson light. 'Myrmidia revels in victory, but there is no shame in retreat before a superior foe. We may very well be the last of our Order, and you would cast your lives away? Master Vaskar died to protect our traditions, our knowledge. To protect *you*.'

Her comrades stood as if cut from ash-streaked obsidian. None would meet her gaze.

'We can hide amidst the mountains, perhaps even find shelter with the Hermdar.' Frustration edged Anaea's words. 'While but one knight survives, the Order cannot die.'

'Some things are more important than survival.' Master Karon turned away from her, his voice booming across the courtyard. 'Arm yourselves, clear the battlements. We shall sell our lives dearly and break the back of Godspite's host.'

There were nods and affirmations from the other knights as they set about preparing for battle. Anaea stared, unbelieving. Karon was giving a battle speech.

So great shall be our legend that for generations, our foe will shun this place.

Banner in hand, Anaea backed away from her former comrades. They looked so foolish, heads bobbing like coal gulls as they rushed around the courtyard, welcoming the wave of lava that would obliterate them.

They will look upon these walls and shudder, knowing only death awaits them here.

Anaea slipped onto one of the healthier-looking demidroths, grasping the reins to turn it as quietly as she could. The others might be willing to see the Order of the Ardent Star cast into ruin, but Anaea would not let it fall.

She put her heels to the demidroth, and it surged towards the open gate, bowling past a knot of knights trying to secure the broken door. Their surprised shouts were eclipsed by the pounding of blood in Anaea's ears.

She pelted down the switchback, running her mount close to the fires so the smoke would mask their flight. In the distance, Godspite's warband spread like lava across the dunes. It didn't take a master strategist to see they would arrive long before Karon and the others could repair the gates.

Anaea kept her head down, leaning low in her saddle as she unhooked the banner and discarded its pole.

'Forgive me, goddess.' She stuffed the rolled cloth into the front of her breastplate. At least there was one thing she could protect from Godspite's filth.

As if to mock Anaea's hopes, a howl echoed from the soot-smudged cliffs. Drawing Vaskar's sword, she turned to see that a pack of the champion's monstrous hounds had broken from the main horde to give chase.

The beasts fanned out, seeking to surround and harry their prey, eyes glowing like bilious lanterns amidst the smoky shadows. With a shout Anaea urged her mount forward. It bounded up an ash-covered escarpment, stones shifting beneath its hooked claws. Smiling grimly, she bore down on the hounds that sprinted to bar her path.

Anaea might be hunted, but she was *not* prey.

A warhound leapt at her, and Anaea shifted to ram the point of her sword between the beast's slavering jaws. Her demidroth reared to catch another hound in its talons, tearing the snarling creature in half with almost contemptuous ease. But, like their cruel masters, the hounds seemed without end. Two more loped from the gloom to snap at the demidroth's legs.

Anaea swung Vaskar's blade in a low arc, the heavy steel cutting deep into one of her pursuers' necks. The other hound leapt, and Anaea turned too slowly, her strike missing the beast.

It crashed into her. Claws scrabbled on steel plate, its jaws like a vice on Anaea's shoulder. With a tortured shriek her pauldron began to buckle. Anaea felt herself being dragged from the demidroth's back. She tried to bring her blade to bear, but the hound was too close.

Myrmidia taught that there were times for strategy, for skill, but there were also times for brute force.

Teeth clenched against the pain, Anaea hammered the pommel of Vaskar's blade into the hound's skull. Again and again, she brought the heavy weight crashing down, feeling the beast shudder and kick. At last, bone gave way to steel, and the hound tumbled to the blackened stone.

No more beasts slunk from the murky haze, but there was no time for Anaea to catch her breath.

She urged her mount on. The demidroth leapt from boulder to smoking boulder, nimble on the broken terrain of the mountain. Thick smoke stung her nose, and Anaea coughed, guiding her steed up above the flames so she could see the Redoubt once more. She paused upon a cliff to overlook the battlefield.

Godspite had moved quickly. Already, masses of shrieking, foam-flecked ravagers swarmed the approach. The first of the attackers crashed into the thin cordon of knights. Even from here, Anaea could see Godspite in the thick of battle, her jagged blade rising and falling, her daemon chain lashing out to bind and crush.

Anaea squinted through the pall of smoke. She could see gold-armoured shapes fighting upon the battlements, more arrayed across the broken gate. They glittered in the gloom like diamonds tossed upon a muddy field.

It was not too late to join them. Anaea could charge back down the mountain, banner in hand, to test herself against Godspite. Perhaps she might even defeat the Chaos champion. Perhaps her brothers and sisters would carry the day, scattering Godspite's horde to the sands.

But there would be more. There would *always* be more.

Anaea's mount shifted under her, echoing the furious shrieks of its kin. Anaea urged it to silence as the first of her comrades' screams drifted up, carried on winds of ash. Each clash of distant blades seemed a slash across Anaea's flesh, each pained shout an arrow aimed at her heart, but she did not turn away.

She watched her companions dragged down, one by one, rivulets of blood dripping from the walls to puddle on the stony ground. Despite the seemingly numberless foe, despite the knights' wounds and exhaustion, the battle was not over quickly.

Master Karon had been true to his word. The Knights of the Ardent Star died noble deaths, yet still they died.

No matter what, Anaea would remember their sacrifice.

After what seemed an eternity, the killing stopped. A roar of triumph echoed from the cliffs, the howling call ripped from a thousand savage throats. The rightness of Anaea's choice was no balm against the guilt and shame that warred within her chest. She would hide in the mountains, craven and callous as the fyreslayers Master Karon had so reviled.

Head bowed, Anaea nudged her mount away from the Redoubt. The past held nothing but ashes. She tugged off her gauntlet, working her hand beneath her breastplate to grasp a thick handful of the banner.

'*Stella Invicti*.' The words came like a prayer, but she knew Myrmidia did not hear them.

Triumph was all that mattered to the Goddess of War, and survival was the only victory Anaea could yet win.

THE CLAW OF MEMORY

MEMORY

David Annandale

'You are doomed to repeat history,' said Neferata, 'because you are doomed to forget it.'

She looked out upon the conclave, watching the effect as her words sank in, waiting for the first scholar to disagree. She wondered if the objection would be shaped by reason or by fear.

The conclave was taking place in the Ossuary of Rigour. The chamber was a domed semicircle. Neferata presided over the gathering from a raised throne a few yards forward of the back wall. Inlaid in the dome were the interlaced bones of thousands of past Neferatian scholars. To be interred here was to be granted a singular honour, though Neferata did not bestow the gift without exacting a cost. There was no peace in the dome, no rest. Pain and a consciousness like the dreams of fevered sleep rippled through the bones. Even when it was empty, the Ossuary was not silent. From the dome came the susurrus of half-formed thoughts, of unfinished arguments, of the bitterness of fragmentary controversies. The last breath had been taken, but the last word never spoken. Sometimes, the writhing of the souls was so strong that the ceiling seemed to pulse. Now and then, the extremity of intellectual anguish reached such a peak that bone moved. Perhaps a finger twitched, or a jaw parted slightly. The motion was never great, but it was enough to make stone crack.

When the Ossuary was in use, its imprisoned souls were distracted from the agony of their discontent. The dead, confused and broken as they were, listened to the debates, and were compelled to echo them. The back wall of the Ossuary was a single slab of perfectly smooth, polished obsidian. As the discussions ebbed and flowed, so did phantasmal writing. The dark mirror of the stone glowed with the etchings of ghosts, the dying sighs of ideas. Neferata had little need to look back at the wall. She retained everything that was said, but the mortals before her could always see, at a glance, where the current of the debate had taken them, and what ideas were inspiring the strongest reaction.

In the silence that followed her latest words, she saw worried frowns, and knew that the wall had, for the moment, gone blank. Her declaration had cut deeply into the dead as well as the living. Coming from a mortal, the idea could potentially be refuted as easily as any other. But coming from her, the words had much greater weight, because they were backed by much greater knowledge, and much longer memory.

Even so, she was genuinely curious to see what counterargument, if any, would be offered. Her purpose had been twofold in summoning the conclave. There was a prize she sought, but whether she achieved it or not was independent of the actual debates. The other reason was scholarly. She had told these mortals, gathered from across Neferatia, that she wished to discuss the implications of the great loss of history that had occurred as a result of the wars of the Ruinous Powers. This was nothing less than the truth.

There were only mortals in this gathering. Sometimes Neferata wished to discuss with vampires only. Sometimes she mixed the living with the undead. On this occasion, she needed the view of mortals. They and the undead experienced time very differently. The passing of a year for those whose years were numbered was not the same as it was for those who could watch the centuries go by as indifferently as they did a minute, and with little change to themselves. It was not that vampires did not forget too, that they did not lose history too, and through her voluminous writing, she took measures against that danger in her own case. But the loss of history for mortals produced a pain whose acuteness led to particular flavour and vintage of thought. Neferata valued that uniqueness. Her hunger for knowledge, and the power it gave, was as strong as her thirst for blood.

'You present us with an unresolvable paradox,' said white-haired Geya Balanar. 'If what you say is true, then we will have no memory. And because we have forgotten, we cannot experience the truth.'

'I disagree,' said Alrecht Verdurin. He had not journeyed as far as some of the others. He lived in Enthymia, a small, ancient settlement under the protection of Nulahmia. 'Forgetting is not a wave. It is not a uniform condition.'

'Isn't that what the Ruinous Powers have been? A great wave upon our cultures, extinguishing them?'

'But not entirely,' Starin Javeign chimed in, cutting Alrecht off. 'The forgetting is not total. For tragic errors to repeat – and if repetition troubles us, it is because the repetition is tragic – it requires only that a certain number forget. Those who remember will be too few to prevent the tragedy, but they will witness the recurrence.'

'That is an added cruelty to the doom, then,' said Geya, 'if there is always enough memory to recognise the doom but never enough to prevent it.'

'We are not just talking about history that is to be feared and avoided,' said Mela Turvaga. She was even older than Geya. 'I think our queen's statement is true not only in the specific, but in the broader sense. We *are* doomed to forget. Even without the destruction of our cities, our libraries and our places of learning, and the murder of our sages, we would still forget. What the forces of the Ruinous Powers have done is to greatly worsen what was already happening, and is inevitable.'

'But there are still memories,' Alrecht insisted. 'History is not lost altogether.'

'That is a truth so partial as to be almost meaningless,' said Neferata. 'If I find a broken tiller washed up on the shore, can I then declare that the ship has not sunk? Your memories and your histories are lost day by day. Consider even your family's history. Is your line unbroken? Then you may pass down traditions and memories from one generation to the next. But you pass them down imperfectly. Details are forgotten, meanings are misinterpreted. With every ancestor who dies, there is someone else whose knowledge can no longer be consulted. And so little by little, what is passed down becomes distorted, vague, and a lie.'

'But you remember,' said Alrecht.

'Vampires forget too.'

'But *you*, my queen, *you* do not.'

'Don't I?' Neferata smiled, to show she was not denying what he had said.

'I do not believe that you *ever* forget,' said Alrecht.

'If this is so, what flows from that?'

'Then no history is truly lost. What we think we have lost can be recovered, through your generosity.'

Neferata laughed. 'Alrecht Verdurin, you are transparent. I have respect for your work as a sage, but not for your work as a politician. But even if I were as you would invite me to be, your reasoning is still flawed. History is more than a simple act of recall. History is interpretation. What I perceive to be the meaning of an event on one day may be very different from what I believe the next day, and different again the next year, and the next century. Where is your history now? Which of my interpretations would you wish me to give you? But your faith is touching. I wonder how you think I preserve and keep order in infinite memory.'

Alrecht worried he had said too much. He did not want to attract the wrong kind of attention from Neferata. But if he were silent during the conclave, that would draw her suspicions even more certainly. He had meant what he said. His best disguise, he thought, would be to participate as fully and honestly as he could in the discussions. Neferata's smile after the last exchange worried him, though. It felt too pointed. So he contributed less as the night wore on.

This was the second night of the conclave. The debates had been running without pause since it had begun. Neferata did not tire and had been present throughout. The mortal sages needed to rest. There were more than two hundred of them altogether, and though the Ossuary was always crowded, there was also a steady trickle of participants making their way in and out of the chamber. Scholars rose discretely from the rows of stone benches to leave in search of food and drink, or to sleep for a few hours in one of the cells in the halls leading to the Ossuary.

Alrecht waited a few more hours before he withdrew. The conclave would be ending before long. This was his moment. He could not leave the Palace of Seven Vultures until Neferata had dismissed her sages. Neither could he imagine returning to the Ossuary, and feeling her gaze, after he had done what he planned. He had to act while he knew where she would be, and then leave the palace right away.

He rose, timing his departure so that he was just a few steps behind another scholar, and he made his way out of the Ossuary. He turned left and walked down the hall, glancing in each of the cells as if he were looking for someone. He put more and more distance between himself and the other sages. When he reached the far end of the hall, he was alone. Without looking back, without speeding up, walking as if he knew where he was going and had every right to go there, he turned into the branching corridor.

There was no one here. He moved faster now, as quickly as he could while keeping silent. At every intersection, he clung to the shadows and peered around the corners, watching for guards. The further he went, the more confident he became that he would not be seen. He was seeking the way to Neferata's private library, and there would be no guards there, because that tower of the palace was hidden by the Mortarch's arcane arts. The grand library of the Palace of Seven Vultures was renowned across Neferatia and beyond. The private one, though, was a profound secret. As far as Alrecht knew, no one but Neferata was aware that it existed.

No one except the Verdurins.

Neferata was right about the decay of family history. Alrecht did not know how many generations back it was that his ancestor Karlet found the way into the library. He did not even know if the discovery had been the result of a search or lucky chance. It had been, Alrecht thought, so long ago that the defences of the library must have changed greatly. No other Verdurin had been able to find the way in since, yet every few generations, one of them tried. The family was a small one, its means modest. The Verdurins were not nobles. They were small merchants and scholars, and their most revered ancestor had committed a single act of theft. Karlet had seen wonders in the library. What those wonders were grew with every retelling of his legend. Alrecht doubted everything about the stories except for two things. He believed that the library contained limitless knowledge, and he believed that it was true that Karlet had been inside. He believed the first thing because he had to. His family's entire history was shaped by the belief in the power that knowledge would grant. He believed the second thing because he had proof. Karlet had stolen a single sheet of parchment from the library.

The writing on the parchment was in no language Alrecht could read. The runes, perfectly and elegantly shaped, had never been deciphered, though the Verdurins had tried for centuries to solve their puzzle. It was this effort that had gradually pushed the family closer and closer to poverty, as all pursuits except the scholarly fell away. Alrecht would be satisfied if all he took away from the Palace of Seven Vultures was a key, even just a hint, that would unlock the secrets of the parchment. In order to do that, though, he had to find the library, and he had to get in. All of Karlet's other descendants had failed. Most had simply returned home in disappointment, their souls eaten away by the doubt that Karlet had ever succeeded. Some vanished, and their disappearances kept the faith in Karlet alive, as did the parchment, the greatest of heirlooms, passed down from parent to child along with all the confusing, contradictory, frustratingly incomplete family lore.

Alrecht thought he would succeed. Things would be different for him because of the risk he was taking. He had the parchment with him. It was hidden inside the lining of his robe, nestled against his chest. No one had ever taken the parchment from the vault in which it was kept. Nothing could ever be allowed to happen to the Verdurins' most precious treasure. The idea of bringing the parchment to the palace had first come to Alrecht ten years ago. He had weighed the decision every day since then. Finally, knowing that if he failed, he would only be remembered as a traitor to the family, he decided the risk was worth taking. What use was the parchment without a key? None. What had it ever done for the Verdurins other than being the source of their obsession? Nothing.

Everyone had failed but Karlet, and what was different about Karlet? The presence of the parchment. Alrecht knew the logic made no sense. Karlet did not have the parchment *before* finding the library. It was the fact that the relic was present in Karlet's story that was enough for Alrecht. He had no sound reasons to think he was right. But he was convinced he was.

Within minutes of leaving the Ossuary of Rigour, he *knew* he was right.

There was no way to know where the library was. Karlet's legend said it was hidden in a tower. If that was so, there was nothing in the exterior of the palace that would suggest which one. The other inheritance of the Verdurins, accumulated over the generations of failed searches, was a map of much of the interior. That was as useless a heritage as having the parchment sealed in the vault. They were hardly alone in knowing their way around the palace. Having a sense of where he was would be essential when he wished to leave, but it did nothing to help him find the library.

The parchment was helping him, though. He felt it begin

to pull once he left the Ossuary behind. He followed where it wanted to go, and the pull became stronger. Now it was so powerful, he thought the parchment might tear through his robe and fly down the halls on its own. It was behaving like a dowsing rod. It wanted to return to the library, and it was using Alrecht as its tool to get there. He was happy to submit to its will.

He was almost giddy as he ran from shadow to shadow, down one corridor after another. His footing was sure, though it was growing hard to see. Wall sconces were becoming rare. The halls were thick with darkness. This was not a region of the palace anyone but the queen would have reason to enter. He stopped to catch his breath at one intersection. He squinted, looking back and forth. The damp stones of the walls were phantoms to him now. The gloom pressed against his eyes, clammy and smothering.

Alrecht didn't know where he was. He was too deep in the maze of the palace. His knowledge of Neferata's home, he now realised, was hopelessly superficial, a trap in itself. He wondered if he should turn around.

He looked back the way he had come. It was as dark as the path forward. Even if he made it as far as the previous intersection, he didn't know where to go from there. He was lost.

He would have panicked, but the tugging of the parchment was so strong, it submerged his fear. I'll find my way out, he told himself. Karlet took the parchment, and he found the way. The logic was as flimsy as his reason for bringing the parchment. No matter. He had been right to do that. He would be right again. He was close to finding the library. Conviction and obsession held the fear at bay.

Alrecht moved on through pitch darkness. The stone under his palm felt uncomfortably like the rough flesh of some

reptilian beast. The air was musty and dank, as if he were
heading into a region of the palace that was never used, and
was mouldering in neglect. This is another defence, he thought.
Alrecht wondered why there had been no barriers to him. He
had not stumbled over any wards. If the floor dropped away
ahead of him, he would have no warning. The simplest trap
would kill him.

He kept moving. The floor was solid. There were no traps.
He turned yet another corner, and the darkness lifted. There
was a door ahead of him: tall, iron, outlined by a thin glow
the colour of angry blood. Alrecht approached it. There were
shapes in the iron, but the light was too dim for him to make
out details. There was a suggestion of wings, of dark movement
arrested in metal. He felt a gaze upon him. He swallowed hard,
and pushed the door open.

The chamber beyond was suffused with the dim red glow.
Tens of thousands of books lined the curved walls of the tower,
and a staircase spiralled up the wall to its full, dizzying height.
Alrecht stumbled into the library, craning his head back. There
was too much to take in. The tower of books seemed to extend
to infinity. He approached the shelves nearest to the door. The
bindings looked odd, yet horribly familiar. He reached out and
touched a spine, then recoiled from the feel of a corpse. The
bindings were human flesh. He shuddered, swallowing bile.

The revulsion faded quickly. Knowledge and power drew
him on.

He did not know where to begin. The runes on the spines of
the volumes were the same incomprehensible markings as on
the parchment. Where should he look to find a key?

What if there isn't one?

He mustn't let himself believe that. He mustn't give up on
centuries of his family's singular hope.

Alrecht reached out for a book at random. At the last moment, he jerked his hand away as if burned. The thoughts contained between the covers seemed to be leaching out of the binding. The air was charged with a dark storm waiting to strike. The knowledge here was that powerful.

Who do you think you are? he thought. Leave this place. You cannot hope to master what is here. We have been lying to ourselves for every generation since Karlet.

He stared at the books, raising his head again to follow the spiral of power. He noticed now that the markings on the spines were clearly made by the same hand. Neferata had written everything he saw in this chamber. The wealth of thought before him was overwhelming.

Leave, he thought again.

He did not. He refused to give up on his family's dream. He refused to be the one to kill it. Somewhere in here was the key to the parchment.

Alrecht turned away from the wall. In the centre of the library stood a lectern. The stand was one of Neferata's victims, mummified and held in a position of eternal agony. An open book rested on the lectern, an invitation to the curious. Alrecht wondered if this was how Karlet had stolen the parchment so long ago. Tingling with anticipation, he approached the lectern and bent over the book. The page it was open to was blank except for a single sentence. This, Alrecht could read without a key.

RETURN WHAT IS MINE

Alrecht gasped. He wanted to flee but was frozen in place.

'You seem disappointed,' said Neferata.

Alrecht looked up. The Mortarch of Blood was walking down the staircase, her movements unhurried and graceful. She wore the same black robes she had at the conclave, but in the crimson light of the library, runes glowed on them, identical to the ones on the parchment, whipping Alrecht with silent mockery.

A monster glided down the stairs just ahead of Neferata. A dark, heavy shroud covered a body of bones and ghostly essence. A horse's skull protruded from the cloth, its empty eye sockets fixed on Alrecht. It clutched a long glaive, its notched blade carved with sigils. An unfelt wind stirred the tattered edges of the shroud. The jaws of the skull parted slightly, as if it would speak to Alrecht and promise him terrors.

'You are the first of your family since Karlet Verdurin to have entered the Claw of Memory,' said Neferata. 'You would be right to think that means you are also only the second mortal to set foot here. For Karlet's crime, I cursed your family. You have laboured in futility ever since. But none of Karlet's descendants brought the stolen page within my reach until you. So I must shape your fate differently. I hope you will not be disappointed.' She gestured at the horror that accompanied her. 'This is the first part of your reward. For this glaivewraith stalker, there is no one in this realm as important as you.' Her teeth gleamed.

Alrecht staggered back from the lectern. His robe caught on a spike protruding from beneath the book. The tortured face of the mummy screamed mutely at him. He tried to pull free, and it was as if the tome were holding him fast. Alrecht reached inside his robe as he struggled and pulled out the parchment. He threw the page at Neferata. It fluttered in the air and fell only a few feet from the lectern.

Alrecht wrenched himself free, tearing his robe, leaving a long strip of cloth hanging from the lectern. He ran for the door to the Claw of Memory. It had opened easily for him. Now it remained stubbornly closed. Sobbing, he yanked at it, too terrified to look back and see what was coming for him. His neck prickled in anticipation of the touch of a blade.

Then the door ground open. As Alrecht slipped through, he did look back. He saw Neferata holding up the cloth to the stalker. Then he was running.

The glow from the Claw of Memory followed him, lighting his way. He ran without thought or plan. He thought he had been lost before. Now, he truly was. Everything was lost to him.

He did not know how he got out of the palace. His flight was a blur of dark corridors and the distant laughter of Neferata ringing in his ears. But he was out, and in the streets of Nulahmia. He could think again, though that only increased his terror, because he knew why Neferata had not killed him in the Claw of Memory. She had chosen to toy with him. It would have been a mercy to die in the library. Instead, that *thing* was going to come for him. He would live with the torment of dread until then. He could feel the spectre's approach, picture its unhurried, relentless glide towards its appointment with him. There was nothing he could do to stop it.

But maybe he could end the curse. Perhaps he could redeem the centuries of futility, his family's unending expiation for Karlet's theft. Alrecht had failed his ancestors, and they had failed too. He swore he would not fail his son. Alrecht would give Lorron and his descendants the legacy of a true history, one they must never forget.

Nulahmia surrounded him with shadow. Every darkened alley and every gaping threshold of every house and every vault threatened to reveal the stalker. He moved as quickly as he could, running when he had the breath. He stuck to the great boulevards, hiding himself in the crowds. He tried to measure his progress against his memory of the hunter's unhurried movement. From stables at the western wall of the city, he paid for a horse and rode the beast to exhaustion. The wind in his ears was the keen of air through the skull of the glaivewraith stalker, and if he listened more closely than he dared, he would still hear Neferata's laughter.

Alrecht reached his house in Enthymia the following night. At the door, he looked around for the gliding, shrouded form. It was not upon him yet. 'Let there be time,' he muttered. 'Please, let there be time.' He did not know to whom he was pleading.

He slammed the door and barred it, though he knew the gesture was useless, and ran past his startled wife to his study.

Hallaya followed him. 'What is it?' she asked. 'Did you succeed?'

'Lies,' he told her. 'All lies.' He sat at his desk and snatched up a quill and a handful of vellum sheets. 'Where is Lorron?'

'In bed. Asleep.'

'Lock his door, and this one.' He grasped Hallaya's hand. 'I'm sorry,' he said, tears coursing down his cheeks. 'I'm so sorry. My time has come. This is the last thing I can do for you and Lorron. I love you both so much, and that is why I must do this.'

Hallaya ran from the room, and Alrecht turned to his task. He wrote frenziedly. There was too much he had to say, too much to explain, in order to bring this to an end. His hand shook, and his writing was a barely legible scrawl. Words came out in a jumble. He had no time to shape a careful argument. Each moment might be his last. When the door opened again, he yelped and dropped the quill.

It was Hallaya, come back to lock the door on this side.

'No!' Alrecht said. 'You have to leave me! You mustn't be here when it comes!'

'When what comes? I don't understand.' She came and threw her arms around him.

I don't understand. That was his fear. That was the terror that surpassed even that of his coming end – that she would not understand, that Lorron would not understand, that no one would understand. His life had been in vain. His death might be too.

Alrecht pulled free of Hallaya's embrace. 'I have to write this,' he said. 'I have to finish.'

The door flew off its hinges. The glaivewraith stalker floated into the room, its blade pointed at Alrecht's heart, its eye sockets empty yet filled with dreadful purpose.

Neferata entered the boy's bedroom. Lorron Verdurin couldn't have been more than eight years old. He was sitting up in bed, holding the rough woollen blanket up to his chin. His eyes were wide with fear, but when he saw Neferata, wonder suffused his face too.

Neferata smiled and shut the door, muffling the screams and the sound of ripping coming from Alrecht's study. She walked over to Lorron, sat on the side of his bed and stroked his hair. 'Don't be afraid,' she said. 'You are safe.'

'Who are you?' the boy croaked. 'Are you a queen?'

'I am. I am *your* queen. And I have come with a gift for you. And a secret.'

The screams stopped. The glaivewraith stalker had completed its task. Now there were only Hallaya's sobs.

'Do you want to know the secret?' Neferata asked Lorron, distracting him from the sounds of his mother's distress.

'What is it?' he asked.

'Tomorrow, your mother will tell you things about your father, and she will be wrong. She will try to understand, and try to help you understand, some things your father has written. She will not be able to, because they cannot be understood. I am sorry to tell you this, but it is the truth.' She soothed and mesmerised as she spoke. The child stared and nodded. 'So that is the secret. No matter what people say, remember that there is nothing to understand in your father's writings. You must turn all of your thoughts to my gift... Would you like to see it?'

Lorron nodded again.

Neferata opened a scroll tube and removed the parchment inside. She gave it to Lorron. 'This,' she said, 'is one of my most precious treasures. When you are wise enough, you will come to know what it means.'

She had to fight back laughter as she told the great lie. The second purpose of the conclave was fulfilled. She had lured Alrecht Verdurin to the palace, and he, at long last, had been the member of his clan to bring the stolen page with him. The archives of the Claw of Memory were complete once more. But the punishment of the Verdurins would not end. They had paid for Karlet's theft with generations of futile effort. Now they would have a new page to drive them to madness, one she had written for them. The runes on the parchment had no meaning, but they seemed to. They gestured towards a great revelation that did not exist. And Lorron's childhood memory of this night and his encounter with her would grow and poison all his descendants to come.

She leaned forwards and kissed the boy's cheek. 'Study and grow wise,' she whispered, 'until the day comes when you can read your gift.'

THE LEARNING

David Guymer

ONE

I

The *isharann* fane was a long way from their home in Túrach. His mother held his hand. Monsters swam free around the *túrscoll*, she had warned him, and it would not do to get lost. The thought of monsters did not frighten him, but he decided not to tell her that. If she thought that he was unafraid then she might let go of his hand. He sensed that when she let go, it would be for the last time. He did not understand. Through darkness and cold, they swam. Through silence. Through shoals of translucent fish that were all teeth and spines and which burst into individual fleeing shapes at their approach, his grip tiny but firm in hers.

After a time that did not feel long enough, they arrived at the temple. He sensed the size of it, smelled the coral from which the structure had been grown. He could hear the scrabbling of the little things that lived inside, the restless murmuring of the kelp gardens in the currents that came in off the open ocean. He tried to look back. His mother would not let him.

They set down before a bivalve doorway. It was ribbed and grey, and appeared to be breathing slowly. Blind aelves with huge swords and straps around their arms and chests stood in front of it. Five of them. *Namarti*. They looked unfriendly. He drew back into his mother.

'All will be well, Ubraich.'

She lifted him in the water until their faces were level. Her face was eyeless, smooth skin growing over the hollows, just like the warriors. She stroked his face around his eyes, just as she had done since he had been small. It had always seemed to make her happy, and sad.

Like now.

'You go to a better life,' she said.

'When will I be allowed to come home?'

She hugged him tightly.

'I love you, my brave isharann.'

II

He never saw his mother again.

He tried not to look as though her removal from his life had taken from inside him everything that was warm and strewn it over the walls of his little cell. The isharann masters punished such emotion, and in pretending not to feel it, it did become easier to ignore. The cold helped too. The isolation. The dark. Even if he did still stroke his eyes until he fell asleep each night. Isharann, he had learned by that time, were aelves of pure soul who had been judged by the soulscryers as being gifted in magic. Those better suited to the warlike arts had been sent instead to the azydrazor to become akhelian. Pure soul. He was starting to understand what that meant too. How it had made him different.

There was tutelage of a sort, but it passed in a blur of homesickness and misery. He was taught the healing stones of the *tru'heas*, the foundation songs of the chorralus, how to track a single soul across a thousand leagues of ocean, to tear a soul from a mortal's body or to bend one to his will. With no explanation given, the faces around him began to fall away. Gone were the lessons in soulrending and tidecasting. Instead he learned the names fangmora, allopex and leviadon. He learned what they were, how to mistreat them, how to train them.

He learned how to hunt them.

III

He became an embailor the night his master came into his cell with a knife.

The tide was late and he had been sound asleep when they burst in. Three eyeless thralls, their bodies sculpted and lean, covered in cruel-linking ink calligraphy and scars. The musk of the embailor quarter entered with them. Ubraich started from his shelf, but he was confused, still half asleep, and they knew what they were about. Two namarti took his arms. He struggled, but he was a boy. He was outnumbered and the namarti were both strong. A third hung in the water with arms folded across his chest. Since he had been old enough to understand the difference between isharann and akhelian and the soulless namarti, Ubraich had puzzled over why it was that the latter needed to lose their eyes.

He wondered if it was so they could not look into another's soul and feel pity.

An old aelf entered behind them.

Everything about his appearance conferred a greyed-out hollowness. He wore an armoured robe of steelglass and black nacre that seemed too large for his frame. His cheeks were drawn and scarred. The faded semicircle of an allopex bite cut his face in half. His neck was so withdrawn it had become paper over dry bones. His hair was colourless. It floated out behind him in a tail. The skin beneath one of his eyes was a scarred mess.

'Do you know who I am?' he asked. Even his voice was empty.

Ubraich nodded.

Giléan Six-Eyes.

Ubraich recognised him from his lessons in beastmastery. It would not do to say that he had enjoyed those lessons. Such feelings were discouraged. But he had excelled in them and been satisfied in himself. He had sought no praise from his masters, and none had been forthcoming.

Until, perhaps, now.

The old embailor held out the staff that he was carrying. It appeared to have been fashioned from the fused vertebrae of something very large, possibly a fangmora. The pumiced bones had been painted black and carved with *druhíri* dread-runes, an ancient aelf form that existed solely as an expression of pain.

'Do you know what this is?' he asked.

Ubraich shook his head dumbly.

'It is an embailor pain-stave. And it is yours.'

'It is too large for me.'

The embailor looked him up and down. 'You will grow.'

Swimming between the looming namarti, Giléan let the staff drift towards the wall of the cell and drew in alongside Ubraich's shelf. With one aged talon of a finger, he traced a line down Ubraich's cheek. Ubraich shivered. The two namarti held him down.

'Your scars will heal, but you, like the beasts you will tame, will never forget the pain of this night,' said Giléan, as he drew a hooked and rune-heavy knife. 'This is the first lesson my master taught to me. It will be the first that I teach to you.'

IV

The túrscoll was a creation of living coral, coaxed into its current form by the spells of the isharann chorralus, those with the talent for shaping the native materials of the idoneth's ocean home. It glowed, and as his embailor powers grew, so too did his ability to discern every tiny being that dwelled there. He could see their souls. The idoneth economy, he knew, turned on souls. The miniscule lives of the coral-dwellers might have been too small to interest the *incubati* who tended to the infant namarti, but there were those who earned their living from harvesting them, trading them to craftsmen who would use the soul material to make healing gems, soul-lights and restorative potions. The embailors were central to the industry. Most could be wealthy if they chose to be.

Even the unearthly splendour of the coral, however, paled before the creations of the *ishratisar*. Artists and artisans of the isharann, their magic left an immortal imprint of their own souls on the works they left behind, and made them glow in the senses of the sightless. Even to an aelf numbed to sensation by his own environment, the statues were wondrous: giants in silver, depicting heroes of the cythai, the sea-aelves of the first oceans. The beasts they had ridden were creatures that no embailor had ever described to him, with huge wings or legs instead of fins, and clad in metal in the style of the surface races. They bore names like *asglir* and *caldai* – Silver Helms and Dragon Knights.

Over the tides that followed, Giléan Six-Eyes proved a reluctant mentor, stirring himself from seclusion only rarely. It was
to the aelves shown to him by the ishratisar that Ubraich found
himself drawn for solace or guidance. They looked so proud,
so wise, as if the solution to all problems had once been theirs.
They rode their wondrous beasts without saddle or harness.

To aspire towards such nobility was as natural as breathing.

V

'Why did Teclis not make the cythai perfect?'

Giléan, on those rare occasions when he roused himself from
isolation, betrayed a fondness for thought puzzles and rid-
dles. He believed them to be the most elegant expression of
eolas. The word was of the cythai, and it had several meanings.
Knowledge. Teaching. Another name for the god Teclis himself.

Most often, however, it was understood as 'The Learning.'

He turned his brutalised face to look back at Ubraich.

The two embailors were swimming through the pens. The
globed nets rippled and bulged like jellyfish, glowing inter-
nally with the souls of the monsters they held. The billion tiny
gems of the túrscoll and, some way beyond it, Túrach itself,
were brilliant and austere. Like a moonrise. Giléan preferred
to pen his most monstrous beasts here. There were two reasons: it kept those beasts well away from the túrscoll, and it
served as a deterrent to all but the largest of ocean predators
that might otherwise be drawn to the enclave.

Ubraich paused, his arm in a bushel of fish. A hungry allopex
beat its snout against the inside of the net. The globe bulged. It
gnashed its teeth furiously, trying for purchase. Its eyes were
glassy and yellow, glaring through the diamond pattern in the
net.

'Perhaps Teclis is not perfect?' he guessed.

Giléan cocked his head, as though considering, but Ubraich knew him well enough to know that that was not the answer he was seeking.

Ubraich proceeded to feed the allopex.

'Or maybe the cythai were never meant to be perfect,' Giléan said.

'Why would a creator god do such a thing?'

Giléan grinned, pleased to have been asked. 'So that we must strive for the Light that blinded the cythai. That we might learn again, however painful.' The old embailor swam to the next net. His pain-stave was larger than Ubraich's and far more elaborate. Its structure incorporated the vertebrae of more than one beast, greatly enhancing the range and scope of its powers. It was topped by an enormous splayed fin that the embailor seemed to be relying on more heavily than usual.

'Are you injured, teacher?' Ubraich asked.

Giléan glanced at his arm and presented a rueful expression. 'A beast that I have not yet broken in thirty years of trying. It had the better of our encounter again.' He looked back at Ubraich, his gaze appraising. 'You will be able to assist me, I think. When your magic is strong enough.'

VI

The corral was the heart of the túrscoll's embailor quarter. Circular and roofed with a thick accumulation of nets, it was large enough to confine a whole battalion of leviadon. The walls were high and silvered by ishratisar panelling, a living diorama of laagering knights so vivid that the thunderous silence of their hooves was disorienting.

'Have you ever broken a deepmare before?'

Lady Sithilien frowned at him through the narrow slits in her helmet. The akhelian knight was fully clad in blue scales, a shield of organically shaped coral worn across her back. A bundle of delicate white hair emerged from beneath a coif of turquoise mail, dancing in the weak currents of the corral floor. She held a voltspear disinterestedly.

Giléan sneered.

Ubraich did not answer.

There were those races in the Mortal Realms that knew an innate and equal bond with the beasts they rode. He had been told tales about them at the fane. The Stormcast Eternals and their Celestial dracoths. Fyreslayers and their magmadroths. Even the brutish beastclaw ogors and their mournfangs. For reasons that no isharann had been able to explain to him, an animal had never yielded willingly to the idoneth. They had to be broken. Deepmares were the most dangerous and difficult. Too fiercely intelligent to be courted by promises of friendship. Too mean-spirited and guileful to be dominated easily by the embailor's arts. They were also the mount most desired by akhelian nobles raised on the soul-memory of the old *asur*, images of asglir and caldai and Teclis' eolas. Giléan had broken deepmares for two Túrach queens and a king. He wore the six eyes he had taken from them on a string around his neck.

'He will not be breaking this one,' said Giléan, his face turned upwards. 'He will be assisting me, and perhaps learning something.'

The akhelian swept the fringe from Ubraich's face with the back of her hand and studied him. It was little more than a brush of knuckles on skin, but to the sensation-deprived it was like being bitten by an electric fangmora. Ubraich did his best to suppress a shudder.

'Leave my apprentice be, akhelian,' said Giléan.

'He is very young,' said Sithilien, staring hard into his eyes.

'They all begin that way, I am told.'

The akhelian chuckled blackly and released Ubraich's face.

'You are nervous,' said Giléan. 'You are making the boy nervous.'

'Nervous? Either your beast will kill me, and probably both of you, or we will break it and I will be begged to join the highest rank of Túrach's warrior nobility, a place within the *asglir'akhelian* itself. Why ever should I be nervous?'

Even through her blank helm and cold eyes, Ubraich could sense the ferocity of her smile. His pale skin blushed a diffuse shade of indigo, and he averted his eyes.

To see an older woman betray her feelings so...

The Lady Sithilien laughed without pity. 'Have you never been to the surface, child? Have you swum in the aethersea?'

'No, lady. What would a taker of beasts do on the surface?'

Giléan nodded, possibly approving.

'Those who have raided have a different perspective on things,' she said. 'I have stepped outside our ocean and seen it from beyond. I have felt the sun warm my skin and seen light in all its colours. It is an experience that changes you. Not all emotion is to be feared or sensation to be avoided.' She subjected Ubraich to a new, more deeply discomforting appraisal. 'I have eight children, you know. All of them namarti.'

Ubraich's mouth worked soundlessly.

'He is a hundred years too young for you,' said Giléan.

'And you are a hundred years too old.' She produced a smile such as Ubraich had only seen on hungry allopexes.

'I will give you a deepmare,' said Giléan. 'Any ambitions beyond that must wait for another tide.'

The old embailor nodded upwards.

Ubraich, and then finally Sithilien, turned to follow his gaze.

A shoal of muscular namarti converged over the great nets above the corral as they watched. They swam like fish with arms at their sides and legs together, long hair slicked back in tails. Their souls were a constellation of muddy colours. Stunted hybrids of aelf and human, aelf and duardin, aelf and orruk, fused together so that those unfortunates born without souls might persist beyond infancy. Those namarti fortunate enough to have received the souls of aelves taken in the surface raids were favoured as personal servants and guards, but even they were noticeably diminished to Ubraich's senses. There had been a time when he had perceived the namarti differently.

It was difficult for him to imagine such a time now. The differences between them were too stark.

With ropes knotted around their waists, the namarti drew one of the rippling globe nets down from the beast pens in the water above. They docked it to the corral roof. Other namarti swam in quickly to secure the two sets of nets together with metal rings. Ubraich felt the tension in the namarti rising. He fidgeted with his pain-stave and saw Sithilien doing something similar with her voltspear. This was where so many namarti of the embailor túrscoll earned their scars. He watched them dart through the holes in the nets, threading them with the ropes tied around their waists. They unwound them, transferring the knots over to the netting. They fastened them tight, then drew knives to begin cutting away the ropes that held the two bodies of netting separate. Coral-encrusted ropes fell away. The two netted enclosures effectively merged to become one, and the namarti scattered like startled prey as the beast swam into its enlarged pen.

Ubraich clutched his pain-stave to his breast. Trepidation and fear tingled uncertainly under his skin.

It was a gulchmare, one of the rarest and most dangerous

breeds of deepmare to be found in the oceans of Ghyran. It was half again as large as the monster that Giléan had broken to Queen Anaer's saddle. Its clawed fins and tail spines were the restless green of seaweed, but it had no single colour. Its flanks were rainbow swatches of armoured reef. The rippling, wriggling, puckering creatures that had colonised those encrustations conferred a sense of fevered energy and menace to the beast's every movement. Ubraich lost a moment to awe. It was majestic. The gulchmare looped and rolled, swimming foalishly around the larger enclosure.

It had not yet noticed the three idoneth in its midst.

'Bounties of Mathlann!' Sithilien crowed.

Her voice rose in pitch to a keen of whalesong as she kicked off the corral floor and shot towards the gulchmare. The beast turned towards her, then tossed its head as though something had just crawled inside. With one hand on his pain-stave, Giléan held the other outstretched. His face was a rictus of concentration. Sithilien deftly evaded the distracted beast's fin-claws, then gave a whoop as she swung herself onto its back. The gulchmare arched its spine and roared, but Sithilien had wedged herself firmly between the beast's spikes and held on. The akhelian then set about with the butt of her spear.

Giléan turned to Ubraich.

'It is a defiant beast. Only through pain and the fear of pain can its walls be broken and its soul dominated. I cannot both cloud its wits and break its defiance. I need you to confound its mind, Ubraich, while I get in close and aid the Lady Sithilien.'

'I-I will try.'

The old embailor appeared to consider Ubraich a moment, then thrust his pain-stave into his ribs. A firm blow from such a weapon could cripple a leviadon. The idoneth, trained by abnegation and privation, had an altogether more delicate nervous system. Even a touch could be lethal. It was like being burned alive. Being shocked repeatedly by fangmora. Being eaten alive by sawfish while he screamed. It was all of those things and yet, at the same time, none. It was purely internal. It was pain of a sort that would chew through a body to inflict every suffering imaginable short of actual death.

It was pain that an aelf would say or do anything to avoid experiencing twice.

'What are you going to do?' Giléan asked calmly.

'Confound its mind,' Ubraich gasped.

Ignoring his apprentice, Giléan kicked off after Sithilien and the gulchmare.

Ubraich carefully unfolded his body from the foetal position it had unconsciously curled itself into. He tentatively quested out with his beast magic. The gulchmare's soul was a writhing knot of angry defiance, an apex monster that an aelf, in his arrogance, had put in a cage. Ubraich touched its mind at the same moment that Giléan's pain-stave cracked into its shoulder. Its soul halo turned ugly. The beast emitted a shriek of agony. Its mind folded in on itself, instinctively seeking an escape from the pain. It felt the link to Ubraich's soul, and like a school of fish bursting from the closing jaws of an allopex it attacked.

Ubraich grunted. The muscles of his face tightened as he struggled to hold the gulchmare's tortured soul at bay. With the fin-claws and teeth of its mind it savaged him, real wounds opening up his chest and his forearms, while leaving his journeyman leathers undamaged. He screamed as a lash of the beast's tail tore the meat of his thigh. Blood ripped outwards from his leg in a narrow jet.

'Hold it,' Giléan snarled, and struck it another blow.

The gulchmare's torment was staggering. For a moment it was as if Ubraich's mind and the beast's fell into each other's embrace, too beaten and wearied to fight any further. It was so far removed from the principles of eolas that Ubraich almost fainted from the dissonance of it. This was not how it was supposed to be.

What would the cythai have made of the embailor's art, he wondered?

Or the asur?

He shrieked as a soul maddened by agonies beyond all comprehension savaged at his. Had the gulchmare been lucid enough to actively desire him harm, then it might have slain him on the spot. A mauling proved adequate to appease its rage, and he was flung physically back through a compressed fog of dark blood and tiny bubbles. His body cracked against the ishratisar panelling of the corral wall.

The gulchmare's mind landed firmly back into its own body. It was furious, and free to act on it. It snapped Giléan up in its jaws and shook the master embailor violently back and forth. He lost his pain-stave. 'You belong to me!' Sithilien yelled. She attacked the gulchmare's head this time with the bladed end of her voltspear, but its armour encrustations spoiled each of her blows.

Truly, it was a mount deserving of Túrach's asglir'akhelian.

Ubraich pushed himself from the corral wall with a whimper. His body trembled with unpleasant sensations. It was the most intensely he had felt since his mother had left him at the gates of the túrscoll. He made the connection unthinkingly. There was no longer any pain attached to that memory. It had been crushed by time and desolation. Just the idea of *feeling* made his body respond as though threatened by unseen predators.

He looked at Giléan, flailing in a murky red compress of his own blood.

He looked at the beast.

Something arrogant and prideful awoke in his soul-memory. He would break the beast where Giléan had failed. It would be *his* name that future generations of isharann would learn alongside Lotann and Mor'u when they studied the masters of ages past. He extended his beast magic towards the gulchmare once more. The master embailor was already the centre of its attentions, the taste of his lifeblood filling its mouth. Through the connection that Ubraich had already formed between their minds it was simplicity itself to bid the predator to sink its every thought into the devouring of his former master.

'Do not let go, Lady Sithilien.'

Kicking off from the wall of the corral, he swam at the distracted gulchmare. Sithilien had her thighs clamped around the beast's flanks, holding on to the mineral encrustations of its neck with one hand while continuing to stab at its neck with the other. Ubraich came up beneath it and drew back his pain-stave.

The blow crunched into the rock armour of its hip. The beast's back arched, pain shredding outwards and coursing up the monster's spine to its brain. Sithilien whooped as the creature's convulsions exposed bare skin at the base of its throat, and she drove her voltspear into it. Blood squirted from the wound. Its soul flared with confusion and pain. Ubraich reversed his grip on his pain-stave, striking the gulchmare two-handed across its hindquarters. It released Giléan's carcass from its jaws, a thin scream of tiny bubbles issuing from its mouth.

Ubraich planted his foot against the monster's flank and pushed himself back.

'Command it,' he hissed. 'Assert your soul's dominance over its.'

'Yield!' Sithilien crowed, hooking her arm under the beast's throat as if to throttle it into submission.

The gulchmare snapped its jaws in a futile bid to dislodge the akhelian straddling the back of its neck. Its gouged eyes found Ubraich. Its nostrils flared, the muscles in its neck tensing. Ubraich had been inside the monster's mind. He knew what instincts drove it.

'She said *yield*.'

He held his hand to the gulchmare's gaping jaws, and the beast recoiled as though from a master's pain-stave. Baring his teeth in effort, he bent his will against the last shred of the monster's defiance, his magic a tool to leverage its pain. Where he found rebelliousness, Ubraich expunged it mercilessly, excruciating entire swathes of the creature's mind to leave dead soul wherever free will might bloom.

Slowly, reluctantly, the gulchmare closed its jaws.

Sithilien sank as the tension left its spine.

She began to laugh.

'Yes, Ubraich. *Yes!*'

Ubraich glowed with the first words of praise he had ever received.

He found he liked it.

TWO

I

Ubraich sat back into the rippling flesh of the giant calroir clam, gently kneading the muscle of his thigh. His expression was rueful. It had been twenty years since his encounter with the gulchmare, yet the wounds he had taken that day had never closed. It was a soul injury, according to the tru'heas, and such wounds seldom healed well; they had been known to pass from parent to child, and even to recur in distant generations. The constant and quite obvious pain it caused had made him something of a pariah, for the idoneth found extremes of any kind disturbing. This had not troubled Ubraich unduly. Something in the idoneth's nature bade them to seek out seclusion, and none more so than those drawn to the embailor's arts. He settled into his bound-beast's gently quivering gill-sac, allowing its simplistic soul to form a protective mesh about his own as he toyed idly with the necklace of eight deepmare eyes resting against his chest.

In the corral below, three young isharann took turns to bait an allopex, notionally working in tandem to bring the beast down, but idoneth did not work naturally in groups. As he listened, Irimé, the eldest, broke from the others to lay a blow. Her pain-stave crunched into the allopex's shoulder, convulsing it.

'A well-struck blow, Irimé,' Ubraich called down.

He had been experimenting with praise and found it to be effective. As with anything, it was best indulged in moderation.

Irimé was a vigorous girl, when passion was allowed her, and so she relished these opportunities in the corral. The study of beast magic and of the ishratisar's illuminated bestiaries bored her. Ubraich had been forced to face down the angry young isharann more than once. There were those in the túrscoll who would tut, as much at her intensity as his unspoken indulgence of it. 'Send her to the *azydrazor* to learn the ways of the soul-render,' they often said. For their ways were not dissimilar and the soulscryers who assigned young children to their respective fanes were not immune to mistakes. Where the embailor strove to bend a soul to his will, the akhelian-schooled soul-render tore it wholesale from a being's flesh. But Ubraich did not wish for that. He knew that, once unleashed, the difficulty lay in restraining her.

'Back now, Irimé. I would see what the others can do.'

With a scowl, she withdrew.

Flowain and Valhanir were of a similar age, and as close as twins. Both were more naturally cautious, and though they lacked Irimé's talent, they also lacked her scars. Flowain, in particular, would still let fear show when paired with a particularly difficult beast, and had probably felt Ubraich's wrath as often as Irimé. In that, at least, the two were evenly matched. She had a gift, however, and Ubraich was loath to be rid of her entirely. He had once watched her floating on her back in the tru'heas herb gardens, arms extended to the wild ocean, singing down a flock of spinelbuds. They had come to her through the arbour nets of the túrscoll, mindless of the predators they held, to enamel her waiting hands in ruby-coloured florets. Her laugh had been as carefree as a cythai queen.

Ubraich had taken no pleasure in punishing her for her sense of wonder.

All three would make fine embailors, for he demanded no less.

The allopex reared suddenly to snap at Valhanir. The monster's jaw was bound in rubbery kelp, preventing it from opening its mouth much beyond an arm's width, but the boy started all the same. He cried out as he stumbled back. The allopex surged, butting its flat nose into the young isharann's stomach. Valhanir dropped his pain-stave. Ubraich frowned in displeasure. Before he could offer a chastisement, Irimé pounced. She leapt at the allopex from behind, beating its back and tail with such a flurry of blows that the monster almost broke its own spine with its convulsions.

'Enough, Irimé!' The young isharann was snarling as she drew back her pain-stave for another blow. '*Enough.*'

From across the corral, Flowain cocked her head, then made a gesture with her foot that Ubraich would not have noticed had he not seen it many times before. Mirroring it almost exactly, the allopex swatted Irimé with its tail, crashing her into the walls of the corral.

Ubraich winced to see the ishratisar soul-pigment of the asglir that had been rendered there crack.

Only then did his concern shift to his pupil.

'Should I dispatch a namarti for the tru'heas?'

Paddling furiously, Irimé rolled herself upright. She thrust her pain-stave accusingly at Flowain. The younger embailor noticeably shrank from it. Valhanir looked between them. He was a swift learner. One lesson had been enough to teach him to stay well clear of Irimé's temper.

'I know that was you, Flowain!'

Gripping the edges of his calroir shell, Ubraich rose, trying and failing to suppress the quiver of pain that ran through his leg. He settled instead for ignoring it, letting it suffer in isolation from his spirit. The calroir emitted a wheeze to compensate its buoyancy for the shift in weight.

'You earned that blow, Irimé,' he said.

'But she–'

'Imagine, if you prefer, that the blow was mine. I would have tasked her with delivering it had she not done so freely.' Irimé snorted at that. 'I tire of your distemper. You may retire to the seclusion cells until I deem it to have passed.'

'But–'

Ubraich lifted his pain-stave, and the young isharann quietly set about gathering her things. 'And you two.' Ubraich added snap to his voice. 'Remove this thing.' He pointed to the quivering allopex with his staff. 'See that it is fed *your* rations this eve and its wounds are treated. Tomorrow, I think, it will be ready to break.'

'It is all quite different from Giléan's regime, is it not?' Lady Sithilien observed drily as her gulchmare drew in alongside his calroir.

Princess Sithilien, Ubraich reminded himself.

Her claiming of the gulchmare had impressed not only the Túrach's akhelian order, but the royal house of Anaer as well, and they had quickly seen her wed to one of the royal bloodline's innumerable namarti bastards. She wore a coat of scalloped armour emblazoned with the spiked fist of Anaer arms. Her helm was tall and silver, in the old asglir style, leaving her proud, lined face uncovered. The gulchmare too was cloaked in heraldry and mail. A hundred and forty years old, and she had never looked more powerful. Ubraich seldom kept himself up to date with the whisperings of court, but he knew that Sithilien had recently given birth to her fourteenth child. Another namarti. Nobody was entirely certain as to the identity of the father. Nobody was entirely interested. Least of all her prince. The idoneth were dogged if not enthusiastic breeders: they prized fecundity far more than fidelity.

His royal patron and occasional lover settled into a companionable silence that Ubraich rebuffed with a frown. He fondled the eight-eyed necklace thoughtfully as the princess spoke again.

'Giléan would have made an example of Irimé for her aggression. He would have punished Flowain for her cowardice, and Valhanir for his ineptitude.'

'I decided long ago that I would surpass Giléan,' Ubraich said.

She laughed, and Ubraich noted how it had been hoarsened by her years. 'Giléan was good enough. His skills earned him the favour of the akhelian.'

'I do not desire their favour.'

Her smile thinned. 'There are those who wonder by what right you wear the Eight-Eyes' necklace.'

'Six-Eyes,' Ubraich corrected her. 'His name was Six-Eyes.'

'Not if you heed the aelves at court.'

'There is a reason I do not.' Fastening his jaw, he settled into his mount's flesh as if resolving to ignore the akhelian princess. '*I* broke the gulchmare you ride now.' He glared askance at her and the beast whinnied as if remembering the cut of his mind, forcing Sithilien into an inelegant touch on the reins. His abilities had only grown since that day. 'Not Giléan.'

'I remember. It is why I am here now. You are proud, Ubraich, and I am old. I would see you continue to enjoy favour when my soul rests in the chorrileum.'

Ubraich said nothing, choosing instead to watch as Valhanir set nets around the allopex to prepare it for moving.

'Are you not even going to ask?'

Ubraich frowned up at her.

Sithilien mirrored the expression. 'I am recently returned from a raid on the Blight of Gullyrion. On my return, I lost several namarti scouts to a deepmare of a kind whose description confounded the isharann in my phalanx.'

'Tidecasters and soul wardens,' Ubraich muttered. 'What would they know of a beast?'

'It was shelled after the fashion of a leviadon, they claimed, though narrower in shape and not quite as large. It moved swiftly too, they said. Whatever it was, it dispatched forty namarti reavers.'

'Where was this?' Ubraich tore his gaze from his apprentices to regard the princess fully. 'And when?'

'In the shallow seas, near to Dwy-Hor.'

'The shallows,' Ubraich mused. 'It would be rare to find a truly great beast there. Does anybody else know of it?'

Sithilien unsheathed her grin. 'For a reclusive people, we are little able to keep a secret amongst ourselves. The túrscoll is abuzz with talk of this beast, as you would know if you spent any time there. Several embailors and their apprentices are already making plans to claim the monster.'

'They will need the support of the akhelian.' Ubraich's mind was already moving, plotting, visualising the long-overdue eclipse of his former master's legend by his own. 'Without the strength of the battalions they will never make it as far as Dwy-Hor.'

Sithilien's harness creaked as she leaned towards him. The

smile on her face was much the same as Giléan would wear, in his unguarded moments, when he had succeeded in imparting some wisdom.

'Know you of an embailor in Túrach who could command such backing?'

Ubraich scowled. His right hand found its way to his face. With forefinger extended, he started to make rings around his eyes. It was an old habit. He could not recall when he had started doing it, or why, but whenever he felt emotion threatening to get the better of him, it reminded him of a time, a place, where he had felt safe.

He let his hand float to his side, and sighed.

'How long will you need to get ready?'

II

The idoneth were a puritan people, little given to carnival or splendour. If there was an unearthly beauty to their enclaves, then it was because the reef and shell from which they had been created were possessed of it. And if their armed hosts appeared to be things of sublimity, then it was because their composites too had a beauty all of their own. This was as true for the namarti thralls as it was for their akhelian lords, for sickly and withered of soul though they were, they were perfect of body as only aelves could be.

The namarti battalion of Princess Sithilien assembled before the shell-encrusted tidegate of Túrach, not in the dressed ranks and files of a landed host, but as a school of beautifully scaled fish in a bowl. They swam freely, armed with lanmari greatswords or short whisperbows, confined only by the cohesion of the school itself and by the softly glowing coral spires that jutted above them like the spines of a god-beast.

Neither Ubraich nor Sithilien had made any prior announcement, and yet a small crowd had grown organically to witness the hunt's departure. Namarti carters and pickers and labourers paused in their efforts. Lords and their favoured servants watched from coral shelves and verandas that grew from the great spires. A rawness of energy suffused them. Cold and withdrawn the idoneth may have been, but there was something buried deep in their spirit that longed to cut loose on a wild hunt.

Sithilien swept up her spear to rally her schooling battalion.

She did not need to say anything. When the phalanxes raided the shores that bordered their oceans for mortal souls, all knew why. When the akhelian mustered their battalions to bring home a great beast, all knew why.

Ubraich turned to his apprentices and his own small band of stern-looking thralls. Irimé was eager, her face made crooked by a fierce smile. Flowain and Valhanir looked trepidatious, but excited. All three were dressed for the open ocean. Finned leather boots for distance swimming. Lightweight kelp jackets stuffed with pockets and with shells sewn in for added protection. Valhanir had his arm draped over a pack beast. The sea snail was the first in a train of six, their spiralling shells festooned with netting that held provisions: rune-stones for heating, healing and meditation; ropes; chains; herbs; more nets and spare weapons for the namarti. The three isharann all carried their pain-staves.

They required no words either.

Ubraich turned back from them, letting his soul-sight drift out of focus over the mountain of cultivated reefs.

It was his first return to Túrach that he could recall. He was not sure what he was hoping to see there. Or who. Only namarti dwelled in Túrach. The one in one hundred of pure soul would be in the palaces and castles of the great coral-spires, or in the blessed seclusion of the túrscoll. He clutched his pain-stave and drew a steadying breath. Already his leg was beginning to ache, just from treading water. He wondered if he had chosen unwisely in leaving his calroir behind. It was pride that had made him insist that he could swim, for it was a long journey ahead of them and he would not force an entire battalion to the clam's pace.

An isharann tidecaster that Ubraich did not recognise swam through the flitting namarti. She was tall and glitteringly austere, cloaked in white, garlanded in lapis shell and aquamarine. As she descended to join Sithilien, clad almost entirely in asglir silver and mounted on her gulchmare, she raised her pelagic staff to test the prevailing currents through the tidegate and declared them favourable. Eager cheers ran through the watching workers and then, like the tide, the isharann withdrew.

Sithilien gave the command.

The hunt rode out from Túrach.

III

The open ocean was no place for the idoneth.

Though they claimed everything bound within or touched by it, they ruled little beyond the meagre confines of their enclaves. When the phalanxes raided land they voyaged through the aethersea, cast far by the isharann magic of the tidecasters and soulscryers. On those rare instances when the wish or need was there to journey to another enclave or answer the call of assembral, then they travelled through the whirlways, the network of Realmgates that confluenced in the Gaelus Ocean in Hysh, the mythical birthplace of the cythai.

There were five idoneth enclaves in the Green Gulch of

Ghyran, all descended from the original Ionrach colonisation. Elgaen, the White City, whose nacreous towers had earned it a reputation for austere beauty and unearthly splendour. Dwy-Hor, with its verdant underwater forests, where sylvaneth might occasionally be spied beneath wave-dappled sunlight. Guethen, renowned for the barrenness of its stone and the hardiness of its warriors. And Túrach of course, the City of Spines, once pre-eminent, before the rise of Briomdar and its isharann queen. They were motes of civilising influence, scattered across a black and crushing void. In the ocean, there was no light. No ishratisar art defined its walls and edifices. No chorralus builders existed to order its beauty. The pulse of life choked the ocean's surface with algal mats the size of continents, but the deep places remained forever hostile. It was another symptom of the unformed magic that resided there. Physically, the oceans belonged to Ghyran still, but in reality...

Guided only by the meandering soul-lines of the namarti marching columns, Ubraich made it a point of ritual to pause, breathe deeply and imbibe of the crushing emptiness that abounded him. The desolation was absolute, primal; it was almost spiritual.

They lost six namarti to the first tide. Eight the next. Then eighteen, one of Ubraich's own hunters included. Sithilien grew increasingly embittered and wary as the toll steepened, but Ubraich had known that the distance between the Túrach tidegate and the emptiness to which they were destined would come at a cost. He tried to explain, but the akhelian had been borne only to land, on the aetherwaves of the tidecasters, and could not comprehend. A thousand miles of forsaken water separated Túrach from Dwy-Hor, naught but ancient beasts and dreamless magic to fill it.

The mood amongst the namarti was more than usually bleak

as they made camp on the turning of the fourth tide. Huge fish-scale awnings were unfurled, providing shelter from the icy currents and some degree of camouflage for the namarti to huddle beneath, away from the occasional prowling predator. Ubraich bade his namarti to release bushels of sentinel fish into the ocean. They swirled around the forsaken camp, each of them broken and bound to Ubraich's soul and hesitant to be parted from it. They would be easy enough to recapture when the tide turned again and would emit an intense emerald light when threatened: a natural defence mechanism, and useful forewarning in the event of an attack.

At Ubraich's insistence, the entire business was conducted in silence.

Tracking a beast through open ocean was no simple task. There were no broken twigs or footprints to follow, no abandoned kills or droppings to signpost a trail. They had only their ears, their noses and, if they were possessed of the power and knew what to search for, their soul-sense.

Once Ubraich was satisfied, and Sithilien had murmured her assent, the embailors made off from the newly struck camp to divine for the trail of the beast.

Valhanir struck two stones together. Light burst from them. Ubraich grunted. Only the namarti hunters that accompanied them, physically lacking eyes, gave no reaction at all. Ubraich blinked as the light burst faded to tolerable levels. Rocky hills and mesas bulged from the ocean floor, barren even of the simplest vegetation.

'There is nothing here,' said Irimé.

'Do you not sense that?' said Ubraich.

'I do, teacher,' said Flowain.

Irimé screwed up her face as she sought to force her senses further.

'There is another soul in the water,' Valhanir murmured. 'Is it our prey?'

Ubraich shook his head. 'It is not just one. Look again. *Namarti!*'

The namarti hunters swam forwards, raising their whisper-bows, arrows already nocked.

'I see them!' Irimé cried.

Silver-bodied havaklir streamed from a cleft in the rock ahead of them like an eruption from a gaseous vent. The fish were scavengers, but only out of deference to the behemoths that ruled the ocean's brutal food chains. Each was twenty feet long and three high, but so preposterously thin that to face one head-on was like looking down the length of a blade, all cruel serrations and silvered lines. Grimacing in concentration, Ubraich drove a wave of power into the shoal, scattering the flotsam of their tiny thoughts and breaking the school into a confusion of individual minds. Fish snapped at empty water, swimming furiously after the implanted suggestion of prey.

'What are you waiting for?' he said.

There was a *twang* of vibration as the namarti hunters loosed arrows into the convulsing shoal, and Irimé needed no further encouragement.

Her pain-stave crushed into a flat body. The creature locked stiff, its tail muscles and fins frozen in agony. It cartwheeled stiffly, head over tail, as Irimé spun gracefully in the water and hammered the length of her staff into its side. The pain-stave was not designed to be a lethal implement, but swung with enough force it was as effective as any mace or cudgel. Blood puffed from cracked scales and clotted gills as it spun back from her.

Ubraich hefted his pain-stave. Irimé had focused the predators' minds. The scattered elements of the school were shaking off Ubraich's spell of suggestion, looping back around and swimming ferociously towards the taste of blood in the water and the wriggling of live prey. One went at Irimé like a thrusting sword. Ubraich reached out for it and made a tugging gesture. It was a simple creature with only the dimmest awareness of self. Its soul was but weakly tethered, and Ubraich's spell wrenched it from its body to dissolve into the ocean. The havaklir's mouth and eyes opened wide, a dead thing now in a living body.

The rest of the school swirled about him. A namarti's bow-stave was bitten in half. Another lost her head to a single bite, her body disintegrating as more havaklir converged over her corpse. Ubraich lashed at them with his pain-stave. The school bruised with purples and blues as pain wracked their souls. Agony of his own flared up in his mutilated leg. He welcomed it. It fed him with more, and worse, to inflict upon his prey. A scream pealed through the seething maelstrom and Ubraich risked a look back to see Flowain breaking from the melee, swimming for the open ocean in panic. He summoned one of his surviving hunters.

'Bring her back here.'

'Master.' The namarti bowed.

'Defend me, Valhanir.'

Freed of the need to concentrate on defence, Ubraich drove another harrowing pulse through the havaklir's minds. This time, the school had suffered enough that it broke up completely under his power, individual shards of silver scattering into the ocean.

Ubraich slumped, slapping away Valhanir's helping hand.

'Gather the corpses,' he panted. 'Sithilien and her battalion will eat well this tide if nothing else.'

'I have never seen havaklir in such numbers,' Valhanir murmured.

'Teacher,' Irimé called, before Ubraich could reply.

The isharann was, as she always conspired to be, some distance ahead. She lay on her stomach above the cleft from which the havaklir school had emerged, her upper body swarmed by obsidian-dark hair. Wearily, Ubraich swam to join her. The others followed.

A monstrous striped fish, big enough to glut even a havaklir swarm to satiation, lay in the lee of the rocks, partially buried under grit and sand. It was a sunken head and a scrap of tail, held together by about eighty feet of crushed bone.

'That is why,' said Irimé. 'They were defending their kill.'

'The havaklir did not kill this.'

Ubraich hovered his hands over the fish's remains and channelled his beast magic. The various bite marks upon its body suddenly inflamed. Valhanir gasped as the oval-shaped indents flared up silvery white.

'Namarti. A knife.'

The hunter behind him wordlessly presented his blade by the handle. With an equal absence of ceremony, Ubraich took it and carved a fillet from the tail.

'What is it?' Irimé breasted lower to see for herself.

'A bite.'

Holding up the fillet to her, Ubraich traced the strange, undulating crescent shape with his blade.

'From what?' said Irimé.

Ubraich smiled, but before he could answer her, the namarti he had dispatched from the battle returned with Flowain struggling in his strong grip. Ubraich sighed. He noted Valhanir, and even Irimé, were no longer looking.

'Bring her to me.'

'Please, teacher,' said Flowain, as the thrall obeyed. 'Forgive me.'

'Shush.' Ubraich pressed the flat edge of the namarti knife to the girl's cheek. She whimpered, tried to turn her head away, but the namarti that held her knew his master well and caught her head in an arm lock. One eye stared upwards, the other buried in pectoral muscle. 'I will not have a student of mine show such fear in her eyes. Not with Princess Sithilien here.'

'It will not happen again, teacher.'

'No, it will not.'

Ubraich withdrew the knife and then, serpent swift, plunged it into Flowain's eye. She screamed, convulsing in the namarti's rigid lock, as Ubraich wrenched the knife out, her face spewing blood and tears and compressed ropes of jellylike fluids.

'Pain is what Teclis gave to us that we might learn, and find our way back to his light.'

He returned the knife. 'Go and rouse Sithilien,' he told the namarti, ignoring his apprentice's increasingly inchoate screams. She would thank him one day. 'Tell her that we take the beast tonight.'

IV

The bite mark was better than a footprint in the ground. It was a compass that pointed neither north nor south, nor to the wild energies that coursed around the realm's edge. It pointed to the soul of a single beast. When they strayed from true, a tremor in the chewed fillet in Ubraich's hand guided them back. Valhanir broke another light stone. The barren cliffs of mountains rose and rose beyond the edge of the light. Irimé ranged ahead with the remaining namarti, forcing them all to swim a little harder to match her impatience. But even with Teclis' own will behind him, Ubraich would never be as swift in the water as he had been before the gulchmare, and Sithilien caught up to them just as the tide was beginning to turn.

DAVID GUYMER

The akhelian princess came mounted on her gulchmare, pennons streaming from her voltspear and mingling with the silver-white cloud of her hair. Ubraich's hunter returned with her, along with an entourage of greatsword-wielding thralls and bow-armed reavers twenty strong. Between them and Ubraich's túrscoll hunters, they numbered twenty-five.

He hoped that there would be enough bodies to distract the beast's attention while he broke its mind.

This, he reminded himself, was merely the hunt. Most embailors would agree that it was the easy part. Giléan had captured Sithilien's gulchmare easily enough, but it had taken him thirty years to finally break its will. That long and dangerous process would come later. It would need to be stabled, acclimatised. It would need to surrender its eyes. And as soon as an akhelian with the courage to make the attempt was found, then it could begin.

Ubraich looked forward to it with relish. He regarded the ruined soul that moved underneath Sithilien's saddle with pride. The gulchmare had been a wild and tempestuous beast. Now there was not enough independent spirit left to twitch without Sithilien's implicit command. It was a mutilated once-animal spirit in a mighty body, all but its basest instincts muzzled by fear and the memory of pain.

'I see something ahead,' said Sithilien.

Immediately on her arrival, she had taken charge, and despite her age she had an aelf's eyes, her vision honed by decades spent hounding smaller prey. Her gulchmare pulled her to the front of the group as she spoke. It had a scent. An animal's sense for the presence of a mightier beast than itself in its waters. It was agitated. To Ubraich's wonder it was even demonstrating enough free will to resist Sithilien's reins. She pulled angrily, opening up the old wounds where Giléan had hooked the original harness into the gulchmare's flesh. The beast emitted a near-constant whinnying vibration that ground through Ubraich's teeth and set all of the younger isharann on edge. Irimé gave the monster a sideways look, fondling her pain-stave thoughtfully, before Sithilien caught her eye and withered her temper with a glare.

Ubraich was impressed.

'What do you see?' Ubraich asked her.

'The mountain we passed earlier is part of a range that cuts across the Green Gulch,' said Sithilien. 'I have heard of it, though I do not think any aelf has ever seen it with their own eyes. We come now to its foothills. I see a cave ahead.'

'I see it too,' said Flowain quickly, eager to please.

Ubraich patted her shoulder and she flinched.

'Do we wait it out?' asked Valhanir. 'Or do we lure it to us?'

'Allow me to go inside, teacher,' said Irimé.

'No, I will go!' said Flowain.

'Neither of you will go,' said Ubraich.

'No indeed,' said Sithilien, rising contemptuously in her ornate saddle. 'Foolish girl. You are isharann. Do you think I bed myself to half of Túrach to sire endless namarti brats so that a pure soul can bait herself for a beast? You do? Then let me help you, girl. I can gut you here and cast your entrails into the pit that the beast might follow them to us.' The gulchmare dropped its lower jaw, displaying a hideous grin of emerald-coloured teeth.

Irimé swam hastily back. Ubraich covered his smirk with his hand.

'No, girl.' Sithilien lowered her spear, then regally raised a hand. With a wave of the fore and middle fingers, she summoned a lanmari-armed thrall. 'See what is in there,' she ordered.

Ubraich muttered a few phrases over his beastmark, then passed it to the namarti before he swam off towards the cave.

They fell to silence as the warrior vanished into the opening.

'What did you say over that skin you gave him?' Sithilien asked softly.

'It has a power entirely separate from mine. The words I spoke merely awakened that power. It will draw the beast to its mark, as it drew us to the beast.'

Sithilien smiled to herself.

'I knew you were as good as Giléan, Ubraich. Nothing pleases me like being right.'

Waves of ink-black water erupted from the cave mouth before Ubraich could answer. The namarti thrall flailed helplessly against the sudden torrent, tossed around like a gloomtide wreck caught up in waves of denser, darker water. Ubraich felt something rising. He made a pained sound and bent suddenly, pressing his hand to his forehead. It was titanic. Ancient. The idoneth could be pitiless and uncaring, often mistaken as cruel, but the depth of malevolence he felt from this creature was enough to make him bare his teeth and grip his pain-stave until his knuckles whitened. Flowain howled like a frustrated predator, shortly followed by Irimé and Valhanir, as the monster surged from its lair.

Some way distant, it still managed to be huge, rippled and distorted by squalling water, but not to Ubraich's soul-sight. The basic body plan of a deepmare was there; the long horn that jutted from the middle of its forehead, the clawed forelimbs, the triplet of tails, but altered by the centuries and the ancient magic of its environment into something scarcely recognisable.

Colossal forelimbs encased in chitinous exo-armour and terminating in pincer claws snipped the struggling namarti neatly in half. Legs disappeared into a segmented, chute-like mouth. A still-living, still-screaming upper body, innards held inside the torso by the crushing in-pressure of the ocean floor, spun away in the whirlpool that the titan's emergence had left in its wake. The gulchmare issued a terrified whinny. Ubraich was dimly aware of Sithilien screaming at it, rallying namarti reavers to loose and her thralls to close.

How would it be to sit bestride such a beast? To stand upon that armoured back, heavy chains in hand? He would be as the caldai of the mythic asur, mounted on the reptilian god-beasts of the skies-that-were.

As Teclis the Wise had always wished his children to aspire.

He reeled his mind back from his grand visions of eolas with a tremble of effort. While he had indulged it, battle had been joined.

Sithilien's reavers peppered the monster with arrows that scattered harmlessly off its carapace. The lanmari-wielding thralls availed of themselves better, chipping away at the monster's armour, though at a cost in blood. Every flex of its limbs crushed bones, knocked blades from hands and sent muscular namarti aelves tumbling through the water. It pincered its claws menacingly, but the namarti were too agile and too wily to be drawn.

'For Túrach. For Mathlann. For the pride of Anaer!'

Sithilien aimed her voltspear, the gulchmare already hurtling forwards. The two monsters crashed together. Akhelian voltspear split crustacean-like armour and drove deep. The ancient deepmare was easily three times the gulchmare's size but the moment of the charge sent them both spinning through the cordon of namarti. They grappled savagely as namarti were flung aside. The gulchmare raked carapace with fin-claws. The ancient fought back with chitin-bladed forelimbs. The gulchmare whipped the monster's underbelly with its tails. It was how the embailors trained deepmares to battle leviadon, but unlike that warbeast, there was no weakness to its armour there. The ancient emitted a screaming pulse of sound that rippled out from it in a wave. Sithilien screamed as though she could not hear her own voice. Then the monster pincered through two of the gulchmare's tails. Her mount scrabbled at the behemoth in a furious panic, breaking a fin-claw on its armour, before Sithilien, hands clapped to her ears, kicked her heels into her mount's ribs.

It swam away, leaving the akhelian's voltspear sticking from the side of the titan's head. Arrows continued to loop in as thralls swept back to harry the monster with lanmari blades, buying their princess time to escape and regroup.

'It is a defiant beast!' Ubraich turned towards the embattled giant, kicking his legs harder for more speed. It did not occur to him that he spoke now in his own teacher's voice. 'Only through pain and the fear of pain can its walls be broken and its soul dominated. I cannot both cloud its wits and break its defiance. Confound its mind, my students, while I get close and aid the Lady Sithilien.'

He heard no reply. His attention was too firmly fixed on his quarry. This would be the realisation of his dreams, the affirmation of the status he had always craved, even before he had known he craved it. The túrscolls of the entire Green Gulch and beyond would come to revere his name.

A namarti fell diagonally into two pieces as Ubraich swam towards her, through the cloud of blood that stretched thinner and thinner between the departing halves.

He drew back his pain-stave, and then stove it into the side of the monster's head. Its eye splattered under his blow. Then... nothing. He stared in disbelief. The deepmare's ancient nervous system was buried deep under an armoured shell. It was immune to the pain-stave. A panicked stream of bubbles escaped from between his lips as the monster turned towards him.

He bashed at its snout with his stave, paddled back with both feet. At his command, debilitating waves of enervation and despair thundered from his psyche and through the alien mind of the monster. A tail looped around his ankle. He gasped in shock. It dragged him back towards the deepmare's mouth. He sensed the disturbance in the water of the approaching pincer, struck at it as if with an asglir lance, and wedged his pain-stave into the closing claw. It withstood the monstrous pressure for a split second before exploding. Bone fragments formed a grainy white cloud. His arm scissored off from his shoulder, sweeping through the cloud and away. He looked down.

He screamed.

Then he screamed again.

A thrall hacked through the tail that held Ubraich's ankle with his lanmari greatsword before the stump whipped into her gut. The thrall coughed up pulped organs as she drifted away.

Irimé swam in.

'Take its other eye, Irimé! Take it, and we will claim this beast together.'

The young isharann extended a hand towards the deepmare as she swam. Power shivered through the intervening water. The master embailor was already the centre of the deepmare's attentions, the taste of his lifeblood filling its mouth.

It was simplicity itself to bid the predator to sink its every thought into the devouring of her former master.

Ubraich screamed as the deepmare tore off his leg and sent him spinning into higher water. In the dimmest sense, he was aware of Irimé crashing blows against the monster's head, Sithilien exhorting her as the akhelian princess came around for another pass at the beast.

Embraced by the cold and the dark of oblivion, the screams of battle becoming muted, Ubraich smiled as the life poured from his wounded flesh. Like the cythai before him, like Teclis himself, he had been shown a great truth, and like those exalted antecedents, he had been blinded by it. He smiled because he understood it now, and if there was a lesson to be taken from eolas, then it was that one was never too old to learn.

He smiled because one day Irimé would find herself usurped by her own creation too.

THE LIGHTNING GOLEM

Nick Kyme

Rassia trembled in his arms.

'Rest now,' he said.

She half turned her head, her dark eyes blinking.

'Rest, and fight no more.'

Issakian Swordborne gently stroked the gryph-hound's flank, his armoured fingers stopping before they touched the arrow that had killed her. He felt her heart thudding weakly.

Rassia opened her beak. Her purple tongue lolled against her sharp teeth.

'Rest,' Issakian said again as he cradled her head in one hand. 'No more pain.'

She shuddered once and breathed her last breath.

Issakian bowed his head, and fought down the grief. She had been with him since he joined the Celestial Knights, a bond that had lasted many years.

'You have served me faithfully, Rassia,' he whispered. 'I could not have wished for better.' Anguish turned to anger, and his fingers clenched into fists as he rose to his feet. He cut through the fog as he swirled his blood-red cloak. It was the same colour as the pteruges of his night-blue armour. The cloak revealed a sheathed sword. He uttered three words.

'Judgement is coming.'

Then he drew the blade, which shone like twilight. He knew they would see it. He wanted them to see it.

A cry pierced the fog, ululating through the ruins of Harobard. Hammered footsteps came after, followed by panting.

A brawny figure burst into being, tendrils of pinkish vapour clinging to his body like grasping fingers. Blood matted his beard. His bare flesh had the tattoo of the Hektate rune inked onto it, the hook and eye wreathed in flame. Feathers pierced his skin, pink and blue and purple. Eyes, wild and delirious, glared at Issakian from behind a half-bird mask.

The axe whistled as it cut the air, arcing straight for Issakian's head. The edge looked stained, notched. Well used.

Issakian put his bracer in the way and the axe raked across it, spitting sparks like starbursts before the haft gave way and snapped. The axe head spiralled off as Issakian filled the Hektate's gut with a foot of gleaming sigmarite.

Scowling at the muddying of his blade, he shucked the Hektate loose as another of the barbarians came screaming for his blood. Issakian dropped to a crouch and impaled this one through the groin. He then rose to meet a third, hacking off a hand that had clenched a heavy hammer, before taking the head and ending the Hektate's plaintive wailing. A jet of dark arterial blood shone brightly as it struck the Stormcast's white shoulder guard.

A fourth Hektate wielded a double-handed axe and let out an avian shriek as he swung for a killing blow. Issakian leaned aside a moment before the axe landed. The Hektate had overcommitted and pitched forwards, overbalanced and vulnerable. His head rolled off his shoulders a moment later. Issakian barely gave the wretch a second glance as he pressed further into the fog.

By now, he had caught the faint echoes of the battle. Somewhere in this filth, Vasselius and his warriors fought hard. A muted lightning arc lit the sky, softened by the haze.

'I am coming, brother,' said Issakian.

He sought out the fifth attacker, the archer whose missile had ended Rassia's life. A hastily notched arrow was turned aside by Issakian's bracer. The archer retreated in fear, hoping to escape in the pink miasma.

Issakian had a different fate in mind.

'This is judgement,' he said. 'This is Sigmar!' He hurled his sword like a spear and the blade struck the Hektate in the chest.

Issakian closed the distance between them at a run, his pace inhuman. He wrenched his sword loose with a spurt of blood and plunged it into the Hektate's throat before the wretch could fall. Death followed. Revenge felt hollow. The Hektate tribe, though corrupt, were not his prey. He had come here seeking something else, a creature more than a man, but he would not find it in this abysmal cloud. It had settled quickly, drowning out the larger battle and separating Vasselius' forces, of which Issakian counted himself a part.

He breathed hard, painting the inside of his helm with flecks of spittle, and tried not to take in too much of the fog. It put Issakian's teeth on edge. He set his will against it. Magic threaded the air. He could taste it like acid on his tongue. His mind briefly filled with psychedelic images... *The Summoner with the head of a purple crow... A cloak of variegated feathers... The lightning golem*. He shook it off. He had seen them before, *dreamed* them before. He focused on his purpose. Vasselius would not be far.

'Rassia, lantern,' he called out, and then cursed under his breath. 'Fool…'

Issakian found the lantern where he had left it, thrust into the hard earth, shining like a beacon.

He raised it high upon its staff, his arm fully extended.

'Sorcery,' he bellowed, 'I abjure thee!'

The unearthly fog recoiled as if burned. It *shrieked*, and like morning mist before the sun it steadily diminished until it was no more. The sight and sound of battle rushed in, abruptly renewed.

All around him, Harobard burned. Its wooden arbours were aflame, its streets thronged with desperate fighters. Skirmishes had erupted throughout the city, the Stormcasts scattered by the fog and only now regaining some kind of coherency.

Issakian found Vasselius amongst the warriors, right in the teeth of the battle. A warrior-god clad in the ivory armour and blue pauldrons of his Stormhost. He fought at the foot of the temple stairs against the dwindling Hektates. Statues carved out of glittering marble honouring the great beasts of the land rose up on either side of him, framing rugged stone steps. Vasselius quickly gained the stairway with his men and forced the horde back behind raised shields and cutting swords.

On one flank were the pale-armoured warriors of the Knights Excelsior, on the other the spearmen of the Bruhghar Kings in thick furs and skull helms, who fought with the fury of the recently liberated, letting off horn blasts and setting up a thunderous drum tattoo.

Issakian made for the narrow gap between the beast statues, where the fighting was at its fiercest.

Nigh on a hundred Stormcasts battled shoulder to shoulder, pushing into arrows and flung spears. Now they were freed of the fog's taint, nothing could stop them, though Issakian saw a white-clad warrior struck in the throat. He fell, lost to sight, before a lightning arc cascaded upwards.

It was to be a last act of defiance.

The Hektates broke and scattered, unable to match the ferocity of the Stormcasts or the warriors whose lands they had usurped.

The Bruhghar roared, exultant. Stormcast Heraldors trumpeted the victory, shaking the very earth.

Vasselius gave a shout that sent hunters into the skies and the ruins to seek out the fleeing Hektates and make sure they were dead. He turned, and raised his hammer aloft in triumph.

Issakian raised his own sword in salute as he met him at the foot of the temple steps.

'Don't rest yet, brother,' Vasselius told him. The Lord-Celestant went bareheaded, his red hair as bright and vivid as fire against his ivory armour, his eyes wild with the promise of further battle.

'Ever since we met, you have bent towards violence, Vasselius.'

'And you are too soft of heart, Issakian,' he said with good humour. 'A fine pair we make, eh?'

'That we do.'

Vasselius gestured with his hammer to the ruins beyond the temple.

'My hunters are hard at work. Shall we join them? There are many of these wretches that yet live, despoiling Sigmar's fine lands.'

Issakian nodded. 'I'll follow you into the ruins, but leave the killing to you, Lord Ironshield.'

'Still on the hunt then?' asked Vasselius.

'I haven't found him yet. But if he's here, if *it's* here, I will.' Issakian sheathed his sword. 'I saw captives amongst the Hektate horde. Who will save them if you're about the killing?'

Vasselius smiled broadly, but his sharp green eyes betrayed a little of his inner sadness. 'I'd say we best leave that to you.'

Issakian gave a short bark of laughter.

'That sounds like wisdom.'

Vasselius didn't reply. He grinned, revealing pearl-white teeth, and turned on his heel. He called out to his warriors and the Bruhghar, who needed little encouragement, urging them on.

Issakian followed more slowly, leaving his lantern behind. No Hektate, if they even returned to this part of the city, could touch it. He didn't need it for the moment and it was too unwieldy to carry into the narrow places created by the ruination of Harobard.

As he searched, Issakian heard the slaughtering of the Hektates. A necessary task, but a grim one that left him wondering how much humanity the Stormcasts had surrendered to the lightning. How much of the soul remained each time he rode the storm?

His thoughts clouded his senses enough that he almost missed the girl taking shelter under a half-collapsed arch. It had been a bridge once, but the Hektates had destroyed it. Only rubble and the broken arch remained.

The girl, half shrouded in shadow, looked up as Issakian approached. She appeared scared and clutched something she had been playing with to her chest, as if afraid he would steal it.

'It's all right, child,' said Issakian, crouching down as he lifted up his ands to show the girl he was unarmed, and then slowly removed his helm. His close-cut hair and beard felt damp with sweat, but a human face was preferable to one forged of unfeeling sigmarite.

She appeared to relax, loosening her grip on the wooden toy and proffering it to Issakian.

'What is your name, ch–' he began, but found his eye drawn

to the toy. He had seen its like before: a zoetrope, a cylinder that spun upon its central axis, with tiny apertures cut into its surface that, when looked through, would reveal a moving image lit by a solitary candle flame.

This device had exactly the same design, and the girl had already set it spinning.

'Look…' she invited, her voice soft and infantile. 'See…'

Issakian caught the edge of the flickering candle flame, and the smallest glimpse of the moving images within. He drew closer, thinking to earn the girl's trust, but then felt a compulsion to watch the shadow play unfolding against the zoetrope's cylinder walls.

The scratchy man totters on sharp and scratchy legs. He walks and walks and walks, until he is struck by a bolt from the heavens and becomes the night-clad king. His head spits forks of lightning and he holds a starlit sword.

Smash, smash, smash goes the night-clad king, smiting every monster and horror of the land until he finds the lightning golem and the purple crow upon its shoulder. And lo upon the slopes of the claw-handed mountain do the night-clad king and the lightning golem give battle.

Swish goes the night-clad king's sword; crash goes the lightning golem's thunder; caw, caw speaks the purple crow, delighted at such spectacle. The mountain trembles and the night-clad king fights with all his strength, but he cannot best the lightning golem.

Bleeding black, scratchy blood, the night-clad king can fight no more. He kneels before the lightning golem, powerless against it. And as the purple crow looks on, the lightning golem opens its maw as wide as a cave and swallows the night-clad king whole.

Then there is only the lightning golem, a purple crow upon its shoulder, and the night-clad king is no more.

Issakian gasped, suddenly starved of breath. He leaned over, sucking in great gulps of air as he tried to banish a heavy sense of foreboding. His left hand was shaking. He felt sore, as if from battle.

The girl had gone, though when he heard footsteps approaching he turned and drew his sword.

'Lord-Veritant,' said one of Vasselius' men. He carried a chipped shield, and a chin flecked with peppery stubble jutted out where part of his helm's mask was missing. It had been hacked off during the battle. The mouth curled in surprise. The Knight-Excelsior had half drawn his sword. Issakian heard it thrum with Azyrite power.

'How long have you been standing there?'

'Only a moment, Lord-Veritant. I was sent by Lord Ironshield,' he explained. 'They have him…' Now the face changed again, surprise turning into the eagerness for retribution. A dark smile turned his lips. 'The Hektate shaman.'

Issakian donned his helm.

'Take me there. Now.'

The shaman kneeled in the blood and filth of the battle's aftermath, his dead around him.

One of Vasselius' warriors, Agrevaine, had her axe blade against the shaman's neck. Her eyes were storm-grey and thunderous. She wanted to kill him.

'He is the last of them,' declared Vasselius. He stood with the Bruhghar Kings, a little way off from where the shaman knelt in defeat. The prisoner looked cowed, like a beaten dog.

Issakian walked up to him, urging the shaman to lift his chin with the tip of his sword.

'Thunder and lightning… Thunder and lightning…' murmured the shaman. An avian skull with a feathered headdress lay split and scattered nearby. He was old, his wiry beard painted blue and pink to please his god. Fever burned in his eyes. Issakian had heard the Hektates brewed potions to improve their prowess in battle and the potency of their sorcery. It had not availed them in the end. He met the shaman's eyes and peered deeply. None alive could hide their true nature from the Lords-Veritant. He turned away, lowering his sword.

'It's not him,' he said, unable to hide the frustration in his voice.

Vasselius looked as if he were about to argue, but thought better of it. He nodded to Agrevaine. 'Finish it.'

She raised her axe for the killing cut, before the shaman spoke and she hesitated.

'The purple crow…' he rasped. 'The purple crow and the lightning golem.'

Issakian spun around and rushed up to the shaman.

Agrevaine's axe hovered, stuck mid-execution.

'What do you mean by that?' demanded Issakian.

'The purple crow…' said the shaman, 'and the night-clad king is no more…' Then he laughed, shrill like a death scream.

Issakian stepped back, both disturbed and enraged.

Agrevaine's axe fell. The laughter stopped.

Issakian barely heard it. He had turned his back, walking away into the ruins where Rassia was waiting.

She lay still, and Issakian confessed to a private hope that he might have been wrong and that she yet lived. It was not to be.

Kneeling by her side, he unclasped his cloak and laid it down. Then he took off his helm and set that down too.

Reverently, Issakian wrapped Rassia in his cloak. Then he laid his hand upon her body, closed his eyes and sang softly of his lament. He stayed like that for a while, remembering but also trying to forget what he had seen in the zoetrope. It haunted him, but he could not ignore its significance.

'No arc of lightning for her,' said Issakian as he heard Vasselius approach.

'Perhaps not,' answered the Lord-Celestant, offering a gauntleted hand, which Issakian accepted as he got to his feet, 'but she will be reforged in our memory.'

'A good thought.'

'I hoped so.' Vasselius had not come alone. The hunter, Agrevaine, joined them. She had a mane of white hair with a sheathed hand-axe and boltstorm pistol at her belt. She had cleaned her blade since dealing with the shaman. 'Agrevaine, see that Lord Swordborne's companion is properly tended to.'

'Of course, Lord Ironshield.'

She spared a glance for Issakian, lingering only a moment before she went to the body and gently lifted it, cloak and all, into her arms.

'I am sorry...' she whispered, and then she carried Rassia away.

'I'll see to it she is given proper burial and honour,' said Vasselius once Agrevaine had gone. 'I sense you and I are about to part ways soon and will have little time for such observances.'

'You have good instincts,' Issakian replied, looking out into the horizon where a savage land beckoned. 'Have you heard of a mountain in these parts,' he held up his hand and made the shape of it, 'like this, like a claw?'

Vasselius considered the question, then nodded.

'I've *seen* it. The Ironshields have fought in Bruhghar for a while. We passed a mountain like that a few months ago, before you joined us. It's near a realm-edge, where Ghur meets Aqshy.' He sucked at his teeth, as if assessing Issakian's mood. 'What interest does it hold for you?'

'I... *saw* it. Have seen it. I don't know. Dreams, prophecies... These are odd times. Portents are as thick on the air as fire and death these days.'

'A little melancholy, aren't you? You have always struck me as more hopeful than that, Issakian.'

'I am. Then I lost Rassia. Hope lives on, but it is still recovering from that blow.'

'You dreamt of it, the mountain?'

Issakian nodded.

'And you think it is... what? Providence?' asked Vasselius. 'It will lead you to the Summoner?'

'The lords of the Silver Tower are cunning but even they can't escape my sight forever. This is Sigmar's will. I can't just ignore it.'

Vasselius rubbed his clean-shaven jaw, thinking. 'No, I suppose you cannot. The lands beyond the Bruhghar borders are perilous. There are beasts.'

'I seek a beast.'

Vasselius laughed. 'I don't doubt it, or that you'll find one.' He looked to the darkening horizon. 'We'll make camp here tonight. I doubt the Bruhghar will allow us to do anything else.'

'They are... exuberant.'

'Indeed. You should stay. Rest before your journey.'

Issakian considered it. He wanted to be on his way, but there were certain ties here that would keep him. At least for the night. He agreed.

'Good. Very good,' said Vasselius, evidently pleased. 'And in the morning you'll take some of my warriors with you. You shouldn't travel alone. Not out here. Besides, they know where the mountain is. They can take you to it.'

Issakian smiled. 'It's almost as if you knew I would object.'

'Did I convince you?'

Issakian held out his arm.

'It has been an honour,' he said.

Vasselius clasped it, and each grasped the other's forearm in the manner of warriors.

'No, Lord Swordborne,' he said, nodding, 'the honour is mine.'

Lightning speared the heavens in a brief storm of six bolts, one slightly after the other.

His head spits forks of lightning.

'You've lost brothers here, Vasselius. Too many.'

'Ah, they will return. They always return,' he said, unconcerned as they looked into the sky and tried to imagine Sigmaron somewhere beyond it.

'At a cost.'

'Yes,' Vasselius nodded sadly, 'at a cost. We are all just spirits of the lightning now, whether we choose to acknowledge it or not,' he said, walking away.

'And do you?' asked Issakian, calling out. 'Acknowledge it?'

'Oh,' said Vasselius, still walking, 'I try not to worry.'

'That sounds like wisdom.'

'You should heed it.'

'Perhaps I will,' Issakian replied softly as another bolt of lightning cut the sky.

Issakian awoke, his naked body covered in sweat. The dream. Again.

And the night-clad king is no more…

The words came back, gradually resolving in his mind. He tried to steady his breathing, slow the hammering of his heart… Then he felt a light touch upon his shoulder, delicate but strong, and the pain eased.

'I hoped you would sleep,' said Agrevaine, and slid up beside him.

Her bare skin felt warm, welcoming. Issakian touched her hand with his then leaned over to softly kiss her fingers.

'I did for a while,' he said, and listened to the howl of the wind outside their tent. The leather creaked ominously; the ropes pulled but held. 'But I am glad I can wake up to you.'

She gently turned his head, so he was facing her.

Issakian frowned. 'You seem sad.'

'You are leaving in the morning.'

'And you will miss me,' he laughed, gently mocking. Her thigh poked out from underneath the bedroll and he traced its supple curve with his finger.

Agrevaine hastily looked away.

'You are too flippant,' she said, angry.

'Come now,' Issakian replied, smiling as he tucked a strand of errant white hair back around her ear. 'We have this night.'

'Let me come with you,' she said, meeting his gaze.

Issakian's shoulders slumped ever so slightly. He shook his head.

'I cannot ask that of you.'

'I offer it freely.'

'Then I cannot accept it.'

'Then you are a fool!'

'No,' he said, and tenderly cradled her cheek, 'I would be a fool if I let you. I cannot take you where I am going. I won't risk it.'

Now it was Agrevaine's turn to laugh. She had drawn a blade, no longer than a dagger, and held it up to Issakian's throat. 'It is hardly your decision. I am born of the lightning, as you are.'

'And as fierce, I know. I don't doubt your blade or your courage. It's why I love you, Agrevaine. But I have seen… *darkness*. This portent, it bodes ill. I am bound to it, to whatever fate it leads me to. Do not force me to make you a part of it.'

Agrevaine glared, but after a few moments relented.

'Damn you,' she murmured.

'I will admit,' Issakian said, eyeing the blade warily, 'this is not how I thought this would unfold.'

Agrevaine scowled, but lowered the knife.

'We have this night,' he said softly.

'We do,' she whispered, drawing close to him. 'My blood, the thunder…'

'My heart, the lightning.'

The flap of the tent parted, prised loose by the wind. Night scents washed in, redolent of wood smoke and presaging rain. Issakian and Agrevaine barely noticed as they drew together, their bodies limned by the moonlight.

The mountain rose up in the distance, a monstrous and ugly thing. Its five peaks did indeed put Issakian in mind of a clawed hand, and he scowled at the thought of it.

'How far?' he asked as a scout alighted on the rocky promontory where Issakian had made his vantage.

'Another day hence,' came the gruff reply, the scout folding lightning-wreathed pinions behind his back as he approached the Lord-Veritant. His name was Leonus.

Issakian nodded. 'Good. I'll not fail again.'

'Do we rest tonight?'

The night drew in, sweeping soft and deadly. Issakian briefly thought of Agrevaine, but the memory faded quickly with the calls of the nocturnes, the beasts that preyed in the darkness. One such creature turned on a spit, its flensed flanks cooking slowly. The smell was not appetising but it was still meat.

Issakian's eyes were drawn to the meagre feast, and to the eight warriors sat around it whose armour glinted gold in the firelight, their violet spaulders dark like patches of twilight.

One of the warriors looked up. Vitus. He had a recent scar that went from cheek to brow in a ragged line. Like the others', his sigmarite armour was chipped and hastily repaired in places. A shrine stood nearby. It was just beyond the glow of the fire, but still visible. It comprised a notched shield, strapped to a sword that had once belonged to Lord Brightclaw. Marks had been cut into the shield's face. They numbered almost thirty now.

Issakian met the hardened gaze of the warrior and felt the smallest pang of regret. They were not the first to die in service to his quest. He felt the tremor again in his left hand, his lantern-bearing hand, but mastered it. Vasselius' words returned to him. *We are all just spirits of the lightning now.*

That seemed a lifetime ago.

'Let's eat, Leonus, and march again in the morning,' Issakian told the scout.

'Should I post a watch, Lord Swordborne?'

Issakian looked out into the darkness. His eyes took a moment to adjust after staring at the fire, but eventually he saw the shadows of the nocturnes creeping in. Long-limbed, with grey, pallid skin and lamprey mouths, they chattered excitedly as they drew nearer.

'We won't need it. They'll be upon us soon.'

A cloying mist lay upon the ground the next morning as five warriors reached the foot of the mountain. A narrow pass led to a cleft in the mountainside, the only way in that Issakian knew of.

A hollow wind blew through the pass, cold and desolate. It sang to the Stormcasts' heavy hearts.

Issakian looked to the peak. Between wreathes of cloud, a slate-grey sky promised snow.

'We should not linger,' he told Vitus, who had taken up position just behind the Lord-Veritant. 'It's half a day through the pass, and if snow comes it will be treacherous. And without Leonus to watch over us from above we could be easy prey.'

Vitus called to the men, declaring a forced march up the pass.

They left all unnecessary trappings behind, their food and shelter, spare weapons. A sigmarite treasure hoard glittered in their wake, a notched shield and sword sat on top like a sacrificial offering.

Issakian entered a large cavern through a jagged mouth of stone in the mountain. He was glad to be out of the wind. Snow clung to his cloak like mould and he brushed it loose.

The storm had risen swiftly and without warning. As Vitus and the other two survivors joined him, Issakian lifted his lantern.

Sharp, gilded light described a grand chamber. Its depths went well beyond the lantern's reach but at the periphery of the light, a host of ivory statues looked on stoically. They resembled warriors, but of an Order unknown to Issakian. Stone flags defined a processional that led to a throne. Upon it sat a knight in frostbitten trappings. He wore a tabard over his armour, the sigil of a chalice still discernible despite its threadbare state. His skin was deathly grey and rimed with thick ice. The crown upon his head suggested nobility. A sword rested in his hand, the blade touching the floor. A shield sat against one arm of the throne and displayed the knight's heraldry, a lion rampant.

Issakian was about to make for the throne when he felt a hand upon his shoulder.

'What is it, Vitus?'

He gestured to the ground where the shadows grew thickest.

'Bones...' he murmured. 'Some beast has made this place its lair.'

'It may have moved on,' suggested Issakian, 'but we take no chances.'

The Stormcasts drew their weapons and the air sang to the crackle of sigmarite.

'Spread out,' said Issakian. 'Search this place. I will have an answer. I *must* have an answer.'

Warily, they began to search the chamber. Breath misted the air through the mouth slits of their helmets.

Issakian reached the throne and crouched down by its incumbent, surprised at how well the knight had been preserved. His greying skin suggested profound age. It had not decayed though, merely withered.

Then he spoke.

Issakian recoiled in shock.

'*You should not have come...*' the knight rasped, the voice of a revenant. '*Turn back... Turn back...*'

If the others had heard this, they gave no sign. Issakian looked up and caught the figure of Vitus disappearing into the darkness. He returned his attention to the knight.

'How are you alive?' asked Issakian. 'Are you cursed?'

'*Turn back... You should not have come.*'

'I cannot. This is my path. I have sworn to find the Summoner, the purple crow. Tell me, what do you know of it?'

'*Turn back... or be consumed by the lightning golem.*'

'I fear no monster. I have killed many to get here. Know that I will not relent. I have already lost so much. This place came to me in a vision. You are the only living thing in this mountain. Now. Tell me!'

The knight grasped Issakian's vambrace before the Stormcast could stop him. He tried to free himself, but the revenant's grip was strong.

'*You doom yourself, warrior,*' he said, and regarded Issakian as if for the first time. '*What manner of champion are you? I have never seen the like, but then I have dwelled here for what seems like aeons. Are you here to break this curse, I wonder?*'

Issakian tried to answer, but his tongue felt leaden in his mouth. A cold vice had closed around his body and drew tight.

'*Find him...*' said the knight. '*Kill him.*'

'W-where?' Issakian snarled through clenched teeth.

The knight smiled as coldly as a winter storm.

'*Closer...*' he said, '*and I will tell you.*'

Issakian leaned in and listened as the knight whispered into his ear.

A low rumble sounded from somewhere in the depths. Then came shouting and the clatter of blades.

Issakian looked up, startled. The pain lifted. He was free. It was as if the knight had not moved at all, and Issakian began to question if what he had experienced was even real.

'*Turn back... You should not have come.*'

'Turn back!' he cried out to the others, standing and about to raise the lantern. He was too late.

A Stormcast flew across the chamber, hitting one of the statues and shattering it. He crumpled in a heap of broken stone and sigmarite. He tried to rise, reaching for his hammer but fell back, his breastplate a red ruin of protruding bone. The lightning arc hurt Issakian's eyes as it hurtled skywards and tore the ceiling in half.

'Beast!' roared Vitus, emerging from the shadows at a run. Another warrior followed a few paces beyond, unleashing crackling lightning arrows at something huge and looming behind him.

Realising his arrows could not prevail, the archer turned. A massive hoof crushed him before he could flee any further.

The beast reared up, its shaggy hide thrown into stark relief by a bolt of coruscating light from the archer's death. It bellowed, half in pain, half in fury, a feral snarl upon its brutish face.

'Stonehorn!' Vitus yelled, brandishing both swords as the beast towered over him.

Armour festooned with studs and spikes sheathed its muscular shoulders, but the true threat lay in the long horns that protruded from its snout. Formed of overlapping plates of hardened bone, they curved into a wicked points as sharp as flint-ice.

It stank of dank places, of hoar frost and dead meat.

And it wasn't alone.

Another stonehorn thundered out of the darkness. It stood before the entrance to the chamber, crushing any hopes of retreat.

The cavern had begun to collapse. Hunks of rock plummeted from the roof. One struck Vitus, who fell to his knees. The first stonehorn gored him through the chest, piercing his armour as if it were parchment not thrice-blessed sigmarite.

As Vitus died, Issakian wrenched off his helm and touched his sword to his lips.

'For Sigmar and Azyr,' he breathed, provoking an old memory. 'Agrevaine...'

He caught a last glimpse of the ancient knight before the end, silent but his lips moving to form a familiar phrase.

Turn back... You should not have come... Turn back...

And then the mountain collapsed and Issakian had but a moment to consider the knight's words before the rocks crushed him.

'We should turn back...'

Endal Cogfinger hung from the rigging with one hand, his iron-shod boots braced against the raised lip of the foredeck. He held a spyglass against the left eye-lens of his mask and leaned out fearlessly into the wind.

They rode low, skirting the crests of lava waves. Fire caressed the keel of the *Drekka-Duraz* and cast its golden filigree in a hellish glow. A stern ship, laden with guns and with a rune-etched hull formed of steam-bolted plates, even the ancestor figurehead at its prow snarled.

A smouldering, undulating landscape stretched out in every cardinal direction and as far as any mortal eye could see. The Magmaric Sea writhed below, spitting flame and geysering smoke, as volatile and unpredictable as a battlefield. Red-tinged clouds glowered overhead, close to the dirigible's upper fin, a roiling mass of angry cumulonimbus, threaded with bursts of lightning that lit their insides like incandescent veins.

'Bah, is it water or iron in your stomach, lad?' asked Fulson Aethereye. 'Your father, I swear by the Code, would never have baulked from a storm.'

'It is no ordinary storm, Fulson,' said Endal. 'See for yourself.' He handed him the glass, but the ship's aetheric navigator had one of his own.

'Keep your trinket, arkanaut,' he grumbled, and took out an arcane device from his trappings. He glanced over his shoulder at the frigate's sole passenger and muttered proudly, 'Zephyrscope.'

Fulson also wore a mask. Wrought from iron, chased with gold, it resembled a duardin face. The beard curled, unnecessarily extravagant. The left eye-lens telescoped to examine a sphere clasped to the end of a complex metal armature – the aforementioned zephyrscope.

'The aether currents *are* turbulent,' he admitted. 'This deep into the firetides… the updraughts are unpredictable, captain. Lad might have a point.'

'I have been told,' interrupted the passenger, 'that the Kharadron do not renege on a bargain once one is struck.' Issakian Swordborne turned his head to regard the ship's captain. 'Or am I mistaken?'

Arms folded, legs braced apart, Zhargan Irynheart looked down from the forecastle at the main deck, where the Stormcast and most of his crew were standing.

Issakian felt the anger in the captain's stare, even behind the duardin's mask.

Embers crackled on the hot breeze, underpinning the silence. Ash and cinder lay thick on air that had become hard to breathe.

'Half before, half after,' Issakian reminded him, unflinching before the duardin's contempt. 'That was our agreement. Do you deny it?'

Zhargan's mask was more ornate than those of his crew. It signified seniority. His ship, his law.

'We'll see it done,' he growled. 'Let it be known that no ship of Barak-Urbaz ever refuses profit. But no purse is worth the destruction of this vessel. I'll sooner throw you to the firetides than court that fate.'

If Issakian felt anything about the thinly veiled threat, his helm hid it well enough.

'You will be well compensated for the risk.'

'Aye,' said the captain, 'but unlike the *blessed* of your God-King, we duardin are not reborn from thunder and lightning. We are not so profligate with our lives, Stormcast.'

The ship pitched to its starboard side, dragged by a violent aether current, but soon righted again. The Kharadron hardly seemed to notice. Nor did Issakian.

'You sound afraid, Irynheart. Are you?'

The arming of several aethershot rifles clacked noisily as the Grundstok thunderers on the main deck took exception to the slighting of their captain.

Issakian held still. He clenched his left hand to stop it from shaking.

Zhargan waved them back. 'Six guns aimed and you scarcely take a breath. It's true then, is it, that your kind have lightning instead of blood running through your veins?'

'I asked if you were afraid.'

Zhargan gave a slow and rueful shake of the head.

'Yes, I'm afraid. Any sane person would be. You'll need to do better than that to raise my ire, though.'

'The sea-aelves who bore me the first time I undertook this journey appeared sane enough, and they did not look scared of the fire.'

With a muttered curse, Zhargan pulled a volley pistol from its holster and pointed it right at Issakian's head.

'Oh, now you're warming up.'

Issakian merely looked back, his face as impassive as the one carved into the mask he wore.

Zhargan snorted, and lowered the weapon.

'How many ships refused your offer before you came to mine, eh? I'm guessing more than one.'

'On this occasion? All of them,' Issakian replied. 'You alone agreed to take my charter.'

'Lucky bloody me.'

Zhargan jabbed a gauntleted finger, gesturing to beyond the frigate's prow. 'I know why I'm sailing towards that. Greed. I like aether-gold. I want more of it. Being rich is worth a little fear. But you...' He nodded, and Issakian thought the duardin might have hawked up a gobbet of spit had he not been fully helmed. 'Why are you doing it?'

'I seek a creature. I have sought it for a long time. Years, I think. The purple crow, the Summoner.'

'All this to kill a witch?'

'It is prophesied. I dreamt of it. I *still* dream of it.'

A pennant tied to the airship's uppermost vane snapped noisily, drawing Issakian's eye. It reminded him of a white mane, gently rippling in the breeze.

'Breath of Grungni,' hissed Zhargan, 'you *are* insane.'

Issakian looked southwards to the maelstrom.

'No, I'm not. Not yet.'

The sea churned around the maelstrom. It turned, spilling inwards, caught in a slowly narrowing gyre that fed down to dark oblivion at its nadir. Smoke plumed from this wound in the sea, like air rushing from a pierced lung, and hung over it in a black pall.

'"The heart of fire", uttered Issakian, bringing the revenant's words to mind. It had become harder to remember them since that first time, and he sometimes wondered what else he had sacrificed to keep them. '"Seek out the heart of fire, where the ocean sinks and the air is black as sackcloth." It *has* to be here.'

'We will find out soon enough,' said Zhargan, as the air began to burn. He called down to Endal. 'Endrinmaster, signal the crew. We enter the maelstrom.'

Endal nodded, perhaps reluctant, but gave a curt salute. His heavy armour clanged loudly as he leapt onto the main deck. He swung a massive steam hammer onto his shoulder.

'All hands to stations,' he cried, and the crew set to their orders. 'Roll out the heavy guns, and stoke up the aether-vaults. Make ready those belaying valves.'

'Do you know what they call this place? What it is?' said Zhargan to Issakian, but did not wait for an answer. 'Helmaw. It is a Realmgate, but I have no idea where it leads. Do you, Stormcast?'

Issakian didn't answer. As the *Drekka-Duraz* flew into the black smoke he raised his lantern. Light spilled forth from the open shutter, reflecting off fiery embers in the darkness.

'There is debris in the cloud,' cried Fulson, straining to be heard over the swirling fury of the maelstrom.

Carving through walls of smoke, pitching and yawing amidst the savage updraughts, the frigate fought through the burning air until it hovered, unsteadily, right over the heart of Helmaw.

Issakian drew his sword as his mind revisited familiar horrors. 'That is not debris.'

Embers became eyes. The darkness came alive and the daemons descended. Ragged wings beat the air in slow, ponderous sweeps. Distended mouths opened, revealing shiny pin-like teeth. Flayed flesh rippled with heat.

The bark and fizz of aether-rifles tore the air, warring with the infernal shrieking of the damned.

Zhargan looked down into the maelstrom, drawing his cutter and volley pistol. He turned to Issakian, his eyes hidden behind the cold blue of his lenses, and roared.

'For glory... For plunder... *Dive!*'

The *Drekka-Duraz* dropped violently, cutting through veils of smoke. Gobbets of lava sizzled against the hull, spat from the churning walls of the maelstrom.

Down plunged the ship, and Issakian had to brace himself just to stay on his feet. He lashed his lantern to the main dirigible stanchion, the 'endrin mast' Zhargan had called it.

Hot cinder raked his armour, carried on burning wind, scorching the sigmarite.

It was nothing compared to the winged furies emerging from the fire itself. Like scraps of smoke given form and with blazing coals for eyes, they swept upon the ship's crew, as voracious as a plague.

Issakian watched as a rifleman disappeared into the darkness, carried up and away, screaming and fighting. The stink of burning brimstone weighed upon the air, as heavy as a curse. Every taken breath was searing agony.

Something arrowed out of the darkness, shrieking as it came for him. Issakian cut its left pinion and it spiralled madly before clattering into the deck. A pistol shot put the daemon down for good, shattering its skull and reducing it to smeared essence.

Zhargan caught Issakian's gaze and nodded.

Issakian reciprocated, and then the captain turned, about to extol his crew to even greater efforts, just as a flock of furies took him. One moment Zhargan had been there, fighting hard, bellowing orders; the next, only his cutter remained, dropped as he was carried off. It had landed blade down, embedded in the deck like a grave marker.

Discipline began to waver, but the ship plunged all the same, shuddering and creaking as unnatural forces sought to tear it apart. The roar of fire grew deafening, the heat so intense Issakian could barely breathe. He sank to his knees, dimly aware of the shrieking overhead and the hull cracking below.

And then... nothing.

Darkness.

Shadow.

Aldrineth trod carefully, trying to gauge the strength of the bridge. One misplaced step and the chasmal depths below would embrace her. She saw spirits writhing in the shadows, incorporeal and angry. She subconsciously touched the talisman around her neck, glad of its presence. Her boots scraped against one of the slats underfoot.

'It is bone... The bridge is made of bone,' she said to the others, but didn't look back.

Don't ever look back, not in this place, not in Shyish.

A harsh, abrading sand swept down off the hills ahead. It cast Aldrineth's black attire and scalemail armour in an amethyst patina. There were voices in the sand, of the lost. Aldrineth shut them out.

'Everything in this benighted realm is bone, sister,' said Rhethor, tugging his dark cloak more tightly around his shoulders. He kept his sword drawn, but close to his body.

'Do you smell that?' asked Valdred, scowling. He had an arrow notched to his shadewood bow, and watched the shadows with a wary disquiet.

'It's the dead,' offered Issakian, a few paces behind the rangers. He had been looking at his left hand but regarded the aelves now. 'Beyond the bridge, and just past those hills, is the Endless Pyre. That's where the dead go to burn. They never stop burning.'

Burning… The ship aflame. The duardin screaming in terror… A descent into shadow and the prize awaiting him…

'A cheery thought,' muttered Rhethor.

'I thought we were guiding *you*, Stormcast,' said Valdred, his eyes and his bow on Aldrineth as she slowly traversed the bone bridge.

'I have been this far before,' said Issakian. 'But no further – the dead linger in those hills, too.'

'They are not hills,' said Rhethor.

'No,' Issakian agreed. 'They are not.'

'We'll have to go around,' said Valdred, sighing with relief as Aldrineth reached the other side of the bridge alive and with soul intact. She urged the others on, just as the sand around the hills began to stir…

Valdred cried out a warning, but Aldrineth was already turning and drawing an arrow from her quiver. She loosed three times in close succession as a monster of bone and scraps of decaying hide hauled itself forth. Immense, it dwarfed the aelf as it bore down on her. Aldrineth's arrows tore through one of its wings. Its leathery skin sheared like wet parchment, but it gave no cry of pain or discomfort.

Rhethor threw open his cloak and hurried for the bridge as Valdred took aim.

'Save your arrows,' Issakian told him.

Valdred looked askance at him, face angry.

'And do nothing!' he snapped. 'Your blood may be ice, Storm-cast, but those are my kin.'

'Save your arrows for them.' Issakian gestured to a horde of lesser creatures pulling their rancid bodies from the burial mounds. They were pallid, grey and hungry, and cold earth clung to their rangy frames. Aldrineth was trying to fight them off and face the terrorgheist.

Valdred snarled. 'Flesh-eaters.'

Issakian went after Rhethor, his sword trailing starlight.

Rhethor made it halfway across the bridge before the dead took him. The spirits simply reached up, their angry and despairing voices joining the aelf's as a host of spectral fingers coiled around him. First the ankles as he hacked and slashed ineffectually at the phantoms, then the legs and abdomen, followed by the torso and arms. Rhethor had begun screaming, shrill and childlike, but the spirits smothered his face and carried him off the bridge into the shadows below.

The screaming persisted as Issakian gained the bridge; his raised lantern – now separated from its staff and clutched in his gauntleted fist – kept the spirits at bay.

The dead on the other side were another matter.

The ghouls recoiled from the light, hissing their pain through withered mouths stuffed with spiny teeth. The skeletal terror-gheist seemed less perturbed by it and lashed out at Issakian with a bony claw.

He leapt aside, narrowly avoiding being impaled but dropping his lantern. The light went out, and at once the ghouls swarmed.

He swept his blade out, cutting dry flesh, severing a hand from a wrist, opening up an emaciated chest. The ghouls snarled.

Aldrineth lay dead, her corpse cradled beneath the terror-gheist's claw, as though the creature were a hunter jealously guarding its kill. She had been crushed, her armour split apart, her bow snapped in half and trapped under her body. He felt a momentary ache, something only half forgotten, but that quickly faded.

Issakian heard a cry of anguish, and knew then that Valdred had seen what he had seen.

Arrows whipped through the air. At least the aelf had the presence of mind to aim for the ghouls. He shot one through the neck, another through the eye. Dark, old blood splashed the burial mound.

It did not deter them. Hunger had become a greater motivator than the threat of death.

Issakian cut another of the creatures down as the terrorgheist beat its huge but ragged wings and took to the sky. He looked up as a monstrous shadow fell across him.

'The tower, inverted, spearing down into the underworld,' he murmured, trying to commit the image to memory. It had been etched onto a stone tablet, lying at the bottom of Helmaw like sunken treasure. Not a Realmgate, as such, but a near-inaccessible vault. A crew of duardin privateers had given their lives so he could obtain this knowledge. He had to keep it. For when he returned…

The terrorgheist bore down on him, claws outstretched to shred him sigmarite from bone.

Issakian raised his sword.

Then lightning struck.

A bolt of pure Azyrite, hurled from Sigmaron itself, sheared the monster in half. It fell out of the sky in a hail of bones, as if whatever darkness had held it together had come unstitched.

Further lightning strikes hit the chasm, hammering the spirits harboured there and chasing them into the deepest dark.

And in the storm's wake... Warriors clad in ivory sigmarite, their spaulders as blue as summer rain.

The Knights Excelsior. It felt like several lifetimes since Issakian had seen them. They set about the flesh-eaters swiftly, cutting them down with hammer and blade. Azyrite arrows crackled and spat cascades of sparks. The horde fled, what few of their kind remained, and from out of this righteous slaughter there came a general riding a fierce gryph-charger, its flanks grey and white, with green feathers around its fore-limbs. She carried a spear, though tied it at once to the beast's saddle when she saw Issakian, and leapt off her mount.

A hand-axe and boltstorm pistol slapped gently against her armoured thighs as she approached him.

'Palladors!' she cried. 'Make sure those creatures are gone for good.'

A host of more lightly armed cavalry on gryph-chargers went immediately to do her bidding. Lord-Aquilor, they called her, but as she took off her helmet and allowed her long white hair to cascade onto her shoulders, Issakian realised he knew her by a different name. He had to reach for it in his mind, like catching a snowflake before it melted in his hand. It took a few moments.

'Agrevaine...'

He knew her, but chasms of memory kept them apart.

The briefest shadow of sadness passed over her face, before she mastered it. Agrevaine rested her hand on the pommel of her axe.

'Issakian, I did not expect to see you here.'

'I seek the Summoner.'

Agrevaine tried to hide her surprise.

'Still?'

'It has been a long road, and the storm,' he uttered, 'has been... taxing.'

Agrevaine looked as though she were about to say something, but caught her breath. She touched his armoured cheek and whispered, 'Are you still flesh under that mask, Issakian?'

Issakian did not respond. He remembered the tablet.

'The tower, inverted, spearing down into the underworld.'

Agrevaine let her hand fall.

'Is that what you seek?'

'It is his lair. The creature I have followed through death, through the storm.'

Agrevaine nodded then clenched her teeth. She looked as if she were in pain, though Issakian could discern no injury.

'We are bound for the Blackstone Gate,' she said, 'and from there to a city called Glymmsforge. A muster is gathering. Rumours say that war unbound is coming to Shyish. We shall play a part.' She paused, as if trying to see through the mask Issakian wore. He could not remember the last time he had removed it. Perhaps he never had, but he found her gaze curious all the same. 'Come with us,' she said. 'I shall have need of a Lord-Veritant. You would be very welcome in our ranks, Issakian.'

'Abandon my mission?'

'Before it takes everything you once were, yes. Abandon the mission.'

Issakian was incredulous. 'I cannot. I have come too far to give up. I have sacrificed...'

'Obsession drives you now, not duty. Please... Come with us.' Agrevaine reached out for him, but Issakian stepped back.

'The tower, inverted, spearing down into the underworld... I will find it, and I will kill the thing that makes its lair within.'

The Palladors had returned, both beasts and their riders eager for the hunt.

'I cannot stay,' said Agrevaine. She donned her helmet.

'Nor I,' Issakian replied.

'We will be at Blackstone Gate for three days, awaiting Lord Ironshield and his men...' She let the implication of that statement linger.

'That sounds like wisdom,' said Issakian.

She paused, as if discerning some greater meaning from the words, and whispered.

'My blood, the thunder...'

Issakian looked back blankly, unsure how to respond.

Her eyes hardened behind her mask. He heard her fist clench.

'Farewell, Issakian Swordborne,' she said at length, something in her voice making her sound hollow. Then she turned and deftly leapt onto her mount.

Issakian watched her go, leading off the Palladors at a fearsome pace. In moments they were gone, lost in the distance behind an amethyst sand cloud.

Valdred had taken him the rest of the way. The dead did not bother them. They were in hiding after the storm, but would return soon enough.

Issakian stood facing the tower, its crooked roof stabbing upwards like a dagger thrust, and balanced impossibly on a raised shelf of amethyst sand. A narrow causeway of violet-tinged stone led to an outer door framed by a skull-studded arch.

As Issakian took his first step on the causeway, he heard Valdred slip away. The aelf had done his part. Let him mourn for the dead.

Spectral fog wreathed the tower, thickest at its roof. Incorporeal faces swam in this miasma, reaching up at Issakian from beneath the causeway but almost afraid to touch him.

He felt the storm within, like lightning in his veins instead of blood. His thoughts turned to his prey and a long hunt at last drawing to its end.

Crossing the causeway, Issakian stepped through the arch and let darkness take him.

He saw well enough, but found the halls of the tower lonely and cold. His footsteps echoed. They almost sounded like the voices of the lost. A presence lingered here. Issakian felt it. Slowly, he closed in on it, the instinct that all Veritants have coming to the fore.

'I seek that which is hidden, the daemon and the sorcerer...' he murmured. 'I shine the light where darkness clings deepest.'

He raised the lantern, though it made his hand ache. Its pearlescent light described the edge of a circular dais. Smooth steps led down to a massive chamber, hewn from the same violet-tinged stone as the causeway. The dais lay in the centre, the lines of the chamber's three walls converging and connecting at this point.

A figure knelt inside the dais with her back to Issakian, scribing on the floor with a piece of purple chalk that had coloured her fingers in the same dust.

The girl. Issakian dimly remembered her and the zoetrope, turning and turning as it revealed its shadow play to him.

'You are no child...' he began, and drew his sword.

The girl snickered, and as she turned and rose to her feet, she grew. Her bones lengthened, her skin turned a pale, mottled blue, tinged with pink. Her eyes split, multiplying as horns pushed out from her forehead. A third arm sprouted out of her back and her legs bled together, gaudy and iridescent, until they flowed and became robes.

'Summoner...' breathed Issakian, recognising the creature now it had transformed utterly. He threw himself at it, prepared to impale the wretch on the point of his sword and...

…pierced nothing except purple dust. It veiled his armour, giving it an ugly amethyst sheen. The reek of dank, mildew and old, dusty places fell heavy on the air.

Cackling laughter echoed from the shadows around the dais, and an old, withered man in a black robe shuffled into the light.

Issakian went to confront him but dark energies curling from the Shyish runes etched in the dais kept him firmly rooted.

'You are persistent,' said the old man in a reedy voice that cracked like dry parchment. He shuffled closer, leaning on a gnarled staff with three finger bones tied to it. 'Curious, isn't it,' he went on, walking round the edge of the dais and inspecting Issakian from every angle, as if appraising a laboratory specimen, 'how you can die so many deaths and still come back? I find that interesting.'

'Release me and I will give you a swift death,' Issakian promised, his grip tightening around the hilt of his sword. The lightning prickled his skin. He felt its power, and knew he could unleash it if he wanted to.

The old man laughed. He laughed so hard he doubled over and began to cough.

'Death,' he rasped when he had recovered. 'This *is* death. Shyish is death. You offer me nothing by way of trade. But I don't seek to bargain. I wish to study.' He leaned closer and outstretched a bony finger to claw at the dark energy caging Issakian. It shrieked to his touch, like nails running across slate.

'I can smell the magic in you…' he hissed. 'The power reforged, remade. Did you think you could escape *his* gaze? Such arrogance. The hourglass has already tipped, bearer of the storm. Its sands run inexorably towards your end.' He reached into his filthy robes and brought forth an emaciated bird, its feathers the same hue as the chalk dust. It cawed once in a thin, almost human voice. 'The purple crow...' The old man nodded to Issakian, '...and the lightning golem.'

Issakian roared. Anger, hot and indignant, rushed through his veins. His left hand burned, trembling with Celestial fire. He slammed his sword into the dais and a great storm erupted from the pommel. Lightning lashed out, bright and violent, but as it touched the edge of the darkness, it reflected inwards. The storm struck Issakian repeatedly. A hail of thunderbolts tore at him, stripping back his armour, burning away his flesh and turning bone to ash, until... nothing.

He died again, but as the storm within tried to leap up and arc for Azyr, it could not. The darkness turned into smoke and then glass, bottling lightning behind a host of potent enchantments. And within the glass was the crackling shape of a man, a lightning golem.

'And the night-clad king is no more,' said the old man, shuffling off into the shadows. As the darkness swallowed him, he rasped, 'How much we will learn... and the God-King's arrogance shall be his undoing.'

The laughter faded and then the footsteps, until Issakian was alone with his mindless self-pity. He had *become* the storm, lightning without the lightning rod, rampant and angry.

But a word resounded amidst the impotent rage, the only word the lightning golem could remember.

Agrevaine...

THE SANDS OF GRIEF

Guy Haley

'I don't like it here, master. Please, let us go. Too much magic, hurts my bones.'

'Hush, Shattercap, they are nearly done, and then we can leave. Be patient.'

The second speaker was Maesa, a proud aelf prince in the bronze armour and green-and-grey clothing of the wayfarer peoples. The first was a vicious spite, a small, gangrel creature of ill intent. His appearance did nothing to disguise his nature. He was a clutch of bones and twiggy fingers, garbed in wizened green skin. From a small, apelike face, his button black eyes peered at the world with fearful malice, in marked contrast to the calm benevolence radiated by his keeper. But though a captive, Shattercap was more or less content to live among the folds of the prince's cloak.

Content, because the aelf offered a way out of wickedness, and Shattercap desired that in a half-grasped way. Less, because the prince and the spite were at that time within the shop of Erasmus Throck and Durdek Grimmson, providers of the finest alchemical instruments in Glymmsforge in the Realm of Shyish, a place Shattercap feared greatly.

Throck and Grimmson were comical opposites. Grimmson was a stout duardin with a blue beard and bald head. Throck was a tall scrap of a man with a shock of white hair and clean-shaven chin. The duardin rooted about behind the counter near the floor. The man was balanced upon rolling steps, searching cubbyholes high up by the ceiling.

Grimmson hauled out a leather-covered box and placed it on the glass countertop.

'This is it, aelfling, the soul glass you wished for.'

Throck tutted from the top of the steps at his colleague.

'Come now, Durdek! Prince Maesa is high-born and worthy of respect.'

Durdek's granitic face maintained its scowl. 'He's an aelf, and I call it as I see it, Erasmus.'

Throck shook his head, and pulled the wheeled ladder along to the next stack of cubbyholes.

'Don't worry, your worthiness,' said Grimmson to Maesa. 'I've outdone myself for you. Look at this.'

With a delicacy his massive fingers seemed incapable of, Grimmson took out a tiny hourglass. Its bulbs were no bigger than a child's clenched fists, decorated with delicate fretwork of silver and gold.

Durdek flicked open a lid in the glass' top. 'Life sand goes in here. Seal it. Tip it over when it's near run out. Keep on with that to prolong the life within. Away you go. Very simple concept, but simple usage is no reason for drab work.'

'We pride ourselves on the finest equipment,' said Throck. 'Durdek here makes the devices...'

'...and it's him as does the enchanting,' said Durdek.

'It is a beautiful piece,' said Maesa. He took the hourglass from Grimmson and turned it over in his hands. 'Such fine workmanship.'

Grimmson hooked his fingers into his belt, gave a loud sniff and pulled himself up proudly.

'We do what we can.'

'Aha! Here is the other item,' said Throck. He jumped from the ladder. From a soft velvet bag, he took out a complex compass. It too had a lid in the top, covering over a small compartment. 'A soul seeker. This should lead you to the realmstone deposit you seek.'

Grimmson took the glass and placed it carefully back into the box so Maesa could examine the compass.

Eight nested circles of gold, each free moving against the other, surrounded the central lidded well. On one side of the well was an indicator made in the shape of the hooked symbol of Shyish. Maesa pushed it with his finger. It spun silently through many revolutions at the gentlest touch.

'It floats on a bath of ghostsilver,' said Throck. 'Very good work.'

'Should be,' said Shattercap. 'For the money you are being paid.'

'You get what you pay for,' Grimmson growled. 'Quality. We are Glymmsforge's foremost makers of such devices.'

'We are expensive, I admit, but you will find none better,' said Throck.

'Indeed,' said Maesa. 'I have no issue with the cost. Ignore my servant, he has yet to learn manners.' He handed the compass back and produced a white leather pouch from his belt. 'Five hundred black diamond chips, from the Realm of Ulgu, as you required.'

Grimmson took the bag from Maesa's hand and tugged at the drawstring ready to count the contents.

Throck patted his partner's burly arm. 'That won't be necessary. I am sure the prince is good to his word.' Throck was awed by the prince's breeding, and couldn't help but give a short bow. Maesa returned the gesture with a graceful inclination of his head. Grimmson looked at them both fiercely.

'You best be careful out there,' the duardin said. 'We sell maybe eight or nine of these a year, but the folks that buy them don't always come to the best end. Most go out into the Sands of Grief, and vanish.'

'How do you know they work then?' said Shattercap, slinking around the back of Maesa's head from one shoulder to the other.

'Ahem,' Throck looked apologetic. 'Their ghosts come back to tell us.'

'Ghosts? Ghosts! Master!' squealed Shattercap. 'Why did we come here?'

'I trust you have supernatural means of sustenance?' said Throck amiably. 'I do not mean to pry into your business, but where you intend to go is no place for the living. There is no water, no food, no life of any kind, only the dead, and storms of wild magic. We can provide the necessary protections – amulets, enchanted vittles, all you would require – if you have none of your own.'

'Oh, no!' Shattercap shrieked again. Maesa ignored him.

'I have what I need. My kind have wandered in every place. This realm is no alien land to me. I shall return in person to inform you how well your goods performed.' Maesa bowed and picked up his packages. 'My thanks, and good day to you, sirs.'

The door of the shop banged closed behind the prince. Shattercap cowered from the strange sights of Glymmsforge. The sky was a bruised purple, forever brooding, its long night scattered with amethyst stars. Outside the walls were afterlives ruined by the war with Chaos, and haunted by broken souls. But the streets of the young city were full of life, bathed in the light of magical lanterns that held back the dark.

Throck and Grimmson's shop was located on Thaumaturgy Way, along with dozens of other purveyors of magical goods. Market stalls narrowed the street, leaving only a slender cobbled passage down the centre. Humans, aelves, duardin and all manner of other creatures thronged the market, and not only the living, but the shades of the dead also, for Glymmsforge was situated in the afterlife of Lyria, where some vestiges of past glory still clung.

The crowd moved slowly. People browsed goods, creating hard knots in the flow that eddied irritably around each other. Maesa could pass through a thicket of brambles without disturbing a twig, but his aelven gifts were of no use in that place, and he was forced to shove through the crowd along with the rest.

'Market days, I hate market days!' hissed Shattercap. 'So many people. Where is the forest quiet? Where is the mossy silence?'

'You will yearn for their fellowship where we are going, small evil,' said Maesa. He slipped through a gaggle of ebon-skinned men of Ghur haggling over an imp imprisoned in a bottle, and reached the relative quiet of the main street.

Free of the overhanging eaves of Thaumaturgy Way, more of the city was visible. Concentric rings of walls soared to touch the sky. The innermost held within their compass the Shimmergate, a blue slash of light high up in the dark sky. Shattercap and Maesa were in the second district, thus close to the Stormkeep, the College of Amethyst and all the other wonders of the deepest ward.

Maesa turned his back on the central spires. His destination lay outside the city.

He returned to their lodgings in the fourth ward, and there arranged his equipment for the journey while Shattercap fretted in the corner. The spite could have bolted at any time, and for that reason Maesa had kept the thing chained for the first part of their association. As the days passed, a bond had grown between them. Besides, Shattercap was too cowardly to flee, so Maesa had abandoned the fetters.

Maesa packed his saddlebags with food, drink and sustenance of a less mundane kind. He stowed his unstrung bow into its case on the outside of his quiver. The compass from Throck and Grimmson he hung about his neck in its bag, and he stored the hourglass carefully in his packs. Lastly, he took from the table his most prized possession – the skull of his dead love, Ellamar – and placed it carefully into a light knapsack woven from the silk of forest spiders.

He called the house boy to take the bags to the stables, and followed him down.

The inn's stable block housed every sort of riding beast imaginable. At one end of the stalls was a mighty gryph-charger that rattled its beak in conversation with a pair of its lesser demi-gryph kin stabled next to it. Dozens of horses, flightless birds, great cats and more all whinnied, growled, squawked and screeched. As the air was a confusion of different calls, so the smell of the stables was a mighty animal reek composed of many bestial perfumes.

There was only a single great stag in the stable. His name was Aelphis and he was Maesa's mount. He waited for his master, aloofly enduring the clumsy efforts of the grooms to saddle him.

'Aelphis,' said Maesa softly.

The giant stag bowed his head and snorted gladly at the prince's greeting. He dropped to his knees to allow Maesa to load him with the baggage.

'I am sorry, my lord, but I do not think I have your saddle right,' said the head groom. 'I have never tacked up a creature like he before.'

'No matter,' said Maesa. Although the groom had made a poor job of it, he was genuinely apologetic. The prince adjusted the saddle while the groom looked on, and Maesa welcomed his desire to learn. When all was as it should be, Maesa leapt nimbly upon Aelphis' back. The stag let out a lusty bellow and rose up to his full, majestic height.

'We shall return,' said Maesa, and took his helm from a groom. Its spread of bronze antlers mirrored the magnificence of Aelphis' rack. Armoured, he and the beast were perfectly matched.

Maesa rode from the inn's yard. He would dearly have liked to give Aelphis his head, and let the beast break into its springing run, but the streets of the fourth ward were as crowded as those of the second. Beast and rider were forced to keep their patience until they reached the eastern outgate.

A permit was required to leave the walls at night. Maesa duly provided his papers to the gate captain, who scrutinised them carefully.

No one else was leaving.

'All is in order,' said the captain reluctantly.

At a shout from the captain, the gates swung wide. The road leading away from Glymmsforge was empty. Not one soul walked the level paving. A channel of purple salt cut through the road surface a hundred yards out, interrupting its journey into desert nowheres devoid of living souls.

The walls were patrolled by keen-eyed men armed with sorcerous guns. Two of them barred Maesa's exit.

'You must be an influential man to secure exit from the city
at night,' said the captain, handing back the papers. 'I advise
you to wait for the day.'

'I am eager to be away.'

'I have a suspicion of where you are bound, prince,' said
the captain. 'I've seen plenty of creatures with the same look
you have in your eyes. They are not to be dissuaded, so I will
not try. I will give you the warning that all free-thinking folk
receive from me. At the line of salt out there, the protection of
Sigmar ends. There are perils aplenty beyond these walls. This
gate is the frontier of life. Out there is only death and undeath.
Are you sure whatever reason you are going out there for is
worth your soul?'

'It is a price I will gladly pay,' said Maesa.

'Then Sigmar watch over you. There are no others that can,'
said the captain.

'Your warning is noted, captain,' said Maesa. 'But I have nothing to fear.'

The men stepped aside at a nod from the captain.

Maesa's trilling song set Aelphis bounding out into the empty
desert, joyful to be free of the confines of the city.

The road entered the low hills some miles from Glymmsforge,
and there it petered out at a half-finished cutting. Construction gear lay around, awaiting the day and the work gangs.
Night-time was altogether too dangerous for mortal labour.
As the stag left smooth paving for the sand, Maesa directed
him up the slope and pulled him to a stop.

Dust kicked up by the stag's hooves blew away on a cold
wind. Maesa turned back for one last look upon Glymmsforge.

From the vantage of the hillside, it was set out like a model for him to examine.

The Shimmergate gleamed in the sky, surrounded by the gossamer traceries of the stairs leading to its threshold. The Realmgate reflected in the Glass Mere, the broad lake encompassed by the fortifications. Monumental buildings stretched spires skywards, taller even than the walls, all ablaze with fires and shining mage-light. Among the finest were the cathedral-like mausolea of the Celestial saints, the relics of a dozen creatures whose holy power kept back evil, joined together by trenches of the purple salt. The twelve-pointed star the mausolea and the sand trench made was the reason for the city's survival, being a barrier to all wicked things.

Around this oasis city, the Zircona Desert stretched its gloomy grey expanses. The haunting cries of tormented spirits blended with the fluting wind.

'Look back at the city, small evil,' Maesa said to Shattercap. 'It will be our last sight of life ere our task is done.'

Tiny, whistling snores answered. Shattercap was a relaxed weight in the bottom of Maesa's hood.

Quietly, so as not to disturb the slumbering spite, Maesa urged Aelphis into a run.

Zircona's desert ran for leagues. Aelphis covered its distances without tiring. He cut straight across the landscape, bounding as quickly over crags and shattered badlands as he ran over the flats. Day's watery light came and went, and Maesa did not pause. Every third night he would rest, for aelven kind are hardier than mortal men, and sleep rules their lives with a looser hand. Aelphis slept when the prince did while Shattercap kept watch. Trusting terror to keep the spite vigilant, aelf and stag rested without misgiving.

There were ruins in the wastes. Shattered cities dotted the lands, though whether raised by the living or the dead it was impossible to say. The metaphysics of Shyish were complicated. Before the Age of Chaos cast them into ruin, many lesser after-lives had occupied the desert. As time went on, the living had come into those places also, and lived alongside those who had been born and died in other places and come to Shyish for their reward. In the south of Glymmsforge, towards the heartlands of Shyish, there were mighty realms yet, but towards realm's edge where Maesa headed, only ruins remained, haunted by the shrieking gheists of the Dispossessed.

None of these wandering shades dared come near him. To the sight of the dead, Prince Maesa shone with baleful power. His sword, the soul-drinking Song of Thorns, would bring their end with a single cut, and Maesa had other magical arts to command should it fail him.

They passed a great city whose walls were whole and aglow with corpse-light. No sound issued from the place. There was no sense of vitality, only an ominous watchfulness. The city filled the valley it occupied from side to side, and Maesa was forced to travel uneasily within the shadow of its fortifications.

A wail went up from the gatehouse as he approached, answered by others sounding from the towers in the curtain wall. Aelphis pranced and snorted at the din. Shattercap gibbered in miserable fright. Disturbed, Maesa spurred Aelphis on. The wailing harrowed their ears as they galloped by, but nothing came out from the city, not phantom nor spectral arrow, and as Maesa passed, the ghostly shrieks died one by one, until terrible silence fell.

They quickly left the city behind. Afterwards, the character of the land changed for the worse.

* * *

During the night that followed, they camped. All were weary, for the land took a toll on their spirits. Shattercap puled miserably and tugged at Maesa's hair.

'Master, master,' he whined. 'I feel so ill, not good at all.'

Maesa squatted at Aelphis' side. The giant stag was sleeping, its huge flanks pumping like bellows, gusting breaths whose warmth the bitter lands swiftly stole. Maesa took Shattercap from his shoulder and looked at him carefully. The spite's skin had gone dry and grey. Maesa too was ailing. His pale face had lost its alabaster sheen, becoming pasty. Dark rings shaded his almond eyes.

'It is the land. The nearer the edge we go, the less forgiving to mortal flesh it is, even to those like we, small evil, who are blessed with boundless lifespans.'

Shattercap coughed. Maesa cradled him in the crook of his arm like a sick lamb as he hunted through his bags with his free hand.

'It is time. For you especially, a creature born of the magic of life, this place is hard. I have something here for you to ensure your survival.'

He took out a round flask protected by a net of cord. Contained in the glass was a clear liquid that glowed faintly with yellow light. As Maesa uncorked it, it flared, lighting up the bones and veins in his fine hands. He held the bottle to Shattercap's lips.

'Water from the Lifewells of Ghyran,' Maesa explained. 'Drawn long before the Plague God's corruption. Take but one drop. Any more will change you, and we have but a little.'

Shattercap dipped his pink tongue into the glass. When it touched the blessed water, he let out a relieved sigh.

'It tastes of the forests. It tastes of the rivers and the seas. It tastes of home!'

Maesa set Shattercap down and wet his own lips with the water. His skin tingled. His face glowed with renewed life, and the dark rings faded. He dabbed a little on his forefinger, to rub on the gums of the sleeping stag, then corked the flask and put it away.

A miserable moaning sang out of the night.

'Best keep this out of sight,' Maesa said. 'The dead here are cold, and will seek out a source of life such as this.'

They went further edgewards, heading away from the heartlands of Shyish. At night, the dark was full of desperate howls. Cold winds blew, carrying whispers that chilled the marrow. Thunderous storms cracked the sky with displays of purple lightning. No rain fell. Nothing lived. The days grew shorter with every league they went, the sun paler, until they passed some fateful meridian, and went into lands clothed perpetually in shadow.

Where the light died, the sky changed. Beneath amethyst chips of stars a new desert began. Zircona was a wasteland, but it was part of a living world. This new desert was wholly a dead place.

Maesa slipped from Aelphis' saddle.

'We have reached the Sands of Grief. Now is the time for the magic of Throck and Grimmson,' he said. He took out the gold compass, and set it on a stone. From a velvet bag he removed the skull of Ellamar and unwound its wrappings, set it on the ground, and knelt beside it.

'Forgive me, my love,' he said. Delicately, he took up the brown skull, and pinched a tooth between forefinger and thumb. 'I apologise for this insult to your remains. I shall replace it with the brightest silver.'

Grimacing at what he must do, he drew the tooth. It came free with a dry scraping.

He set the tooth aside, rewrapped his precious relic and returned it to the back of his saddle. Then he opened up the lid of the compass-box and placed the tooth within.

'Let us see if it works.'

He held the compass up to his face.

Slowly, the pointer swung about, left, then right, then left, before coming to a stop. Maesa moved the compass. The pointer remained fixed unwaveringly on the desert.

'Success?' said Shattercap.

'Success,' said Maesa in relief.

Daylight receded from recollection. Shifting dunes crowded the mind as much as the landscape, and Maesa put all his formidable will into remembering who he was, and why he was there. Had he not, his sanity would have faded, and he would have wandered the desert forever.

Time without day loses meaning. The compass did not move from its position. Hours or lifetimes could have gone by. The desert landscape changed slowly, but it did change. Maesa came out of his fugue to find himself looking down into a gorge where shapes marched in two lines from one horizon to another. One line headed deeper into the desert and the realm's edge, the other oppositely towards the heartlands of Shyish.

The sight was enough to shake Maesa from his torpor. Shattercap stirred.

'What is it?' asked Shattercap. His voice was weak.

'Skeletons. Animate remains of the dead,' said Maesa. The percussive click of dry joints and the whisper of fleshless feet echoed from the gorge's sides. Purple starlight glinted from ancient bone.

'What are they doing?' said Shattercap.

'I have no idea,' said Maesa. 'But we must cross their march.'

'Master!' said Shattercap. 'Please, no. This is too much.'

Maesa urged Aelphis on. The great stag was weary, and stumbled upon the scree. Stones loosened by his feet sent a shower of rock before him that barged through the lines of skeletons and took two down with a hollow clatter. The skin of magic holding the skeletons together burst. Bones scattered. Like ants on their way to their nest, the animates stepped around the scene of the catastrophe, and continued on their silent way.

'Oh, no,' whimpered Shattercap.

'Be not afraid,' said Maesa. 'They see nothing. They are set upon a single task. They will not harm us.' He drew Aelphis up alongside the line, and rode against its direction. The skeletons heading outwards marched with their arms at their sides, but those going inwards each held one hand high in front of eyeless sockets, thumb and forefinger pinched upon an invisible burden.

Shattercap snuffled at them. 'Oh, I see! I see! They carry realmstone, such small motes of power I can hardly perceive them. Why, master, why?'

'I know not,' said Maesa, though the revelation filled him with unease. Nervously, he checked his compass, in case the undead carried off that which he sought, but the compass arrow remained pointing the same direction as always. 'I have no wish to discover why. Few beings could animate so many of the dead. We should be away from here.'

They left the name unsaid, but it was to Nagash, lord of undeath, Maesa referred. To whisper his name would call his attention onto them, and in that place Maesa had no power to oppose him.

'Come, Aelphis, through the line.'

The king of stags bounded through a gap. The skeletons were blind to the aelven prince. With exaggerated, mechanical care, they trooped through the endless night, bearing their tiny cargoes onwards.

They passed several skeleton columns over the coming days. Always, they marched in two directions, one corewards, the other to the edge. They followed the lie of the land and, like water, wore it away with their feet where they passed, forming a branching of dry tributaries carrying flows of bone. Not once did the skeletons notice them, and soon the companions' crossing of the lines became routine. The compass turned gradually away from their current path. By then notions of edgewards and corewards had lost all meaning. They knew the direction changed simply because they found themselves coming against the skeleton columns diagonally, then, as the compass shifted again, walking alongside them to the deeper desert. For safety's sake, Maesa withdrew a little from the column the compass demanded he follow, shadowing it at a mile's distance. Time ran on. The line of skeletons did not break or waver, but stamped on, on, on towards Shyish's centre, each step a progression of the one behind, so the skeletons were like so many drawings pulled from a child's zoetrope.

Some time later – neither Maesa nor Shattercap knew how long – they witnessed a new sight. In a lonely hollow they spied a figure. On impulse Maesa turned Aelphis away from their route to investigate.

A human male squatted in the dust, a prospector's pan in one hand. From the other he let a slow trickle of sand patter into the pan, then sifted it carefully around the pan while croaking minor words of power. Sometimes he would take a speck of sand out and put it into something near his feet. More often he would tip the load aside.

'Good evening,' said Maesa. It was dangerous approaching

anyone in the wastes, but even the prince, who had spent solitary decades in his wandering, felt the need for company.

'Eh, eh? Evening? Always night-time. What do you want?' said the man. He did not look up from his work.

Maesa saw no reason to lie. 'I seek the life sands of my lost love. I hope to bring her back, and be with her again.'

'Mmm, hmmm, yes. Many come here for the realm sand, the crystallised essence of mortal years,' said the necromancer, pawing at the ground. He mumbled something unintelligible, then suddenly looked around, eyes wide. His skin was pallid. A peculiar smell rose from him. 'You must be a great practitioner of the arts of necromancy to attempt to find a particular vein, though I doubt it. I never met an aelf with a knack for the wind of Shyish. But I, Qualos the Astute, necromancer supreme, I will have my own life soon bottled in this glass! By reversing it, I shall live forever. I alone have the art to exploit the Sands of Grief, whereas you shall fail!' He chuckled madly. 'What do you think of that?'

'It is most impressive,' said Maesa.

The smile dropped from Qualos' face, his eyes widened. 'Oh, you best be careful! He doesn't like it when souls are taken! You take the one you're looking for, even a part, and he'll come for you. He'll not let you be until your bones march in his legions and your spirit shrieks in his host.' He looked about, then whispered. 'I speak of Nagash.'

The whisper streamed from his lips and away over the dunes, growing louder the further it travelled. Thunder boomed far away. Aelphis shied.

'Not I, though. I have this! Within is my life! My soul is none but my own.' He held up the bottom bulb of an hourglass. The neck was snapped, the top lost. The glass was scratched to the point of opacity. No sand would run in that vessel, unless it was to fall out.

'I see,' said Maesa neutrally.

'The man is mad!' hissed Shattercap.

'Just a few grains more, then I will be heading back,' said Qualos. 'All the peoples of Eska will marvel at my feat!' he said. He licked his lips with a tongue dry and black as old leather. 'I don't think you can do it, not like me.' He cradled his broken glass to his chest.

'We shall see,' said Maesa.

'Well, on your way!' said the necromancer, his face transformed by a snarl. 'You distract me from my task. Get ye gone.'

Aelphis plodded slowly by the man. As they passed him, Maesa glimpsed white shining inside his open robes. Shattercap growled.

Qualos' ribs poked through desiccated flesh. Splintered bone trapped a dark hole where his heart had beaten, now gone.

'He is dead!' whispered Shattercap.

'Yes,' said Maesa.

Shattercap scrambled across Maesa's shoulders to look behind. 'You knew?'

'Only when he spoke,' admitted Maesa. 'I thought him alive, at first.'

'Should we not tell him?' asked Shattercap.

'I do not think it would make any difference, and it may put us in danger. His fate is not our business. The lord of undeath has him in his thrall. A cruel joke.'

Maesa directed Aelphis back upon their course and rode for a while. When he was sure they were out of sight of Qualos, Maesa pulled out Ghyran's bottled life and regarded it critically.

'The lack of this, however, is a cause for concern. There is enough for a few more days,' he said. He looked towards the centre of Shyish, estimating the ride to more hospitable lands. 'No more than that.'

'What do we do when we run out?' whimpered Shattercap.
Maesa would not answer.

Maesa and his companions were dying. Not a sharp, blade-cut
end, but the slow drip of souls weeping from broken hearts.

Grey dunes rolled away to chill eternities. Aelphis stumbled
up slopes and down slip faces, his antlers drooped to his feet.
Maesa swayed listlessly in the saddle. Shattercap was silent. A
few drops of Ghyran's life-giving waters remained to sustain
them. They would have to return soon, or they would die.

At the same time, they grew hopeful. Increasingly in the dust
they saw glittering streams of coarse grains of green, black,
amethyst and other gemstone colours. These were realmstones
of Shyish – life sands, each streak on the dunes the crystallised
essence of a life, a grain for every week or so. Maesa looked at
his compass often, hoping against hope that the needle would
turn and point to one of the deposits, but he was disappointed.
The needle aimed towards the horizon always. None of the coloured streaks were Ellamar's mortal days.

And then, the miraculous occurred. After what felt like years,
and could have been, the needle on the compass twitched.
Maesa stared dumbly at the device cupped in his hands. The
needle was moving, swinging away from their line of travel.

'Shattercap!' said Maesa, his voice cracked from days of
disuse.

'Master?' replied the spite, a breath of words no louder than
the whisper of the windblown sand.

'We approach! We are near!'

Maesa spurred Aelphis into life. Huffing wearily, the king of
stags lumbered into a trot.

'To the right, Aelphis! There!' said Maesa, intent upon the
dial.

Their path took them closer to the line of skeletons. At last, the source of the animates' burdens became apparent. Where realmstone gathered most thickly, a depression had been carved.

Within the bowl of a great quarry, the two lines of skeletons joined into one. They entered, looped round, bent without slowing to peck at the sand, then walked around the back of the bowl and thence out again, carrying their dot of treasure away to their master. In the dim starlight, Maesa spied many such pits, some worked out, some alive with the flash of dead bones.

A moment of horror gripped him. If Ellamar's sands were in one of those pits...

Relief came from the compass. It spun a little to the left, then as Aelphis followed, to the right. The compass rotated slowly around and around. Maesa brought Aelphis to a halt and slid from his back.

Sand shifted under his feet. Rivulets of it ran from the dunes' sides to fill his footsteps. The grey dust comprised the lesser part of it, much was realmstone. Many colours were mingled there. Many lives blended.

The prince stooped low, the compass held to the sand. By lifting individual grains to the compass rose and watching its spin, he ascertained that Ellamar's life was of an indigo hue. One grain set the compass twirling sharply. A handful made it blur.

'Fitting,' he said. 'Indigo was her favourite colour.' He took out the last of the life water, and roused the spite. 'Shattercap.'

'Good prince?'

'We shall finish this. We shall need all our strength. The servants of Nagash will come.' He took a sip, gave a drink to Shattercap, and then tipped the last of the water into Aelphis' mouth. The stag huffed and stood taller as vitality returned.

'Help me. Pluck up this indigo sand.' He drew out the hourglass from his saddlebags and placed it on the desert floor. He opened up the lid. 'Fill it up. Carefully. Not one other grain, only hers.'

When lowered to the sand, Shattercap mewled. 'It burns me, master!'

'Bear the pain, and you shall be four steps closer to freedom,' said the prince sternly. 'Hurry!'

Together the aelf and spite worked, fastidiously plucking single grains of the glittering sand from the dust and depositing them in the hourglass.

The bottom bulb was almost full, and the grains becoming harder to sift from the rest, when a piercing shriek rose over the desert.

Shattercap's head whipped up. His hands opened and closed nervously.

'Master...' he whimpered. 'We are noticed.'

Another shriek sounded, then a third, each one nearer than the last. The ceaseless, gentle wind of the desert gusted fiercely.

'Fill it, spite!' commanded Maesa. He drew the Song of Thorns. The woody edge of the living sword sparked with starlight. 'Get it all. I shall hold them back.'

Howling with outrage, a wraith came flying over the ridge of a nearby dune. It had no legs, but trailed streamers of magic from black robes in place of lower limbs. Its face was a skull locked into a permanent roar. Its hands bore a scythe. This, unlike the aethereal bearer, was solid enough, a shaft of worm-eaten wood and a blade of rusted metal with a terrible bite. Other wraiths came skimming over the sands, their corpse-light shining from the tiny jewels of other creature's lives.

The first wraith raised its weapon, and bore down on the

prince. Moving with the grace native to all aelves, Maesa side-
stepped and with a single precise cut, sliced the spirit in two.
It screamed its last, the shreds of its soul sucked within the
Song of Thorns. Another came, swooping around and around
Aelphis and Maesa before plunging arrow-swift at the prince.
Maesa was faster, and ended it. The Song of Thorns glowed
with the power of the stolen spirits.

More wraiths were coming. A chorus of shrieks sounded
from every direction. The undead burst from the sand, they
swooped down from the sky. The watchdogs of Nagash were
alert for thieves taking their master's property, and responded
to the alarm with alacrity.

'Quickly, Shattercap!'

Maesa slew another, and another. The Song of Thorns was
anathema to things such as the wraiths, but there were hundreds of them gathering in a tempest of phantoms. The spite
scrabbled at the ground, his earlier finesse gone as he shov-
elled Ellamar's life sands into the glass.

'Be careful not to mix the grains!' the prince shouted, cleav-
ing the head of another wraith from its owner.

'I am trying!' squeaked the spite.

'I cannot fight all these things,' said Maesa. He was right.
Now the wraiths saw the danger the Song of Thorns posed,
they turned their attacks against Aelphis and Shattercap, and it
took all of Maesa's skill to keep them from harm. Aelphis reared
and pawed at the wraiths, but all he could do was deflect their
weapons from his hide. When his hooves hit their bodies, they
passed through, leaving wakes of glowing mist.

'I have it all!' said Shattercap, ducking the raking hand of a
wraith. He slammed closed the lid atop the hourglass.

'You are sure? You have checked the compass?'

'Yes!' squealed Shattercap.

The prince danced around the stag, snatching up hourglass and compass in one hand while killing with the other. Shatter-cap leapt from the sand to the prince's arm. Maesa jumped onto the back of the stag, cutting away the head of a scythe in mid-air, then reversing his stroke as he landed in the saddle to render another phantom into shreds of ectoplasm.

Aelphis reared. Maesa slashed from left to right. Braying loudly, the stag leapt forward.

Invigorated by Ghyran's waters of life, Aelphis ran as fast as the wind. The wraiths set up pursuit, and more streamed from the depths of the desert to join them. Maesa slew all that came against him. He cried out when a scythe blade nicked his arm, numbing it with the grave's chill. The wraiths screeched to see his discomfort and they closed in for the kill, but Maesa yelled the war cries of his ancestors and fought on.

It seemed as if the great stag flew. The wraiths were outpaced. Their dark shapes were left behind. No more came from the wastes.

Aelphis ran on. Light grew ahead. The vastness of the Sands of Grief were coming to an end. Desert of a more ordinary sort blended into its edges. At last, Maesa came to a place where dawn stood still upon the edge of the world, and pale sun lit upon his face. At the margins of a wadi, dry grasses rattled in the wind – life had returned. They had gone far from the lines of skeletons and their ghoulish mines. Maesa brought Aelphis to a stop.

The stag snorted. Froth lathered his skin. He shuddered from antlers to tail, spraying foam across the rocks, then settled and blared out his throaty call in pleasure at their escape.

Maesa held up the hourglass. He looked with wonder at the indigo sand within.

'The first part of the task is done,' he said. 'With this, when

Ellamar returns, she will not age. She will be forever at my side.'

'Yes, my master,' said Shattercap. 'But the lord of undeath will not rest until he has brought you to account for your crime, and we must find a way to steal her back from whatever place she languishes within first.'

'Let Nagash's servants come,' said Maesa. He sheathed the Song of Thorns. It vibrated with strange warmth from its feast, passing its strength into him. 'I will be ready. You did well, Shattercap. You are learning.'

'Learning to be good?'

'Learning to be useful. Goodness comes later.'

'Thank you, kind prince,' said the spite. He snuggled down into Maesa's hood. But though his words were fawning, his heart retained a little flinty wickedness. His tiny fist was clenched. In it he held a single grain of Ellamar's soul dust, kept for himself.

Unaware of his companion's thievery, Maesa set his joyous face into the dawn, and rode out full of hope.

SHIPRATS

C L Werner

Carefully, the heavyset duardin warrior raised his weapon. His eyes narrowed, fixating on his victim. He appeared unfazed by the gloom of the darkened hold, his vision sharp enough to pick out a marrow-hawk soaring through a thunderstorm. The duardin judged the distance, allowed for the air currents that buffeted the moored aether-ship and estimated how much strength to bring to bear against his foe.

The shovel came cracking down, striking the deck with such force that a metallic ping was sent echoing through the hold. Drumark cursed as the target of the descending spade leapt upwards and squeaked in fright. The brown rat landed on his foot, squeaked again, then scampered off deeper into the hold.

Furious, Drumark turned and glowered at the other spade-carrying duardin gathered in the *Iron Dragon*'s hold. Arka-nauts, endrinriggers, aether-tenders and even a few of the ship's officers gave the angry sergeant anxious stares.

'Right! Now they are just begging to be shot! I am getting my decksweeper!' Drumark swore, not for the first time.

Brokrin, the *Iron Dragon*'s captain, stepped towards Drumark. 'You are not shooting holes in the bottom of my ship,' he snapped at him. 'We have enough problems with the rats. If you go shooting holes in the hull we won't be able to take on any aether-gold even if we do find a rich cloud-vein.'

Drumark jabbed a thumb down at his boot. 'It peed on my foot. Only respect for you, cap'n, keeps me from getting a good fire going and smoking the vermin out.'

'That is some sound thinking,' Horgarr, the *Iron Dragon*'s endrinmaster scoffed. He pressed his shovel against the deck and leaned against it as he turned towards Drumark. 'Start a fire in the ship's belly. Nothing bad could happen from that. Except the fifty-odd things that immediately come to mind.'

Brokrin shook his head as Drumark told Horgarr exactly what he thought of the endrinmaster's mind. No duardin had any affection for rats, but Drumark's hatred of them was almost a mania. His father had died fighting the pestiferous skaven and every time he looked at a rat he was reminded of their larger kin. It made him surly and quick to anger. This would be the third fight between the two he would have to break up since coming down into the *Iron Dragon*'s holds. Unable to find any aether-gold, the ironclad had put in at Greypeak, a walled human city with which Barak-Zilfin had a trading compact. The grain the city's farmers cultivated was well regarded by the Kharadron and would fetch a good price in the skyhold. Not as much as a good vein, but at least there would be something for the aether-ship's backers.

At least there would be if the rats that had embarked along with the grain left anything in good enough condition to sell. There were more than a few Kharadron who claimed that the

SHIPRATS

Iron Dragon was jinxed and that her captain was under a curse. Sometimes he found himself wondering if his detractors were right. This was not the first time Brokrin's ship had suffered an infestation of vermin, but he could not recall any that had been so tenacious as these. Whatever they did to try to protect their cargo, the rats found some way around it. They were too clever for the traps old Mortrimm set for them, too cunning to accept the poisoned biscuits Lodri made for them. Even the cat Gotramm had brought aboard had been useless – after its first tussle with one of the rats it had found itself a spot up in the main endrin's cupola and would claw anyone who tried to send it below deck again.

'These swine must have iron teeth.' The bitter observation was given voice by Skaggi, the expedition's logisticator. Tasked with balancing profit against expense and safeguarding the investment of the expedition's backers, every ounce of grain despoiled by the rodents stung Skaggi to the quick. He held a heavy net of copper wire in his hands, extending it towards Brokrin so he could see the holes the rats had gnawed. 'So much for keeping them out of the grain. We will be lucky if they do not start in for the beer next.'

Skaggi's dour prediction made Drumark completely forget about his argument with Horgarr. He looked in horror at Skaggi. An instant later, he raised the shovel overhead and flung it to the floor.

'That is it!' Drumark declared. 'I am bringing my lads down here and we will settle these parasites here and now!' He turned to Brokrin, determination etched across his face. 'You tell Grundstok thunderers to hunt rats, then that is just what we will do. But we will do it the way we know best.'

Skaggi's eyes went wide with alarm, his mind turning over the expense of patching over the holes the thunderers would leave if they started blasting away at the rats. He swung around to Brokrin, his tone almost frantic. 'We will be ruined,' he groaned. 'No profit, barely enough to pay off the backers.'

Drumark reached out and took hold of the copper net Skaggi was holding. 'If they can chew through this, they can chew their way into the beer barrels. Me and my thunderers are not going dry while these rats get drunk!'

The sound of shovels slapping against the floor died down as the rest of the duardin in the hold paused in their efforts to hear what Drumark was shouting about. Many of them were from his Grundstok company and looked more than ready to side with their sergeant and trade spades for guns.

'The rats will not bother the beer while they still have grain to eat,' Brokrin stated, making sure his words were loud enough to carry to every crewman in the hold. How much truth there was in the statement, he did not know. He did know it was what Drumark and the others needed to hear right now.

'All due respect, cap'n,' Drumark said, 'but how long will that be? Swatting them with shovels just isn't enough and we have tried everything else except shooting them.'

Brokrin gave Drumark a stern look. 'Others have said it, now I am saying it. You are not shooting holes in *my* ship.' The chastened sergeant held Brokrin's gaze for a moment, then averted his eyes. The point had been made.

'What are we going to do?' Gotramm asked. The youthful leader of the *Iron Dragon*'s arkanauts, he had watched with pointed interest the exchange between Brokrin and Drumark.

'I know one thing,' Horgarr said, pulling back his sleeve and showing the many scratches on his arm. 'That cat is staying right where it is.' The remark brought laughs from all who heard it, even cracking Drumark's sullen mood.

Brokrin was more pensive. Something Drumark had said earlier had spurred a memory. It was only now that his recollection fell into place. 'The toads,' he finally said. The newer members of the crew glanced in confusion at their captain, but those who had served on the *Iron Dragon* before her escape from the monster Ghazul knew his meaning.

'Some years ago,' Brokrin explained to them, 'we sailed through a Grimesturm and a rain of toads fell on our decks. They were everywhere, even worse than these rats. You could not sit without squashing one or take a sip of ale without having one hop into your mug.

'To rid the ship of her infestation,' Brokrin continued, 'we put in at the lamasery of Kheitar. The lamas prepared a mixture of herbs, which we burned in smudge pots. The smoke vexed the toads so much that they jumped overboard of their own accord.'

'You think the lamas could whip up something to scare off rats?' Gotramm asked.

Brokrin nodded. 'Kheitar is not far out of our way. There would be little to lose by diverting our course and paying the lamasery a visit.'

'Kheitar is built into the side of a mountain,' Horgarr said. 'Certainly it will offer as good an anchorage as the peak we're moored to now.'

Skaggi's eyes lit up, an avaricious smile pulling at his beard. 'The lamas are renowned for their artistic tapestries as well as their herbalism. If we could bargain with them and get them to part with even one tapestry we could recover the loss of what the rats have already ruined.'

'Then it is decided,' Brokrin said. 'Our next port of call is Kheitar.'

The lamasery's reception hall was a stark contrast to the confined cabins and holds of the *Iron Dragon*. Great pillars of lacquered wood richly carved with elaborate glyphs soared up from the teak floor to clasp the vaulted roof with timber claws. Lavish hangings hung from the walls, each beautifully woven with scenes from legend and lore. Great urns flanked each doorway, their basins filled with a wondrously translucent sand in which tangles of incense sticks slowly smouldered. Perfumed smoke wafted sluggishly through the room, visible as a slight haze where it condensed around the great platform at the rear of the chamber. Upon that platform stood a gigantic joss, a golden statue beaten into the semblance of an immensely fat man, his mouth distorted by great tusks and his head adorned by a nest of horns. In one clawed hand the joss held forward a flower, his other resting across his lap with the remains of a broken sword in his palm.

Brokrin could never help feeling a tinge of revulsion when he looked at Kheitar's idol. Whoever had crafted it, their attention to detail had been morbid. The legend at the root of the lamas' faith spoke of a heinous daemon from the Age of Chaos that had set aside its evil ways to find enlightenment in the ways of purity and asceticism. Looking at the joss, Brokrin felt less a sense of evil redeemed than he did that of evil biding its time. The duardin with him looked similarly perturbed, all except Skaggi, who was already casting a greedy look at the tapestries on the walls.

The young initiate who guided the duardin into the hall stepped aside as Brokrin and his companions entered. He bowed his shaved head towards a bronze gong hanging just to the left of the entrance. He took the striker tethered to the gong's wooden stand and gave the instrument three solid hits, each blow sending a dull reverberation echoing through the chamber.

'Take it easy,' Brokrin whispered when he saw Gotramm

from the corner of his eye. The young arkanaut had reached for his pistol the moment the gong's notes were sounded. 'If we aggravate the lamas they might not help get rid of the rats.'

Gotramm let his hand drop away from the gun holstered on his belt. He nodded towards the joss at the other end of the hall. 'That gargoyle is not the sort of thing to make me feel at ease,' he said.

'The cap'n is not saying to close your eyes,' old Mortrimm the navigator told Gotramm. 'He is just saying do not be hasty drawing a weapon. Abide by the Code – be sure who you set your axe against, and why.'

Brokrin frowned. 'Let us hope it does not come to axes. Barak-Zilfin has a long history trading with the lamas.' Even as he said the words, they felt strangely hollow to him. Something had changed about Kheitar. What it was, he could not say. It was not something he could see or hear, but rather a faintly familiar smell. He turned his eyes again to the daemon-faced joss, wondering what secrets it was hiding inside that golden head.

Movement drew Brokrin's attention away from the joss. From behind one of the hangings at the far end of the hall, a tall and sparingly built human emerged. He wore the saffron robes of Kheitar's lamas, but to this was added a wide sash of green that swept down across his left shoulder before circling his waist. It was the symbol that denoted the high lama himself. The uneasy feeling Brokrin had intensified, given something solid upon which to focus. The man who came out from behind the tapestry was middle-aged, his features long and drawn. He certainly was not the fat, elderly Piu who had been high lama the last time the *Iron Dragon* visited Kheitar.

The lama walked towards the duardin, but did not acknowledge their presence until after he had reached the middle of the hall and turned towards the joss. Bowing and clapping his hands four times, he made obeisance to the idol. When he turned back towards the duardin, his expression was that of sincerity itself.

'Peace and wisdom upon your path,' the lama declared, clapping his hands together once more. A regretful smile drew at the corners of his mouth. 'Is it too much to hope that the Kharadron overlords have descended from the heavens to seek enlightenment?' He shook his head. 'But such, I sense, is not the path that has led you to us. If it is not the comfort of wisdom you would take away from here, then what comfort is it that we can extend to you?'

Although Brokrin was the *Iron Dragon*'s captain, it was Skaggi who stepped forwards to address the lama. Of all the ship's crew, the logisticator had the glibbest tongue. 'Please forgive any intrusion, your eminence,' he said. 'It is only dire need which causes us to intrude upon your solitude. Our ship has been beset by an infestation of noxious pests. Terrible rats that seek...'

The lama's serenity faltered when Skaggi began to describe the situation. A regretful look crept into his eyes. 'We of Kheitar are a peaceful order. Neither meat nor milk may pass our lips. Our hands are not raised in violence, for like Zomoth-tulku, we have forsaken the sword. To smite any living thing is to stumble on the path to ascension.'

Brokrin came forwards to stand beside Skaggi. 'Your Order helped us once before, when hail-toads plagued my ship. The high lama, Piu, understood the necessity of removing them.'

The lama closed his eyes. 'Piu-tulku was a wise and holy man. Cho cannot claim even a measure of his enlightenment.' Cho opened his eyes again and nodded to Brokrin. 'There are herbs which could be prepared. Rendered down they can be burned in smudge pots and used to fumigate your ship.' A deep sigh ran through him. 'The smoke will drive the rats to flee. Would it be too great an imposition to ask that you leave them a way to escape? Perhaps keep your vessel moored here so they can flee down the ropes and reach solid ground.'

Skaggi's eyes went wide in shock. 'That would cause the lamasery to become infested.' He pointed at the lavish hangings on the walls. 'Those filthy devils would ruin this place in a fortnight! Think of all that potential profit being lost!'

Cho placed a hand against his shoulder. 'It would remove a stain from my conscience if you would indulge my hopes. The death of even so small a creature would impair my own aspirations of transcendence.'

'My conscience would not permit me to cause such misery to my benefactors,' Brokrin stated. 'But upon my honour and my beard, I vow that I will not use whatever herbs you provide us without ensuring the rats can make landfall without undue hazard.'

'It pleases me to hear those words,' Cho said. 'I know the word of your people is etched in stone. I am content. It will take us a day to prepare the herbs. Your ship will be safe where it is moored?'

'We are tied to the tower above your western gate,' Mortrimm stated. He gestured with his thumb at Brokrin. 'The cap'n insisted we keep far enough away that the rats wouldn't smell food and come slinking down the guide ropes.'

'Such consideration and concern does you credit, captain,' Cho declared. He suddenly turned towards Skaggi. 'If it is not an imposition, would it be acceptable to inquire if the tapestries we weave here still find favour among your people?'

The question took Skaggi by such surprise that the logisticator allowed excitement to shine in his eyes before gaining control of himself and resuming an air of indifference. Brokrin could tell that he was about to undervalue the worth of Kheitar's artistry. It was a prudent tactic when considering profit but an abominable one when thinking in terms of honour.

'Your work is applauded in Barak-Zilfin,' Brokrin said before Skaggi could find his voice. The logisticator gave him an imploring look, but he continued just the same. 'There are many guildhalls that have used your tapestries to adorn their assemblies, and poor is the noble house that has not at least one hanging from Kheitar on its walls.'

With each word he spoke, Brokrin saw Skaggi grow more perturbed. Cho remained implacable, exhibiting no alteration in his demeanour. Then the high lama turned towards the wall from which he had emerged. Clapping his hands together in rapid succession, he looked aside at the duardin.

'I thank you for your forthrightness,' Cho said. 'Your honesty makes you someone we can trust.' There was more, but even Brokrin lost the flow of Cho's speech when the hangings on the walls were pushed aside and a group of ten lamas entered the hall. Each pair carried an immense tapestry rolled into a bundle across their shoulders. To bring only a few tapestries out of Kheitar was considered a rewarding voyage. Was Cho truly offering the duardin five of them?

Cho noted the disbelief that shone on the faces of his guests. He swung around to Skaggi. 'I have noticed that you admire our work. I will leave it to you to judge the value of the wares I would offer you.' At a gesture from the high lama, the foremost of his followers came near and unrolled their burden. Skaggi didn't quite stifle the gasp that bubbled up from his throat.

The background of the tapestry was a rich burgundy in colour and across its thirty-foot length vibrant images were woven from threads of sapphire blue, emerald green and amber yellow.

Geometric patterns that transfixed the eye formed a border around visions of opulent splendour and natural wonder. Soaring mountains with snowy peaks rose above wooded hills. Holy kings held court from gilded thrones, their crowns picked out with tiny slivers of jade wound between the threads. Through the centre of the tapestry a stream formed from crushed pearl flowed into a silver sea.

'Magnificent,' the logisticator sputtered before recovering his composure.

'It gladdens me that you are content with our poor offerings,' Cho told Skaggi. He looked back towards Brokrin. 'It is my hope that you would agree to take this cargo back to your city. Whatever price you gain from their sale, I only ask that you return half of that amount to the lamasery.'

'Well... there are our expenses to be taken into account...' Skaggi started. However good a deal seemed, the logisticator was quick to find a way to make it better.

'Of course you should be compensated for your labours,' Cho said, conceding the point without argument. 'Captain, are you agreeable to my offer?'

'It is very generous and I would be a fool to look askance at your offer,' Brokrin replied. 'It may be some months before we can return here with your share.'

'That is understood,' Cho said. He gestured again to the lamas carrying the tapestries. 'Pack the hangings for their journey. Then take them to the Kharadron ship.'

The unaccountable uneasiness that had been nagging at Brokrin asserted itself once more. 'I will send one of my crew to guide your people and show them the best place to put your wares.' He turned to Mortrimm. 'Go with them and keep your wits about you,' he whispered.

'You expect trouble?' Mortrimm asked.

Brokrin scratched his beard. 'No, but what is it the Chuitsek nomads say? "A gift horse sometimes bites." Just make sure all they do is put the tapestries aboard.'

Nodding his understanding, Mortrimm took his position at the head of the procession of lamas. Because of their heavy burdens, the navigator was easily able to match their pace despite one of his legs being in an aetheric brace. Brokrin and the other duardin watched as the tapestries were conducted out of the hall.

'Should I go with them, cap'n?' Skaggi asked. 'Make certain they do not mar the merchandise when they bring it aboard?'

'I think these lamas know their business,' Gotramm retorted. 'They are the ones who sweated to make the things and they have just as much to lose as we do if they get damaged.'

Unlike the banter between Drumark and Horgarr, there was a bitter edge to what passed between Gotramm and Skaggi. There was no respect between them, only a kind of tolerant contempt. Brokrin started to intercede when something Cho had said suddenly rose to mind. He turned towards the high lama. 'You called your predecessor Piu-tulku? Is not tulku your word for the revered dead?'

'The holy ascended,' Cho corrected him. 'Among the vulgar it is translated as "living god". You have yourself seen the ancient tulkus who have followed Zomoth-tulku's transcendence.'

Brokrin shuddered at the recollection. Deep within the lamasery there were halls filled with niches, each containing the mummified husk of a human. They were holy men who had gradually poisoned themselves, embalming their own bodies while they were still alive in a desperate search for immortality. The lamas considered each of the corpses to still be alive, tending their clothes and setting bowls of food and drink before them each morning. He thought of Piu and the last time he had seen the man. There had been no hint that he had been undergoing this ghastly process of self-mummification.

'I was unaware Piu had chosen such a path,' Brokrin apologised.

Cho smiled and shook his head. 'Piu-tulku did not choose the path. The path chose him. A wondrous miracle, for he has transcended the toils of mortality yet still permits his wisdom to be shared with those who have yet to ascend to a higher enlightenment.' His smile broadened. 'Perhaps if you were to see him, speak with him, you would understand the wisdom of our Order.'

That warning feeling was even more persistent now, but Brokrin resisted the urge to play things safe. Something had changed at Kheitar and whatever it was, he would bet it had to do with Piu's unexpected ascension. Glancing over at Gotramm and then at Skaggi, he made his decision. 'We would like very much to meet with Piu-tulku.'

Cho motioned for the initiate by the door to come over to them. 'I am certain Piu-tulku will impart much wisdom to you, but to enter his august presence you must set aside your tools of death.' He pointed at the axes and swords the duardin carried. 'Leave those behind if you would see the tulku. I can allow no blades in his chambers.'

Brokrin nodded. 'You have nothing to fear, your grace. Our Code prohibits us from doing harm to any who are engaged in fair trade with us.' He slowly unbuckled his sword and proffered it to the initiate. 'We will follow your custom.'

Slowly the three duardin removed their blades, setting them on the floor. Gotramm started to do the same with his pistol, but Cho had already turned away. Brokrin set a restraining hand on Gotramm's.

'He said blades,' Brokrin whispered. 'Unless asked, keep your pistol.' He brushed his hand across the repeater holstered on his own belt. 'We will respect their custom, as far as they ask it of us.'

Brokrin gave a hard look at Cho's back as the high lama preceded them out of the hall. 'If he is being honest with us, it will make no difference. If he is not, it might make all the difference in the realms.'

Drumark escorted the lamas down into the *Iron Dragon*'s hold. He had tried to choose the cleanest compartment in which to put the precious cargo, but even here there was the fug of rat in the air. 'This is the best one,' he said. 'You can put them down here.'

'You think they will be safe?' asked Mortrimm. Like the sergeant, he could smell the stink of rat. He looked uneasily at the bamboo crates the lamas carried, wondering how long it would take a rat to gnaw its way through the boxes.

'As long as there is grain, the little devils will keep eating that,' Drumark spat, glowering at a fat, brown body that went scooting behind a crate when the light from his lantern shone upon it. 'It will be a while before they start nibbling on this stuff.' He turned his light on the sallow-faced lamas as they carefully set down the crates and started to leave the hold. 'Tell your friends to get that poison ready on the quick. If we do not smoke out these vermin, your tapestries will be gnawed so badly we will have to sell them as thread.'

The warning put a certain haste in the lamas' step as they withdrew from the hold. Mortrimm started to follow them as the men made their way back onto the deck. He had only taken a few steps when he noticed that Drumark was still standing down near the tapestries.

'Are you coming?' Mortrimm asked.

'In a bit,' Drumark answered, waving him away. Mortrimm shook his head and left the hold.

Alone in the rat-infested hold, Drumark glowered at the shadows. The stink of vermin surrounded him, making his skin crawl. Instead of withdrawing from the stench, he let his revulsion swell, feeding into the hate that boiled deep inside him. Rats! Pestiferous, murderous fiends! Whatever size they came in, they had to be stamped out wherever they were found. He would happily do his part. He owed that much to his father, burned down by the foul magics of the loathsome skaven.

Drumark looked at the crates and then back at the noisy shadows. Despite his talk with Mortrimm and the lamas, he was anything but certain the rats would spare the tapestries. The vermin were perverse creatures and might gnaw on the precious hangings out of sheer spite. Well, if they did, they would find a very irritable duardin waiting for them.

Checking one last time to be certain Mortrimm was gone, Drumark walked over to a dark corner near the door and retrieved the object he had secreted there without Brokrin's knowledge. He patted the heavy stock of his decksweeper. 'Some work for you before too long,' he told it. Returning to his original position, he doused the lantern. Instantly the hold was plunged into darkness. Drumark could hear the creaking of the guide ropes as the ship swayed in its mooring, the groan of the engines that powered the ironclad's huge endrin, the scratch of little claws as they came creeping across the planks.

Gradually his eyes adjusted to the gloom and Drumark could see little shapes scurrying around the hold. Soon the shapes became more distinct as his eyes became accustomed to the dark. Rats, as fat and evil as he had ever seen. There must be a dozen of them, all scurrying about, crawling over barrels, peeping into boxes, even gnawing at the planks. He kept his eyes on the crates with the tapestries, all laid out in a nice little row. The moment one of the rats started to nibble at them he would start shooting.

But the rats did not nibble the crates. Indeed, Drumark began to appreciate that the animals were conspicuously avoiding them. At first he thought it was simply because they were new, a change in their environment that the vermin would have to become comfortable with first. Then one of the rats did stray towards the row, fleeing the ire of one of its larger kin. The wayward rodent paused in mid-retreat, rearing up and sniffing at the crates.

Drumark could not know what the rat smelled, but he did know whatever it was had given the rodent a fright. It went scampering off, squeaking like a thing possessed. The rest of the vermin were soon following it, scrambling to their boltholes and scurrying away to other parts of the ship. Soon Drumark could not hear their scratching claws any more.

Keeping his decksweeper at the ready, Drumark sat down beside the door. He stayed silent as he watched the crated tapestries, his body as rigid as that of a statue. In the darkness, he waited.

The wait was not a long one. A flutter of motion spread through the rolled tapestry at the end of the row. Faint at first, it increased in its agitation, becoming a wild thrashing after a few moments, the cloth slapping against the bamboo that enclosed it. Someone – or something – was inside the rolled tapestry and trying to work its way out. Eyes riveted on the movement, Drumark rose and walked forwards. He aimed his decksweeper at the tapestry. Whatever had hidden itself inside, it would find a warm reception when it emerged.

The thrashing persisted, growing more wild but making no headway against the framework that surrounded the tapestry. Whatever was inside was unable to free itself. Or unwilling. A horrible suspicion gripped Drumark. There were four more tapestries and while his attention was focused on this one, he was unable to watch the others.

Drumark swung around just as a dark shape came leaping at him from the shadows.

The decksweeper bellowed as he fired into his attacker. Drumark saw a furry body go spinning across the hold, slamming into the wall with a bone-crunching impact. He had only a vague impression of the thing he had shot. He got a better look at the creature that came lunging at him from one of the other crates.

Thin hands with clawed fingers scrabbled at Drumark as the creature leapt on him. Its filthy nails raked at his face, pulling hair from his beard. A ratlike face with hideous red eyes glared at him before snapping at his throat with chisel-like fangs. He could feel a long tail slapping at his legs, trying to hit his knees and knock him to the floor.

Drumark brought the hot barrel of his decksweeper cracking up into the monster's jaw, breaking its teeth. The creature whimpered and tried to wrest free from his grip, but he caught hold of its arm and gave it a brutal twist, popping it out of joint. The crippled creature twisted away, plunging back down on top of the crates.

Any sense of victory Drumark might have felt vanished when he raised his eyes from the enormous rat he had overcome. Six more of its kind had crawled out from their hiding places in the tapestries, and unlike the one he had already fought, these each had knives in their paw-like hands. They stood upright on their hind legs, chittering malignantly as they started towards the lone duardin.

'Skaven!'

The cry came from the doorway behind Drumark. The discharge of his decksweeper had brought Horgarr and several others of the crew rushing into the hold, concerned that the sergeant had finally lost all restraint with the rats infesting the ship. Instead they found a far more infernal pestilence aboard.

The arrival of the other duardin dulled the confidence that shone in the eyes of the skaven infiltrators. The mocking squeaks took on an uncertain quality. Ready to pounce en masse on Drumark a moment before, now the creatures hesitated.

'What are you waiting for, lads!' Drumark shouted to Horgarr and the others. 'The bigger the rat, the more of our beer it will drink! Get the scum!'

The sergeant's shouts overcame the surprise that held the other duardin. Armed with shovels and axes, Horgarr led the crew charging across the hold. Their backs against the wall, the skaven had no choice but to make a fight of it.

As he rearmed his decksweeper and made ready to return to the fray, a terrible thought occurred to Drumark. The tapestries and their devious passengers had come from the lamasery. A place from which Captain Brokrin had not yet returned.

'Hold them here!' Drumark told Horgarr. 'I have to alert the rest of the ship and see if we can help the cap'n!'

The young initiate held the ornate door open for Cho and the duardin as they entered the shrine wherein Piu-tulku had been entombed after his ascension. The room was smaller than the grand reception hall, but even more opulently appointed. The hangings that covered its walls were adorned with glittering jewels; the pillars that supported its roof were carved from blackest ebony and highlighted with designs painted in gold. The varnished floor creaked with a musical cadence as the visitors crossed it, sending lyrical echoes wafting up into the vaulted heights of its arched ceiling.

Ensconced upon a great dais flanked by hangings that depicted the wingless dragon and the fiery phoenix, the living god of Kheitar reposed. Piu was still a fat man, but his flesh had lost its rich colour, fading to a parchment-like hue. He wore black robes with a sash of vivid blue – the same raiment that had been given to the mummies Brokrin had seen in the lamasery's vaults. Yet Piu was not content to remain in motionless silence. Just as the duardin had decided that the lamas were delusional and that their late leader was simply dead, the body seated atop the dais opened its eyes and spoke.

'Enter and welcome,' the thing on the dais said. The voice was dull and dry with a strange reverberation running through it. 'Duardin-friends always-ever welcome in Kheitar.' It moved its head, fixing its empty gaze in Cho's general direction. 'Have you given help-aid to our guests?'

'Yes, holy tulku!' Cho said, bowing before the dais. 'The tapestries have been sent to their ship, as you commanded.'

The thing swung its head back around, facing towards the duardin. It extended its hands in a supplicating gesture. The effect was marred by the jerky way in which the arms moved. Brokrin could hear a faint, unnatural sound as Piu moved its head and hands, something between a pop and a whir. He had seen such artificial motion before, heard similar mechanical sounds. The tulku was similar to an aetheric musician he'd seen in the great manor of Grand Admiral Thorgraad, a wondrous machine crafted in the semblance of a duardin bard. The only blight on the incredible automaton's music had been the sound of the pumps inside it sending fuel through its pipes and hoses.

Whatever the esoteric beliefs of Kheitar, what sat upon the dais was not an ascended holy man. It was only a machine.

Piu began to speak again. 'It is to be hope-prayed that we shall all profit-gain from–'

Brokrin stepped past Cho and glared at the thing on the dais. 'I do not know who you are, but I will not waste words with a puppet.' The outburst brought a gasp of horror from the initiate at the door. Cho raced forwards, prostrating himself before the dais and pleading with Piu to forgive him for such insult.

Brokrin gave the offended lamas small notice. His attention was fixed to the hangings behind Piu's dais. There was a ripple of motion from behind one of them. Pushing aside the snake-like dragon, a loathsome figure stalked into view. He was taller than the duardin but more leanly built, his wiry body covered in grey fur peppered with black. A rough sort of metal hauberk clung to his chest while a strange helm of copper encased most of his rodent-like head. Only the fanged muzzle and the angry red eyes were left uncovered. A crazed array of pouches and tools swung from belts and bandoleers, but across one shoulder the humanoid rat wore a brilliant blue sash – the same as that which adorned Piu.

'Now you may speak-beg,' the ratman growled as he stood beside Piu. His hairless tail lashed about in malicious amusement as he smelled the shock rising off the duardin.

'Mighty Kilvolt-tulku,' Cho cried out. 'Forgive me. I did not know they were such barbarians.'

Kilvolt waved aside the high lama's apology. He fixed his gruesome attention on Brokrin. 'No defiance, beard-thing,' he snarled, pointing a claw at either side of the room. From behind the hangings a pack of armoured skaven crept into view, each carrying a vicious halberd in its claws. 'Listen-hear. I know-learn about your port-nest. Your clan-kin make-build ships that fly-climb higher than any others. I want-demand that secret.'

'Even if I knew it,' Brokrin snapped at Kilvolt, 'I would not give it to you.'

The skaven bared his fangs, his tail lashing angrily from side to side. 'Then I take-tear what I want-need! Already you let-bring my warriors into your ship.' He waved his paw at Cho. 'The tapestries this fool-meat gave you.' He gestured again with his paws, waving at the skaven guards that now surrounded the duardin. 'If they fail-fall, then I have hostages to buy the secret of your ship. Torture or ransom will give-bring what I...'

Kilvolt's fur suddenly stood on end, a sour odour rising from his glands. His eyes were fixed on the pistols hanging from the belts Brokrin and Gotramm wore. He swung around on Cho, wrenching a monstrous gun of his own from one of the bandoleers. 'I order-say take-fetch all-all weapons!' The skaven punctuated his words by pulling the trigger and exploding Cho's head in a burst of blood and bone.

The violent destruction of the lama spurred the duardin into action. With the skaven distracted by the murder on the dais, Brokrin and Gotramm drew their pistols. Before the ratmen could react, the arkanaut captain burned one down with a shot to its chest, the aetheric charge searing a hole through its armour. Brokrin turned towards Kilvolt, but the skaven took one glance at the multi-barrelled volley pistol and darted behind the seated Piu-tulku.

Instead Brokrin swung around and discharged his weapon into the skaven guards to his right. The volley dropped two of the rushing ratmen and sent another pair squeaking back to the doorways hidden behind the hangings, their fur dripping with blood. Gotramm was firing again, but the skaven were more wary of their foes now, ducking around the pillars and trying to use them as cover while they advanced.

'We are done for,' Skaggi groaned, keeping close to the other duardin. Alone among them, the logisticator really had come into the room unarmed. 'We have to negotiate!' he pleaded with Brokrin.

'The only things I have to say to skaven come out of here,'

Brokrin told Skaggi, aiming his volley pistol at the guards trying to circle around him. The ratmen were unaware the weapon had no charge and seeing it aimed in their direction had them falling over themselves to gain cover.

A crackle from the dais presaged the grisly impact that sent an electric shock rushing through Brokrin. The armour on his back had been struck by a blast from Kilvolt himself. Feeling secure that the duardin were distracted by his henchrats, he returned to the attack. The oversized rings that adorned one of his paws pulsated with a sickly green glow, a light that throbbed down to them via a series of hoses that wrapped around his arm before dipping down to a cannister on his belt.

The heavy armour Brokrin wore guarded him against the worst of the synthetic lightning. He turned his volley pistol towards the dais. Kilvolt flinched, ducking back behind the phoney tulku. As he did, the ratman's eyes fixated on something behind the duardin captain.

'The boy-thing!' Kilvolt snarled from behind Piu. 'Stop-kill boy-thing, you fool-meat!'

Brokrin risked a glance towards the door. It had been flung open and the initiate was racing into the hall outside, screaming at the top of his lungs. Immediately half a dozen of the skaven were charging after him, determined to stop him from alerting the other lamas about what was happening in Piu's shrine.

The ratmen made it as far as the door before a duardin fusillade smashed into them. Skaven bodies were flung back into the shrine, battered and bloodied by a concentrated salvo of gunfire. Just behind them came their executioners, Drumark leading his Grundstok thunderers.

The surviving guards squeaked in fright at the unexpected appearance of so many duardin and the vicious dispatch of their comrades. The creatures turned and fled, scurrying back into their holes behind the wall hangings. A few shots from the thunderers encouraged them to keep running.

'The leader is up there!' Brokrin told his crew, waving his pistol at the dais. 'There are tunnels behind the tapestries. Keep him from reaching them.'

Even as Brokrin gave the command, Kilvolt came darting out from behind the dais. His retreat would have ended in disaster, but the skaven had one last trick to play. To cover his flight, he had sent a final pawn into the fray. Piu-tulku rose from its seat and came lurching towards the duardin. There was no doubting the mechanical nature of the thing now. Every jerky motion of its limbs was accompanied by a buzzing whirr and the sour smell of leaking lubricants. Its hands were curled into claws as it stumbled towards Brokrin, but the face of Piu still wore the same expression of contemplative serenity.

'Right! That is far enough!' Drumark cried out, levelling his decksweeper at the automaton. When the Piu-thing continued its mindless approach, he emptied every barrel into it. The shot ripped through the thing's shell of flesh and cloth. In crafting his 'tulku' Kilvolt had stitched the flayed skin of Piu over a metal armature. The armature was now exposed by Drumark's blast as well as the nest of hoses and wires that swirled through its body.

Despite the damage inflicted on it, the automaton staggered onwards. Drumark glared at it in silent fury, as though it were a personal affront that it remained on its feet. While the sergeant fumed, Brokrin took command. 'Thunderers!' he called out. 'Aim for its spine! Concentrate your shots there!'

The thunderers obeyed Brokrin's order, fixing their aim at the core of the Piu-thing. Shots echoed through the shrine as round after round struck the automaton. Under the vicious barrage, the thing was cut in half, its torso severed and sent crashing to the floor. The legs stumbled on for several steps before slopping over onto their side and kicking futilely at the floor.

'And stay down!' Drumark bellowed, spitting on the fallen automaton.

Gotramm seized hold of the sergeant's arm. 'We have to get back to the ship! There are more of them in the hold with those tapestries!'

'Already sorted out,' Drumark declared. 'By now Horgarr should be done tossing their carcasses overboard. I figured you might be having trouble over here so me and the lads grabbed one of the lamas and found out where you were.'

Brokrin felt a surge of relief sweep through him. The *Iron Dragon* was safe. At least for now. He turned his eyes to the dragon tapestry and the tunnel Kilvolt had escaped into. Even now the skaven were probably regrouping to make another attack.

'Everybody back to the ship,' Brokrin said. 'The sooner we are away from here the better.' He gave Skaggi an almost sympathetic look. 'When we get back we will have to dump the tapestries over the side as well. We can't take the chance the skaven put some kind of poison or pestilence on them.'

Skaggi clenched his fist and rushed to the wall. With a savage tug he brought one of the hangings crashing down to the floor. 'If we have to throw out the others then we had better grab some replacements on our way out!' Catching his intention, Gotramm and some of the thunderers helped Skaggi pull down the other tapestries. The hangings were quickly gathered up and slung across the shoulders of the duardin.

'What about the rat poison, cap'n?' Drumark asked as they hurried through halls that were empty of either lamas or skaven.

'We cannot trust that either,' Brokrin told him. 'We must do without it.' He gave the sergeant a grim smile. 'I hope you remember where you put your spade.'

Drumark sighed and shook his head. 'I remember, but overall I would rather stay here and shoot skaven than play whack-a-rat with a shovel.'

A DIRGE OF
DUST AND STEEL

Josh Reynolds

Eerie shrieks pierced the gloom.

They reverberated through the broken field of toppled pillars and dust-shrouded statuary, riding the night wind. To Sathphren Swiftblade's ears, there was both damnable pleasure and promise in those cries. The Lord-Aquilor repressed a shudder and bent forwards in his saddle. 'Faster, Gwyllth,' he murmured into his mount's ear. 'We're almost there.'

The long-limbed, avian-headed gryph-charger squalled in reply, and increased her speed, despite the weight of the fully armoured Stormcast Eternal she carried on her broad back. Sathphren glanced back, checking on his warriors. Half a dozen armoured Vanguard-Palladors rode hard to either side of him. Like the Lord-Aquilor, they wore the silver-and-azure war-plate of the Hallowed Knights Stormhost, and rode atop lean, leonine gryph-chargers. The beasts were galloping flat out, the magic that flowed through their muscular frames enabling them to easily outpace their pursuers.

As one, they bounded over the fallen statue of some long-forgotten warden king. The square, bearded face glared sightlessly at the silver-armoured riders and their steeds as they raced on across the broken ground. The duardin had once ruled this unforgiving ground. Before the coming of Chaos, the Oasis of Gazul had provided shelter for traders and pilgrims alike. Now, it was a daemon-haunted ruin, shrouded in shadows and dust.

Out of the corner of his eye, Sathphren caught a glimpse of a pack of lithe, inhuman shapes as they raced along parallel to the Hallowed Knights. The creatures, at once serpentine and avian, leapt and scrambled over fallen pillars and broken walls, moving with a speed that defied comprehension. They were urged on by their cackling riders – slim, hideously sensual daemonettes, the Handmaidens of Slaanesh.

The daemonettes resembled women, with thick manes of snaky locks and pitiless, androgynous faces. Chitinous claws snapped wildly at the air, as the creatures gesticulated obscenely. The Hounds of Pleasure were on the hunt, and Sathphren and his warriors were their quarry. 'Looks like they've caught up with us at last, eh, Feysha?' Sathphren called out.

'Took them long enough,' Feysha, his second in command, replied. The Pallador-Prime peered back over her shoulder. 'Though I've not seen such a pack of beasts since the Bitterbark. Every daemon in this desert must be on our tail.'

'Good. The more of them the better.' Sathphren glanced back, following her gaze. Behind them, daemons raced across the dust dunes with quicksilver grace. Brutal beastkin loped in their wake, braying to the Wraith Moon above. There were mortals among them as well – strange figures those, clad in everything from silks to furs, bearing weapons and musical instruments in their tattooed hands. Some rode atop daemonic steeds, while others capered through the dust. Golden stand-ards, decorated with looted tapestries, mirrors and flayed hides, bobbed above the monstrous cavalcade.

It was not an army. A horde, at best. A moveable feast of fren-zied indulgence. A celebration of blood and pain. And at its head, crouched atop a massive chariot, made from bone and gold and pulled by a darting, hissing herd of daemon-steeds, was the host – the creature known as Amin'Hrith, the Soulflayer.

The Keeper of Secrets was a monster among monsters. It tow-ered over the tallest of its followers, even squatting as it did on its nightmarish conveyance. Its elongated torso bore a quar-tet of long, milk-pale arms. One of these ended in a vicious, snapping claw, while the hands of the others rested upon the bejewelled hilts of the various blades sheathed about its per-son, beneath the cloak of skins it wore. Its head was that of a bull, with great, curving horns capped with gold, and a ring of silver in its wide, flat nose. A mane of thick spines draped across the back of its neck, and its pale form was covered in the marks of ritual scarification, as well as various gemstones clinging to its chest like barnacles.

Sathphren's gaze was drawn to the largest of these – a massive ruby, set between the daemon's uppermost pectorals. Some-thing flashed within the facets of the gem, and he turned away, frowning. 'Into the oasis – go!'

Lone pillars and broken statues gave way to more substan-tial ruins – stone watercourses and shattered aqueducts cast elongated shadows in the moonlight. And beyond them, the high, narrow summit of Gazul-Baraz. The ruins spread out around the immense tower of limestone, spilling forth from the caverns beneath it, following the ancient watercourses. There were greater ruins by far within those caverns, stretch-ing into the deep darkness. This was but the uppermost level of that vast fiefdom. One the Soulflayer had destroyed, and now claimed as its own.

'Swiftblade – beware!'

Feysha's shout was all the warning he needed. He ducked low, folding himself over Gwyllth's neck. A crustacean-like claw snapped closed where his head had been, as a daemon-steed drove itself into Gwyllth's side. The gryph-charger stumbled and spun, shrieking in rage. Sathphren hauled back on the reins, and snatched his boltstorm pistol from its holster. He levelled the weapon at the daemonette rider and loosed a bolt. The bolt struck it in the eye and sent it tumbling from the saddle. Its serpentine steed staggered, off balance, and Gwyllth smashed it from its feet, tearing open its elongated neck.

More daemons closed in, moving quickly. Sathphren holstered his pistol and unsheathed his starbound blade. The blade gleamed like a distant star as he parried a darting claw, and removed a daemonette's head. It spun away, trailing gory locks.

The rest swirled about him, cackling and shrieking, and he dealt with them swiftly. Even in death, they laughed, as if pain and pleasure were both but a singular sensation. The stink of strange incense rose from their glistening flesh. Black eyes, empty of all save malice, bored into him and their smiles were at once alluring and repulsive. Their claws gouged his silver war-plate, but failed to penetrate. 'Who will ride more swiftly than the storm-winds?' he roared, laying about him.

'Only the faithful,' came the response, as the boltstorm pistols of the others cracked and starstrike javelins hissed, further distracting his pursuers. A moment later, Feysha's lunar blade joined his own, as her gryph-charger bore a squealing daemon-steed to the ground. The surviving daemonettes retreated in disorder, a frustrated tenor to their shrieks. Sathphren hauled Gwyllth around and thumped her ribs. The gryph-charger leapt back into motion, speeding to join the others, followed closely by Feysha. 'Keep moving,' Sathphren bellowed. 'Our allies are waiting.'

They led their pursuers down a slope into a narrow defile, between twinned limestone crags that acted as a gateway into the cavern-city beyond. The crags had felt the touch of hammer and chisel at some point in antiquity, and alcoves had been carved into their inner slopes. Immense statues occupied these alcoves – ancient duardin kings and heroes, Sathphren thought. Their countenances were uniformly, grimly stoic, as if humour were somehow taboo among their folk.

Having met them, Sathphren could well believe it. The Gazul-Zagaz were a sombre folk, as befitted those who worshipped death. Their ancestors had taken the name of their fallen god for their own, in the dim, ancient epoch when Nagash, the Undying King, had warred with the old gods of death and emerged supreme.

Theirs was a society built on a legendary defeat, and the bones of those it had claimed. Where they had once ruled, they now merely persisted... huddled in the ruins of former glory, waiting out the days. Hunted by creatures like those even now pursuing him and his warriors. The servants of the Soulflayer had made these ruins their playground. But not for long. Not if Sathphren's gambit was successful.

It was a simple enough plan. Bait the foe in and chew them apart, piecemeal. With the aid of Sathphren and his warriors, the Gazul-Zagaz might rule the Sea of Dust once more. And in return, they would help the Swiftblades complete their mission. 'So far, so good,' he muttered, as they passed through the shattered gateways and into the cavern-city beyond.

It had been hacked from the stalactites and stalagmites of the vast caverns, built into the very bedrock. Despite the situation, he could not help but marvel at the extent of that ancient undertaking. Crumbled structures and ruptured aqueducts rose over sloped avenues. Moonlight shone through great wells carved in the uppermost reaches of the cavern. The silvery radiance was reflected in the sluggish waters that still slithered through the broken aqueducts, and poured down into the ruins in haphazard waterfalls.

'Look,' Feysha called out. She pointed. Sathphren laughed.

'It appears our new-found allies are as good as their word.'

A line of duardin waited for them, their stocky, armoured forms set in a rough battle line. They were clad in coats and cowls of burnished gromril. Each wore a steel war-mask wrought in the shape of a stylised skull, and carried a heavy, baroque hand cannon. Dust sifted off the broad forms of the duardin Irondrakes as they raised their weapons. '*Uzkul-ha!*' they roared, as one.

The ancient drakeguns belched fire as the Vanguard-Palladors leapt over their wielders. The volley cut through the front rank of daemons and mortals like a scythe of fire. Mortals fell screaming from their abominable mounts, and daemons were ripped to shimmering rags. In the ensuing confusion, the duardin fell back into the ruins, reloading their weapons with a speed born of precision and experience, clearing the path.

Monstrous chariots rattled on in pursuit, over the broken bodies of the fallen. These were bombarded from on high, by hurled chunks of stone. Many slewed wildly, crashing into one another or flipping and rolling. Daemon-steeds screamed as they were pulled to the ground or crushed beneath the tumbling chariots. Even the Soulflayer's massive carriage was brought to a halt, as a chunk of stone shattered one of its wheels, and killed several of the beasts pulling it. The Keeper of Secrets leapt from the wreck with a bellow of frustration.

'Remind them that we're here, brothers and sisters,' Sathphren shouted. As one, the Hallowed Knights emptied their boltstorm pistols into the stalled horde. The Lord-Aquilor took aim at the Soulflayer, and sent a shot smashing into its chest. The daemon whipped around, eyes narrowing. Sathphren gave a mocking wave and glanced at Feysha. 'Think that'll do it? I'd hate to think the beast is getting bored of us.'

The daemon flung out a claw and bellowed. Its followers surged past it, clambering over the wreckage in their eagerness to catch their prey. Feysha jerked on the reins of her gryph-charger and turned the beast about. 'I think so, my lord,' she said. Sathphren laughed and jolted Gwyllth into motion.

Drakeguns spat death from the ruins, as the Irondrakes fired again. Followed by the echoes of that volley, the Vanguard-Palladors split up. Several turned back, arrowing through the ruins. They would harass the flanks, and bleed the enemy, striking and fading as only they could. It was what they had been forged for. The rest continued on, racing down what had once been a grand avenue, pursued by the main body of the enemy.

Sathphren looked ahead. At the end of the avenue, between two crumbled structures, a shield wall of duardin warriors waited. '*Gazul-akit-ha!*' The words echoed through the cavern, accompanied by the crash of weapons against shields. '*Uzkul! Uzkul! Uzkul!*' The wall of duardin shields parted, allowing the Stormcast Eternals to pass through.

Mourning bells, mounted on iron standard poles, tolled grimly as the duardin beat on their shields. Warriors wearing white vestments over their armour and golden war-masks, lifted stone tablets marked with crudely carved runes. As they paced up and down behind the battle line, they began to sing an eerie dirge. The sound rolled across the line, and sent a chill down Sathphren's spine.

'That doesn't sound like any duardin battle-song I've ever heard,' Feysha said. The Vanguard-Palladors slewed to a halt behind the shield wall, their gryph-chargers yowling in protest. The beasts hated standing still, almost as much as their riders.

'They're mourning the dead yet to be,' Sathphren said. 'Singing their souls to the caverns of their god.'

'Their god is dead.'

'I don't think they care.' He gestured to the duardin. 'Can you support them until Thalkun gets his Vanguard-Raptors into position?'

Cadres of Stormcast marksmen were even now scaling the broken heights of the oasis-city, seeking the best vantage points to deliver their lethal volleys. They would further bleed the foe, dispersing their strength. The enemy was caught fast in the jaws of the trap now, though they didn't yet realise it.

Feysha nodded. 'Aye, if we must. I still think one of us should go with you, at least.'

'One soul more or less won't make a difference.' He gestured. 'Remember, don't fight too hard. Let the beast through. If we're to win this, it must reach the oasis.' The shield wall was only there to blunt the initial rush of the foe. Once they'd bloodied them, the duardin would retreat, as the Irondrakes had, and regroup in the ruins.

'You can count on us,' Feysha said. 'It's the duardin I'm worried about. They look set on dying here.' The dirge swelled up, rolling through the ruins. The song of a dying folk, as they made what might be their last stand. Sathphren frowned and shook his head.

'They know what's at stake, as well as you.' The Gazul-Zagaz had set the price for their aid, though it meant duardin blood would be shed, as well as that of his warriors. For centuries, they had suffered the depredations of the Soulflayer. Now, at last, they had a chance to free themselves. Whatever the cost.

Feysha met his gaze solemnly. 'Much is demanded...' she said.

'Of those to whom much is given,' he replied, completing the canticle. They clasped forearms. 'Fight well, sister. And don't let them catch you standing still.'

'Never,' Feysha said, cheerfully. 'Hup!' She thumped her steed, and the gryph-charger leapt into motion. Sathphren watched her. She would circle through the ruins in order to flank the horde flooding down the avenue. Several of the remaining Vanguard-Palladors followed her, while the rest readied their javelins and drew their boltstorm pistols.

Sathphren twitched the reins and urged Gwyllth deeper into the ruins, seeking their heart. The beast growled low, unhappy at being denied the chance to savage the enemy. 'Soon enough, old girl,' he said, stroking the bright green plumage on her neck. 'Now let's go bait ourselves a trap, eh?'

Traps within traps. That was how the Swiftblades waged war. Sathphren had learned the art of the oblique approach in those harsh, bloody days before he had been called to Sigmar's side. Those lessons had stayed with him, even as he had been reforged, body and soul, on the Anvil of Apotheosis.

And if there was one place where such an approach was needed, it was Shyish. The Sea of Dust was a harsh land of broken mountains and dust storms that could strip flesh from bone, as easily as gilt from sigmarite. It had its secret roads and hidden paths, and the Swiftblades had sniffed them out, one by one. This was not merely aimless wandering on their part, but a quest given to them by the God-King himself.

The Swiftblades had been sent to Shyish to find the ruins of Caddow, the City of Crows. And in that broken city was the

Corvine Gate – an ancient Realmgate linking Shyish with Azyr. Only a scant few such transdimensional apertures remained, in the wake of the War of Death and Heaven. Sigmar had commanded that it be rediscovered and reopened. Sathphren did not know why they sought it, or what might await them there. Nor, in truth, did he care. That the quarry was named was enough. He would find it, or perish in the attempt, and explain his failure to the God-King in person.

But first, he had a daemon to slay. And a bargain to make good on.

He smiled. It was the Soulflayer he'd set this trap for, and it had proved very obliging, thus far. The creature had been easy to provoke – one whiff of fresh prey, and it had been on their trail. Then, in his experience, daemons were many things, but rarely shrewd. They had teased it for days, leading it into the ruins. Now, it was time for the trap to snap shut. A thrill of premature satisfaction surged through him. He forced it down. The hunt wasn't done yet.

Gwyllth loped through the ruins, carrying him down long, aqueduct-lined avenues towards the central plaza, where the waters of the oasis still ran fresh and clean within the great temple of Gazul. The remains of that edifice rose up around the softly bubbling spring like a forest of stone. It was a massive rotunda of pillars and glowering statues – as with everywhere in the city, the faces of the dead had been captured forever in stone.

Sathphren could hear the soft susurrus of the water as it swirled about its stony prison, deep within the forest of pillars. It filled the watercourses, which stretched from the base of the temple and connected to the closest aqueducts. He hauled back on the reins, bringing Gwyllth to a stop before the vast, flat steps leading up into the temple. A group of duardin awaited him. They wore soot-blackened robes and armour, and their beards and hair were covered in ashes. Some carried weapons, but most had their hands free. They were rune-singers – the last members of an ancient priesthood. Once, they had guided their kin through life. Now, they warded their souls in death.

One of them stepped forwards. 'You have returned.' The War-Mourner of the Gazul-Zagaz was clad in black, and his armour was bronze. Several heavy tomes were chained to him, the cover of each marked with the Khazalid rune of death. He bore an iron staff, surmounted by a dirge-bell and a heavy hammer. Unlike his companions, he wore no mask, though his face had been painted with ash and soot to resemble a skull.

'As I promised, Elder Judd,' Sathphren said as he slid from Gwyllth's back. Heart pounding, he could hear the whistle-crack echo of the hurricane crossbows wielded by the Vanguard-Raptors. Thalkun and his warriors were unleashing a blistering fusillade against the pleasure-maddened warriors flooding into the ruins. But even that wouldn't hold the Soulflayer back for long. Nor did he wish it to. 'Is our trap ready?'

'It waits, manling.' Judd frowned. 'Are you certain the Soul-flayer will come?'

A roar of frustration echoed across the ruins. Sathphren smiled. 'Fairly certain.' He clapped Gwyllth on the haunch. 'Go. You know what to do.' The gryph-charger screeched and turned, scraping its beak against his war-mask. He caught hold of its feathered skull. 'Go, sister. And wait for my call.'

The great beast squalled and loped swiftly into the forest of pillars, tail lashing. Sathphren drew his starbound blade and laid it across his shoulder. The avenue trembled beneath his feet. He turned, keen gaze sweeping across the ruins. He felt no fear. Only the anticipation of a hunter who closes fast on his moment to make a kill. 'Take your kin, and get out of sight, rune-singer. Best we not distract our prey.'

Judd hesitated. The duardin was old, even by the standards of his people. So old that he might have witnessed his kind's fall in person. His hair and beard were the colour of ash mixed with snow, and his weather-beaten flesh resembled worn leather. But his voice was strong, as were his shoulders. 'Are you certain you wish to do this, manling? It may well mean your death.'

'Then we are in the right realm for it, no?' Sathphren looked down at him. 'I swore an oath. And I will hold to it, with every breath in my body.'

Judd nodded. 'Aye, you did at that. And so did we. If we are victorious, we will guide you to the ruins of the City of Crows. And we will aid you in opening the way for your kin, as best we can.' He patted the hammer that rested in the crook of his arm. 'And if we fail – we will add your name to the Great Dirge.' He smiled mirthlessly. 'It is the least we can do.'

Sathphren laughed. 'Don't start singing yet. There's never been a foe to catch me, if I didn't wish to be caught.' He jerked his head. 'Go. It's close. As soon as I lead it into the temple…'

'We know what to do, manling. And so do they.' Judd glanced meaningfully at the statues that glared down at them. Sathphren grunted, trying to ignore the chill that swept through him. In Shyish, the dead did not rest easy, whatever their race.

'Let us hope so. I have no wish to fight the dead, as well as a daemon.'

Judd gave him a gap-toothed grin. 'Have no fear on that score. They know their enemy.' He turned and barked an order in his own tongue. Swiftly, the rune-singers disappeared into the ruins. The duardin of Gazul-Baraz had learned well the art of vanishing from sight. So skilled were they that even Sathphren's warriors had been impressed.

'We have much to learn from each other,' he murmured. 'Perhaps after this is over.' An old refrain, but a comforting one. It implied an end to strife. Something he had not truly believed possible in his mortal life. But now, he had hope. That, in the end, was perhaps the greatest gift that Sigmar had bestowed upon him.

He sank to one knee and planted his sword point first into the stones before him. Somewhere in the cavern, he heard the tolling of dirge-bells. He could see the battle lines breaking in his mind's eye. The duardin would retreat, and the foe would splinter, greedy for victory. Softly, he began to pray. As a mortal, his faith had not extended itself to prayers. Here, now, it was another weapon in his arsenal. Each canticle was a wall, a gate, a tower – defending him from what was to come.

He was still praying when the first of the daemons burst into view. Smoothly, without missing a beat, he rose, starbound blade hissing out. A daemonette fell, its unnatural skull cleft in two. Another leapt on him, claws clacking. He swept it off him, and sent it crashing into a pillar. Before it could rise, he pinned it to the pillar with his blade. He twisted the sword, silencing its shrieks.

Two more came at him and met their end. More of them loped down the avenue – some bore wounds, their limbs stained with black ichor. Over their sibilant cries, he could hear the crash of steel and the shouts of his warriors, echoing through the cavern. They had fallen back, as he ordered, opening the way for his prey. He smiled and lunged to meet the daemonettes.

Before he could reach them, a sudden jangle of bells caused them to stop short. With disconsolate hisses, the creatures retreated. They flowed back up the avenue, around a massive form that strode into view. 'You have teeth, then. Good.'

The Soulflayer.

The daemon's voice was like syrup over coals. 'It is always better, when the prey has teeth. A bit of fight makes the triumph all the sweeter.' It flung back the edge of a cloak of mortal flesh and hair, heavy with plundered duardin gold, and clashed its bronze bracers, setting the dozens of bells that hung from them ringing. 'You've led me a pretty chase, little glow-bug. I've followed your scent for days. The stink of your soul teases me in exquisite ways. It is like lightning on the tongue.'

'You haven't caught me yet,' Sathphren said. His hand dropped to his boltstorm pistol. 'But here I am. Come and get me.' He studied the gems that marked the daemon's flesh. Each one flickered with an inner light, some of them brighter than the rest. Thanks to Elder Judd, he knew that the gemstones held the souls of those slain by the daemon. It was called the Soulflayer for good reason.

The Keeper of Secrets bared lupine teeth in a hideous parody of a smile. 'I will. But in my own time. The hunt is ever more pleasing than the kill.' It spread its uppermost arms. 'Why else would I leave the stunted inhabitants of this wasteland with their souls intact?'

'Not all of them,' Sathphren said. The stink of the daemon flooded his nostrils. It was a cloying fug, like perfume over rot. He shook his head to clear it.

The daemon's head twitched, like a bull shaking away flies. 'Ah. Does word of my magnificence reach so far, then?' A bifurcated tongue slid across the thicket of fangs. 'I am flattered.' A claw-tip caressed the ruby. In its facets, something that might have been a face, contorted in agony, formed briefly before dissipating. 'Yes. I took their prince. The last prince of Gazul-Baraz. He is precious to me. I keep him with me always and will until the day I grow bored of these arid lands, and the scuttling prey that inhabits it.'

Sathphren laughed. 'That's not the story I heard.'

'Oh?'

'I heard that you remained here out of fear.' Sathphren forced a laugh. 'Shyish has claimed so many of your kind. They say that Amin'Hrith hides in the wastes, hoping the war will pass him by. That the Soulflayer is nothing more than a scavenger, picking the bones left behind by more faithful celebrants.'

The daemon snarled. It thrust its chitinous claw at Sathphren. 'Choose your words with care, little glow-bug. You are alone.'

'I'm done with words.' Sathphren snatched his boltstorm pistol free of its holster and loosed a shot. One of the gemstones on the daemon's abdomen burst as the bolt struck home. Amin'Hrith shrilled in rage as a soft will-o'-the-wisp of soul-light fluttered upwards, through the daemon's grasping hands.

'Thief!' The daemon capered, trying to catch the light as it swam upwards and away towards the roof of the cavern above. Sathphren fired again and again, backing away with each shot. Gems burst like blisters, releasing soft puffs of radiance – souls, long denied their rest by the daemon's greed. With every shattered bauble, the daemon grew more enraged. It loped after him.

'I will tear your soul to pieces, to replace that which you have taken,' it screamed. It drew the blades that hung from its war-harness as it ran, and slashed apart a nearby pillar in a fit of petulance. Sathphren raced up the steps and into the temple through the slabbed archway that marked the entrance.

The rotunda was full of pillars, each carved with thousands of runes – names, he knew. Or so the Gazul-Zagaz had claimed. The names of the dead, going back to the founding of the city. At the heart of the rotunda was the vast pool from which all the water in the city was drawn. It bubbled and flowed, as fresh as the day the first duardin had discovered it. A colossal statue of Gazul sat atop a dais of dark stone, overlooking the waters. The god's statue was draped in a burial shroud of shadows and dust, his features obscured.

Sathphren lost himself among the pillars, moving as quietly as possible. He could hear the clop of the daemon's hooves on the stone floor. 'I can taste your fear and your desire on the wind,' it growled. Its voice was thick with silky menace and promise, all in one. It echoed through the pillars. 'I will add your soul to my collection, little glow-bug. You will dangle 'pon my chest, and your screams will soothe me to sleep, ere I grow tired of my games.'

Sathphren didn't answer. He heard a voice chanting – Elder Judd. The rune-singers were gathering outside the temple now. They had waited centuries for this day. The jaws of the trap were clashing shut. He heard the scrape of chitin on stone, and tensed. It was close.

'Why do you not answer me, little glow-bug? I thought your kind liked to talk. So boastful, you storm-riders. You wield declarations like swords.' It chuckled again, and he could almost see the ghastly smile on its twisted features. 'Do you tremble at the thought of my gentle touch, glow-bug? As well you should.'

A fug of perfumed musk suddenly enveloped Sathphren. He spun. A chitinous claw thrust itself towards him. He leapt aside. The claw gouged a pillar in half, casting rubble across the floor. The Keeper of Secrets lunged into view, hauling itself around another pillar. Its eyes blazed with a monstrous greed. 'Oh, I have such sights to show you,' it snarled. 'Nightmares and ecstasies beyond any you can conceive. I will flay your soul from the meat. I will make adornments from your bones, and wear your screaming skull into the eternities yet to come.'

Sathphren lunged, his starbound blade licking out across the daemon's taunting muzzle. Amin'Hrith jerked back with a shriek of pain. Sathphren twisted aside, narrowly avoiding a wild slash from the daemon's blade. He whistled sharply, and Gwyllth leapt down from the top of the pillars, where she had been waiting. The gryph-charger's weight caught the daemon by surprise, and knocked it stumbling. The great beast clung to the daemon's broad back, tail lashing. Her beak stabbed down into the alabaster flesh, releasing a spurt of sickly-sweet ichor.

Amin'Hrith shrieked, clawing at its attacker. Sathphren ducked beneath a flailing claw and drove his sword into the daemon's elongated torso, twisting it upwards with all his strength. It gave a tooth-rattling shriek and dropped a heavy fist onto him, driving him to one knee. A second blow caught him on the chest, and sent him skidding backwards. The daemon tore the screeching gryph-charger from her perch and hurled her into a pillar. She crumpled to the ground with a muted whine.

Sathphren rolled onto his stomach. Pain beat at his temples, and his chest felt as if it had been caved in. He coughed, and tasted blood. The chanting was louder now, beating at the air like hammer strokes. The air felt heavy with something – anticipation, he thought. He glanced towards the statue of Gazul, and it seemed as if the god's eyes were gleaming.

It was time. The trap snapped shut.

Amin'Hrith touched the ragged wounds opened in its flesh with something akin to wonder. 'How exquisite. It has been centuries since my flesh was ravaged so.' It fixed Sathphren with its yellow gaze. 'I thank you, glow-bug. Let me show you my gratitude properly.'

'Let me show you mine, first,' Sathphren wheezed, hauling himself upright. He rose to one knee, spots swimming across his vision. 'For the gift.'

'Gift?' The daemon hesitated, head tilted.

Sathphren held up the ruby. He'd managed to chop it loose, just before the daemon had swatted him aside. It pulsed with an unsettling warmth, as if there were a fire within its crimson facets. Amin'Hrith looked down at its chest, and then back at him. It took a heavy step towards him, claw extended. 'Give it back, glow-bug. Or I will ensure your torments are legendary, even by the heady standards of the Pavilions of Pleasure.'

'A kind offer, but not one I care to take.' Sathphren slammed the flickering gemstone down on the stone floor, shattering it. Outside the temple, the song of the rune-singers rose to a rolling crescendo, shaking the very stones underfoot. They fell silent as the echoes of the ruby's demise faded.

In the quiet that followed, Amin'Hrith laughed, and Sathphren felt his sense of triumph ebb. 'And what was that supposed to achieve?' the daemon sneered. 'What did you think would happen, glow-bug? I am no mere courtesan, to be banished at the whim of a mortal. I am Amin'Hrith, the Soulflayer. I have wallowed in the dust of a thousand worlds, and seen reality itself shatter beneath the awful weight of my lord's gentle gaze. I have worn ghosts as baubles and hunted entire peoples to extinction, in the World-That-Was. And I will do the same here. I–'

The shards of ruby shone suddenly with a soft light, interrupting the daemon. Blood-red shadows crawled across the pillars and floor. Curls of cerise smoke rose from the fragments, twisting and coalescing with one another, until they became a vaguely duardin-shaped mass. Something that might have been a face turned towards the daemon, and twisted into a wrathful expression. A wordless cry boomed out of the stones and air, and the daemon stepped back. 'What is this? You could not challenge me while you lived, little prince. What makes you think you can do so now?'

The smoky shape took a step forwards, its hunched form sprouting an amorphous shield and something resembling an axe. The temple seemed to shake with its tread. Sathphren caught sight of ghostly shapes drifting through the pillars – the dead, come to answer their long-lost prince's call. 'He isn't alone,' Sathphren said.

While the daemon held the soul of their prince captive, the Gazul-Zagaz had been unable to act against it. Now, with the ruby shattered, and the soul free, the dead of Gazul-Baraz, raised up by the song of the rune-singers, could have their long-delayed vengeance. Sathphren smiled. A good plan. A fitting plan.

A grim dirge rose from the spectres as they gathered, encircling the daemon in a ring of insubstantial bodies. Sathphren could hear the faint crash of steel, and the crack of stone. Motes of pale light floated within ghostly skulls – the eyes of the dead, fixed on the author of their torment. *Uzkul*, they moaned, as one. *Uzkul. Uzkul. Uzkul.*

The Keeper of Secrets turned, trying to keep all of the gathering spirits in sight. 'Begone, shades. There is no joy to be had from your pallid essences.' It swept out a claw dismissively, trying to disperse the horde. The dead struck, as the claw passed through them. Ghostly axes and hammers caught the limb, and ichor spurted. Amin'Hrith screamed in rage and pain. The daemon jerked its injured limb back. 'No. No, this isn't right.' It whirled, eyes fixed on Sathphren. 'What have you done?'

'What I do best,' Sathphren said, as he rose to his feet. Gwyllth was on her feet as well, if somewhat battered. He caught hold of her and hauled himself into the saddle. 'And now, I leave you to it.' He thumped the gryph-charger in the ribs, and she leapt away with a shriek, even as the daemon lunged for them.

Amin'Hrith crashed awkwardly into a pillar as they avoided its grasp, and screamed in fury. It clattered after them, smashing rubble aside in its haste, and the ghosts boiled up around it like storm clouds. A typhoon of spirits – led by the crimson essence of the prince – surrounded the blundering daemon, striking at it from all sides and angles. They blinded it, slowed it. Trapped it.

And there was another presence there as well, something greater than any ghost, and mightier than any daemon. It seemed to gather itself in the limits of the temple, readying itself as Sathphren urged Gwyllth towards the entrance. The shadows thickened and the voices of the dead were echoed by a deep tolling, rising up from somewhere below. Not a bell, this, but a wordless cry, like the crash of stone into the sea.

It roared out as the gryph-charger leapt through the archway and down the steps. Sathphren turned his steed about, sword in hand, to face the archway. The Keeper of Secrets clawed at the entrance, hands gripping either side of the aperture. It strained, as if against unseen bonds. Its mouth was open, but Sathphren could hear nothing save that roaring cry.

A wind rose up from somewhere and caught at the creature, forcing it back. Beneath the roar came a grinding sound, like stone rasping against stone. One by one, the remaining gemstones on the daemon's flesh burst. Ghostly hands clutched at the Soulflayer's limbs and head. The daemon's eyes bulged as it fought against the dead.

'*Uzkul. Uzkul. Uzkul.*'

Sathphren glanced around. Judd and the other rune-singers chanted as they approached, their bells tolling sombrely. With every peal of the bells, the daemon's grip on the aperture seemed to grow weaker, its claws digging deep trenches in the stone. Then, with a final thunderclap, a dark shape, massive and indistinct, caught hold of the Soulflayer and jerked it backwards, into the dark of the temple and out of sight.

It did not even have a chance to scream.

The rune-singers ceased their song. The sound of the bells faded. All was silence, save for the burble of water. Judd thumped the ground with the ferrule of his staff. Slowly, the spirits of the dead emerged from the darkness. Their prince stood among them, his form as indistinct as before, recognisable only by the raw, red radiance.

Judd lifted his staff, and murmured. The spirits of the dead duardin wavered like smoke and dispersed, in shreds and tangles. They drifted upwards, towards the roof of the cavern and the moonlight streaming through. Something like thunder rumbled in the depths, and Sathphren felt its reverberations in his bones. He thought it might be laughter.

Judd smiled sadly. 'Gazul is pleased. Our oath is fulfilled at last.'

Sathphren looked at him. 'They say Nagash devoured the other gods of the dead, and added their might to his own.'

'Yes, that is what they say.' Judd shrugged. 'And yet, what is death to a god?' He scooped up a handful of dust, and let the wind pull it from his hand. 'Dust, and less than dust.' He sighed and looked at Sathphren. 'But that is a matter for another day. For now, we will fulfil our oath to you. We will lead you where you wish to go.'

Sathphren nodded solemnly. 'I expected no less.' He laughed suddenly and turned Gwyllth about, towards the sounds of fighting. 'But first – our task is not yet done. There are still daemons to hunt, and an oasis to free. As I promised.'

ONE, UNTENDED

David Guymer

Master,

The artefact is within my grasp, but there have been complications and I am unable to report to you as requested. I can only hope that this note will be recovered by another of your agents and returned to you in my stead. I am still within the bounds of the Twin-Tailed City and appear likely to remain so for some time. I just need more time.

I will not fail you.

Still and eternally the faithful servant of Azyr,

Maleneth Witchblade

'Get back, aelfling,' Gotrek scowled. 'This is not something that your pretty little eyes need to see.'

Maleneth rolled her 'pretty little' eyes as Gotrek bent over the open sewer that ran along the back yard of the Missed Striking, one hand on the ivy-scrawled corner of a brick wall. She watched with a casual anatomist's fascination as the immense muscle groups that corded his back rippled and flexed. The duardin turned to look over the single plate of black armour fixed across his left shoulder.

His one good eye was virulently bloodshot, his preternaturally aged skin slacker and more haggard even than usual. His huge blade of gold-struck orange hair drooped over the armour's leonine features, sodden with stale beer where he had slept with his head against a trestle table. 'I told you–' His throat suddenly clenched. His face blanched. Red light from the street lamps slithered across it. 'Grungni's beard.'

Then he was violently, messily sick into the sewer.

Maleneth patted the thickly creased skin at the back of his head.

'There, there.'

'I hate you, aelfling,' Gotrek said between ructions. 'I hate you and all your darkling kin.'

'I know.'

After a few minutes the duardin's heaves subsided, and he spat the last chunks of a green sausage and ghyrvole egg supper into the ditch.

'This has never happened to me before.'

'I am sure that you say that to all of the girls.'

Gotrek glared at her.

'A joke,' she said.

'I think there was something nasty in my beer,' Gotrek complained.

Maleneth nodded sympathetically. There had indeed been something nasty in the Slayer's beer. Several somethings. Duardin were notoriously resistant to poisoning, but the amount of gravelock, heartcease and scarlet clover that Gotrek Gurnisson had obligingly consumed over the last day and a half would have killed a gargant. He should have been curled up on the weed-filled yard bleeding out of every orifice rather than complaining of an upset stomach.

Maleneth looked up at the night sky, trying to judge the time. The moons were swathed in autumnal colours. Even the realm's cohort of satellites responded to the life song of the Everqueen, and on a clear night Maleneth could see foliage stirring in another world's winds. This was not such a night. Scraps of dark cloud raced across their faces. A thin mist shrouded the creaking wooden tenement runs and lean-tos of the Stranglevines, and even Maleneth's inhumanly chill breath fogged the air in front of her face. It was past midnight.

She sighed as the Slayer began to dry retch over the ditch. He should have been dead three times over already. But even in his current condition she was not sure that she wanted to risk hurrying things along. She had fought the duardin twice before, and on both occasions had barely escaped with her life. And that had been before he had acquired the fyreslayers' master rune, multiplying his already formidable strength severalfold. The rune smouldered quiescently from the scarred, fire-ruined meat of his chest. Occasionally, when the Slayer had drunk enough to pass out and sleep, it also whispered, though not in any language that Maleneth had ever heard. No. She belonged to a fantastically long-lived race. Barring a knife in the back she could afford a little patience.

'Come on, Gotrek,' she said. 'I think you left a beer untended in there.'

'Give me a moment here, damn you.'

Before she could try to cajole the duardin any further, the tavern's back door opened. Another posse of drunks stumbled through the rectangle of wobbly warmth and light and into the moonlit yard. They appeared to be armed, in some distress and without exception, drunk. Not an agreeable combination in Maleneth's experience, even in the most salubrious of establishments. And even in the Stranglevines of Hammerhal Ghyra, establishments did not come more insalubrious than the Missed Striking. Gotrek had found his way through its doors the way a blind woman found her own bed.

Eager to avoid any trouble with the local ruffians, Maleneth nodded across the yard to them, as though standing over a retching duardin in the dead of night was the most natural activity in Ghyran. To her relief they ignored her utterly, too intent on their own whispered arguments to mark even Gotrek's outlandish appearance.

A young woman in a nightdress and a thin shawl ran barefoot into the yard after the gang of armed drunks. Tears streamed down her reddened cheeks as she screamed something about a 'Tambrin'. It was her distress, rather than her peasant prettiness and state of undress, that made Maleneth forgo her earlier misgivings about attracting attention and turn to watch. She had come a long way from the girl who would murder the row's cats and kidnap the neighbours' children, but she still found other people's pain arresting. A burly man in a sweat-stained linen vest tried to put a coat over her. His head looked like an executioner's block, all nicks and bloodstains with strange chunks missing. The woman beat her fists against his chest until he gave up. The other drunks, clearly as embarrassed by the display as Maleneth was enthralled, fussed over strappings and buckles.

There were two of them, both human, both what Maleneth would call old despite being at least a century her junior.

One was clad in leaves of delicate, lightly scuffed mail that appeared to have more of a decorative function than offering any real protection. A laurel of dried leaves and flowers sat nestled on a coarse stubble of grey hair. He carried a long-handled hammer. The next step in the cultural surrender of Ghyran, Maleneth thought. Azyrite might was irresistible, in all its forms. The old faiths had adapted to and appropriated from the doctrines of Azyr to remain relevant to the new order, or else had simply been assimilated wholesale into the Sigmarite faith. The warrior-priest of Alarielle was an extreme example.

Maleneth felt herself uniquely qualified to judge – a shadow-blade of Khaine, now an agent of the Order of Azyr. Or at least she had been. Her failure to return to the Order with the master rune would have done little to ease her superior's understandable distrust.

The second figure was more difficult to make out in detail. She kept to the darkest parts of the yard, as if out of habit. Her hood was drawn tight against the cold, not a single strand of hair falling free. Her cloak was made from woven leaves, and real ones, not the steel likenesses worn by the warrior-priest. They changed colour with the light, turning from black to autumnal red with the streaking of the clouds across the moons. Despite that exotic quality the garment was well worn, stained by sweat, soil and beer, and had probably never been anything but functional to begin with. The only thing to distinguish the woman from another common footpad or down-on-her-luck highwayman was a string of campaign badges on her collar. They marked her as ex-Freeguild. Perhaps even one of the Living City Rangers, judging by the raiment, well known throughout Ghyran as the best scouts and trackers in the Mortal Realms. Maleneth recognised some of the battles. The most recent had been fought about fifteen years ago.

'What's going on over there?' said Gotrek.

'Nothing.'

'Really? Because it *sounds* as if someone's mislaid a child.'

'As I said,' said Maleneth. 'Nothing.' But the Slayer was already stomping towards the armed gathering. Maleneth swore. Talk about something that he actually wanted to hear and Gotrek's ears were as keen as any darkling aelf's.

'You were supposed to be watching them while I visited the night market, Junas,' the distraught woman yelled as Gotrek walked over.

'It was a rough-looking crowd tonight, Madga,' said the big man, Junas, defensively. 'Helmlan wanted more help on the door. What was I supposed to say?'

'Speaking of rough-looking crowds,' muttered the warrior-priest, his eyes widening at the sight of Gotrek's sagging crest. He shuffled smartly out of the Slayer's way.

'I hear that someone has lost a child,' said Gotrek, in a tired voice that sounded like a slab of granite dropped into a conversation.

'What's it to you?' said Junas. 'I don't know who you are.'

Madga slapped him. Maleneth saw the brawler's biceps tense. Her hand strayed to her knife belt, but whatever anger he was containing he found room for a little more.

'I know you,' said the ex-Freeguilder, slowly. 'You're the fyre-slayer that slept the night on Helmlan's table.'

A glitter of malice in Gotrek's one eye made the old veteran step back.

'I am no fyreslayer, woman.'

'My mistake, master duardin.' The ranger bowed.

'Aye. It was.'

'My name is Madga,' said the young woman, wiping the tears from her face on the sleeve of her nightdress as though to make herself presentable for the permanently dishevelled Slayer. 'This is my husband, Junas.' The tavern brawler crossed his arms over his chest. Maleneth recognised a display of threatened masculinity when she saw one. All bulging neck muscles and scowls. Like a feral alley starwyrm. 'The priest is Alanaer.' The older man painstakingly put together a drunken bow, leafmail twinkling under the light of the moons. 'The Freeguild ranger is called Halik.' The woman so named nodded curtly. 'Anyone who drinks often enough in the Missed Striking to be on first-name terms with my husband isn't the sort I'd want to trust my family to, but anyone who'd drop it all in the dead of night to go looking for a boy can't be all bad, can they?'

Maleneth did not think that the girl had intended it as a question, but the hopeful inflection she gave it made it sound like one. The priest, Alanaer, smiled faintly, as if remembering the last time he had been spoken of so highly.

'Do you have children?' Madga asked.

Gotrek scoffed. 'Take another look, girl. If this one ever got her claws on a child, she would probably skin it alive. And eat it.'

Maleneth nodded.

The young woman blanched. 'I... I actually meant you, master duardin.'

Gotrek grimaced, as though pained by an old tooth. He grumbled something in his own archaic form of the Dispossessed tongue, his breath misting the midnight air. He stamped his boots on the cobblestones, taking small but obvious comfort in crushing the small flowers that sprouted between them.

'It is quite the collection of arms you carry for a missing child,' said Maleneth.

'Someone saw the boy heading towards one of the catacomb entrances,' said Halik.

Gotrek raised an eyebrow, and turned to Junas. He shook his head slowly. 'You live a stone's throw from the entrance to such a place and you would leave your child untended?'

The big man coloured. 'The entrances are all locked,' he protested. 'And patrolled by the watch.'

'It was the ghost of Hanberra!' Madga wailed. 'He's taken my Tambrin.'

Some of the gloom lifted from Gotrek's complexion.

Trust the Slayer to be revived by talk of spirits and monsters, Maleneth thought. 'Ghost?' she asked, casting a furtive look over her shoulder.

There was not much in this world that she truly feared. It was coldness, she often supposed, rather than genuine courage. But as a devotee of the God of Murder, the undead stirred a peculiar revulsion in her which, on a night as dark as this one, might have been mistaken for fear.

Alanaer shook his head. 'A folk myth, pedalled by some of the Sigmarites.'

'It's true though,' Junas murmured. He touched the small hammer he wore around his neck. 'Hanberra was a hero of the old city. The one that stood here before Hammerhal. Before the War Storm. He fell defending it from Chaos. Sigmar tried to take him, for his Stormhosts, but he refused, because there were still folk in the city he could save.'

'His children,' cried Madga. 'He defied the lightning to go back for his children. And he looks for them still.'

'It's just an old tale,' said Alanaer. 'One the Azyrheimers have latched on to, to warn about what happens to those who turn their backs on Sigmar.'

Halik, Maleneth noticed, looked unconvinced, but she nodded. 'True or not, Tambrin was seen alone. Heading towards the Downs.'

Madga started to sob.

'I'm going to bring him back, Madga,' said Junas.

Halik and Alanaer both grunted their agreement.

'Please, master duardin,' Madga sniffed. 'Will you help? Please?'

Gotrek scowled, but nodded. 'Aye. I'll help find your boy.'

Maleneth sighed.

With any luck, a little light exertion would be just what the various poisons in the duardin's body needed to do their work. And failing that, there was every chance that the monsters of the catacombs or the ghost of Hanberra could do what she had been unable to.

Kill Gotrek Gurnisson.

The stairs into the catacombs went down forever. It seemed that way to Maleneth, at least, after a second hour had elapsed with no end in sight.

Maleneth wondered if Madga was still up there, waiting. Probably. For a moment it had looked as though the peasant woman would come with them, and it had only been a word from Alanaer that had dissuaded her.

At least there was little chance of her being discovered and moved on by the watch. Their patrols were laughably infrequent, and could almost have been designed to give the entrances to the catacombs as wide a berth as possible. Maleneth had not harboured any elevated expectations of the local law enforcement and so had not been disappointed.

Maleneth tried to recall the pretty, tear-soaked face that had watched them disappear into the old sewers beneath the Stranglevines Downs, but could not seem to call it back to memory. She sighed. She could have used some cheering up.

Even this deep under the earth of the city, the brickwork was florid with life. Weeds and scruffy flowers matted the steps. Tuberous roots broke through the walls and ceiling, forcing everyone except Gotrek to walk with a crouch lest they strike their heads. More than once a particular brute of an obstacle funnelled the adventurers down to single file to slither over the crumbling, weed-carpeted steps on their bellies. Maleneth appreciated those interludes even if Junas, Halik, Alanaer and Gotrek manifestly did not. They were a chance for her to sit down and rub her aching thighs while the others caught up, struggling and cursing behind her.

What sustenance do these plants draw from this grey place? Maleneth wondered. *Where do they turn in lieu of sunlight?* In Azyrheim, too, the days were often dark. The city had no sun, but bathed in the light of Sigendil, the High Star, at the very heart of the cosmos, it shared in the brilliance of a trillion stars. Perhaps it was the song of the Everqueen alone that bade them grow.

She could see in near-perfect darkness. Her senses of hearing and intuition were so acute that she could fare reasonably well even without vision. But even she was starting to miss the cheap, imported illumination of the Stranglevines' street lamps.

The ranger, Halik, bore a torch, but she had not lit it.

There had been no need.

The only light that had followed them into this forgotten corner of Alarielle's realm was that of Gotrek's axe. Zangrom-thaz, it was called, in the language of the *unbaki* fyreslayers who had crafted it. The forgeflames bound up in the huge fyrestorm greataxe licked at his flesh and at the hairs of his beard without finding a purchase on either. Another effect of the fyreslayers' ur-gold on his body, Maleneth thought. She could feel the axe's heat perfectly. Sweat beaded her forehead. The palms of her hands were damp, to the extent that she almost feared she would be unable to draw a weapon should the need arise. The tangling vegetation shrivelled back from him, much to the Slayer's childish glee.

The weight of rock above Maleneth's head seemed to close in. It dawned on Maleneth that it was this, rather than the darkness, that was truly disturbing her.

In her duties for the Temple there had been no dungeon so

deep that she could not penetrate it, no arcane fortress warded so completely that she could not reach its heart. There was an aspect of killer instinct at play there, but largely it came down to preparation. Since she had been an acolyte, Maleneth had known never to open a door without first knowing of at least two others by which she could flee. Following Gotrek wherever the idiot duardin chose to swing his axe denied her that. It was simply not possible to carry the same sigmarite-clad self-assurance that she was accustomed to when she had no idea where she was or what she was supposed to be doing.

Her hand strayed over the array of knives sheathed to the lightweight, drakespawn leather plate of her thigh. Her neck itched as though she were being watched. Like a zephyrat in a sadist's maze. She almost feared to look back, stricken by the bizarre certainty that she would see a million tons of Ghyran-ite rock crashing over the stairs behind her if she did.

Forcing herself to swallow her phobias and face them, she glanced over her shoulder. Junas walked behind her, hunched, scared, stroking the hammer pendant that hung from his neck and muttering a prayer to Sigmar. For himself or for his child, Maleneth could not quite make out. Maleneth's hand moved involuntarily from her knife belt to the device at her own neck. The locket was in the form of a silver heart bound in chains. A small window between revealed a quantity of blood inside.

It had belonged to her former mistress.

'What other choice did I have, my lady?' she whispered. 'Let the Slayer go? Return to Azyrheim empty-handed? The Order would cast me onto the streets and to the tender mercies of the Temple. I fear that the last person who would have granted me a painless end died when I murdered you.' She smiled, heartened somewhat by the memory of the last Lady Witchblade drowning in the blood of her own cauldron.

'Who are you talking to, aelfling?' said Gotrek.

'The dead,' she said.

The Slayer snorted, but for several hours thereafter said no more.

The vegetation started to become yellower and sicker. Halik drew her hood tighter. Junas' mashed-up face contorted further in disgust, finding breathing into his own elbow pit preferable to the rancid sweetness of the decaying plantlife. Alanaer spoke prayer after prayer until his voice gave out, but only the axe-fire of Zangrom-thaz seemed able to purge the plants of their blight. This mercy Gotrek delivered with apparent relish and no sign of weariness.

Maleneth's sense of smell was many times keener than any of theirs, and she decided not to mention how deep into the stones the contagion ran. If she did then even Junas might have second thoughts and turn back. Getting the Slayer killed was one thing, but surviving long enough to cut the master rune from his flesh and escape with it was another. It was a task that would undoubtedly benefit from having another warrior or two between her and whatever monster it was that had finally bested the old duardin.

'A corruption has taken root here,' Halik murmured.

'Really?' Maleneth asked, as a cackling Gotrek Gurnisson burned another mushy curtain of vines from their path. 'What makes you think that?'

The ranger pursed her lips, but said nothing.

Maleneth decided not to rile the woman any further. Sometimes, she just could not help herself.

'Who built these stairs?' Gotrek asked. He looked down. The steps wound on away from him, as if a gigantic god-beast had driven a drill into the heart of Ghyran only to see it become entrapped in its rich soil. 'They bear the mark of dwarven crafts-manship. The age of these worlds of yours is hard even for one who's seen as much as this dwarf to conceive. Even the works of my people would falter if abandoned for such a span of years.'

'That's impossible,' said Junas. 'The folk of the Mortal Realms lived in ignorance until the first coming of Sigmar. He taught them how to raise their cities and to build great monuments.' The big man looked defensive as Halik and Alanaer turned to him. 'I can't read, but you think I can't listen?'

'Maybe that's so,' Gotrek mused, sniffing at the great depth of blackness beyond the reach of his axe. 'But who do you think taught *him?*'

Gotrek lowered himself gruffly to one knee, rubbing at his thigh with a scowl.

The ground at the base of the stairs was buckled. Pale weeds and stalk-like flowers had pushed the flagstones out of true. But after the hours they had spent on the stairs it looked as though it had been levelled flat by the Six Smiths of Grungni themselves. Alanaer sat against one of the mossy pillars that framed the mouth of the stairwell, red-faced, mouth hanging open, his knees pulled up to his leafmail coat. He was probably regretting the beer he had consumed earlier. Or perhaps he was simply regretting following Junas and Halik at all.

Maleneth realised that she did not know her companions on this adventure very well. And if the catacombs were half as dangerous as she had heard them to be then she probably never would.

Even the Stormcast Eternals had been unable to cleanse them of all evil.

Gotrek thumped his thigh and issued a curse in consonant-heavy Dispossessed duardin.

'Cramp?' Maleneth asked.

'I'd like to see how spry you are when you get to be this age, aelfling.' Gotrek nodded his flattened crest towards the tumble-down architecture around them. His nose chain tinkled loudly in the enclosed space. 'I'm twice as old as this ruin. I think I've held up well, all things considered.'

Halik lowered her torch to the rune-fuelled brazier at the heart of Gotrek's fyrestorm greataxe and lit it. She lifted it as she padded past. Its wavering light pushed into the darkness, revealing a hallway flanked by massive granite columns. Some of them had been carved into figures. Their identities however had been long hidden beneath blotching mould and withered creepers. Like the staircase before it, it seemed to go on forever.

'Could the boy have… have got this far?' Alanaer panted, sitting up with effort.

'He could be no more than an hour ahead of us,' said Junas.

Which means he has been dead for no more than an hour, Maleneth thought, but chose to keep it to herself.

'We've not passed him,' said Halik. 'A small child may have been able to move faster. He would have had less difficulty on the stairs.'

'You are talking about a four-year-old boy,' Maleneth said aloud. 'Walking alone for hours in the dark. Why would he not stop? Or turn back?'

No one had an answer. At least, not one they liked.

'I don't know,' Halik admitted.

The ranger crouched with only a slight protestation of old bones, and brushed worn fingertips over a patch of flattened stems and crushed flowers. Maleneth knew that she was not the equal of a Living City Ranger when it came to the tracking of quarry, but she knew how to read a spoor. It was a footprint. A small footprint. Such as might be made by a child.

'Unbelievable,' said Maleneth. 'He really did come this way.'

'If you doubted it, aelfling, then why come?' said Gotrek.

Maleneth chose not to dignify that with an answer.

'There are some older prints here.' Halik waved her hand over the pale grasses. 'But Tambrin's is the only one to have been made recently.'

'So he wandered down here alone,' said Junas, relieved.

'It looks like it,' said Halik, rising stiffly. 'And much less than an hour ahead of us I would say.'

'Let's be moving then,' said Gotrek.

'Tambrin!' Junas yelled.

After the hours they had spent with just the occasional furtive whisper between them, the sudden shout startled Maleneth. The syllables rang from the columns and down the hall. Even Halik's torch seemed spooked, cavorting back from the out-breath, making shadows flap around them like bats. Maleneth swore in Druhíri, reaching for her knife belt, even as Junas ran past her to charge bow-legged down the desolate hall.

'Tambrin!' he yelled.

'Quiet, you idiot,' Maleneth hissed.

'Let him shout, aelfling,' Gotrek grumbled. 'Sound travels in strange ways below ground. And if the ground-sniffer says the boy's close then he's probably close.'

'And if something else hears?'

Gotrek grinned, broken teeth flashing yellow and red in the firelight. 'Good.'

'Fair enough,' said Maleneth. 'So long as we understand one another.'

'Tambri–'

A wooden club swung out from behind a pillar before Junas could finish. It mashed into the middle of his face with a horrible wet sound. The big man dropped like a sack of grain. A

squeal went up as the brawler hit the flagstones, ratman warriors pouring from myriad hiding places amidst the crumbling
stonework and hanging plant life. Their robes were soiled and
mangy. Deep hoods concealed their faces but for dripping
noses and rotten, elongated mouths filled with cracked and
yellowing teeth.

'Skaven!' Maleneth yelled. 'Plague monks!'

It dawned on her that the monks had selected this hall for their
lair with good reason. They would have known that any would-be
adventurer wishing to brave the catacombs from the Stranglevines Downs, already exhausted by the descent, would have
first to pass through it. The preponderance of clubs and nets in
their scabrous paws told her the monks' intentions for such fools.

'They mean to take us alive,' she said.

'Hah!'

With a roar Gotrek barrelled towards the oncoming horde,
his axe held high. Fire trailed from the monstrous weapon like
a comet's tail. A single blow cleaved a plague monk in two and
incinerated it. Three more armed with quarterstaves and maces
pounced on him while he was still wreathed and half blinded
by crimson smoke.

Maleneth heard a rapid flurry of blows, followed by an angry
shout.

She decided to leave the Slayer to it.

A plague monk charged at her with a squeal.

Yellow froth bubbled up from toothless black lips, staining
the creature's hood. Maleneth let it come within arm's reach,
then vaulted its hunched back with an aerial cartwheel. With
one hand she drew a knife. With the other she took hold of the
foetid folds of cloth at the back of the monk's hood. It shrieked
in dismay, but was still running as she landed. She yanked back.
The monk's footpaws flew out from under it as it fell backward

onto its tail. She dropped to one knee and then turned, plunging the knife into the belly of the monk that had been scurrying in behind the first. Its own momentum drove its heart and lungs down onto the blade. Forged from celestite and etched with the murderous blessings of Khaine, it was enough to kill even those most resistant to death with but a nick.

Except for the one life she most wished it to take, it seemed.

Maleneth relished the horror on the plague monk's face as it expired.

She turned again.

The monk she had thrown to the floor was already on its footpaws. Skaven were fast. As fast as her, if not faster. It came at her with bared teeth, on all fours like a rabid dog. There was a *hiss*, a *thunk*, and an arrow exploded from the monk's eye socket. It jerked once, as though surprised by something on its shoulder, and then fell over.

Halik grunted, as if surprised to see that she was still strong enough to draw a bow and sharp enough to aim it, then turned to loose a second arrow into the fray.

It skewed high.

Maleneth's lips pricked into a smile. With a long fingernail, she tapped on the silver talisman at her collar. Little wonder that the Azyrite Hags go to such lengths to stay young.

The skaven appeared to be focusing their considerable numbers on killing Gotrek. The monks' leaders had apparently concluded that despatching the Slayer quickly would allow them to capture the three humans and the aelf more easily. They were probably right. Maleneth would have come to a similar conclusion in their position.

A monk in more ornate robes than the rest crouched on a pedestal of rubble just at the limits of Gotrek's wildly dancing axe-light. It wore creamy yellow robes and a mitre, decorated with fly eggs, dung pellets and spider's silk. With two bandage-wound paws it waved a censer-topped stave, the effect of which was to fill that end of the corridor with greenish fumes that drove the monks caught in the haze to new heights of rabid insanity.

Gotrek bellowed, trying to get at the skaven priest, but found himself hemmed in by the sheer mass of foes that surrounded him.

From the stairs behind them, Alanaer began to chant, words of sylvanspeak that had the diseased roots behind the walls writhing in agony. Dust rained from the ceiling, and for a moment Maleneth feared that the warrior-priest meant to bring the entire hall down on their heads.

Then the grey-haired priest lifted his open palm to his lips and blew. A mighty gale flurried down the halls with a swirl of sepulchral leaves. The battering-ram force hurled skaven from their footpaws, bludgeoning through a corridor all the way to their malefic leader. The plague priest hacked as the fumes from its own censer were blown back into its face by the warrior-priest's scouring wind.

Maleneth saw the opening and took it.

She sprinted, hurdling stricken monks between herself and their priest as they picked themselves off the ground. She was fast, practically a blur as she covered the hundred or so feet in a matter of seconds. The last dozen she turned into a leap, a knife appearing in her off-hand as she dropped.

'For Khaine!'

She slashed the knife across the skaven's throat, intending to gizzard it, only to see her blade *thunk* into the mouldy wood of the priest's staff. Its reflexes were astonishing. The priest hissed, fangs bared, and swung up the butt of its staff. Maleneth twisted to one side. The staff whooshed across her chest.

The priest spun, cackling like a fanatic, his censer emitting a weary drone as he spun it overhead, then turned to bring it whirring back towards her.

'For Sigmar!'

She roundhoused the priest, a heel-kick across the snout, deliberately unbalancing herself and falling to the ground as the plague censer droned overhead. The big bronze censer crushed the flagstone behind the one she was sprawled over. Whizzing fragments ripped her drakespawn leathers. Noxious fumes rushed over her. Her eyes filled with stinging tears. The skin bared by her torn armour itched. Coughing, she crawled away from the plague fumes on her back.

The priest tittered as it jumped off its rubble mound to follow.

This was, she acknowledged, not turning into the incisive decapitating stroke that she had envisioned.

Already, the monks that Alanaer's prayer had thrown down were rallying. Several were even peeling away from Gotrek, drawn by the commotion and their priest's shrill laughter. She cursed, glancing back at the Slayer, and in doing so identified another good reason for the wilier of the plague monks to abandon that particular prize in search of another.

Gotrek Gurnisson was on fire. He was liquid gold, sparks hissing, poured into the cast of a duardin form. The flames grew fiercer as the Slayer butchered his way through the squealing plague monks, feeding off his fury and feeding it in kind. His greataxe moved with such speed that it looked to Maleneth as though he wielded two of them, the air around him webbed with fiery after-traces. The heat was so incredible that Halik and Alanaer could no longer even contribute to the fight at all. They had retreated to the shelter of the stairwell. The occasional refrain of a prayer rose over the roar of the flames, but otherwise the Slayer had effectively cut off his, and Maleneth's, only means of aid. It was a testament to the unholy durability of the plague monks that they were able to endure the Slayer's proximity and still fight.

With an ugly snarl, Maleneth tore her gaze from the approaching plague priest and looked around. A way out. A place to hide. *Anything.* What she found, recessed behind two thick, ivy-strangled columns, was so subtly worked into the wall and well hidden that she almost failed to see it at all. It was an arch. A feeling of bleakness and unreasoning dread emanated from it, a chill finding its way through her violet eyes, and from there along rarely used ways to her heart. Her snarl became a shiver. Something about the arch urged the eye to move on, and discouraged any thought of approaching. But Maleneth had nowhere left to run.

Even as she ignored her own disquiet to sprint towards it, the ratmen on her heels fell off the chase with squeals of terror. Maleneth turned to look over her shoulder. The plague priest jabbed a claw at Maleneth and shrieked at the cowering monks. Maleneth did not understand the chittering speech, which was a small tragedy on the priest's part for it was one of the last acts it would ever perform.

Gotrek reared up behind it.

The Slayer had grown massive. Muscles bulged with rune-forged might. His good eye blazed like a freshly minted coin. Even his eyepatch was limned by a halo of golden brilliance. Flames wreathed him.

Maleneth had known many great wielders of power. She had witnessed the awesome rituals performed by the magisters of the Collegiate Arcane, and had ended the life of more than one rogue wizard in her time. But even the last, desperate conjurations of sorcerers driven mad by the promises of Chaos had been tame and controlled compared to what Maleneth beheld now. It was as though someone, or some*thing*, breathed dragonfire against the thin skein separating Ghyran from the aether that swirled beyond its sphere in the cosmos. Unveiling the dead stars and wrathful deities that lingered there in all their awful magnificence.

The sooner I get that rune out of him the better, Maleneth thought.

With a howl that shook the roots of Ghyran, Gotrek cut the plague priest in half. The two halves of its diseased body consumed themselves in flame before they could hit the ground. The Slayer breathed it in, exhaling it like sparks from a furnace. Those skaven bright enough to have been directing their efforts elsewhere squealed in terror at the sight. They broke, scampering off down the long hall.

Maleneth did not expect them to come back. She noted, however, that despite being for many the closest avenue of escape, none of them had tried to flee down the side tunnel behind her.

With a deep breath, Halik emerged from her hiding place behind the stairs. She cast a wary look at Gotrek as she padded down the hall. But the Slayer did not move. He was hunched over the rubble of the priest's pedestal. It was a cairn now, burnt to twisted plates of unreflective glass by the intensity of the heat and magic that he had unwittingly unleashed upon it. The glassy lump creaked under Gotrek's weight, splintering and popping as it cooled. He was breathing hard, steam curling off his crisped, cooling skin.

It was probably optimistic to hope that it was the cocktail of poisons in his blood finally starting to tell. If there was a toxin anywhere in the planes of existence that could have endured such runefire then it was under the jealous protection of the Hags of Azyr – held against the day that Sigmar himself needed to feel the knife of Khaine.

'What in Sigmar's Storm was that?' said Halik.

Maleneth smiled weakly and shook her head. That was a longer story than she had the strength for, and one that she was not entirely sure of the end of herself.

Alanaer crouched by Junas.

'He's alive,' the warrior-priest declared. He pulled the big man up to sitting, and smiled ruefully as the brawler spat out another tooth. 'But I doubt he'll be breaking any more young ladies' hearts with this face.'

Halik managed a nervous chuckle. 'Skaven,' she muttered, as it left her.

'More of Thanquol's craven minions, I expect.' Gotrek moved like a statue taking life, slowly, vitrified gore and dust trickling from his shoulders. He drew in a shuddering breath, then coughed it up. He wiped blood from his bottom lip on his thumb, then lifted it to his eye. He grunted and stuck it in his mouth. 'Leftovers from the war on the other side of the Storm-rift Gate. With skaven you never can kill them all.'

'No.' Alanaer shook his head. 'The servants of the Great Corruptor have long coveted my Queen's realm. I expect that their presence here predates the Grey Lord's invasions of Hammer-hal Aqsha by some time.'

'What have you found here, darkling?' Halik looked up at the archway that Maleneth had discovered. Her footsteps slowed noticeably as she looked on it. She shivered as she reached out to run her hand along the inside of the stone arch, hesitating, finally bringing the hand back to her side unused. 'Tambrin passed this way,' she breathed. 'The ground here is marked, and not by skaven paws. And.' The ranger paused, ear cocked. 'Can you hear that?'

Maleneth listened, then nodded, impressed. The ranger was good.

For a human.

'Footsteps,' she said.

'And still only one set,' said Halik.

'He has somehow bypassed a locked door, a watch patrol and now a skaven ambush as well,' said Maleneth. 'He belongs in a temple of Khaine, this child.' She turned to join the old ranger in her study of the arch. 'It reeks of soulblight and carrion. Whatever dwells beyond this portal, I fear it is beyond even Khaine's reach now. Such things are best left buried.'

Gotrek heaved himself to his feet with a clink of gold chain and a dying splutter of half-seen flame. Maleneth had to marvel at his determination. And all this for the myth of an ancient ghost, for surely Gotrek Gurnisson cared less for this Tambrin boy than even she did, and she cared nothing at all. It was with a mixture of amazement and frustration she was lately becoming painfully familiar with that she watched the Slayer limp towards her.

'What are you all standing about for?' he said. 'There's black work ahead of us yet.'

After what he had inflicted on the plague monks, nobody felt inclined to argue.

A chill blue light shone from the passage beyond the archway. The languid movements of the mist that filled the corridor diffused and scattered it. It was like being submerged in water. Maleneth felt her breath starting to come quick and shallow. She studied the walls. Frost prickled the weeds and mosses that encrusted their ancient stonework. But aside from the chill the plants looked healthy. The air in this part of the dungeon smelled clean. For some reason, that pristine quality troubled her more than the rank despoliation in the chamber that had preceded it. It was the sterility of abandonment. Nothing had moved in to claim these halls. That alone was enough to give Maleneth's heart jitters.

There was a tired creak as Halik raised her bow.

The ranger's aim wavered.

'Sigmar preserve us.'

Maleneth drew her hand from the frost-stippled wall and looked up. Her eyes were sharper than those of the human ranger. At that precise moment she wished they were not.

Between her looking away and turning back the mists ahead had parted. Or rather, something had drawn them apart. They clung to the walls of the passage in a way that was wholly unnatural, trembling like cold skin, and bathed in blueish light. A taller-than-human figure stood revealed in the ankle-deep mist. Its body was formed of crackling energy. A long cloak and a suit of ribbed, holly-like armour filtered its fell glow. It turned its head to look back over its shoulder and Maleneth felt that her heart would stop. A black helmet masked its face with coiling shadows. In one fizzing blue hand it led a small boy. Were one to mentally unbox the ears and reset the nose then the resemblance to Junas would have been striking. For all that he was standing upright, the boy seemed to be sound asleep.

'Thambrin,' said Junas, the most recent break to his nose making his voice come out as a frightened honk. 'Praith Thigmar.' He shook off Alanaer's supporting arm and tottered forwards, hand outstretched to his son. 'I'm here, Thambrin.'

The shade drew the boy in close.

'Begone, spirit.' Gotrek hefted his axe. Its forgefires chased the shadows from his face, filling its creases with new ones. 'Release the child and walk amongst the living no longer.'

The shade turned to regard them fully, pushing the boy behind its back. It flickered rather than moved, its outline stuttering in and out of focus with a horrible vibration as though it were only weakly tethered to the living realm.

'What are you waiting for?' Junas snarled. 'Thoot it.'

Maleneth was not sure if Halik did as Junas demanded or if terror had simply loosened her hold on her bowstring.

A foot away from the ragged armour of its chest her arrow disintegrated. Aged a thousand years in the blink of an eye, the shaft fell to dust like a stick fed into a Kharadron steam-shredder. A brittle wedge of rusted and barely recognisable steel dinked on the spirit's breastplate and dropped to the floor. The apparition crunched it under one icy boot. It looked up. Maleneth gasped in horror as its helmet melted back. A skull face glared out from a hood of shadow, eyes blazing with malefic lightning. The breath that Maleneth had taken caught. It refused to come out. She felt it freeze in her lungs where it hid, icicles creeping outwards into her heart. Her mouth stretched into a silent scream, her black hair turning slowly white.

Then the ghost screamed.

It hit Maleneth like a lightning bolt. Something inside her braced, clinging on to meat and bone like a drowning woman to a wrecked ship in a storm. From the corner of her eye she saw Halik as her soul was blasted from her body. Pale and ephemeral, its hands grasped for the ranger's body, but passed through, unable to prevent the corpse from toppling. With a plaintive wail the disembodied soul dissolved into the aether. Maleneth grit her teeth. Junas had folded to the ground, his hands over his ears. Alanaer was screaming. Over and over. As if to block out the banshee cry with the terrified sound of his own voice.

'It is the ghost of Hanberra!' the warrior-priest wailed, holding his hammer before him as if its crossed shadow would ward the visitation from his sight. 'By the light of my Queen, it is true. The hero who broke free from Sigmar's lightning to go back for his family!'

Even without the benefit of a dark legend, Maleneth would have known that this was no ordinary shade. The empty halls. The skaven's terror. Its bearing and raiment – all made it clear that this had been the spirit of a great hero in life. But death had eroded him until only the deepest core of the warrior's former personality remained.

A solitary purpose.

'I said unhand him,' said Gotrek.

Unlike the others, the Slayer simply looked weary, as though having been burned once by the purple sun of Uthan Barrowalker, the winds of Shyish could no longer touch him. Maleneth looked for the warning flicker of runefire, but in vain. The master rune was cool in the Slayer's chest. It was, perhaps, a sign of the tremendous power it contained that once unleashed it took time to recharge. Not that that came as any great solace to Maleneth at that moment.

'Give me my thon,' snarled Junas. 'He'th mine, not yours.'

'He's mine. Not yours.'

The words echoed back at them as if from a deep well.

Maleneth shuddered.

The ghost of Hanberra did not move. One moment it was upright. Then it was turned away, hunched over the sleepwalking boy. And then it was facing its mortal pursuers again, the boy held in its arms, drifting away from them as though drawn on the freezing in-breath of the deep earth itself.

'Thambrin!'

Junas lurched into a charge.

Gotrek caught his scuffed and damaged wrist with one hand. Despite barely coming up to the big man's chest, the duardin stopped him without effort.

'Don't be an idiot, manling,' he said in a voice like stone. 'You've failed the boy once today already. Don't fail him again by dying now.' The Slayer pulled back on Junas' arm, dragging him easily to the floor at his feet. He looked down the passageway towards the towering wraith. 'Your boy is dead, spirit, as are you. Unhand this one and face a dwarf nearer your own age. My axe will grant you the release you seek.'

The spirit issued a sepulchral moan.

'Release.'

Its cloak flapped about it like the wings of a bat and a warhammer of truly monstrous proportion appeared in one gauntleted fist. With the other hand, it cosseted the still-sleeping infant to its chest.

Then with a hiss it swung.

Gotrek ducked his head at the last moment.

The hammer punched a hole through the roof of his crest and pulverised a block from the wall. Masonry dust rained through the embittered shade. It painted the Slayer grey. Gotrek shook it off his head, shortened his grip on his axe, and punched it straight up into the spirit's body. The red runes on its fyresteel blades glowed like coals plucked from a fire. The shade flickered and the fyrestorm greataxe cleaved through scraps of aether. The wraith rematerialised a dozen feet away. Swifter than Maleneth could follow it moved again, its hammer no longer *there*, embedded in stone beside the Slayer's face, but *here*, poised above its own crackling skull at the apex of a downswing.

Gotrek threw himself to one side as the hammer stove in the flagstone he had been standing on. He landed on his back with a crunch of armour and a gravelly curse. The duardin was insanely tough, but nimble he was not.

Alanaer began to chant.

The ice that caked the stonework around Hanberra's feet

cracked and hissed. Vines groped from the thaw to tug on the
harder edges of the spectre's armour. A tendril wound its way
up his leg to reach for the sleeping child.

The shade pulled Tambrin in close and hissed. 'He's mine. Not
yours.' It drew in a breath of amethyst-flecked magic, turned
towards the warrior-priest and screamed.

Alanaer was lifted from his feet and thrown back down the
passageway. He landed on his back and rolled. Unconscious
or dead, Maleneth did not know. Either way he did not get
up again.

Taking full advantage of the distraction, Gotrek hacked
at the shade's ankle from prone. The fyresteel blade passed
through the spirit's leg, leaving a flickering line of blue energy
and golden fire where it had crossed. The shade stuttered in
and out of form, screeching in outrage. Maleneth covered
her sensitive ears as the ghost of Hanberra kicked Gotrek in
the ribs. There was a blast of sound and pressure as if from a
thunderbolt and the Slayer was hurled across the passageway,
plunging into the mist like a brick into water before crunch-
ing into the stonework behind it.

Shaking masonry from his crest, Gotrek pulled himself back
up.

This is it, Maleneth thought. The Slayer's doom.

Finally he could die. She could recover the rune from his
remains and, if she was quick about it, return to Azyr late in
some kind of triumph.

Hanberra drifted back. Its hammer blinked to a defensive
position as Gotrek shrugged off the last of the wall and barrelled towards it with a roar. Maleneth frowned. She could see
that Hanberra was not fighting to its utmost. The ghost actually seemed more intent on shielding the child in its arms than
it was on actually defeating Gotrek.

And that, Maleneth thought, is just not going to be good enough.

She rifled through what was left in her various pouches and pockets. Her long mission had kept her away from the blood markets of Azyrheim, and her fruitless efforts to concoct a poison that would actually kill Gotrek Gurnisson had depleted her supplies still further. But she still had a few herbs. Poisons that she had not yet thought to try. Her fingers closed around the hard nut of a wightclove and she withdrew it from her pocket. It was tough, ridged and white as bone. She kissed it for Khaine's blessing and then crushed it to a powder against the back of her hand.

Leaping into the midst of the contest with a yell, Maleneth struck the powder from the back of her hand and across Hanberra's arm. The arm that held the boy.

The spirit shrieked as its arm and shoulder wavered.

A concentrated and properly delivered dose of freshly harvested wightclove would banish a spirit and, though Maleneth would not like to test it, cause severe discomfort to a Mortarch. With a single dried clove the best she could hope for was a temporary loss of corporeality, but that was all she wanted. The shade tried desperately to keep a hold of the child, but its efforts were as fruitless as those of Halik's spirit had been on her own body. Its arm had taken on the consistency of mist. The child fell through it. Maleneth dived as the spirit cried out in anguish, intercepting the boy before he could hit the ground, and then rolled, curling to protect his body with her own.

She broke from her roll just before she hit the wall, braking with an out-turned foot. The boy lay beneath her, pudgy arms and legs spread out. Unbelievably, he was still asleep.

Behind her, the spirit raged.

Aether rose off the ragged figure like smoke. It clenched

its fist, finding it once again solid, and took its massive war-hammer in a two-handed grip. It stuttered back and forth around its streaming outline, screaming in rage.

'Thambrin!' Junas cried, but made no move to intervene.

Maleneth bared perfect teeth in a grin.

This is more like it, she thought. A little more of this and you might rid me of this burdensome Slayer yet.

Exhausted beyond even his own awesome strength, but defiant to the last, Gotrek looked up to meet his doom. His one eye met Hanberra's and for some reason that was not immediately apparent to Maleneth, the shade hesitated. An unlikely understanding seemed to pass between ancient duardin and lost soul. A pain they had both shared. A pain that had broken one and made the other.

'He's mine. Not yours.'

'No,' said Gotrek. 'This one is still of the living. Begone, spirit. Seek your boy in the Lands of the Dead.'

'Dead...'

Hanberra's hand flickered to its eye sockets. The shade's corposant skull stared at them as if seeing them as they were for the first time in a thousand years. Its warhammer burst into a cloud of rising ash above its head. Its armour began to peel away, lightning seething about the trapped human shape underneath.

'Dead...'

'Aye,' said Gotrek. 'Aye, he's gone and it was your fault. And no. It doesn't get any better. So begone, spirit. Begone and be at peace.'

'Hangharth was his name,' the spirit said, as though remembering a precious revelation it had thought long forgotten. *'Sigmar forgive me.'* Its dissolution accelerated. There was a muffled *crump*, as if of lightning striking somewhere far below

ground, and the ghost of Hanberra vanished in a puff of smoke, its last words a breath on a dead wind. *'I should never have left.'*

Maleneth stared at the thinning cloud in horror.

From somewhere behind her, she could hear Alanaer coughing as the warrior-priest stirred.

'That was brave, aelfling,' said Gotrek. The duardin picked himself up and walked stiffly towards her. She offered no protest as he bent to take the child from her. Tambrin was a stocky boy, and was clearly going to grow into a large man, but tucked into the crook of the Slayer's huge arm he looked gangly and long-limbed. His lips smacked together as he started to stir. Gotrek shushed him with a few gravelly consonants of what might, to ears attuned to the sounds of picks on stone and hammers on anvils, have been a lullaby. A grin, unsettling in its strange lack of hostility, spread across his scarred face. 'Maybe there's hope for you yet, eh?'

'Gotrek…' said Maleneth.

The duardin's expression hardened. 'Come on, aelfling. Let's go on back.'

'Do you mean, do you *honestly* mean, that the ill-tempered old Slayer I knew genuinely came down here to save a human child?'

Gotrek glanced fleetingly at the child in his arms. 'Of course not.' Grumbling under his breath, he deposited the boy into Junas' crushing embrace. 'But you said I left a beer untended up there.'

BLOOD GOLD

Gav Thorpe

The foothills seethed with movement – like a crust of red and black constantly breaking and reforming, a mass of Blood-bound warriors poured over slopes and crests in a continuous wave.

Their goal stood before them. The dark flanks of the immense pinnacle known as Vostargi Mont. It was not so much a mountain as a cloud-piercing edifice that defied the eye to judge its height. Countless lifetimes of spewed molten rock had grown the volcano into a titan amongst its kind, and from a thousand calderas and fumaroles the flame-ridden forces at its heart continued to burst into the world.

But the mount was not a dead place. Its surface was covered in great battlements and walls, guarding gates reached by winding, tower-flanked roads.

Those gates protected a labyrinth of tunnels, caverns and mineworks so vast that it was impossible for a single mind to know them all; so complex and ancient that even the annals of their inhabitants covered but a fraction of their full extent. Vostargi Mont was the ancestral home of the fyreslayers, fierce descendants of the stout duardin race who had been forged in the bowels of the World-That-Was.

Before the Gate of Endless Defiance, one of the lesser portals into the lower runeholds, the rocks themselves seemed alive. As the hills moved with the teeming horde of the Blood God's howling servants, so the ridged slope of the mountain was also home to an army.

They were unlike any other duardin, unique among the fyreslayers even. Their flesh was like solidifying lava, a dark grey-black that cracked as they moved, showing glimpses of red-and-yellow heat from within. Ten thousand eyes that gleamed with the flame of a volcano's heart watched the approaching Bloodbound.

Like all of their kind, they wore little armour. Their helms were split at the scalp, allowing great crests of fire-like hair to jut through, sculpted in extravagant designs, hung with clasps and rune-beads. Their beards were likewise a fall of orange and yellow hair-fire, plaited and knotted in intricate patterns and ringed with pale gold.

The air shimmered with heat haze. Their sheer presence brought a crackle of flames, and a smog carried on their breath.

At the fore waited Ungrimmsson Drakkazak, runefather of the clan, descended in direct lineage from their earliest progenitors. Like all of his kin his appearance was of volcanic rage given flesh, bound with golden torques and high helm, his beard forked many times by complex knotwork. The axe he held in one hand was almost as tall as he was, save for the great bifurcated crests of his hair, its blade edge dancing with undulating blue flame. As with many fyreslayers, his flesh was hammered with runes of ur-gold – mystic shards believed to be the fragments of the duardin warrior-god Grimnir, whose immortal form had been showered across the realms. Sigils of fortitude, strength, courage and power gleamed with an inner light from where they nestled in bicep and thigh, pectoral and shoulder. From belt loops and bracelets hung amulets and keys denoting his many ranks and titles amongst the Zharrthagi clan.

His eyes glowed with flame as he gazed at the mass of rage-driven humanity that surged across the foothills. A movement to his left caught his eye and he saw one of the fyreslayers, a young Vulkite Berzerker, bending one knee. The youthful warrior rubbed his hand in the dirt and then curled his fingers about the haft of his pick as he rejoined the line of his kin.

'One of my runesons teach you that?' Ungrimmsson asked. 'Better for grip, eh?'

The Vulkite Berzerker nodded, the single binding of his short beard clattering against a gorget he wore about his neck. He looked away, staring out at the horde that approached. His fingers flexed on the haft of his pick again and the fyreslayer darted another look towards his runefather before fixing his eyes on the Bloodbound once more.

'Come here, Alvi,' said the runefather, beckoning with his axe. He knew every one of his kin by name. The fyreslayer approached with quick strides.

'Yes, lodge-sire?'

'You seem agitated.'

'I'm not afraid, lodge-sire!' the warrior protested.

'I didn't say you were afraid, Alvi. Agitated. Something's vexing you.'

'It's not important,' the fyreslayer told him. 'I shouldn't be troubling you.'

The Vulkite Berzerker took a step back towards his companions, but Ungrimmsson stopped him with a disapproving grunt.

'I'll decide what's troubling me. Spit it out, lad.'

'When I came to my first battle you said you were going to tell me about the Zharrthagi curse, lodge-sire. But you never got around to it. I asked the others but they said I needed to hear the tale from you.'

'Why is it bothering you now?'

'If I die, I'd like to know first, is all,' confessed the fyreslayer. He flexed his arm and the skin cracked, leaving a crease of fire in the crook of his elbow. 'I'd like to know why we're the way we are.'

'Well, there's a thing,' said Ungrimmsson. 'First off, you'll not be dying today. I promise you that. Second, you're right, I do owe you the tale. You're of age now, you should know.'

Ungrimmsson cocked an eye towards the red-armoured barbarians and gave the youngster a wink. 'I figure we've got a bit of time to kill and here's as good a place as any. The Zharrthagi curse, the fire in our bodies, goes back a long time, to before the Red Feast when the Great Parch was gripped by the ravages of the Blood God unleashed by that lord of slaughter, Khorgos Khul. The runefather of the Angastaz Lodge, as the clan was known then, was one Brynnson Drakkazak. A prouder nor more stubborn runefather has yet to walk the halls of Vostargi Mont...'

Sigmar's reign held relative peace over the lands of the Great Parch and a great many other regions over many realms. Even so, the children of Grimnir were not ones to be idle and we warred with orruks and ogors and even the humans on occasion. Their holds were raided by grotz, and even bands of aelves would occasionally seek to take their overland territories. Even so, there were also times when the lodges fell to conflict with each other, though only rarely did such disputes end in battle, even amongst hot-headed fyreslayers. Sometimes runesons and runefathers might duel each other to prove a point or settle an argument.

The Ironfists were more aggressive than most, spending years at a time on the surface seeking ur-gold while others delved deep into the spine of the mountain to find the shards of Grimnir. It was good that they did, for often disagreement followed when they returned to Vostargi Mont. The Ironfists were not the most numerous nor the wealthiest lodge, but Brynnson Drakkazak was determined that they would have great reputation all the same. In ferocity it was said there was nothing like an Ironfist, and it was joked that the fire of the world-salamander, Vulcatrix, had mixed with the blood of Grimnir to make them. Perhaps those jests contained more truth than mockery. Brynnson certainly did nothing to quell these chattermouths, and took some delight in the bloodthirsty tales told of his exploits, whether true or not.

Matters did not sit well with the councils and runefathers of the other lodges. It seemed to them that Brynnson's belli-cose nature courted disaster for all the people of Vostargi Mont and the Great Parch. He would likely lead his clan into war against one of the human powers like the Aridians, Aspirians or Bataari. Though the Fatherspire would be safe, such outright war between the fyreslayers and the pre-eminent empires of the humans would be disastrous for both, and would bite deep into the truce with Sigmar also.

'Faint-hearts and fair-weather warriors!' Brynnson called his peers when his presence was demanded at the High Temple. He did not like the summons one bit and the accusations of the other runefathers were wearisome in the extreme. 'Grimnir would cover his eyes 'fore he'd look at the likes of you. Had he the guts of his lesser sons, Vulcatrix would have devoured him and the realms would burn eternal.'

But the other runefathers were not cowed by his venomous words and demanded of Brynnson an oath pledging the Ironfists to not raise arms against the civilisations of the humans, or risk being named *ufdaz* – less than duardin. The lodges were bound to one another by lineage and home, but Brynnson did not care for the tone of the other runefathers, nor the threat that his people would be dispossessed by their peers.

'None put words upon my tongue, nor oaths upon my back,' Brynnson roared at them. They had gathered by the Firewell in the heart of the eternal mountain, and before its flames Brynnson raised his fist and pledged his own pact. 'Cross waste and mere, mountain and valley, sea and ice, I will not rest while there is ur-gold to be claimed. Our godlord demands it and thus I vow it!'

How the flames leapt at his words! The runefathers grumbled their disapproval and cut their ties with the Ironfists but there was no opprobrium or censure they could level that would pierce the armour of self-righteousness that guarded Brynnson's purpose.

And despite the misgivings of the oldbeards, it seemed no ill came of the Ironfists' exploits over the years that followed. For near a score of summers the prosperity of the lodges increased and the tribes and cities of humans grew in power and influence. Brynnson was a canny leader and though he held true to his oath, he was of enough sense to venture far from the Great Parch for much time, using the Realmgates to prosecute his hunts for the ur-gold across distant lands in Chamon, and even allied and warred with the wraith-aelves of Shyish.

But vows, once made, never break nor age. Brynnson did not forget the words he had spoken before the Firewell of Grimnir, and their echo would return long after their utterance.

* * *

Though they spent a great deal of time abroad on their wars and quests, on occasion the Ironfists returned to the halls of their lodge at Vostargi Mont and would melt down the ur-gold they had collected. Brynnson would meet with the council and boast of the gains he had made on his endeavours, mocking the other runefathers for the scarcity of their ur-gold. Never let it be said that Brynnson was a modest leader, but he never lied either and spoke as he saw. After returning during one particularly scorching season, Brynnson received word to attend to the council of the most senior runefathers. With no patience to weather further scorn or rebuke, he refused to heed their call. It was only when he learned that a stranger had come to Vostargi Mont demanding audience that he relented in his defiance and climbed the winding stairs and long passages from the lodges of the Ironfists to the High Temple, where the Vostarg and other clans would meet with this visitor.

The one that had come was a human, of slender build even for their kind, and garbed in fine robes of purple and grey. His head was bald and patterned with black ink in zigzag patterns. He wore rings through nose and brow and ears, the glint of the gold pleasing to the eyes of the runefathers, and more precious metals and gems adorned wrist and ankle.

'I am Ologhor Sheng, dreamwalker of the southern plains,' he introduced himself, bowing low before the council. 'I have come before the renowned runefathers of the fyreslayers to offer a pact.'

Storbran, runefather of the Vostarg and head of the council, sat upon a granite throne with a broad Grimnir icon in gold above him. The other runefathers likewise were enthroned upon chairs of stone in a semicircle about their petitioner, while at the human's back burned the unending flame of the Firewell.

'It is uncommon for the children of Sigmar to call upon the sons of Grimnir in this way,' said Storbran.

'But not impossible,' replied Sheng. 'I know of the fyreslayers' quest to recover the shards of their ancestor-god, and that their axes are willing to bite in return for it and many other treasures besides.'

'You have travelled far for this pact,' remarked the runefather of the Whitefire Lodge, Nordron-Grim. 'The southlands lie distant to this peak and you have passed many other potential allies to come here. What is it the fyreslayers possess that these others did not?'

'The will to do what must be done,' replied Sheng. From his robes he produced a small nugget that he held out in his palm, the glint of the gold ruddy and lively in the light of the Firewell. 'Ur-gold. And there will be more if we can find common ground.'

The lodgemasters gathered close while Storbran called for his Auric runelord, the widely famed Augun-Skrandin. To their experienced eyes the claims of the human seemed true, but in the matter of ur-gold no duardin takes an assertion at face value. When Augun-Skrandin arrived, Sheng delivered to his hand the piece of metal.

Augun-Skrandin, wise in the ways of ore and seam, proceeded to assay the offering of Sheng. He rubbed a gnarled thumb upon its surface, listening to the sound. He smelt the gold and examined it through the lenses of his Auric scrutineer. Holding the nugget between finger and thumb the Auric runelord touched it with the tip of his tongue and closed his eyes, savouring and assessing the taste.

'Seems right,' he offered as summation of his appraisal, but held up his hand when Sheng made to retrieve his nugget. 'There's one more test and we'll know for sure.'

Holding the alleged ur-gold on a calloused palm he approached Storbran. The runelord lifted his hand close to the rune of ur-gold hammered into the left arm of his liege and all eyes were set upon the small piece of golden metal. As it drew closer it started to shake upon his palm, twisting ever so slightly as iron is wont to do when close to the lodestone. Nearer still the runelord moved his palm and both flesh-runes and nugget began to gleam in sympathetic recognition. From the body of Storbran the ur-gold glowed with an orange hue. Upon the palm of Augun-Skrandin a darker red shone, flickering with tiny black filaments. The elder's brow creased like the deep valleys of the Cynder Peaks.

'Not ur-gold?' whispered his runefather.

''Tis ur-gold, right enough,' the runelord declared, tipping it back into the hand of Sheng. 'Though of a nature I've never seen before.'

'There is more,' announced Sheng, as the lords of Vostargi Mont returned to their stone seats. 'The land of my people is rich with these deposits.'

'Be warned, Ologhor Sheng, that false promise is a crime punishable by death among the fyreslayers,' growled Storbran, but Sheng showed no hesitation.

'Payment will be made, in full.'

'Payment you have offered yet you have not said for what task it will be exchanged.'

'I wish the deaths of my enemies, and only the fyreslayers have the strength and the determination to end them.' Sheng looked at all the gathered runefathers while his hand slipped the ur-gold back into its nestling place within his robe. 'The tribes of the Flamescar Plateau are gathering for an ancient rite. The chieftains of those I wish dead will meet to choose one amongst their number to represent them at this celebration. To have so many leaders of my foes in one place is opportunity too ripe to waste, and so I call upon you to bring your blades with me and lay them upon my enemies at this tribal council, slaying them all at a stroke and scattering their people.'

'It is bloody work indeed,' said Storbran, but he rubbed his chin in contemplation. 'Yet not a task beyond the Vostarg. Who are these people that have so earned the wrath of Ologhor Sheng?'

'They are a powerful tribe who have encroached upon our lands for generation after generation without respite. They are called the Direbrands.'

A shared intake of breath greeted this revelation. The Direbrands were known well amongst the lodges, as a sizeable and powerful people of the Flamescar Plateau and, more importantly, as devout and favoured servants of the Thunder God, Sigmar.

'To move against the Direbrands is to dare the wrath of Sigmar himself,' warned Storbran.

'And yet I thought the fyreslayers only indebted themselves to the memory of Grimnir,' retorted Sheng. 'I did not know Sigmar had cowed the folk of Vostargi Mont so well.'

'Ease your tongue, Ologhor Sheng, and do not think to shame us with words when the deed you ask of us risks war with an ally of our father-god.' Storbran shook his head, the rings and finials of gold in his beard clanging against each other. 'No, it will not be done. Even promise of ur-gold is not worth the shattering of the peace that has been forged here.'

Sheng nodded and shrugged, accepting this judgement with good grace. He said nothing but turned his gaze to the next runefather, Orskard-Nok of the Forgestorm. Orskard-Nok shook his head also.

And so it continued, from one runefather to the next. In turn each silently declined the contract that Sheng offered.

All but one.

'Mithering soft-hearts,' growled Brynnson Drakkazak. He stepped down from his chair and ran a hand through his fine crest, sparks of ur-fire gleaming from his fingers. 'You'd let the shards of our mighty father-god lie in the chests of these mystics rather than bloody your axes?'

'To move on the Direbrands–' began Storbran, but Brynnson did not care for the argument.

'Gold is gold,' the runefather of the Ironfists declared. He pointed to the flames where he had pledged himself to the spirit of Grimnir. 'And ur-gold belongs to us, wherever it has fallen. Would Grimnir have held his blade back? No! And neither shall the Ironfists!'

The condemnation of the others was like the breaking of a storm, but their words troubled Brynnson no more than the patter of rain on the flanks of Vostargi Mont. With Sheng at his side, he left the High Temple to seal the pact.

When Brynnson led his forgesons from the Ironfists' halls it seemed as though the sky itself was a vast sea of embers. That erratic heavenly body that was called the Sky Crucible burned ruddily above, its wayward course taking it over the Flamescar Plateau as it slowly arced from the north. Its scarlet crescent met a swathe of storm clouds that had swept up from the south, as though the tempest had been following Sheng. The human mystic called the waxing orb above the Blood Moon and said its motions across the sky had guided him to Vostargi Mont.

Sheng guided the fyreslayers for many days, while each night the Blood Moon grew larger and larger. The Ironfists did not need much rest, and slept only for a small portion of the night, but when they stopped after each march Sheng would erect a small tent and hide himself away. Strange smells and sounds emanated from this dwelling, and often the human could be heard chanting in some unknown tongue.

Unsettled by this behaviour, Brynnson confronted Sheng and demanded to know what he was doing. The dreamwalker took the runefather into his tent and showed him many crystals of different sizes and shapes: ruby, emerald and sapphire, each carved with small designs of interlocking lines and circles, so that their irregular planes created odd shadows by the firelight, thrown upon a stark white sheet Sheng had drawn across one end of the tent.

Upon a brazier he heated dozens of strangely wrought brands, each as small as a thumbnail and exquisitely fashioned. Brynnson did not recognise the symbols as any language of duardin, human or aelf that he had encountered, but Sheng assured the runefather that they were nothing more than the tools of his rituals.

'By the crystals I step into the dreamworld between the realms, my thoughts travelling on currents of past, present and future. In that state I use the symbol brands to record what I see, in the mystical language of my people. On waking I interpret what I have written.'

He showed Brynnson sheaves of brand-marked paper, the individual runes dark, their accumulation creating whorls and angles and lines of letters that seemed like words.

'And what do these dream-visits tell you?' Brynnson asked.

The human answered with a smile.

'That all goes as I foresaw. The Direbrands are holding conclave, as I told you. One among them has already departed with an honour guard, leaving the gathering of their other leaders perfect for the slaughter.'

'Slaughter?' said Brynnson. He was no soft-heart but had marched forth expecting battle.

'They are protected only by their closest family and few guards.' Sheng's delight was clear, his gold-studded teeth showing in the brazier light. 'The greatest and wisest of the Direbrands will be easy pickings for a throng as ferocious as the Ironfists.'

As Sheng had said, so it was to be.

Three nights later the lodge warriors of Brynnson Drakkazak came upon the encampment of the Direbrands. They were in their revels, celebrating the coming together of their widespread tribe, drunk equally upon strong wine and good humour.

The fyreslayers fell upon the camp with brutal ferocity, led by their runefather. Scores of foes fell in the opening charge, several hundreds more in the following battle. Brynnson let his fury flow as molten metal spills from the forge. His ur-runes blazed with the ire of Grimnir and his axe smote many a bone that bloody night. The Ironfists followed the lead of their runefather and showed no mercy, even as Sheng urged them on with exultant shouts and promises of reward.

By the light of their fires, the Direbrands died. Though set upon by a terrible foe, worse the wear for their drinking and feasting, not one tried to run or surrender. As defiant an enemy as Brynnson had ever seen, the Direbrands fought to the last, man and woman, blades in hands as they were cut down.

Sheng stalked among the dead and spat upon their bodies, joyful at the carnage.

'Enough,' Brynnson called to the man, axe in hand. 'They died well, they deserve no disrespect.'

'Speak not of respect until you have fulfilled your contract,' Sheng replied with a snarl. He pointed to the tents of the Direbrands a short way off from the fires. 'You promised the death of all that attended the gathering.'

Shamed by the accusation of oathbreaking, Brynnson led his warriors upon this second camp. Yet there were children in the camp and even the battle-raged fyreslayers baulked at slaying these innocents.

'You paid for warriors, not murderers,' Brynnson told his employer. 'You have won – the Direbrands will not recover from the blow you have dealt tonight.'

'I want them all dead!' shrieked Sheng, and he raged more, in tongues both understandable and foreign, calling the Ironfists weak-thewed and dishonourable. 'None of them are to survive. The Direbrands will not rise to threaten my lord again.'

'What lord do you serve?' demanded Brynnson, for his pact had been with Sheng and no other patron had been mentioned by the mystic.

'One that will long remember this slight, Brynnson Drak-kazak of the Ironfists.'

The threat was empty though, for Sheng could not force the fyreslayers to turn their weapons on the infants.

'They'll die without care, all the same,' the southerner said eventually. 'The Flamescar Plateau is a cruel bower to sleep in.'

'Do not think to shirk the payment,' Brynnson warned.

'Of course not,' said Sheng, bitter and snarling. From his belongings he brought forth ingots of ur-gold, eight of them as had been agreed. A considerable sum for the effort involved, Brynnson had thought, but now he knew why the price had been so generous.

'Take them and be gone,' Sheng bid the fyreslayers.

Brynnson did not think it boded well for the children for them to be left with Sheng, but he could not raise a weapon against the mystic while their pact was in place.

'Never come again to Vostargi Mont,' he told the dream-walker. 'If you do, you'll find the axe-welcome waiting for you.'

Leaving the remnants of the camp burning in their wake, the Ironfists took their ur-gold from Sheng and departed.

The journey back to Vostargi Mont was one of mixed feelings for Brynnson. The deed performed left ash in his mouth, even as the gentle whisper of the ur-gold he had earned for his lodge soothed his worries. All the while they travelled back to Vostargi Mont the Blood Moon continued to swell to fullness, glaring down upon the Ironfists with its ruddy gaze. The Great Parch seemed to burn beneath its eternal stare, the air hot and still. A latent but potent tension lay upon the world.

Coming back to their halls, Brynnson called upon his rune-lords and runesmiters to smelt the ur-gold and fashion the flesh-runes as swiftly as possible. They warned that the portents were poor for such work, that the forging of runes beneath the swollen Sky Crucible was never wise. Brynnson roared at them to follow his command and against their better judgement the runeworkers complied. The ur-gold from Sheng was melted down and the blessings of Grimnir laid upon it as it cooled in the moulds.

Runefather, runesons and all the Ironfists came to the temples to receive their reward and a great hammering was undertaken, to set ur-gold into flesh as tradition dictated. Brynnson was first and as the shard-flesh of Grimnir touched his skin he felt the power of the warrior-god course into his veins, bringing strength and pain and a deep burning through his body. He did not cry out, for it was against his creed to show any weakness.

And when the ritual was done he bid the runesmiters to labour on his kin as the smouldering runes settled into his muscle and turned sinew to taut iron.

That next night the Blood Moon waxed fullest, a ruddy orb pierced by the summit of Vostargi Mont. The fire in Brynnson's flesh had not settled and the ache of the runes chafed his spirit as he declared a feast of celebration for the lodge. Uneasy in his own skin, Brynnson climbed to the outer galleries of his lodge halls and stood upon the flanks of the mountain.

Looking to the south he saw a terrible tumult in the skies, of a black-clouded storm that boiled upon the far horizon, churning above the southern seas. A flickering face of almighty wrath and terrifying power appeared within the stormhead and it was as though the light of the Sky Crucible above reignited the flames that had smelted the ur-gold, for suddenly his body was ablaze.

The flames burned into Brynnson, and even as his cries resounded from the mountainsides so he heard the anguished bellows and roars of pain from his kin within the lodge halls. In the echo of the clamour he heard a voice, recognising it as Sheng's.

'Your fate is sealed, the curse brought upon you by your treachery against the Lord of Skulls,' that dread voice declared. 'From the ancient rocks of the World-That-Was the duardin were born. Into your flesh that lava-birth is re-enacted! And so for your kin forever more. When Grimnir fought Vulcatrix and was shattered, not all his pieces fell first to the Mortal Realms. The Bloodthirsty Power who had delighted in the battle between god and drake took his toll. He bade the Crimson Smiths that labour in the infernal citadel to bind the ur-gold with brass from the walls of his keep, and so forever made it part of his bloody domain. That reward should have made you stronger than any other, but in shunning the Blood God you have sealed your doom instead. Now the blood-marked ur-gold will turn your flesh to the magma of its birth!'

'Yet the curse was not to slay the Ironfists,' Ungrimmsson told the fyreslayer, gesturing at the lava-form of his own body. 'But still we are fyreslayers, though we have raised axe against ally and our own kind, and are exiled from the mountain of our birth. By Brynnson's oath we are bound, still searching for Grimnir in the ur-gold wherever it has fallen.'

'And that is how we earned the name Zharrthagi, for killing in betrayal?'

'It is,' Ungrimmsson said with a sour look.

'You speak the tale as though you remember it, lodge-sire.'

'I do, for it was not just the Ironfists whose name changed.' A tear of flame ran down Ungrimmsson's cheek. 'It was me that took the payment. And for generation after generation Khorne has kept me alive to know the price of my betrayal.'

Alvi swallowed hard at this revelation, eyes wide with shock. Now the fyreslayer understood the truth behind the name Ungrimmsson – inheritor of the broken oath.

'Back to your blade-brothers, now,' said Ungrimmsson.

The Bloodbound horde was but a hundred paces away, the earth rumbling beneath their feet, their cries and crashing weapons a din that rang back from the gatehouse and mountainside.

Fifty paces distant the army of Khorne's mortal followers slowed and stopped. A single figure emerged from the front line, a warrior taller than any other. She was clad in red-and-black armour, a standard of bones tied to her back, and carried an axe in each hand.

She approached the runefather, but there was no challenge nor charge. The champion of Khorne set her axes into the earth a few paces from Ungrimmsson and brought forth a small sack. She upended it into her palm, where a ruddy light shone from nuggets of metal. Ungrimmsson felt the runes in his body twitch in recognition of tainted ur-gold, the same that had cursed the Zharrthagi.

'Blood is blood, Khorne cares not who sheds it,' said the champion, putting the ur-gold back into the bag before throwing it to Ungrimmsson's feet.

'And gold is gold,' replied Ungrimmsson, stooping to pick up the sack as he turned towards the gates, readying his axe with his other hand.

THE DEEPER SHADE

C L Werner

Mighty waves crashed against the craggy shore, splashing the luminescent boulders with a briny spray. Steam rose from the rocks as the salt evaporated, repulsed by the strange stones. Dun-coloured surf-spiders cast webs across the vapour, greedily drawing the dissolved mineral into their maws with claw-like mandibles. Overhead, flocks of winged lizards circled in search of the squamous molluscs cast up by the tide. Plant-like anemones slowly slithered along the beach, their stinging tendrils ready to stun any lizard that flew too near and their foot-stomachs ready to consume anything left helpless on the sand.

The shores of Gharn were vibrant with strange life. All except one place. A great finger of luminescent stone that projected far out into the bay, curling in upon itself like the horn of a mighty ram. Such was the atmosphere of nameless dread that clung to the spot that not even the surf-spiders were witless enough to trespass there. Only men had so little regard for their own lives.

Thalinosh of Charr ran his fingers through the turquoise feathers that coated his arms and studied the grim outcropping. The curving mass of rocks was just as he had seen it when he had cast the rune-bones and made his auguries. It was always a risk to seek wisdom from daemons, for there was invariably a maliciousness in such transactions, lies hidden inside truth and truth woven within a skein of lies. To gain power, a sorcerer had to quickly learn what to believe and what to reject.

'There it is, my lord. The Claw of Mermedus.' The words came in a low whine from the tortured wreck that had been Thalinosh's apprentice until a few weeks ago. He tried to give his master an ingratiating smile, but his face was too mangled to manage the effort. 'That is where I was attacked. I was fortunate to escape with my life.'

'Yes,' Thalinosh hissed. 'Most fortunate. Even more fortunate that I found you before Carradras.' The sorcerer's hands tightened into fists as he spoke his rival's name. Gratz had grown impatient and ambitious, seeking a master who would advance his knowledge of the black arts more swiftly than Thalinosh. Carradras had promised to meet those desires... for a price.

'The dogs of Chaos always bite their own!' A bitter laugh wracked the battered old man who lay prostrate in the sand at Thalinosh's feet. His face was a mash of bruises and cuts, his once pristine robes now tattered and torn. There was a jewelled chain around his neck, but the symbol that had once hung from it was gone, stamped underfoot by Thalinosh's followers. The hammer of the God-King was not exactly held with fondness by the disciples of Tzeentch.

The old man's speech brought an angry snarl from the creature that stood over him. The fur-covered brute stamped down with his iron-shod hoof and smashed the captive's thigh. Sharga grunted in amusement when the priest cried out in pain. The rest of Thalinosh's warband echoed the beastman's savage laughter.

'No more games,' Thalinosh said, raising one of his feathered hands and commanding his followers to silence. Human and beastkin alike, they knew better than to question the sorcerer's orders. They had the recent example of the priest's torture to remind them of what happened to those who defied Thalinosh.

Thalinosh knelt beside the old man. His touch was almost gentle when he reached out and lifted the priest's face from the sand so they might look one another in the eye. 'This is the place I am meant to be. The place the Changer has sent me to find.' The sorcerer's sallow features drew back in a cold smile. 'Tell me again why your people will not fish in this bay. Why they will not hunt along this shore.' He looked out to the outcropping. 'Why is it that nothing will dare those rocks?'

The old priest returned Thalinosh's gaze. For just an instant, through the mien of defeat and subjugation, the sorcerer detected a glimmer of triumph. The prisoner had let his guard down and now the captor would wrest the truth from his mind.

'You… Will… Speak…' Thalinosh's eyes blazed with energy as he evoked his magic. Some of the feathers on his arms curled up and fell out, rolling across the sand as desiccated, withered things. He could feel the arcane power crawling through his flesh, seeking to transform still more of his body. He redirected that power into his spell, setting his mind against the priest's will.

Weakened by torture and doubt, the priest's defiance was not equal to Thalinosh's magic. Words came spilling off his tongue. 'There is a cave beneath the water where dwells a ravenous phantom. Man or beast, it spares nothing that invades its domain. It pulls its victims asunder, leaving only ragged fragments to be washed in with the tide. The bones are always cracked, the marrow sucked out and only a black slime left within. No ship will dare these waters and no village has long stood upon these shores.'

Thalinosh smiled at the priest's recitation. 'A phantom?' he mused. 'You claim it is some murdering ghost that has wrought such havoc? Yet what need would a ghost have for the marrow in a man's bones? What revenant would squander its wrath upon fish and birds?'

'It has been seen,' the old man whispered. 'Or rather the effect of its attack has been seen. Sailors brought up from the decks of their ships, screaming as spectral hands broke them apart, rending them limb by limb.' He drove his fist against the sand. 'I have seen it happen, watched as my own wife was taken by the accursed fiend!'

The sorcerer laid his hand on his prisoner's head. 'I have seen it too. In my auguries.' He glanced at the cowering Gratz. 'My apprentice has told me something of it, how it tried to snatch him from his boat but instead only succeeded in taking from him the treasure he stole from me. A treasure that has been lost.' Thalinosh gazed out at the bay, his eyes peering at the rolling waves. 'Until now, that is.'

Sharga cocked his goat-like head to one side and peered at Thalinosh with a bulbous, ophidian eye. 'Cave is under water. Cannot fight. You bring ghost out for fight?'

Thalinosh scowled at his bestial underling. 'It is no ghost,' he told Sharga, making sure his voice was loud enough for the rest of the warband to hear. 'And it would serve no purpose to lure our enemy to us. We must face it in its lair.'

'How?' the ebon-armoured Borir asked. The warrior rapped her gauntlet against the steel of her breastplate. 'I have served under your banner for many years, but I did not do so simply to sink and drown.' She turned her skull-masked helm and considered the rest of Thalinosh's dozen followers. 'We are none of us fish, sorcerer. We cannot march into this phantom's watery grave.'

Thalinosh gestured at Borir with a crooked finger. 'We can and we will,' he told her. He stared down at the captive priest. 'With a bit of help from our new friend, we will find the cave.'

The priest howled in terror when he saw the cruel gleam in Thalinosh's eyes.

The priest was a long time in dying. Thalinosh had counted upon that. Some rituals demanded copious amounts of blood, others could be performed only at certain junctures of the constellations. This spell, however, had demanded pain.

Borir had done the cutting, plying the athame with the grisly facility of a butcher. Staked out on the beach at the shore of the bay, the old man was skinned and gutted like a fish, a red ruin of humanity that lingered on only because of the magical sympathy between himself and the pounding waves. With each wet, bloody breath the prisoner drew, a great torrent of water was drawn up from the bay and hurled back into the vastness of the sea. A rippling barrier of force kept the waves from crashing down again, a spiral of eldritch power that defied the raging elements.

Thalinosh gave the dying priest an almost affectionate glance as the bay was drained. Only the diametric opposition of the sacrifice could have endowed the ritual with the power to do what he demanded of it. The pious zealotry of a holy man matched against the profane ambitions of the sorcerer. It was almost beautiful in its poetry of antagonism.

The other component of the sacrifice sat on the sands with his legs folded. Gratz, Thalinosh's apprentice, had been oblivious to his true role in the ritual until much too late. The sorcerer used his former student as a conduit, a channel for the awesome magic he evoked. There was only so much power a frail mantle of mortal flesh could withstand. Gratz was past that limit now. His body had been reduced to a blackened husk, the skin sloughing away from his smouldering bones. Like the priest, the apprentice persisted only because of the ritual's energies; without that his tortured wretchedness would have expired hours ago.

'It is enough,' Thalinosh decided when the bay was drained down to the very dregs. From where he stood on the beach he could see the black fissure that gaped on the opposite side of the emptied bay, at the base of the clawlike rock. The cave mouth stood exposed, a dark cavity in the luminescent stone. A litter of bones and wrecked ships poked up from the muddy floor, the oldest of them coated in thick encrustations of barnacles. The haunter of the bay had been quite busy over the centuries.

'It is enough,' the sorcerer repeated. He motioned to Sharga. The beastman swung his heavy cudgel and mashed the priest's skull with a single blow. The last draw of seawater fell back into the bay, spilling across the mud and pooling in its deepest recesses as the prisoner's pulse was silenced. Gratz howled even louder as the full force of the spell closed upon him. Thalinosh gave his apprentice an appraising scrutiny. There was enough left of the man that he should be good for a few more hours. After that, the barrier between bay and sea would vanish and the waves would come crashing back. Before that happened, his work needed to be finished.

'Stay here and watch over Gratz,' Thalinosh commanded two of his other acolytes. The robed cultists flanked the doomed apprentice, standing guard over him with bared swords. There was small chance of anyone or anything disturbing the ritual now, but it paid to be cautious.

'You are going down to the cave?' Borir asked, a trace of uneasiness in her tone.

'We are going into the cave,' Thalinosh corrected her. His gaze swept across the rest of his retinue. Erudite cultists, barbaric warriors and mutant beastkin, they all shrank before the sorcerer's imperious regard. 'What we have come here to find is in that cave,' he stated. 'And we are not leaving here without it.' He pointed at Gratz's withered body and drew their attention to the man's fading vitality. It was a vivid way to impress on them the essence of urgency.

The warband hastened down into the muck of the bay, sloughing through the mire of mud and sand. They picked their way across the field of skeletons and wrecked ships, drawing towards the black opening of the cave. A warm, evil smell billowed from the fissure, a cloying stench that made the skin crawl. The luminous rock was subdued here, cloaked in a black scum that dripped from the walls. Jumbled bones lay heaped around the cave's mouth, splintered in some uncanny fashion that made them look twisted rather than cracked. Thalinosh paused to examine one. Just as the priest had said, the marrow had been extracted and replaced with a tarry sort of slime.

Leading the way, one of the beastmen was the first to venture into the cave. His terrified bleats were heard a moment later. When Thalinosh reached the cave mouth, the cries collapsed into a sickening gurgle. All that could be seen of the creature were his horns as he was sucked down by a patch of quicksand.

'Bind yourselves together,' Borir ordered as she retrieved a roll of rope from one of the marauders. 'Around the waist and in groups of three.'

Thalinosh declined Borir's offer to tie the sorcerer to herself and Sharga. He had his own methods of escaping the hazards of the cave if it became necessary.

Their precautions taken, the warband resumed their advance into the rank depths of the cave. The layer of slime that coated the walls was patchy, exposing just enough of the luminescent rock to ease the gloom, casting everything in a mousy grey light. The profusion of splintered bones remained persistent, but now they were mingled with other debris. Rusted armour and swords were much in evidence, as were the decaying remains of chests and casks. Goblets and plates of obvious workmanship lay scattered about. Battered coffers rested amidst piles of coins. The gleam of gemstones shone from the mud and slime. All the treasures of sunken ships and demolished villages had been drawn into the cave.

'Something is here,' Borir whispered, her sword clenched tight in her hands. Far from evoking a sense of avarice, seeing the accumulated treasure had instead aroused an increased wariness in the warrior.

'This predator's lair,' Sharga grunted. 'Hunter live here. Bring prey here to eat.' The beastman lifted his head and snorted loudly. 'Cannot tell if smell old or new. Maybe hunter here. Maybe hunter gone.'

Thalinosh made arcane passes with his hands, evoking a minor divination spell. 'What I seek is deeper in the cave,' he declared. 'Whatever is here, be it beast, phantom or daemon, it will not stand in my way.' He waved his hand at the leading group of warriors. 'Onwards, or would you prefer to wait for the sea to come rushing back?'

The threat overcame the misgivings of his followers. Warily, they probed further into the gloom of the grotto. Finally, the leading warrior called back to Thalinosh. 'My lord, the way ahead is still flooded! The tunnel angles downwards and is filled with water.'

Thalinosh moved forwards and inspected the scene. The

tunnel remained wide enough to run a brace of chariots through side by side and the ceiling was still far above them. The floor, however, had taken a sharp decline, angling deeper than it had before. Ahead of them, all that could be seen was the reflection of light across still water. It was here in this flooded cavern, his sorcery told him, that the thing he sought would be found.

'We go on,' Thalinosh said. He pointed at his vanguard and slowly gestured to the flooded tunnel. 'Do not fear. My magic will protect you from whatever waits in the dark.'

Reassured, the warrior and those tied to him by the rope advanced into the ankle-high water. The second group of three followed after them. Thalinosh motioned to Borir and Sharga to wait. Let the others take the risk of drawing out the cave's inhabitant. They could be replaced easily enough. More easily than the magic it would take to really cast protective wards over them.

Thalinosh let the two groups of minions get twenty yards down the flooded tunnel before he ordered his henchmen to follow. The sorcerer kept behind them, his eyes glowing with arcane light as they adjusted to the increasing darkness. The walls here were thick with slime, almost utterly blotting out the luminescent rock beneath. Long strings of black mucus dripped from the ceiling, lending their reek to the clammy, stagnant air.

'Bones under water,' the bird-faced beastman leading the second group of three declared. 'Toes feel bones.'

'Hold your tongue, turnskin,' the vanguard hissed. 'Your racket might wake the phantom.' The warning made the two cultists with him glance around in fear while the scraggly brays in the second group looked behind to gauge how far they would have to run if they had to flee the cave. The bird-faced tzaangor leading them grunted sullenly, but made no further comment.

The cave pushed deeper into the earth. The water level now was chest-high for the warrior leading the way. The walls were so thick with slime that the intruders began slashing at them with their swords and axes to scrape away some of the encrustation and expose patches of luminous rock to provide them a little light.

A sound from ahead stopped the vanguard just as he was swinging his sword to chop at the wall. A loud, wet plop that echoed through the tunnel, it was unlike the faint drips and splashes caused by the mucus falling from the roof.

Thalinosh's magically attuned sight could decipher no more than the mundane vision of his followers. Stifled by the reek in the air, even the bestial senses of his more animalistic minions were unable to detect anything. All they had were their ears, and everyone was silent as they strained to draw some betraying sound from the darkness.

The tense vigil ended in a blood-curdling shriek. The lead warrior screamed and flailed at the water. Before anyone could react, he was yanked under the scummy surface. The cultist behind him howled in terror as the rope grew taut and he too was jerked beneath the water. The last of the trio whipped out his knife and sawed frantically at the rope. He was also pulled under, but unlike his companions, he soon reappeared, gasping and floundering in the flooded tunnel. Freed from the drag of his doomed comrades, the cultist started swimming back towards Thalinosh and the others.

Panicked cries filled the cave. The tzaangor and his brays were clawing at their rope, preferring to risk the quicksand than be drowned by whatever had taken the vanguard. Borir and Sharga had already slashed the cord that connected them, but neither strayed any deeper into the cave.

Thalinosh raised his hand and muttered words of power.

From his palm, a sphere of blue light flashed into being and went streaking down the tunnel. By its glow, the terrified cultist could be seen trudging through the water. Beyond him, a litter of torn flesh bobbed to the surface, remains so ravaged they scarcely could be recognised as human.

'Hold fast!' Thalinosh snarled at his minions. The beastmen gazed at him in confusion. The surviving cultist simply ignored him and continued to flee.

By the magic light, Thalinosh could see the water behind the defiant cultist shiver, disturbed by something moving beneath it. The surface bubbled violently, as though the thing were rising. Yet still there was nothing to be seen.

The cultist shrieked as he was suddenly jerked backwards. Thalinosh watched in wonder as the man was lifted into the air. He flailed about, suspended midway between the water and the dripping roof. The sorcerer could see nothing holding the man. There was a grisly rending sound. An arm popped from its socket and was then torn free. Then the opposite leg was pulled from the man's body.

It was, Thalinosh thought, just as the priest had claimed – havoc wrought by an invisible phantom.

Only one thing marred the impression. When the cultist's other leg was ripped free, Thalinosh saw his midsection collapse as well, pinched as if gripped in a gargant's hand.

'Stay, you fools!' the sorcerer snarled as his remaining followers turned towards the mouth of the cave. 'It is no ghost, and I will prove it to you!'

At his gesture, Thalinosh brought the sphere of light speeding down towards the levitating cultist. Before the orb could reach the body it crashed against some unseen barrier between magic and man. The sphere shattered, dispersing as a wave of crackling blue lightning. As the wave shivered through the air, it followed the contours of the immense bulk that towered over its mangled victim. Thick tentacles were revealed, wrapped about the corpse and its severed limbs. The outlines of a vast body-head were suggested, rearing up from the scummy water.

'Krakigon,' Thalinosh hissed. He had read of such monsters in obscure bestiaries but never had he expected to see one. For one thing, it was reputed that they made themselves invisible by means of the slime they excreted from their pores.

Reeling from the shock of Thalinosh's spell, the krakigon lurched backwards. It hurled the dismembered pieces of its victim away, sending them crashing against the walls. As the sections of carcass struck, patches of slime rubbed away. The luminescent rock was exposed, throwing shafts of light into the cave. Those bits of the krakigon caught in the light stood revealed, taking on a visible solidity. The beast's hide was at once both rubbery and scaly, shaded a dull grey with yellow markings. The tip of each tentacle ended in a bony spear, its edges viciously barbed. Along the underside of each limb were thousands of tiny toothless mouths, each with a sharp tongue as barbed and gruesome as the spears themselves.

Those portions of the krakigon caught in the light swiftly adjusted to the illumination, fading again into invisibility as it matched its hue to the difference. The beast swung its tentacles at the walls, rubbing its slimy skin across the exposed rock to once more smother its light in slime.

'Before it can vanish!' Borir shouted. 'Attack! Kill!' She raised her sickle-bladed sword and charged towards the krakigon. The beastkin, only a moment before on the verge of panic, rallied to her and rushed at the monster in a snarling mass.

Thalinosh drew upon his sorcery to set an aura of energy crackling around Borir before she reached the monster. When the krakigon struck at her, the scaly arm was repulsed by the arcane ward, peeling away like the petals of some gory flower. The limb flailed about in agony, no longer an unseen phantom, but a dead mass of tissue incapable of camouflaging itself.

The tzaangor was not so fortunate as Borir. Without Thalinosh's protection, he was snatched up in the krakigon's coils. The beastman howled as he was pulled from the water and dashed against the roof of the cave. A single blow was enough to turn his birdlike head into bloody mash. One of the brays was caught by an invisible tentacle, his furry body twisted by the unseen grip until it was wrenched in half and sent flying across the cave.

'Under the water!' Thalinosh shouted to his followers. The surviving members of his warband ducked under the scummy surface as the sorcerer stretched forth his hand. From his fingers a writhing sheet of gibbous fire exploded across the tunnel. The outline of the krakigon stood revealed as its gigantic bulk was caught in the blaze. The brute's tentacles lashed through the air as the arcane flames flared across it. The slime coating its limbs sizzled away in the conflagration.

So too did the slime coating the walls and ceiling. Burned away by the sorcerer, the muck exposed the long-hidden luminous rock beneath. The krakigon's smoking body was caught in the light, its charred hide incapable of reacting to the sudden illumination. The monster stood revealed in its totality, a great scaly bulk some fifty feet long with tentacles jutting from its rubbery sides. Four enormous flippers propelled it through the water. The head jutted directly from the top of its roughly ovoid body, a string of eight black eyes flanked by feathery gills.

Thalinosh fixated upon a single spot on the brute's body, a darker patch amidst its greys and yellows, an impossible shadow embedded in its scaly hide. He recognised the object caught there, the artefact that had been stolen from him by his treacherous apprentice. A sliver of shadowy glass the length of his hand. A relic from a lost realm and an eldritch magic.

The sorcerer raised his hand once more, but the immolation he had conjured had taxed his energies and disturbed his concentration. Instead Thalinosh pointed at the artefact. 'The shadeglass,' he snarled at his followers. 'Retrieve the shadeglass!'

Sharga nodded his horned head and bellowed a savage war cry. The beastman leapt upon the krakigon, chopping at it with his axe. At the same time, Borir came against the monster from the side. Her sword licked across one of the tentacles, severing it almost at the root, and sent it squirming mindlessly through the water.

The krakigon lurched forwards; three of its tentacles lashed out and caught the last of the brays. The screaming beastman was wrenched apart by the scaly coils. The gory remains were tossed aside as the monster surged for Borir.

Sharga charged the monster, sinking his axe into the krakigon's hide. He swung his weapon as though it were a mountaineer's pick, using it to ascend the creature's enormity. It flailed about, lashing at him with several tentacles, oblivious to the gashes its spear-like spikes opened in its rubbery flesh.

Borir dived beneath the water to avoid the coils that whipped towards her. Sinking from view, the warrior circled the krakigon to rise behind it. Sighting the monster's enormous eye, she hefted her sword like a javelin and hurled it at the staring orb. The sickle blade raked across the gigantic eye. Pulpy jelly exploded from the ruptured organ and the krakigon shuddered in agonised spasms.

'Sharga! The shadeglass!' Thalinosh shouted to the beastman. The goat-headed henchman was clinging to the writhing krakigon like a horsebreaker riding a wild stallion. Turn and shudder whichever way it might, the tortured monster could not throw Sharga off.

Thalinosh drew upon the dregs of arcane power yet lingering in his drained essence. Again, a crackle of fire leapt from his outstretched hand. No grand conflagration as before, but a mere lance of fiery light. Yet he put the spell to more direct effect. Following Borir's example, he attacked one of the monster's eyes, popping it in a burst of steam and blood.

The krakigon's tentacles whipped across the ceiling, gouging great gaps in the rock. Debris rained down on the creature, slamming into its scaly body. While the pain-maddened brute lashed out at the rocks, Sharga made his move. Plunging away from the grip of his axe and leaving the weapon embedded in the monster's hide, he sought the dark, shimmering sliver of shadeglass. The beastman bellowed as he tore at the trapped artefact. It was wedged deep in the krakigon's flesh, but Sharga's brawny grasp was such that it came free with a single pull.

The beastman toppled into the water with his prize. The krakigon lashed the water around Sharga, but before it could make a more determined assault, a great boulder came crashing down from the roof of its cave. The monster's central mass was smashed beneath the enormous weight, crushed beneath it like an insect. The flailing tentacles groped and slithered against the burden, but try as it might, the mass was too much for the krakigon to budge.

Sharga sloshed his way through the flooded tunnel, water dripping from his fur, blood oozing from his wounds. He held the shadeglass before him, proudly showing it to Thalinosh. Then the beastman stopped. A confused look swept into his eyes. He stared down at his chest, unable to comprehend the blade that had punched through his back and skewered his heart. He bellowed and fell to his knees. His last act was to turn his horned head and stare at his murderer.

Borir ripped the athame free and snatched the shadeglass from Sharga's faltering grip. She stepped back as the beastman collapsed face first into the black water. The warrior flicked his blood from the ceremonial dagger and turned towards Thalinosh.

'Treachery,' the sorcerer stated.

Borir laughed. 'Oh yes, treachery,' she mocked him. 'You should not have expended so much of your power fighting the krakigon. I have been with you long enough to know your limits.' She shook her head. 'I would have waited, but this opportunity was too good to forsake.'

'Carradras must have promised you a great deal,' Thalinosh said. 'When Gratz stole the shadeglass, I suspected he did not act alone. He must have held that secret to the last, thinking you would save him.'

Thalinosh expected Borir to say something. He was surprised when she suddenly threw the dagger at him. The athame flickered as it sped across the tunnel and struck the sorcerer, burying its blade deep in his chest. He staggered back. The sorcerer struck the wall and slowly slid to the floor.

'Carradras is mighty in the esteem of Tzeentch,' Borir declared. 'His star is rising, while yours has most certainly set, Thalinosh of Charr. For all your divinations, you could not see what was right before you!'

It was Thalinosh's turn to laugh. 'If my foresight has failed me, how much more has your own betrayed you, Borir? I am dying, and with me dies my magic. What do you think will hold the sea back when I am gone?'

Borir's eyes went wide as she realised the import of Thalinosh's words. Gratz was simply a vessel, a channel by which the sorcerer's spell was maintained. Without Thalinosh, the enchantment would be broken and the krakigon's cave would be submerged once more!

The warrior did not linger to mock the man she had betrayed. Quickly wrapping the shadeglass in her cloak, she ran down the tunnel. Thalinosh watched her go. Her panic was a thing of true amusement.

Once Borir was out of sight, Thalinosh reached to his chest and withdrew the athame. The dagger had struck true, but it was he who had forged it and his magic that endowed its enchantment. Stabbing him with it was like returning a part of his own body to him. As the blade emerged from his flesh, the wound closed up behind it.

Thalinosh glanced at the trapped krakigon and at the hole it had ripped from the ceiling. He could see the faint twinkle of starlight through that hole. An egress far more convenient than the way he had entered the grotto.

The sorcerer laughed as he thought of Borir racing back through the cave and the frantic climb up the cliff. Even moving at her most frantic, how long would it take her to reach the top? Thalinosh hurried to the hole in the roof of the grotto. He drew the last dregs of power from his body, willing the arcane energies to hasten his ascent.

Sunlight spilled down around Thalinosh as he emerged onto the beach. In the distance he could see the guards standing beside Gratz's withered body. He could see the drained bay and the magical barrier that kept the sea from rushing back in. There was the black mouth of the cave and, just faintly visible, an armoured figure scrambling away from it.

Thalinosh paused as he considered the shadeglass. It was a curious relic, something that would be full of promise once it yielded its secrets to him. It would be a shame to lose it again when it was so nearly his. Yet Borir had spoken truth when she said she knew the limits of his power. He had no magic left to use against her. All he had was the sorcery he had already evoked.

At a gesture from Thalinosh, Gratz fell prostrate into the sand, his body crumbling into chalky dust. The guards fled from the grisly remains, but their panic was magnified still further when they looked out to the bay and saw the barrier extinguished.

A shriek of terror rang out as Thalinosh saw Borir for the last time. The sea came flooding back into the bay, rushing to fill the places his sorcery had drawn it from. The warrior was smashed beneath the deluge, vanishing the instant her shattered body was engulfed by the waves. Perhaps they would carry her back into the cave, leaving her corpse with those of the krakigon's victims.

Thalinosh stared at the swirling, pounding waves that refilled the bay. His eyes penetrated the angry waters, trying to imagine where the shadeglass had been thrown by the tempest. When he rested and recovered his arcane energies, he would make his auguries. He would return to reclaim the relic.

And this time he could content himself that there would be no traitors in the fold.

GHOSTS OF DEMESNUS

Josh Reynolds

The boat carved a slow track through the thick bulrushes. Clouds of insects, disturbed by its passing, rose towards the pale green sky with an audible hum.

The vessel was a flat-bottomed riverboat, its aft deck stacked with cargo. Bales of cloth from Verdia, and bolts of silk from some far, eastern kingdom were stacked precariously beneath a heavy tarpaulin to keep off the weather. Gardus sat on a large cask of sweet wine beneath the tarpaulin, and watched the home he had all but forgotten draw nearer, through the curtain of morning mist.

The Lord-Celestant shifted on his perch, feeling oddly unbalanced without his weighty silver war-plate. The simple tunic and leather jerkin he wore beneath his woollen Nordrathi cloak had been cut especially for his immortal frame, as had his boots. None of it helped him to fit in.

The crew had given him a wide berth since they had left the riverside docks of Hammerhal Ghyra, despite his initial, hesitant attempts to engage them in conversation. Perhaps it was his size. Or the runeblade he wore at his side. The sword was almost as long as one of the oars the crew used to ply the waters, and its wielder was almost twice the size of the tallest crewman.

Regardless of the reason, they had left him alone. He'd half hoped they would encounter a troggoth or some other malign river-beast on the voyage south along the Quamus River, if only to prove that he and his sword meant them no harm. Such an encounter might have kept him from thinking of what awaited him at the end of his journey. He frowned and turned away from the city as it drew closer.

The dreams had started innocuously.

Gardus barely noticed them, so rarely did he sleep. A fact of his new reality was that the needs of mortality had all but abated. But he'd had time, of late, to ponder such things. To think and consider the echoes within his own head.

Such rumination was not encouraged among the ranks of the Stormcast Eternals. Even less so, when one was not simply a Liberator standing in the battle line, but a Lord-Celestant, with all the duties and obligations that came with such a rank. The past was the past – to try to grasp it was a distraction at best, and outright folly at worst. Warriors had perished, seeking the answers to unspoken questions.

Then, death was not an unfamiliar experience for Gardus.

Nonetheless, he'd done as always and sought solace in the movement of the stars. He had climbed the highest peaks of Azyr, and then further still, following the winding celestine bastions of Sigmaron to the uppermost heights, where the blue gave way to the black. Finally, he had wandered the outer rings of the Sigmarabulum, so close to the firmament that he'd fancied he might slip and fall upwards forever.

He'd hoped to find forgetfulness there, or at least a way to calm the sudden turbulence that afflicted his soul. But all he'd found was more dreams. And more time to think about the dreams. He closed his eyes and ran a hand through his shaggy white hair. It had been black, once. Before his second death. Now, it was the hue of moonlit ice.

That wasn't the only change. There were others – some subtle, others not. He could feel the light, shimmering beneath his skin. That strange radiance, pulsing within him. If he relaxed, even for a moment, it would escape. It grew brighter with every passing day, as if seeking to return to wherever it had come from.

He was not the only Stormcast Eternal to change after being reforged on the Anvil of Apotheosis, but he took little comfort from that fact. Some lost memories, or pieces of themselves. Others became hollow, as if they were mechanisms of steel, rather than flesh and blood. He shone like a star, and dreamed strange dreams.

He let his gaze wander across the slow, sunlit waters. The bulrushes clumped thick and long to either side of the boat and stretched away into the morning mist. If he looked hard enough, he could almost make out familiar faces in the swirling vapours. Men and women he had known, and helped – or failed to help.

He heard their voices in his dreams – the voices of the living and the dead, or perhaps those caught somewhere in between. Ghosts of a past that was drawing further away with every decade that slipped unnoticed through his fingers. The ghosts of those he'd laboured among, and laughed with, and even loved, before a crash of lightning had stolen him away.

Gardus felt no resentment. His faith was not a rock to be broken, or iron to rust and chip. His faith was a river, always changing and renewing itself with every passing day. But sometimes, like every river, he felt a need to find the sea.

Perhaps there would be answers there. Or maybe only more questions. In any case, he'd decided to come back to the beginning. His journey had begun in Demesnus. And so, it had brought him back, many centuries after he had left. He felt the hull of the boat scrape against something and opened his eyes.

'Are you awake, then?'

Gardus looked up, as the captain of the riverboat stumped towards him, her round features set in a scowl. The duardin was as broad as all of her kind, but dressed in simple garb, befitting a sailor. Thick iron bracers encased her forearms, and her red hair was bound tight and coiled atop her head in a bun. A small fyresteel axe was thrust through the wide leather belt strapped about her midsection.

'I am awake, Fulda.'

'Good. I hate to throw a sleeping man off my boat.'

Gardus stood. He loomed over her, but she didn't seem unduly concerned. He smiled. 'I trust I have not inconvenienced you overmuch.'

'You mean other than scaring my crew half to death?'

'Yes, other than that.' Gardus looked towards the docks. 'It smells the same.'

Fulda's frown deepened. 'It's Demesnus. It doesn't change. It just sinks a bit deeper into the bulrushes.' She turned her scowl on the city. 'What does one of your sort want here anyway? There's nothing here but mud, fish and moss-lepers.'

Gardus felt a prickle of irritation. 'Demesnus is one of the greatest centres of learning in southern Ghyran.'

Fulda peered up at him. 'Maybe a hundred years ago. Now it's the biggest fish market in southern Ghyran.' She hiked a thumb over her shoulder. 'Which is why I need you off, so I can make room for the load of salted fish I'm taking to the markets in Hammerhal.'

Gardus chuckled. 'I understand.' He held out his hand. Fulda looked at it for a moment, and then clasped it.

'You're an odd one, Azyrite.'

'So I've been told.' Gardus left her shaking her head, and made his way towards the gangplank and the wharf beyond. The crew were already hard at work unloading cargo as he tromped down the wooden boards, but paused to watch his departure warily. Gardus pretended not to notice.

The wharfs stretched along the untidy curve of the Quamus. Berths of varying sizes jutted out into the shallows of the river, alongside raised piers. Warehouses lined the path opposite, their doors flung open as the dockhands and crews went about their duties. Fulda's vessel wasn't alone. Dozens of riverboats crowded the berths. There were flat-bottomed rafts and multistoreyed paddle-wheels, as well as stranger craft – vessels made from woven, living reeds and even a lithe dragger, pulled by a coterie of gigantic, highly vocal waterfowl.

While Demesnus was not the largest port in southern Ghyran, it had carved itself a niche as a necessary stopover along the intersection of several rivers. Or, at least, such had been the case when Gardus had been mortal. It was still as busy as he remembered. Overhead, birds swooped and squalled with raucous disapproval.

As he stepped onto dry land, he saw mortals in the dull ochre uniforms and troggoth-hide armour of the city guard escorting scribes through the crowd. The scribes likely worked for the Rushes – the leading families of Demesnus, who formed the city's ruling council. There was cargo to be inspected, and taxes on foreign goods to be collected.

Several of the warriors studied him with narrowed gazes.

Gardus knew they were taking note of his size and his blade, but they made no move to stop him as he walked along the wharf. Most mortals would take him for an outlander – from the wilds of Ghur, perhaps, or the hinterlands of Aqshy, where some folk grew to great size. Others would recognise him for what he was. Either way, they would steer clear of him.

He made his way along the wharf, moving carefully through the crowd. Over the sounds of ships being unloaded and dock-hands shouting, he heard a sharp cry. At first, he dismissed it for the call of a bird. But when it came again, he recognised it as human. He turned, seeking the origin of the sound.

He saw a flash of movement – too abrupt to be a part of the normal routine of the wharfs – and started towards it. Near a freshly unloaded fishing boat, a trio of men herded a slim, ragged shape against a mooring post. The men were of a sort Gardus had seen in every city – rough-looking and brutal, wearing a mishmash of armour. Sellswords and bravos, of the sort that even the most desperate Freeguild would think twice about contracting.

'Filthy leper,' one of the men spat. 'Ought to burn the lot of you.' His ire was directed at the young woman huddled against the post. She was clad in threadbare robes and rags, that might once have been of better quality. She held a knife in one hand, and jabbed at the air.

'Leave me alone,' she said, her voice high and thin with dismay. 'Someone help me!' Gardus saw nearby fishermen turn away, as the sellswords patted their weapons meaningfully. He stalked towards the confrontation, hands balling into fists.

One of the sellswords leered. 'No one is going to help you, leper. They know better.'

'She is not a leper,' Gardus said, as he caught the closest of the men by the scruff of his neck, and without pause, flung him from the wharf. The second spun, hand falling to the hilt of his sword. Gardus caught his wrist and squeezed. The mortal's eyes bulged. 'There is no sign of moss, no odour,' Gardus continued. He slapped his prisoner from his feet, and sent him tumbling into a nearby pile of fish.

The third man – the one who had threatened the woman – backed away, sword out. It was a cheap, back-alley blade, its length pitted and chipped. 'Stay back,' he shrilled. Gardus lunged, moving more swiftly than mortal eyes could follow. He slapped the sword aside and drove a fist into its wielder's sternum. Bone cracked, and the swordsman folded up into a heap. He wasn't dead, but he would soon wish he was. Gardus turned, looking for the woman. But she was gone – fled as he had dealt with her tormentors. He frowned and shook his head.

He reached down and hauled the second man out of the fish. 'Get your friend to a hospice,' he rumbled, shoving the frightened man towards his downed companion. The man bent hurriedly to do as Gardus had commanded, his injured hand pressed to his chest. Gardus watched them go, noting with some chagrin that he had attracted an undue amount of attention. 'Can't be helped, I suppose,' he murmured.

Behind him, someone cleared their throat. 'Mercy is a sword with two edges. Or so Elim of Vyras had it, in his seminal treatise, *On Clemency*.'

'But an honest man need never fear its cut,' Gardus said, finishing the quote. He smiled and turned. 'Hello, Yare.'

'Hello, Steel Soul. I thought I recognised the rumble of your voice. We were supposed to meet at the northern wharf.' The old man was tall, despite his accumulation of years. A halo of white hair encircled a bald head. Yare's ravaged eye sockets had healed in the years since Gardus had last seen him, forming a thick mask of scar tissue, balanced atop the remnants of a once proud nose.

'Someone was in trouble.'

Yare nodded. 'This is Demesnus, my friend. Someone is always in trouble.' The philosopher wore thick robes of wool and fur against the growing chill of the season, and held a wooden staff. Beside him, a small gryph-hound leaned against his leg, its tail twitching. It shrieked softly in challenge as Gardus neared. Yare patted the creature's wedge-shaped skull. 'Easy, Dullas. The Lord-Celestant means me no harm.'

Gardus looked down at the gryph-hound. Solid black, with feathers the colour of ash, the beast was a stocky mix of leopard and falcon, with a temper to match. He acted as Yare's eyes, when the old man let him. 'He was just a hatchling, when we gifted him to you.'

'He grew quickly. Likes his fish,' Yare said, stroking the beast's feathers. Dullas hissed in pleasure and wound himself about the old man's legs. 'Then, so do I.' Yare smiled and extended his hand. Gardus took it gently, all too aware how fragile Yare was, these days. He had been old when they'd first met, in the slave-pens of Nurgle's Rotbringers. He was ancient now – almost a hundred seasons, but still surprisingly spry.

Gardus studied him. 'You look well, my friend. Better than when I last saw you.'

'Home is a healer,' Yare said. 'And fresh marsh honey is a wonderful preservative. A spoonful a day helps to keep me from feeling the full weight of my years.' He cocked his head. 'Is Angstun with you? He and I have a discussion – several, really – to continue.'

Gardus chuckled. 'I'm sorry, no. But he sends his greetings.'

Yare laughed. 'I bet he does.' The Knight-Vexillor of the Steel Souls and the elderly philosopher had become good friends, in the days following the fall of the Sargasso Citadels. They shared a love of esoteric philosophies, as well as a willingness to argue a point for days on end. Having witnessed some of this verbal sparring first-hand, Gardus couldn't help but feel admiration for the old man's stamina.

A stiff breeze curled in off the wharf. Yare shivered, and Gardus shifted himself so that he stood between the old man and the river. 'You did not have to meet me here, Yare.'

'I know. But I am not an invalid, yet.' Yare smiled. 'My students tell me that the fog is getting thicker. It slouches in off the water in the mornings, and creeps on cat-feet through the maze of streets and alleys, filling them sometimes until noontide.'

Gardus nodded. 'There'll be ice on the river soon, then,' he said. He glanced at the river, remembering. 'I recall those days. Sometimes, the frost on them was so thick, the rushes broke. You could hear them snapping, all throughout the day.'

'The music of winter,' Yare said.

Gardus felt an ache in him as he remembered. He turned away from the water. 'It is good to see you, Yare.'

'And it is good to hear you, my friend.' Yare clutched at Gardus' arm, just for a moment. 'I'm glad you came. I feared that Sigmar had sent you beyond the reach of my letters once again.'

'Not of late. Though there are rumours that we will be descending into the dark of Shyish soon.' A petition had come, to reopen one of the few remaining Realmgates that connected Shyish and Azyr. Gardus had little doubt that Sigmar would grant it, as he had other, similar petitions recently. In the last decade, expeditions had entered the underworlds of Lyria and Shadem, among others. New cities rose, amidst the ghosts and dust.

'Is that why you finally decided to come, then?' Yare tilted his head, as if studying Gardus. 'And clad as a mortal.' He reached out and tugged on Gardus' sleeve. As ever, the blind man's perceptions were sharper than Gardus gave them credit for.

'I would prefer not to go into the lands of death encumbered by malign dreams,' he admitted. He flexed his hands, as a breeze blew in off the river. For a moment, he thought he heard something, in the space where the susurrus of the wind met the slap of water. Voices, rising up and falling away, just at the edge of hearing. He looked at Yare. 'It's still here, then. I thought... I hoped it would not be.'

Yare smiled sadly. 'It took some time to find. I had my students compare half a dozen maps of the city, from this century to the last. The way Demesnus has grown, even since I returned, is startling. New streets appear by the month, new voices, new smells.'

'The light of Azyr brings new growth, even to the Realm of Life.'

Yare chuckled. 'But is it merely growth for the sake of growth?' He raised a hand, forestalling Gardus' reply. 'I know, you didn't come here to debate philosophy, much as I might wish otherwise.'

'Afterwards, my friend. I promise.' Gardus felt gripped by a sudden urgency. 'After I have laid these ghosts to rest, once and for all.'

Yare sighed. 'There have been three Grand Hospices, since yours burned. They are all tangled together, in the histories. The same place, scattered across different locations. The one I knew was destroyed when the servants of the Plague God last attacked. Another was closed when its master fell into disfavour with the Rushes. And the third... the third became a plague pit and was torn down...'

'You found mine, though,' Gardus said. The urgency was all but unbearable. 'The one I built...' He flexed his hands, feeling the ghost of an old ache. He had built it himself. Not alone, but he had worked alongside the others, stacking stones. He remembered the songs the others had sung, as they'd worked, and the prayers the priests had spoken as the foundations had been sunk.

He remembered, but not clearly or well. It was like a particularly vivid dream.

Or a nightmare.

Yare nodded. 'I think so. A set of ruins, on the western edge of the city, overlooking the wharfs there. Overgrown, now, like much of that part of the old city.' He frowned. 'We've lost so much in the centuries since you were mortal. Demesnus was once a major port – a centre of learning and wisdom. There were broadsheets on every corner, and the air bristled with debate. Now...' He shook his head. 'I fear the students I tutor in the art of dialectics and rhetoric will be the last.'

'If you have taught them well, they will not be.'

Yare laughed. 'Let us hope.' He turned his blind gaze westward. 'What you seek is there, Gardus. I am sure of it.'

'Then that is where I must go.'

'Do you wish for company?'

Gardus smiled and clasped the old man's shoulder. 'No, my friend. You have done enough. But when I am done – when I have found what I seek – we will sit and debate.'

Yare patted Gardus' forearm. 'I look forward to it, my friend.'

Demesnus had indeed grown, since Gardus had last seen it.

It did not come as a surprise – Yare's letters had said as much – but reading about something and seeing it first-hand were two different things. But despite the changes, he still recognised the city he had once loved.

The roots of Demesnus were sunk deep in the mud of the

Quamus. It had grown from a scattering of simple bulrush huts, to a thick palisade of marsh-oak and, finally, a city of imported stone, banded on two sides by wharfs and quays. A city of weavers and fisherfolk, ruled by the descendants of the inhabitants of those first bulrush huts.

Gardus forced himself to walk slowly. To amble, rather than march. He let the old smells fill him – the stink of pitch-lanterns and burning moss; of dung and fish; the distinct pong of the tanneries and the wharfs – hoping they might stir his sluggish memories. As he left the river behind, the reek of commerce gave way to the smell of baking bread and flowering orchards. The patter of street vendors duelled with the catcalls of the broadsheet urchins. The folk of Demesnus had an abiding interest in the written word, despite the average citizen being only nominally literate. Yare's fears in that regard seemed unfounded, from what Gardus saw.

The boarded streets of the riverside became flat stones, or rutted dirt paths, carving crooked trails between buildings that still bore the scars of fires set centuries before. It was exactly as he remembered, and yet unfamiliar. There was more green, for one thing.

Demesnus had never truly recovered from the various assaults and sieges that had befallen it during the Chaos incursions of the past century. Unable to rebuild, or simply unwilling, the city's inhabitants had left many buildings as ruins. And as was common in Ghyran, what mortals abandoned, nature soon reclaimed. Whole blocks now faltered under the weight of old growth. Broken structures slumped beneath spreading trees and clinging vines, which created impromptu parks. Many of these had become orchards, or communal gardens. Others were seemingly avoided, and left to whatever vermin might choose to call them home.

Despite this, the city had prospered visibly in recent years. With trade once again flowing along the Quamus, the population had swelled. Every street was crowded with throngs of people, laughing, talking, buying, selling. *Living*.

As Gardus moved through the crowds, tatters of memory stirred, and his head echoed with the dolorous hymn of a hospice – coughing and moaning, prayers and whispered pleas. The sounds of the sick and the dying. The street around him wavered like a desert mirage, and for a moment, he stood elsewhere. The same spot, but many centuries ago.

He smelled again the acrid stink of burning pitch, and heard the ringing of the great river-bell. The ground trembled, as soldiers thundered past, their faces white with fear. The streets were flooded, water pouring down the lanes, as the river broke its banks. The enemy had come, on barques of bone and gristle, sailing a blood-dimmed tide.

Almost against his will, he turned, watching as the echoes of the past raced through the present, overlaying it in his mind's eye. Ghostly fires burned, as street-vendors hawked their wares. Soldiers raced towards the wharf, through heedless carts and crowds.

Garradan... help us...

He pressed on, trying to escape the tangle of recollection. But the past held him tight. He felt a wash of heat, as a building collapsed, spilling burning slates across the street. The air was split by the shriek of primitive artillery – he looked up and saw comets of greasy flame, trailing smoke, arc overhead. He heard the dull boom of the siege engines, assailing the landward gates.

Garradan... please...

Gardus stumbled, narrowly avoiding a tinkerer's cart as it trundled down the street. He stepped back, into an alleyway.

He shook his head, trying to clear it. The hospice. He had to get to the hospice.

Garradan... where are you?...

Around him, the city wavered between what it had been and what it now was. The streets twisted around him, and it was all he could do not to simply freeze in place. The horizon rippled, birthing familiar turrets and towers that vanished moments later. It was as if the world were in flux, caught between past and present, but only for him.

Garradan... save us...

He found himself walking down a familiar crooked lane, lined with marsh-lanterns. Even at midday, they glowed with a pallid light, casting long shadows on the brick walls to either side. The lane widened into a plaza, its surface broken by a carpet of thick, winding roots that stretched in all directions. Twisted trees, with full boughs, rose from craters of broken cobblestones, and birds sang amid the branches.

The sounds of the city were muted here, swallowed up in curtains of green. Ivy snaked across the walls of nearby buildings, and swaddled the weather-worn statues that overlooked the street. Gardus found himself holding his breath, as he walked over the thick patches of weeds and wild bramble.

At the other end of the circular plaza, nestled between buildings to either side, was a crumbled facade. He recognised a high archway of imported stone, rising atop a semicircle of rough-hewn steps, worn smooth in places. The great wooden doors, so visible in his memory, were now nothing more than a few splinters attached to rusty hinges. The two great lantern posts were still there, to each side of the doors, though they were now rusted through. And the carving of the twin-tailed comet over the archway.

Garradan... where are you?...

Gardus stopped, and stared. Remembering. He remembered watching as the comet had been chiselled into the stone. He could feel the weight of the lantern posts as he helped set them into place. He remembered that first day, as he'd welcomed his first patient – a carter who'd been trodden on by a horse. The man had cursed loud and long, as his fellows helped him up the steps. How he'd screamed as Garradan had set his leg.

Garradan... help us...

Overcome, he sank down, head in his hands. He could hear them all, the voices rising, asking, pleading, thanking, cursing. The wind in the trees sounded like the whispers of the dying. They filled him, drowning out all thought. He closed his eyes, and the words came to his lips. Canticles, prayers, the armour of faith.

Then, a new sound. The birds fell silent. The wind died away. And the bells rang. He remembered the bells; it had cost him – cost *Garradan* – the last of his inheritance to have them fashioned, but it was worth every coin. Great bells of bronze, to accompany the songs of the faithful...

He blinked back the beginnings of what might have been tears, as the low tones echoed across the plaza. The bells were still here. After all this time. Still ringing, even after so many years. He stumbled to his feet, and towards the steps, drawn by the sound of the bells. He had to see them again, to hear them above him.

But as he passed through the archway, he heard something else, beneath the bells. The sound of voices, raised in a hymn. The broken stones of the foyer were covered in a carpet of dried rushes, and curtains of the same now occupied the doorways beyond. Braziers of incense smoked in the corners, and mortal forms were huddled along the walls.

Gardus stopped. There were people here. Living ones, not

ghosts. But perhaps not for much longer. Beneath the fug of incense, he smelled the stink of sickness. Of death and the dying. Instinctively, his hand fell to his sword, but he fought the urge to draw it. The sickness he detected was unpleasant, but natural. Familiar. Moss-leprosy and marsh-lung. Wracking coughs accompanied him across the foyer and to the archway that led to the heart of the hospice. Eyes and muted whispers followed his progress, but none of those present made any move to stop him.

There were more of them in the entry chamber beyond. Once, it had been filled with cots and pallets, with the sick and the dying. The sick were still here, but they were not alone. A crowd knelt or sat, filling the chamber, their voices raised in song as the bells rang.

Pilgrims and penitents, devoted and zealots. He saw crones, clad in sackcloth, and men who had carved the sign of the comet and the hammer into their flesh. Others were dressed more sedately, in blue robes that they had obviously dyed themselves. There were men and women and children as well. Infants cried softly as their parents sang.

At the opposite end of the chamber was a statue. It was stained with dirt, but he recognised his own face – or what had been his face, once – lifted to the ceiling, where the remains of the ancient murals a grateful patron had commissioned still clung. It was him, but not – an idealised version of the man he had been. Tall and strong, bearing a great two-handed blade over one shoulder. He stared at it, wondering when it had been carved. And who had done so. Was Garradan remembered, then?

He wanted to speak. But something held him back. Was it fear? Or regret? Who were these people? And why were they here, in this forgotten place?

'It's you.'

Startled, Gardus turned. The woman he'd rescued on the wharfs stood behind him, staring. So preoccupied had he been, he had not noticed her approach. 'Yes,' he said softly, so as not to disturb the prayers of the other mortals. 'I am glad to see that you are unhurt.' Gardus smiled. 'I am Gardus.'

She hesitated. 'Dumala. You're not mortal, are you?'

Gardus avoided the question. 'Do you... live here?'

'We do. Saint Garradan called to us, and we came.' She smiled shyly. 'I saw him once.' Gardus looked at her, and she hastily added, 'In a dream, I mean.'

'Oh? Did he speak?'

She flushed. 'It wasn't that sort of dream.' She looked at the statue, and made the sign of the hammer. 'I... saw him, as he must have been. Ministering to the sick. Feeding the poor. Striking down daemons with his silver blade.'

'It was a candlestick,' Gardus murmured.

'What?'

'Nothing. And so you came here?' He had heard similar stories before. The Devoted of Sigmar often followed in the footsteps of holy men and women who had come before, and long since passed into Celestial sainthood – most were warriors like Orthanc Duln, the Hero of Sawback, or martyrs like Elazar Tesh, who had brought down the pillars of the Red House upon himself and the hounds of slaughter. 'Why?'

'I told you. He called to me. He called to all of us. So we came to sit and pray, as he did, until our purpose reveals itself.' She looked at him. 'Does he call to you as well?' She motioned to the statue. 'They say Sigmar raised him up, and set him in the sky, so that he might always watch over us.' She peered at him. 'Your face... It is familiar, I am certain.'

Gardus turned away. The song had ended, and the bells had

fallen silent. People had noticed him now, and he experienced a twinge of unease as he felt their attentions. 'I doubt it. This place... It used to be a hospice, didn't it?'

'That it did, stranger.'

Gardus turned to see a small figure approach, wrapped in rags and bandages, leaning on a pair of canes. He could smell the stink of illness wafting off of the newcomer. A familiar odour – the soft pungency of moss-leprosy. He could see the grey-green stains on the rags, and the fuzz of moss, peeking through the bandages.

The cancerous moss ate away at flesh and muscle, leaving only clumps, clinging to pitted bone. It was a common ailment here, and throughout the Jade Kingdoms, and one Gardus remembered well from his mortal life. Long had Garradan of Demesnus laboured among the moss-leper colonies, isolated in anchored ships along the river. Thankfully, the lepers could feel nothing as their bodies dissolved.

'I am Carazo, friend,' the leper said, his voice a harsh, wet rasp. 'Might I know you?'

'I am Gardus.'

Carazo peered up at him, his eyes a bright blue within the mass of stained bandages that hid his face. 'A fine name.' He hunched forward suddenly, coughing, his frame wracked by tremors. Instinctively, Gardus reached for him. Carazo twitched back. 'No, my friend,' he wheezed apologetically. 'No. Best not to touch me. What's left of me might well slough off the bone. Very messy.'

'You should not be standing.' Gardus looked down at him. 'How are you standing?'

'Sigmar gives me strength, friend. As he gave Saint Garradan the strength to fight against the slaves of darkness.' Carazo fumbled in his rags, and produced a tarnished medallion, bearing the twin-tailed comet. 'Sigmar guided me across many battlefields in my time, and this is but one more.' He chuckled. 'Though I rather think it shall be my last.' He looked around. 'It is a good place, though.'

'You were a warrior-priest,' Gardus said.

'I had that honour, once. Now I'm just a humble pilgrim, tending to this most holy of places.' Carazo turned to look at the statue. 'I first heard of him when I was a novice in the temple here. He cast down a hundred foes, to defend those he had tended, and when he fell, the enemy wept to see such courage.'

Gardus did not remember them weeping. The Skineaters had not seemed to possess the capacity, nor the inclination. And he had not killed a dozen of them, let alone a hundred. 'And you... venerate him?'

'Just a few of us, for now. But our numbers grow.' Carazo coughed again. Dumala stepped to his side, not quite touching him. There was a concern there, like a child for a parent, and Gardus could not help but wonder at the connection. 'Soon, he might reveal why we are here. When enough of us have come to this sacred place.' He looked at Gardus. 'Until then, we pray and sing, and make do as best we can. Hardship is the whetstone of faith.'

'Some hardships are more difficult than others.' Gardus looked at Dumala. 'Those men who accosted you earlier, on the wharf...'

Carazo stiffened. 'They attacked you again? Why did you not tell me?'

Dumala looked away. 'I did not want to worry you, or the others.' She glanced at Gardus. 'He saved me,' she said. 'Maybe the Saint sent him to help us.'

Gardus looked back and forth between them. 'It has happened before?'

'They think we bring sickness,' Dumala said. 'Many of our number are ill – Saint Garradan watches over the sick – but we keep to ourselves. We grow our own food, where there is space. We endanger no one, save ourselves.' Her voice became heated. 'They have no right to try to drive us from this place! I – we – will not go!'

Heads turned, and people murmured as her words echoed. Carazo waved Dumala to silence. 'It will be well, child. The Saint watches over us. He would not have called us here, merely to see us turned out.' He looked at Gardus. 'Regardless of why you came, I am grateful to you for saving her life.'

Gardus bowed his head. 'I could do no less.'

'Even so, you have my thanks. And I welcome you here, brother. Stay, if you wish. We have food, and there are pallets for those with nowhere else to go. We ask only that you abide by the peace of this place, and perhaps pray with us, at evensong.'

Gardus paused, considering. Then he nodded.

'It would be my honour.'

Gardus sat on the steps as night fell, weaving rushes.

Though he had not done so in a century or more, he found that his hands remembered the way. So he wove, and let his mind wander over what he had seen. The pilgrims had been welcoming of him, if wary. Their days were spent weaving bulrush baskets, or fishing nets, which they sold in the markets to feed themselves. When not at work, they cared for the sick among them, or sang hymns and prayed, seeking enlightenment.

A peaceful existence. And yet, one that left him ill at ease. Why had they come here? Something had drawn them, but what? Did they hear the same voices he did? And if so, what did it mean? He shook his head. Too many questions, but precious few answers.

They were weak with hunger, ravaged by illness, and seemed to subsist as much on prayer as scraps of bread and watery soup. In that regard, they were little different from other pilgrims he'd seen. Hardship was their proof of faith.

Carazo wasn't the only leper among them. Others coughed blood, or shook with fever and chills. A few of them, like Dumala, were healthy, but the rest were almost at the lichedoor. They'd come from as far away as Aqshy, hoping Saint Garradan would heal them.

A rush snapped in his hands. He paused.

'Was that why I was drawn here?' he murmured, selecting a new rush from the pile beside him. 'To minister to the sick once more?' A part of him leapt at the thought. But surely Sigmar would have told him, if he was to be released from his oath of duty. Then, the ways of the God-King were, at times, mysterious.

No. There was something else. He could feel it, like water running beneath the earth, or the air just before a storm. As if he had arrived just before the rain began to fall.

He stopped again. He felt eyes on him.

A familiar face peered at him from a side street. The man he'd thrown off the wharf earlier. And he wasn't alone. Others sidled into the plaza, until there were more than a dozen sellswords lounging among the trees, watching him. A muttered comment elicited harsh laughter.

The laughter died away as he looked at them directly. He considered asking them what their business was, but decided to err on the side of patience. He went back to his work.

A few moments later, his patience was rewarded.

'Rushes are wonderful things. Utilitarian. Practical. You can use them to make seats for chairs, or to fill out coats and pillows. They can be peeled, and the hearts boiled or eaten raw.

Their pollen can be used to thicken flour, for making bread. The local broadsheets use them for paper. Why, the earliest settlers of this place even made their homes from them. Just goes to show, anything can be made useful, with a bit of effort.'

Gardus looked up from his work. A short, thin man stood watching him. He was dressed simply, if richly, in a heavy coat of dark leather, lined with eiderdown, and a shapeless hat of otter fur. A brooch of silver, decorated with a spray of feathers, was pinned to the side of the hat. He leaned on a cane of dark wood, carved with shapes reminiscent of the harvest, and had a short sword sheathed on one narrow hip.

'They tell me you accosted several of my employees.'

Gardus set aside the bulrushes and stood. The sellswords twitched, some reaching for their weapons. But the newcomer did not so much as flinch.

'You're a big fellow, aren't you?' he said. He glanced at the sellswords and waved them back. 'Bigger than these.'

'And with a sword to match.' Gardus let his hand drop to the pommel of his runeblade. The newcomer nodded.

'So I see. I am Sargo Wale.' Wale bowed shallowly, one hand on his hat to hold it in place. 'You might have heard of me?'

'No.'

'You are new to the city, then?'

'No.'

Wale frowned. 'How curious. I should have thought I would have heard of a fellow of your... vigour. And you certainly should have heard of me. My ships line the wharf. My grain and my orchards feed the city, and keep Demesnus from sinking into the mire, like so many of our neighbours.'

Gardus crossed his arms. 'Nonetheless, your name does not ring familiar.'

'May I have yours, then?'

Gardus made to answer, but something held him back. 'No,' he said finally.

Wale smiled and shrugged. 'Ah well, no matter. I'll just call you friend.' He set his cane down and leaned on it, one thin hand atop the other. 'I am here to speak to Carazo. Where is he?'

'Inside. Sleeping.' The old priest had used up what little energy he had leading his people in another hymn. The last Gardus had seen, Dumala had been bullying the old man into laying down somewhere. 'He is ill.'

Wale sighed, and peered up at the sky. 'They all are. This place... It is not healthy. Perhaps in time. But not now.' He thumped the street with his cane. 'The soil is sour, you see. It needs a firm hand to till it, and turn out the stones. You know whereof I speak?'

Gardus said nothing. Wale continued. 'I own this land. I bought it, fair and true, from the council. They were glad to be rid of it.' He frowned. 'I will turn it into something useful. Another orchard, perhaps, or maybe even a park. The soil is still sweet, beneath the sour. Or it can be made so again. With a bit of effort.'

Gardus looked him up and down. Wale's smile widened. 'You think me a liar, sir? Why, I'm no scion of the bulrushes, come from money and privilege. I came here from Aqshy, without a single coin to my name. But I knew how to work the soil.' He held up his hands. They were scarred and muscular. 'These hands were worn bloody on handle of plough and haft of scythe, my friend.' He turned them over, studying them. 'I bargained with treekin and waged war on beasts, to carve out my first fields. And I paid well, and was paid, for the privilege of feeding this growing city. I'm a man of the soil, me. I take what it offers, and give back, when I can.' He gestured with his cane. 'Nothing more.'

'Your men tried to hurt one of the people living here,' Gardus growled, tired of Wale's patter. 'And not for the first time, if what they say is true.'

Wale's smile vanished. 'And you believe them?'

'I have no reason not to.'

'My apologies. Were they a friend of yours?'

'No.'

'Then less reason still to involve yourself in matters that don't concern you.' Wale peered up at him. 'Step aside, and we'll say no more about it.'

Gardus crossed his arms. Wale blinked, but recovered quickly. He glanced back at his men, and then shook his head. 'Ah, well. One must learn to endure what comes.' He looked at Gardus. 'Is it money, then?'

'No.'

'Mm. Something else?'

'I want you to leave.'

'And so I will. But I will return.' Wale looked up at the hospice. 'This place is mine, now. By right, and by law. They can't stay here. Better for everyone if they move along.'

'Because you wish to turn this place into something useful.'

Wale shook his head. 'For their own good. For the good of the city.' He took off his hat and ran a hand through thinning silver hair. 'This was a place of healing, once. A long time ago. Now, it's a graveyard. It needs tending, and not by sickly wretches, coughing out prayers and spreading their ills to honest folk.' He slapped his hat back on his head and looked at Gardus. 'I know what you are, friend. I've been to Hammerhal, aye, and Azyrheim as well, if you can believe it.'

'Then you know these will not be enough to move me, if I decide to stand here.' Gardus indicated the sellswords with a sweep of his hand. A gesture of bravado, but necessary. The sellswords had the look of men who'd just realised that they probably weren't going to be paid.

Wale nodded thoughtfully. 'And yet, I own this land. Mine by right, you see?' He held his hand out. 'You're like a stone, sitting in my field. I can try to dig you out...'

'Or you can go around me.'

Wale smiled thinly. 'Never been one for that. But, never been one to tempt the gods, either.' He hunched forward, leaning on his cane. 'I expect that you came here for a reason, my friend. I expect that reason has to do with them inside. Maybe you can move these stones, where I can't.'

'What do you mean?'

'I came here today to drive them out once and for all. I have warrants from the Rushes, allowing me to use whatever methods I deem best.' He twitched his cane towards the sellswords. 'I'm a simple man, friend. I use what tools are to hand. But I wouldn't say no to a bit of help.'

'You want me to get them to leave.'

'You'd be ensuring their safety. Sigmar's law is on my side, and I'd rather not water this ground in blood.'

Gardus' hand dropped to the hilt of his sword. 'If I say no?'

Wale smiled sadly and shrugged. 'Then these fellows will earn their pay.'

'And if I stand against them?'

'Then they'll die, I imagine.' Several of the sellswords blanched at this. Wale continued, 'But I will have what I'm owed. Even if I have to involve the Rushes, and the city guard.' He frowned. 'I'll hire an entire Freeguild regiment, if that's what it takes. So, you have to ask yourself – am I the stone, or the man who'll move it?'

Gardus said nothing. Wale sighed and peered up at the darkening sky. 'I'll give you until evensong tomorrow. After that, I'll do what must be done.' He turned away. 'As, I imagine, will you.'

Gardus watched the sellswords drift away in ones and twos, as their master departed. They wouldn't go far. And they'd be back, in force. Possibly with help from the city guard, if Wale had been speaking the truth. Gardus had little reason to doubt him.

Mortals like Wale were becoming more common, as Sigmar's influence spilled out into the wider realms. They remade the land in Azyr's image, whether they meant to or not, taming the wilderness and helping the cities of men grow. Gardus had seen it before, and had even aided it, once or twice. That was the Stormcast Eternals' purpose, after all. To drive back the dark, so that the light of Azyr might flourish. To make new what was old.

Men like Wale were necessary, in that regard. They consecrated the ground the Stormcast cleansed in blood and fire, and sowed the seeds for the harvest to come. They raised the cities and rebuilt the roads. Without them, all that warriors like Gardus had achieved would soon fall back into ruin.

But necessity was not always just. He remembered other men, like Wale, from his life as Garradan. Men who wanted lepers burned, and the sick herded onto barges. Men who wielded necessity as a shield, for their own fear and greed.

He turned, and looked up at the ruins of his hospice.

'Sigmar guide me,' he murmured.

'They will return tomorrow at evensong,' Gardus said, as he watched Dumala and others fill bowls of soup for the hungry.

'And we will be here to greet them,' Carazo said. They stood in an antechamber, watching as the pilgrims took their evening meal. Soup and hard, crusty bread, donated by a sympathetic baker. 'Saint Garradan will provide. As he always has.'

'What if he wishes you to leave?'

Carazo looked at him. 'Has he spoken to you, then, brother?'

Gardus looked away. Carazo sighed, and went on. 'Wale never showed an interest in this place until we moved in. Then he decided he needed it.'

'And the Rushes gave it to him.'

Carazo nodded. 'Of course. We are lepers and beggars and fanatics. They don't want us here. But our numbers grow, and they fear what others might say if they turn us out. We are not the only followers of the twin-tailed comet in this city, though most worship the Everqueen, these days.'

'So they hand the problem to Wale.'

Carazo laughed, but it quickly turned into a cough. 'Wale has done much good for the city. I admit that.'

'And you haven't,' Gardus said. Carazo shrugged.

'What is the measure of such a thing? We preach, sometimes, to those who wish to hear. We tend to the sick among us. We sit out of sight, and pray and sing. We are peaceful, as Saint Garradan was peaceful. But like him, we will fight to defend this place, and our way, if we must.'

'I doubt he would want that.' Gardus looked at the old priest. 'Why stay?'

Carazo coughed and dabbed at his bandaged features with a rag. 'The Saint called us here, though we know not why. So we came, and we found a sort of peace in this place.' He looked at the statue. 'I will not leave, until I know why the Saint called me here.'

'Nor will I,' Dumala said firmly. She offered Gardus a bowl of soup.

He waved it aside. 'It is not a question of allow,' he said. 'They will come, and there is little you can do to stop it.' He looked around. 'Wale has the Rushes on his side. He has the law.' The words tasted bitter, even as he said them.

'And we have a higher law,' Carazo said. He made the sign of the hammer. Gardus' reply was interrupted by the sudden scream of an infant. He turned, to see a woman trying to quiet her child, to no avail.

Gardus stepped over to her. 'Let me,' he rumbled. The woman stared up at him, fear in her eyes. Gardus held out his hands. 'Please.'

She looked at Carazo, who nodded. Gingerly, she held out her child, and Gardus took him. He lifted the infant and rocked him gently, quieting his screams. The woman smiled, the exhaustion on her face easing slightly. 'He is quiet,' she said.

'I remember when I, too, was a child,' Gardus said softly. 'All men were children once, and in need of comfort.'

'Some might say we still are,' Carazo said.

Gardus smiled gently. 'Yes.' The infant had settled, and he handed the boy back to his mother. 'He is colicky. A warm bath may help.'

Dumala stared at him. 'How do you know that?'

Gardus looked at her. 'Know what?' He turned to Carazo. 'If you will not leave for your own sake, think of this child – and of the others here. Think of Dumala.'

'I told you – I will not leave,' she began, but Carazo silenced her with a look.

'Perhaps you are right. But it is not a decision I can make lightly. I must pray.' He raised his hands, and the others fell silent. 'We all must pray, and seek answers from Saint Garradan. If it is his will that we go – if it is Sigmar's will – we will go. But we must pray.' He looked at Gardus. 'Will you pray with us, brother?'

Gardus nodded, after a moment. 'I will.'

Perhaps in prayer, he would find the answers he sought.

* * *

GHOSTS OF DEMESNUS

Gardus snapped alert.

He could not say why, but something had drawn him from his meditations. He glanced at Dumala, and saw that she was sleeping beside him. So were Carazo and the others. Prayer had given way to slumber as the night wore on.

He rose, wondering if Wale's men had come early. If so, he would greet them. Quietly, he padded from antechamber to antechamber, searching for the source of the disturbance. But he found nothing, saving the sick and the lost, sleeping fitfully. Did they dream of him, of the man he had been?

Garradan... please...

He turned. 'I hear you,' he said softly. 'I have always heard you. But when will you tell me why you call out to me?'

Garradan... we need you...

He paced through cold corridors, his breath billowing in the chill. Mortals huddled for warmth, shivering and coughing in their sleep. This place was not good for them. They did not light fires for lack of fuel. They had no food, save what could be scavenged. And yet they stayed, in defiance of all common sense.

Garradan... help us...

His hands clenched into fists. Into weapons. Light flickered in an antechamber. Silently, he moved towards it, his every instinct screaming now. Warning him. There was a smell on the air. A sickly smell, worse than any other, but familiar. One he had smelled before, in places men ought not to go.

Garradan... Garradan... Garradan...

His name beat on the air like the wings of a dying bird. It brushed across the edges of his hearing with painful flutters. He ducked beneath an archway, and the ill light washed over him, filling the antechamber. Men and women lay asleep on pallets, tossing and turning.

Something abominable was coiled about them.

Gardus stopped, a prayer caught in his throat.

The thing looked up at him with more faces than mouths, and more mouths than eyes. It was at once a slug and a cloud and a serpent – no, a nest of serpents – a scabrous, shimmering wound in reality. A thing that should not be. Tendrils of glistening mist wound about the sleepers, pulsing red, and Gardus knew that it was feeding on them in some way. Like a vampire, it drew the life from them, and took it into itself.

Time seemed to slow. His hand fell to his sword. It reared, like a snake readying itself to strike, and unfurled in some awful way. Its mouths moved.

Garradan… Garradan… Garradan…

'No,' Gardus said. Light rose from his flesh, a clean light, and the thing shrank back like a startled beast. The whispers were mangled into moans as it squirmed away from him, slithering into the dark. He followed it, moving quickly.

Was this why he had been drawn here? All this time, had he been haunted in truth, and not just by memories? He did not know. All he knew was that the thing – the daemon of plague and murder – held in itself the souls of innocent and damned alike. It slithered away from him, crawling on withered hands, its faces twitching and gaping. He could hear the voices in his head. A silent storm of whispers and moans. Anger, fear and pain, merging into a dolorous hammer stroke – a pulse of unsound that reverberated through the air, undetectable, save by one with a shard of the divine grafted to their soul.

The ground glistened with grave-light where the daemon-spirit passed, and Gardus could smell the sourness it left in its wake. The earth sickened in its presence, and the air became miasmatic. It was no wonder so many of Carazo's followers were ill.

The daemon-spirit stopped in what had once been the central

chamber of the hospice. As Gardus followed, it began to come apart like a cloud caught by a breeze. In slips and tatters, it sank down into the broken soil, until there was no sign it had ever been at all. Gardus dropped to his haunches at the point of its disappearance. Tentatively, he pressed the palm of his hand to the ground. He could feel it, somewhere below him. Like water rushing beneath the earth. Burrowing down, down to... what?

He looked around the chamber. He noted the fire-scarred stones and the ugly, fleshy growths clinging to the blackened timbers that pierced the broken ground like talons. As was the way in Ghyran, life had returned with a vengeance. Tapestries of green hung down the broken walls, rippling gently in the night breeze. Overhead, the shattered remains of the dome of glass had turned a filthy brown, from neglect. Sigmar's face was hidden beneath a mask of grime. Thin pillars of starlight fell across the chamber like the bars of a cage.

He heard rubble shift, behind him. He glanced back, and saw Dumala.

'When I awoke, you were gone,' she said. 'I thought...' She shook her head. 'What are you doing here?'

'What is this place?' he asked, as he stood.

'They buried them here. All of those who died when the hospice burned.' Dumala joined him, her arms wrapped tight about her. She shivered slightly, her eyes wide. 'You can still feel it. That's what Carazo says.'

'Feel what?'

'What happened here.' Dumala looked up at him. 'Can you feel it?'

Gardus did not reply. He stared at the ground, a sick feeling growing within him. All the dead... How long had they been trapped down there, in the stifling dark? Broken souls, changing, made into something else by pain and fear. By a plague that had been more than mere sickness. A plague of the soul, as well as the flesh.

How long had they festered until the scent of new life, new souls, had drawn them questing from their pit? A new thing, born in blood and darkness, and hungry. So hungry.

He felt Dumala flinch away from him, as if startled. Belatedly, he realised that he was shining. Starlight shimmered over him and from within him, turning the greens and browns of the chamber to silver. Dumala had fallen to her knees, hands clasped in prayer. Tears streamed from her eyes and her mouth moved wordlessly. Gardus stepped back, trying to dim his radiance. To hide the light once more. But it was hard. Something about this place, this moment, called out to it, and the light... the light *answered*.

'Garradan...' she whispered, reaching for him. 'Your face... I knew...'

'No,' Gardus said. Softly at first, and then more insistently. 'Garradan is dead. He died here. I am Gardus.' He made to draw her to her feet, but she fell onto her face.

'No, I am not worthy,' she moaned.

Gardus hesitated, momentarily at a loss. Then, with a sigh, he dropped to his haunches. 'Get up, please.'

She looked up at him, tears streaking her face. 'Why didn't you tell us?' she whispered. 'You came, and we did not know – I am not worthy.' She made to fall forward again, but Gardus caught her.

'Up,' he said, helping her to her feet. 'Why would you think that?'

'I... I questioned, I doubted, I thought... I thought...'

'You thought Garradan would not come.'

She nodded. She turned away, shivering. 'I was going to leave.'

'That is why you were at the wharfs.'

'I wanted to leave. To go. But they caught me, and then – and then…' She trailed off. 'My faith was not strong enough. Carazo's faith is like iron. I wish mine was.'

'No. Be like water,' Gardus said softly. 'Water flows and renews.' He tapped his head and his chest. 'Running water never grows stale. When water – when *faith* – stagnates, it becomes something else. Fanaticism. Obsession. It makes your soul and mind sick. You must be water, always flowing into the sea, to rise up as vapour and fall as rain.'

'I-I do not understand,' Dumala said haltingly.

'Faith without question, is not faith. To be truly faithful, you must always question. You must always be flowing away from certainty, for in certainty, there is only stagnation. Perhaps not immediately, but it will come.' Even as he said it, he realised that he had answered his own questions. He had come here seeking some sort of assurance, and found only more uncertainty. And perhaps that was what he had always been meant to find.

'Why did you call us here?' she asked.

'I didn't.' He looked at the ground. 'There is a sickness in this place. Whatever drew you all here, it feeds on you now. If you stay, it will only get stronger.'

She shook her head, not understanding. 'Carazo will not leave. Nor will most of the others.' She frowned. 'Some of them can't. Too sick.'

Gardus nodded. 'I know.'

'Will you stay with us?' She touched his arm. 'Will you help us?'

He looked down at her. 'For one night more, at least.'

Gardus spent the rest of the evening and most of the next day in silent vigil over the gravesite. The daemon-thing would come again. But this time, it would not leave the chamber. He would make certain of it.

Now that he had seen it, it was impossible to ignore the thing's presence below his feet. Waiting for nightfall, when it might rise and feed again. As it had likely done for months. It was no wonder that illness was rampant here.

Others might have seen that as evidence of corruption. Enough, at least, to warrant burning this place to the foundations, and salting the ashes. But Gardus was not others. Sickness was to be fought, here more than anywhere else.

'Was this why I was drawn back here, now, of all times?' he murmured, looking up at the mural of Sigmar. 'To confront hungry ghosts? I should not be surprised, I suppose. We were forged for war, and it seeks us out.' Sigmar, as ever, remained silent as to his intentions. Even on the few occasions Gardus had spoken to the God-King face to face, he had found himself questioning what was said, and whether what he had heard had been what was meant.

Questions and uncertainty. These, not hardship, were the whetstones of faith. He felt that he was where he needed to be, whatever the reason. And so he would wait, and do as Sigmar willed. As he hoped Sigmar willed.

'Patience is something of a burden,' he grumbled. He patted his runeblade in its plain sheath, sitting across his knees. He could feel the heat of the blade, the echo of its forging. Like him, it was more than just a sword. He hoped it would be enough. He hoped *he* would be enough. But only time would tell.

Behind him, he could hear the faithful of Saint Garradan singing an old Verdian hymn. A song of life and renewal, of hope. He closed his eyes, and for a moment, he almost thought himself in Azyr once more, walking the rim of the

Sigmarabulum, listening to the song of the stars. As Dumala had said, Carazo had decided not to leave. Some few had departed, but most of the congregation had stayed.

For her part, Dumala told no one of her realisation, not even Carazo. Her faith in him was somewhat unnerving, even as he made use of it. She and a few others would keep watch for Wale's men, and ring the hospice bells when they spotted them. Gardus suspected that a show of force would be enough to make the sellswords rethink any plans to violence. And if not, he would deal with them, if necessary.

As you dealt with the Skineaters?

The question caused him to stiffen. He was not sure whether he had thought it, or not. He took his sword off his knees and stood. 'I did what I thought was right,' he said.

Right... right... right...

Long shadows crept along the unsettled earth. The night came on, and a chill prickled across the nape of his neck. 'Do you know me?' he asked. He felt foolish as he did so. 'Have you been calling to me, all this time?'

Silence. But he felt as if he were being watched. The air had taken on a pall, as before a storm. He drew his blade, and cast aside his sheath. 'You called. I am here. Answer me.'

Still, no reply. Then...

Garradan...

'Yes,' he said, bringing his runeblade up. 'I hear you. I have been hearing you for a long time, I think. I am sorry I could not come sooner.'

Garradan... help us...

'I will. If I can.' He turned, seeking any sign of the daemon-thing. He'd half hoped his presence would keep it quiescent. It had seemed to fear him, the night before. But there was no fear in its voice now – only a raw, ugly *need*.

In the other chamber, the song rose. He felt the ground shudder beneath his feet, as if the sound pained it. Had their prayers woken it, that first night? Had the hymns stirred some faint memory, and brought what had been growing in the dark to the surface?

Garradan... where are you?... Garradan... please...

'I am here.' He raised his blade, watching the ground. 'I am waiting.'

The song faltered. He spun, as the bells began to ring, and a babble of worry rose. He could hear Carazo trying to keep people calm, and something else – shouts, and the clatter of weapons. He started towards the archway.

Garradan... don't leave us... You can't leave us...

Gardus paused, and turned back as the daemon-spirit erupted from beneath the churning soil, its many mouths open in a manifold scream. Hands and arms sprouted from its serpentine length, like the legs of a centipede. He staggered, and fingers and fists thudded into him, striking with inhuman force, bruising his flesh as he was driven back against a broken support timber. It was at once there and not – incorporeal, but somehow hideously solid. The thing surged up, larger than he'd imagined, and coiled about him, knocking aside fire-scarred rubble in its fury.

Gardus smashed a gibbering, gnawing face, and slashed out with his runeblade. The moist spirit-stuff parted like jelly, rippling and splitting around the edge of the sword, before reforming with a wet splat. Gardus grunted in frustration and redoubled his efforts, chopping at the viscous matter as it rose up around him. As he fought, the whispers of the dead insinuated themselves, burrowing through the walls of his concentration.

Garradan... help us...

My hands... I can't feel my hands...
Dark... So dark... Why can't I see?...
Garradan...
Garradan...

'Silence,' Gardus roared. But the voices continued, doubling and redoubling, drowning out his own thoughts. The daemon's coils convulsed about him, nearly crushing the air from his lungs. He fought to free himself, as fingers and teeth dug into his flesh. Blood ran down his arms and legs, dripping to the broken ground.

He tore himself free of the entity's coils, splitting it in two with a wild blow, and staggered back against another fallen timber. There was blood in his eyes, and his breath was thick in his lungs. The daemon-spirit hissed and writhed, reforming slowly.

He heard a chuckle, from somewhere close by. 'It's strong, for something so young. Then, good soil does wonders with even the smallest seed.'

Wale.

Gardus blinked blood and sweat from his eyes. He could hear screams. The shouts of Wale's men, and the rattle of weapons. 'No,' he said hoarsely.

'I warned you. I gave you a chance. But here it is, evensong, and this stone is still in my field.' Wale sighed. 'I'm no butcher. Just a man of the soil. But this field is mine, by right.' Gardus heard the click of Wale's walking stick, striking a rock. 'As is this harvest. Someone else might have planted the seeds, but the crop is Grandfather's, through and through. I've been waiting for it to ripen for decades.'

The daemon-spirit had finished reforming. It lurched towards him with a slug-like undulation. Faces and hands bulged like blisters on its gelatinous body, biting and groping. The voices of the dead hung on the air like the hum of insects. He felt weak – as if the daemon's miasma were sapping his strength.

'Beautiful,' Wale said. Gardus saw him, standing near the far wall, his hands folded over the head of his cane. 'A new thing, under Grandfather's sun. That's a true joy, that is. Bringing something new into the world.'

The daemon-thing turned at his words, its faces contorted in expressions ranging from confusion to frustration. It snarled, in many voices, and Wale frowned. 'Now, now, little one. None of that. I'm not here to harm you.'

It stretched its upper half towards him, faces splitting and sprouting anew as they extended. Mouths moved, voicing a babble of what might have been questions. Wale gestured, and there was a sudden sickly light. The daemon-thing jerked back, with a startled hiss. 'Go back to your meal, little one. You'll find no nourishment from my withered frame.' The thing turned, and began to slither back towards Gardus.

Gardus lifted his sword. 'Is this your doing, then? Is this monstrosity something you've conjured?'

The daemon-thing undulated closer, mouths opening and closing. Parts of it were singing. Some were praying – to Sigmar, to Khorne – but the words twisted, becoming a paean to Nurgle. Gardus twisted aside as it lunged, its malformed jaws tearing a chunk from the timber behind him.

Garradan... help us...

Wale laughed. 'Me? No. This is the fruit of death, and I'm no killer. Just a farmer. A man of the soil, as I told you. I know a few tricks, but I'm no sorcerer or Rotbringer. But isn't it magnificent? Grandfather loves all things that live and grow, friend. Even this. Even you. You should remember that, should you walk these green places again.'

Garradan... we need you...

The daemon-thing shimmered in the dark, shining with the ugly light of a bruise or an infected wound. The runeblade felt heavy in his hand. The thing seemed to shrug off his strongest blow, and he wondered at the weakness he felt. He touched one of the wounds on his arm, rubbing the blood between his fingers. The thing licked its lips. His blood marked its mouths and limbs, and crimson pulses ran through its semi-opaque form.

It was feeding on him. The mortals had given it the strength to manifest, but it needed more than they could provide. He lowered his sword, as realisation flooded him. Fighting it would only make it stronger. It would bleed him, and leave him a broken husk.

It was greedy, like an infant. And like an infant, it needed comfort.

Garradan... please...

He stabbed his sword into the ground. 'Yes,' he said, stepping forward, weaponless. He spread his arms. 'I hear you.'

It surged towards him, with a murmur of triumph. He heard Wale cackle in pleasure. The daemon-thing engulfed him. It was like being struck by a spray of icy water, and he fought the urge to resist. He felt teeth fasten into his flesh, and fingers clutch at him, with desperate ferocity.

He sank down, drowning in effluvia, and let loose his hold on the light within him. It burst forth, from every pore. It swelled, filling the daemon-thing. The entity screamed in many tongues, and heaved itself away from him, its form writhing. Gardus stumbled after it. The blood that slicked his limbs shimmered like fire, and where it struck the ground, plumes of smoke curled upwards. He caught hold of the daemon-thing and dragged it towards him, as the light grew blinding in its intensity. It squirmed in his grip, babbling.

Garradan... Garradan... Garradan...

'I am here,' he said. 'I am here. I will help you.' It twisted, coming apart in his hands, boiling away to nothing. Faces stretched like clay, bubbled and fell away, leaving only fading moans to mark their passing. His light filled the chamber as he gathered the dissolving remnants to him, hugging it close. He murmured to the struggling entity, whispering words of comfort. 'I did not mean to leave you here,' he said. 'But I will not leave you again.'

Garradan... help us...

He closed his eyes. 'I will.' It beat at him, trying to free itself, but its struggles grew weak, and finally ceased entirely. As it fell silent, he looked down, and saw that he held something frail and broken and pale – something that murmured word-lessly as it came apart in his hands and spilled away like dust.

'No!'

Something caught him on the back of the head, and shattered. He staggered, sinking to one knee. Wale roared and struck him again, with the remains of his cane. Despite his withered frame, the old man was far stronger than he looked – stronger than any mortal. Wale cast aside the fragments of his cane and caught Gardus by the scalp. 'You killed it! Murderer!'

Wale drove him face first into a timber. Gardus slumped, dazed. Wale kicked him in the side, knocking him onto his back. 'What harm did it ever do you? It was no more than a seedling.' The old man drew his sword. The blade was dull and brown with old rust. Ugly runes decorated its length, and Gardus could feel the malignant heat of its magics. He shook his head, trying to clear it.

'It was a monster,' he said hoarsely. 'As are you.'

'Just a farmer, friend,' Wale said, as he raised his blade. 'And after I'm done with you, I'll grow such a crop here as this city has never seen.'

'Gardus!'

Gardus looked up, and saw Dumala. She had his runeblade in both hands and sent it skidding across the ground towards him as Wale spun towards her, face twisted with fury. Gardus caught the hilt, and lunged to his feet. Wale, realising his error, turned back. Their blades connected with a hollow clang. Gardus forced Wale back.

'You'll grow nothing,' he said.

'It's– You can't! This place is mine,' Wale snarled. 'Mine by right!'

'No,' Gardus said. 'It is *mine*.' Wale's blade shattered as Gardus swept it aside. Wale fell back, mouth open in denial. Gardus slammed his sword through Wale's chest, and drove him back against a timber. He loosed the hilt and stepped back, leaving Wale impaled.

Wale clawed at the runeblade as his thin form began to unravel. His coat shed its feathers, as his limbs shed skin and muscle. He crumpled inwards, like fruit gone rotten, and fell away, leaving only one more black stain to mark his passing.

Gardus pulled his blade free, and turned. 'Thank you,' he said.

Dumala nodded. 'Just returning the favour.' She gestured. 'Look,' she said softly.

The chamber had changed. Was changing.

Blue flames danced across black walls, leaving only bare stone in its wake. The unsightly vegetation crumbled away, and new, vibrant growth replaced it. Wherever his blood had fallen, green shoots pushed through the soil, and spread outwards.

His light had seared away the filth. The pall he'd felt was gone, and the whispers of the ghosts had fallen silent. 'Wale's men?' he asked.

'Gone,' Dumala said. 'You were right. They had no stomach for a fight. They ran, the moment we began to resist.' She smiled. 'You should have seen Carazo, waving his canes as if they were warhammers.' Her smile faded as she took in his wounds, and the black mark of Wale's demise. 'What happened here, Garradan– Gardus?'

For a moment, he had no answer for her. 'What was meant to,' he said finally.

She frowned. 'How do you know?'

'I don't.' He looked up at the mural of Sigmar, and smiled. 'But I have faith.'

ABOUT THE AUTHORS

David Guymer wrote the Horus Heresy novella *Dreadwing*, the Primarchs novel *Ferrus Manus: Gorgon of Medusa*, and for Warhammer 40,000 *The Eye of Medusa*, *The Voice of Mars* and the two Beast Arises novels *Echoes of the Long War* and *The Last Son of Dorn*. For Warhammer Age of Sigmar he wrote the novel *Hamilcar: Champion of the Gods*, the audio dramas *The Beasts of Cartha*, *Fist of Mork*, *Fist of Gork*, *Great Red* and *Only the Faithful*. He is also the author of the Gotrek & Felix novels *Slayer*, *Kinslayer* and *City of the Damned* and the Gotrek audio dramas *Realmslayer* and *Realmslayer: Blood of the Old World*. He is a freelance writer and occasional scientist based in the East Riding, and was a finalist in the 2014 David Gemmell Awards for his novel *Headtaker*.

Andy Clark has written the Warhammer 40,000 novels *Kingsblade*, *Knightsblade* and *Shroud of Night*, as well as the novella *Crusade* and the short story 'Whiteout'. He has also written the novels *Gloomspite* and *Blacktalon: First Mark* for Warhammer Age of Sigmar, and the Warhammer Quest Silver Tower novella *Labyrinth of the Lost*. Andy works as a background writer for Games Workshop, crafting the worlds of Warhammer Age of Sigmar and Warhammer 40,000. He lives in Nottingham, UK.

Evan Dicken has written the short story 'The Path to Glory' and the novella *The Red Hours* for Black Library. He has been an avid reader of Black Library novels since he found dog-eared copies of *Trollslayer*, *Xenos* and *First and Only* nestled in the 'Used Fantasy/Sci-fi' rack of his local gaming store. By day, he studies old Japanese maps and crunches data at The Ohio State University.

David Annandale is the author of the novella *The Faith and the Flesh*, which features in the Warhammer Horror portmanteau novel *The Wicked and the Damned*. His work for the Horus Heresy range includes the novels *Ruinstorm* and *The Damnation of Pythos*, and the Primarchs novels *Roboute Guilliman: Lord of Ultramar* and *Vulkan: Lord of Drakes*. For Warhammer 40,000 he has written *Warlord: Fury of the God-Machine*, the Yarrick series, and several stories involving the Grey Knights, as well as titles for The Beast Arises and the Space Marine Battles series. For Warhammer Age of Sigmar he has written *Neferata: Mortarch of Blood* and *Neferata: The Dominion of Bones*. David lectures at a Canadian university, on subjects ranging from English literature to horror films and video games.

Nick Kyme is the author of the Horus Heresy novels
Old Earth, Deathfire, Vulkan Lives and *Sons of the
Forge*, the novellas *Promethean Sun* and *Scorched
Earth*, and the audio dramas *Red-Marked, Censure*
and *Nightfane*. His novella *Feat of Iron* was a *New
York Times* bestseller in the Horus Heresy collection,
The Primarchs. Nick is well known for his popular
Salamanders novels, including *Rebirth*, the Sicarius
novels *Damnos* and *Knights of Macragge*, and
numerous short stories. He has also written fiction
set in the world of Warhammer, most notably the
Warhammer Chronicles novel *The Great Betrayal* and
the Age of Sigmar story 'Borne by the Storm', included
in the novel *War Storm*. More recently he has scripted
the Age of Sigmar audio drama *The Imprecations of
Daemons*. He lives and works in Nottingham.

Guy Haley is the author of the Siege of Terra novel *The Lost and the Damned*, as well as the Horus Heresy novels *Titandeath*, *Wolfsbane* and *Pharos*, and the Primarchs novels *Konrad Curze: The Night Haunter*, *Corax: Lord of Shadows* and *Perturabo: The Hammer of Olympia*. He has also written the Warhammer 40,000 novels *Dark Imperium*, *Dark Imperium: Plague War*, *The Devastation of Baal*, *Dante*, *Baneblade*, *Shadowsword*, *Valedor* and *Death of Integrity*. For the Beast Arises series he has written *Throneworld* and *The Beheading*. His enthusiasm for all things greenskin has also led him to pen the eponymous Warhammer novel *Skarsnik*, as well as the End Times novel *The Rise of the Horned Rat*. He has also written stories set in the Age of Sigmar, included in *War Storm*, *Ghal Maraz* and *Call of Archaon*. He lives in Yorkshire with his wife and son.

C L Werner's Black Library credits include the Age of Sigmar novels *Overlords of the Iron Dragon* and *The Tainted Heart*, the novella 'Scion of the Storm' in *Hammers of Sigmar*, the Warhammer novels *Deathblade*, *Mathias Thulmann: Witch Hunter*, *Runefang* and *Brunner the Bounty Hunter*, the Thanquol and Boneripper series and Time of Legends: The Black Plague series. For Warhammer 40,000 he has written the Space Marine Battles novel *The Siege of Castellax*. Currently living in the American south-west, he continues to write stories of mayhem and madness set in the Warhammer worlds.

Josh Reynolds' extensive Black Library back catalogue includes the Horus Heresy Primarchs novel *Fulgrim: The Palatine Phoenix*, and three Horus Heresy audio dramas featuring the Blackshields. His Warhammer 40,000 work includes the Space Marine Conquests novel *Apocalypse*, *Lukas the Trickster* and the Fabius Bile novels. He has written many stories set in the Age of Sigmar, including the novels *Shadespire: The Mirrored City*, *Soul Wars, Eight Lamentations: Spear of Shadows*, the Hallowed Knights novels *Plague Garden* and *Black Pyramid*, and *Nagash: The Undying King*. His Warhammer Horror story, *The Beast in the Trenches*, is featured in the portmanteau novel *The Wicked and the Damned*, and he has recently penned the Necromunda novel *Kal Jerico: Sinner's Bounty*. He lives and works in Sheffield.

Gav Thorpe is the author of the Horus Heresy novels *Deliverance Lost*, *Angels of Caliban* and *Corax*, as well as the novella *The Lion*, which formed part of the *New York Times* bestselling collection *The Primarchs*, and several audio dramas. He has written many novels for Warhammer 40,000, including *Ashes of Prospero*, *Imperator: Wrath of the Omnissiah* and the Rise of the Ynnari novels *Ghost Warrior* and *Wild Rider*. He also wrote the *Path of the Eldar* and *Legacy of Caliban* trilogies, and two volumes in The Beast Arises series. For Warhammer, Gav has penned the End Times novel *The Curse of Khaine*, the Warhammer Chronicles omnibus *The Sundering*, and recently penned the Age of Sigmar novel *The Red Feast*. In 2017, Gav won the David Gemmell Legend Award for his Age of Sigmar novel *Warbeast*. He lives and works in Nottingham.

YOUR
NEXT READ

NEFERATA: THE DOMINION OF BONES
by David Annandale

With Chaos on one side and Sigmar's Stormcast Eternals on the other, the fate of the undead kingdom of Neferatia hangs in the balance. But even as an enemy rises from within, Neferata's plans to save her realm come to fruition.

An extract from
Neferata: The Dominion of Bones
by David Annandale

Light from the fires of Mausolea rose high along the flanks
of the Sentinel of the Shroud. The city sprawled out from the
western foot of the mountain, a supplicant prostrate before a
towering, unforgiving god. Before the coming of the legions of
the Blood God, Mausolea had been a city for the dead. Its avenues of monuments and vast sepulchres were grander and more
numerous than the streets of the living. Whether entombed or
walking the night, the dead had ruled Mausolea, and the mortals had prospered there only at their sufferance.

The dead ruled no longer. Mausolea had changed from a city
of shadows and silence to a cauldron of flame. Its mortal population had grown under the reign of the lord of Skulldagger
Bastion. Khorne craved blood. To feed that insatiable hunger
required an army and an industry unlike any that Mausolea
or any of the lands and cities of Angaria had ever seen. Tombs
had been opened, vaults had been ransacked, graves had been
turned into primitive forges. Molten iron ran down the gutters

of the streets. Graunos commanded, and an army grew, and from the maws of the industry that created the army came the flames that rose and spread their light on the mountainside.

There were other fires, too. The burning homes and the burning pyres of the day's sacrifices to the throne of brass.

The flames of Mausolea illuminated the slowly changing face of the mountain. Though the structures of the city came very close to the base of the mountain, none were built upon the slopes themselves. None were permitted on the flanks of the turning mountain, and the near-vertical rock face defied any attempt to build upon it. Slowly, relentlessly, the towering pillar of rock rotated on its base, following the rhythm of the days and nights. Its peak hunched forward in the shape of an immense granite hood. When the light of Hysh fell upon the land, the Sentinel's movement seemed to be an agonised turn away from the day, the hood seeking the darkness that had vanished. Then, with the coming of dusk, for all the regions that fell within the shadow of the Sentinel, the abyss within the hood appeared to be the origin of night, and it was from the mountain that the breath of darkness came to fall upon Angaria.

So it had been until Graunos had conquered Angaria and commanded the construction of Skulldagger Bastion. The base of the fortress was in the shape of a colossal skull of brass. It filled the cavern of the hood, and had transformed the Sentinel of the Shroud, giving it a face. No longer did the mountain turn from light and create darkness. Now it looked upon the land below, a gaping, snarling guardian of Chaos. The towers of the citadel rose from the crown of the skull like a forest of brass spikes. The spires of the periphery leaned at sharp angles, jutting into space beyond the skull. The central turrets climbed high above the peak, daggers that stabbed the day and blinded the night.

From the eyes and mouth of the skull came the light of Graunos. The daemon prince had come from Hysh, and he had brought with him his particular strength of anger. He brought, to the land of the dead, the curse of the most terrible, virulent light. The beam was red as blood, if blood burned at the touch. It was brilliant, its intensity dazzling even at the peak of day. At night, it was a sword that cut the darkness, a searing wound.

The light marked a scorched perimeter around Mausolea as the mountain turned. Where it passed, stone burst into flame, and the air rained molten brass. During the hour before it came again, the land remained as hot as the interior of a crematorium.

The tower that jutted from the centre of the skull's brow, leaning the furthest out over the vertiginous fall, held in its peak the Offertory throne room. The chamber was a huge hemisphere. In the centre of the floor was a bowl-shaped combat arena. Here the supplicants of Graunos' favour and the victims of his displeasure fought to the death. A mob of bloodreavers surrounded the arena, their raving howls urging the combatants on. There was no need for them to act as guards. No soul who entered the pit would think of climbing out without the severed head of their enemy, their offering to the figure who sat on the throne of brass and iron.

The throne was huge, a monolithic sculpture whose edges were serrated with claws. The iron talons moved perpetually, with the grinding of protesting metal. They slashed at the air, hungry for the flesh of all who dared approach the lord of the bastion. But massive as the throne was, it was dwarfed by the mound of brass-coated skulls behind it that climbed towards the distant vaulted ceiling of the chamber. Here were the heads of every failed supplicant and condemned prisoner. Though the victors of the pit presented the skulls to the ruler of Angaria, the mound loomed over the throne as a reminder that the offerings were truly meant for Khorne.

Graunos presided over the latest battle to unfold in the pit. Standing to the right of the throne, Kathag, lord of Khorne, divided his attention between the battle and the daemon prince. It served him well to gauge his master's mood, and to study him closely.

One of the gladiators was Antur Kesseng, scion of one of the noble families of Mausolea. He was in a land dispute with House Renteer. His opponent was Sekkana Garthan. She had collapsed with exhaustion at a weapons forge. The only reason she had not been executed on the spot was because her work had been ferocious in the service of Graunos' armies. That her crime and Antur's dispute had no relation to one another was irrelevant. In the Offertory throne room, the judgement in the arena was not for duels. All that mattered was survival or death.

The struggle had already been a long one. The two fighters were ragged, bloody masses, barely distinguishable from one another. They had no blades. Their only weapons were their bare hands and the bones of prior victims that littered the floor of the bowl. Antur seized a femur and swung it at Sekkana. She ducked, and Antur smashed the bone against the wall. It snapped in half, leaving a jagged stump in his hands. He wavered in pain and fatigue. Sekkana made a desperate lunge and shoved at his arms, pushing them back against him and thrusting the spike of bone into his throat. Blood poured over his hands and down his chest. He clawed weakly at the bone. Soaked in gore, it slipped from his grasp, and he fell to his knees. His mouth opened and closed in silent pleas and curses. Sekkana caught him as he slumped forward. She grasped the spike with one hand, his hair with the other, and began to saw back and forth. It took almost as long to cut through all the muscles and tendons as it had to defeat Antur, but at last she tore his head free from his body. She held it up in triumph, and the shouts of the bloodreavers shook the stones of the chamber.

With the head clutched in both hands, arms stretched forward in presentation of the gift, Sekkana marched slowly up the slope of the arena. The bloodreavers parted, clearing the way for her to approach the daemon prince. She stopped and knelt a few feet away from the base of the throne.

Graunos nodded. 'Take command of the forces of House Kesseng,' he said, his voice rumbling like a lava flow. 'Burn House Renteer to the ground and slaughter all its sons and daughters.'

Sekkana looked up, her eyes shining with renewed energy and erupting bloodlust. 'It shall be done, great prince,' she said, and withdrew.

The bloodreavers roared in delight and fury to see Sekkana's violence rewarded.

Kathag watched Graunos use the boon to fuel even more bloody competition for his favour. The word would spread like fire through the ranks. Every warrior in Angaria would burn with the need to gain Graunos' favour. Nothing could withstand an army so driven.

Kathag smiled in anticipation of the fury that would fall upon Neferatia. For Graunos, this would be his next, inevitable conquest. For Kathag, it would be vengeance.

A gust of wind from the south blew through the arched windows of the throne room. The windows were tall, half as high as the ceiling, and ran the entire circumference of the chamber. They looked out in all directions onto the vistas of Angaria, and created the impression that the throne room floated in mid-air. Graunos had hurled many subjects who had displeased him through these windows, sending them flying with a dismissive flick of his wrist, not even granting them the chance to prove themselves in the blood of the pit.

Far to the south, lightning flashed. Then came the distant mutter of thunder. Graunos rose from the throne. 'Leave us!' he commanded, and the bloodreavers rushed to obey, emptying the throne room while Graunos' bellow still echoed.

The daemon prince drew to his full, towering height and strode to the southern windows. He was a colossus. Lord Kathag was tall, his body swollen with the strength Khorne granted to the supremacy of rage. The scar tissue that covered his body was so thick he barely needed the protection of his crimson plate. The horns that had grown when he ascended to the height of Exalted Deathbringer made him loom even more mightily over the legions of the Gorechosen that he commanded. Yet he had to crane his neck to look up at Graunos, who was more than twice his height.

The daemon flapped his huge leathery wings once in displeasure as he faced south. Then he turned his visage back to Kathag. Graunos' features were a mask of terrible enlightenment and blind rage. His eyes were silver, blank and searing orbs that Kathag could not look at for long without being blinded himself. He could not imagine how such things could see. They were weapons. They struck out. Perhaps they consumed what they saw just as fire consumed fuel.

'What is our state of readiness, *Lord* Kathag?' Graunos said. The emphasis he gave Kathag's title was a reminder that the price of failure could be the loss of that title. And worse.

'It won't be long,' said Kathag, telling Graunos what he must already know. 'But I do not think we are ready yet to confront Neferata.'

'Is that caution I hear in your voice?'

'It is.' Kathag would not attempt to dissemble before Graunos. Whether the daemon prince saw with those eyes or not, he perceived everything. He was still a creature of Hysh, and he seemed to shine a violent light into the most hidden secrets of all who confronted him. But Kathag would have answered with the same honesty had Graunos been blind. He would have felt even more compelled to speak the truth. It was important that Graunos fully understood the nature of their opponent. 'Lord Ruhok erred in his attempt to take Nulahmia,' Kathag went on. 'He underestimated Neferata, and we were destroyed. I will not make that same mistake. When we strike, it must be with such overwhelming superiority that the war is decided at its outset.'

Kathag, then an Exalted Deathbringer, was the only one of Ruhok's Gorechosen to escape the catastrophe Neferata had unleashed. A maelstrom had opened up in Nulahmia, swallowing up the entire army, pulling it into an abyss of absolute dissolution. Kathag had looked away as it appeared, and so escaped its pull. But the partial glimpse he had caught still haunted him.

He was haunted too by the shame and the helpless fury he had felt as he staggered through the wasteland beyond the vanished walls of Nulahmia. In order to live, he had done that which had been unthinkable for all his life until that moment. He had fled. The memories were as burning and urgent now as the reality had been. The memories of running through a city turned into a blur of disintegrating wreckage, pulled inexorably into a maelstrom of unbeing, until, at last, he had been safe, alone, walking through the desolation beyond the walls of Nulahmia. He had put the city behind him, but not the humiliation, nor the defeat, nor the returning rage and the need for retribution.

He had fought hard to purge the shame, and to redeem himself in his eyes and in those of his god. He had gathered the broken remains of Ruhok's horde and turned their flight from Neferatia into a slavering raid of vengeance on the lands beyond the Stonepain mountains. He shed new blood for Khorne even while still in retreat. He had built a new warhorde. He never rested. His wrath was always on the ascendant. Flight became raids, and raids became a march of conquest. And one great night, waist-deep in slaughter, tens of thousands of the Bloodbound fighting for him and his favour, he felt the touch of Khorne. He was engulfed in crimson fire, and when the burn faded, leaving him scarred and exhilarated, the weapon in his hands was no longer the ruinous axe that he had wielded as an Exalted Deathbringer. It was a Wrathforged Axe, a weapon that imprisoned a daemon, and it marked him as a lord of Khorne.

It was not long after his elevation that Kathag witnessed the arrival of Graunos. Kathag's conquests had always had one purpose. They were the means to return in vengeance to Neferatia, to hurl the walls of Nulahmia down and to destroy the Mortarch of Blood. In Graunos, Kathag found a being so mighty that his goal came within his grasp. Where Kathag had hordes at his command, Graunos had legions. The daemon prince swept over Angaria, taking it and remaking it in his image. Soon he would reach further. He would destroy Neferata and plunge her subjects into the fires of Khorne. Graunos was doing more than destroying the enemy in the service of his god. He was reshaping Shyish, turning the land not simply into a wasteland but into a self-sustaining empire from which blood would flow in an endless, torrential tribute to the Skull Throne.

When Graunos looked to the west, Kathag saw in the careful gaze how different he was from Ruhok. Like Kathag, Graunos' wrath was sharpened by strategy. He used the illumination of Hysh like a barbed whip. Neferata's arts of deception would not help her this time. Kathag knew what she was. He was prepared, and Graunos listened to his counsel.

Now Graunos said, 'We will not attack until we are ready. Agreed. But when will you know that moment has come? *Can* you know it?' When Kathag hesitated, Graunos added, 'We cannot gauge the full measure of her strength by watching her preparations as we complete ours.'

'True,' said Kathag. 'She will dissemble. She will conceal her might.'

'We will need to test her,' Graunos said, his growl becoming a low, musing rumble.

In the south, lightning flashed again.

'Then there is that,' Graunos said, pointing. 'You know what comes with such a storm.'

'I do.'

'Neferata to our west, Sigmar's Eternals to the south. That has the appearance of strategy.'

'She might have planned this,' said Kathag.

'No. The Lord of Undeath wages war against Sigmar. There is no alliance here.'

'Yet.'

'You think she can create one.'

'If we can imagine such an outcome, we can be certain she does too.'

Graunos nodded. 'If she did not plan this, she may well have waited for this opportunity.' A growl built deep in his chest until the stones in the throne room began to shake with its force. 'If this is her chance, then she will force our hand before we are ready. She is forcing me to react, and I will not have that. It is *my* will that will shape these lands.' He paused for a moment, calculation moving like red lightning through the boiling clouds of his anger. 'Reinforce the southern gate,' he said. 'But do not move beyond it. We shall observe Sigmar's dogs, but we will not divide our attention unnecessarily.'

'They *are* arriving on the far side of the mountains,' Kathag observed.

'Then Angaria is not their immediate goal,' said Graunos. 'Go now. Make fast the south, and prepare in the west. We will find our own opportunity here.'

Once Kathag had left, Graunos circled the throne room, sweeping his gaze over the empire he had built for Khorne and thinking about the war to come. What the lower of Khorne's servants did not understand was that rage, in its great forms, had shape and purpose. Graunos could see the pattern in his existence, and in his presence here. In the Realm of Light, he had been in darkness, and had brought darkness. Now, in this world of death and shadows, he was bringing exterminating light.

In Hysh, he had truly been blind. Cursed and shunned because of this, he had won Khorne's favour with the purity of his anger. He had repaid the gifts of the Blood God with an uncountable tribute of skulls. As a lord of Khorne, he had worn a brass mask that had granted him a form of sight. He had seen what needed to be destroyed, and the more powerful his rage, the more there was to destroy. One of the first conquests had been the city of Lykerna. He had crushed the place of his birth and marched on, unstoppable, and Khorne had raised him higher yet.

Now a daemon prince, he had plunged from the Realm of Light to the Realm of Death, a bright star tearing open the firmament, falling to earth to bring fire, to bring blood, to bring war.